"Cracker Chronicles"

The Confessions of a Weary Cracker

By- R. Wayne Tanner

Order this book online at www.trafford.com
or email orders@trafford.com

Most Trafford titles are also available at major online book retailers.

Many names are mentioned out of the deepest respect for the memory and contribution each
made to making the life I lived and love possible. Their humor, struggles and privacy are held
in the highest regard. My hope is that each enjoy a look back and will laugh with me.

Note for Librarians: A cataloguing record for this book is available from Library
and Archives Canada at www.collectionscanada.ca/amicus/index-e.html

Printed in Victoria, BC, Canada.

ISBN: 978-1-4269-1585-7 (Soft)

*Our mission is to efficiently provide the world's finest, most comprehensive
book publishing service, enabling every author to experience success.
To find out how to publish your book, your way, and have it available
worldwide, visit us online at www.trafford.com*

Trafford rev. 9/4/2009

 www.trafford.com

North America & international
toll-free: 1 888 232 4444 (USA & Canada)
phone: 250 383 6864 ♦ fax: 812 355 4082

Acknowledgment:

Charlotte "Charlie" Tanner for editing my book and not changing the story.

Emmett Tanner, Charles Yates and Ormond Simmons for sitting with me for hours as I asked questions and searching for details. If it had not been for these three men it would have taken longer in producing this book. Thank you.

Thank you to my wife Susan Tanner for the cover.

Dedication

I dedicate this book to two individuals who has meant a lot to me.

First, to the memory of my beloved daughter Sarah Tanner who died January 28, 2009. Her strength and courage motivated me to chase my dream.

Second, to my daddy Emmett O. Tanner Jr. a tutor, disciplinarian, and friend. A man of character, integrity and honor. I love you both and thank you for pushing me forward.

Chapter 1

Danny Whaley stood at the foot of his grandfather's grave. Tears rolled down his check. He was overwhelmed with loneliness and fear. He raised his left hand and wiped the tears from his face, hoping no one saw him crying. The crowd that gathered for the informal funeral walked away from the small cemetery on the northeast bank of Lake Okeechobee. The sun was setting as it cast shadows on the double tombstone, seeming to illuminate the date recently carved there. His heart seemed to skip a beat as he turned and walked slowly toward an old Chevy pick-up truck, the last of his grandfather's cherished possessions. Danny treasured the old truck he had recently inherited. It must have been disappointing to his grandfather, he thought, to have worked all his life with nothing more than the old truck to show for it.

Times had been hard due to the great depression. His grandfather had lost everything he and his grandmother had accumulated during forty-nine years of marriage. With a slight smile and a sense of pride, Danny was confident of one thing. Because of his grandfather, the Whaley name had a good reputation. He knew if he decided to stay and make his life here, he would be successful. Danny's decision had been made, however, and he was heading north as soon as possible.

Stopping just short of the loaded pick-up truck, he turned and watched through the grove of weathered live oak trees as the sun set in the West. One of his greatest joys was watching the shadows fall around the edge of the lake. He listened to the sounds he heard while sitting quietly by the lake. The sound as a fish splashed among the pickler weeds.

1

The feel of gentle breezes blowing toward the shore, and the shrill cry of blue herons taking flight as the birds were startled by his presence. He watched the washing of the small waves as they lapped tranquilly upon the sandy white shore forming a flotilla of white foam. Danny continued to picture in his mind the times he and his grandparents walked the edge of the lake fishing, causing more tears to fall down his face. Danny reached deep into his pocket, grasping a letter that held his only hope of a future away from the demanding life of a commercial fisherman. Withdrawing his hand as he approached the cab, he reached for the door handle. He pulled hard at the rusty door. The door opened with a squeaking noise, breaking the silence that had shrouded him in sorrow again.

Danny questioned himself and wondered deep in his heart if he had made the right decision to leave so soon after his grandfather's death, abandoning the only home Danny had ever known. His plans were to begin by heading north to meet a man he was not even sure was still alive. Even if he were still alive, how would he accept a teenage boy and the challenges that were a part of growing up? The gamble was one Danny was willing to make.

The small amount of money he inherited from his grandfather was nearly depleted when he finally arrived in Kissimmee. He was still not sure the trip would not end in disappointment but the way Will Magrit had written the letter to his grandfather gave him hope. Exhausted from several days of continual driving and having to sleep in his truck he looked forward to finding an end to his journey.

The road was rough and filled with potholes, which caused his very insides to rattle. The roads were not being properly maintained. Danny shook continuously in the old pick-up truck as he sped along a stretch of highway he was convinced would never end. Endless stretches of sandy trails, brick and black top roads winding through and around orange groves and cattle in pastures dotted with cypress heads were left behind him. Cypress strands stretched for miles offering only the occasional shade for the thousands of head of cattle he saw. In spots, Australian Pines shielded the roadway leaving thick blankets of brownish-orange nettles that only moved slightly as the old truck sped by.

Danny was not paying attention when a cow and its calf wandered out of the woods onto the road around Kenansville. The truck hit the cow loosening the front fender. The loose fender's continual rattling was a constant reminder of the accident. The only other damage done to either beast or truck was to Danny's pride. The heat of the engine coming through the floorboard was beginning to affect him but the excitement of finally meeting his uncle would not be dampened.

He was unsure of how many miles of road lay before him and the unfamiliar terrain was, at times, very intimidating. Behind him, he was leaving memories he wanted to fade from his mind as fast as the dust that was being produced by the truck traveling down the old dirt roads.

It was late in the evening when he stopped and camped under a stand of Australian Pines next to the road. He had eaten the last of the canned beans and peaches the night before. He only had a few oranges he had picked from a grove earlier in the day that would have to last until he came across a store along the way. He would buy as many supplies as his money would afford him. He thought to himself, speaking out loud "A good hot meal would really be nice right now". Danny knew even if he could find a store in this remote country, he could not afford all the supplies he would need to finish his journey into his tomorrows.

Before he knew it, he was deep in thought about his grandmother and how he and his family came to visit her home when he was young. He could never remember a time when there was not something cookin' on her kitchen stove. His favorite meal was when she would cook ox tail stew. Danny started feeling the effects of not eating for a while but the need to complete his journey drove him on. At a curve in the road, he spotted a sign that read, "If you're not from here don't be here after dark." A mile past the sign Danny was startled when he saw a truck drive across the road in front of him. He had finally found the settlement of Fort Christmas.

The letter he had in his pocket that his grandfather had received was postmarked "Fort Christmas, 1909". The letter was frayed because of the many times Danny had read it. He shifted in his seat taking the letter from his pocket and reading it one more time.

"Horace,

Hope this finds you well. I want you to know that I have purchased my own place. If you every get back this way you are welcome. Ask anyone in Fort Christmas and they can tell you how to get to my place.

Respectfully, Will".

Danny pulled up in front of the store at the crossroads, a cloud of dust testifying how long it had been since it had last rained. He walked up to the man standing behind the counter and asked if he knew Will Everett Magrit? The man was verbally short in his response to Danny and told him the last time he heard he was in the hospital. "Do you know how I can get hold of him?" asked the nervous boy. The old man answered harshly, "Know how ta use the telephone? Ring it and they 'll hep ya."

The phone rang for the forth time when a woman answered and said, "Mosquito County Infirmary, Ms. Lottie speakin'. How ken I hep ya?" "Yes, my name's Danny Whaley and I am lookin' for Mr. Will Everett Magrit. Is he there?" With aggravation in her voice she said, "He was, but he aint no more. I aint his keeper either. He was with the doc and couldn't speak". With that bit of wisdom, she hung up the phone. Surprised, Danny called back to be reconnected with the public phone out in front of Hodge's General Merchandise Store. Tired and slightly irritated, he leaned against the post the phone hung on and waited for the connection on the other end. "Mosquito County Infirmary, Ms. Lottie speakin', how ken I hep ya?" Before she could finish her introduction Danny spoke "Please don't hang up again. I'm lookin' for Mr. Will Magrit and I really need to find him, please." "I wush you'd leave me lone, he aint here. The doctor told him not to go but he left anyhow. Why you gots to know where he is any way?" Danny was confused because just a few minutes before she had told him that Mr. Magrit was there and now he's not. Along with explaining to her his need in finding him, he made the fatal mistake of asking one too many questions. The result was not pretty and it angered Danny, but he was taught to be respectful. Before their conversation ended, she told him "I ust told ya he left here and if'n he just left means he's still a livin." Danny spoke quick because he could tell the woman was getting annoyed and would probably soon hang up on him again. "Do you know where he was go'in and could you give me directions?" With a little sass in her voice, she told Danny that he still lived at the big creek at the end of State Road13. She didn't know if the gate would be locked and she really didn't even care. With that, she hung up.

Danny turned and looked at the road leading from Orlando and wondered aloud, "Where the hell's Highway 13?" Just then, he heard a soft voice with a deep Southern drawl. When he turned, he saw a young girl about his age. "Where ya go'in?" she asked. Embarrassed Danny cleared his throat, quickly apologized for the slip of his words, and politely said, "I'm lookin' for Highway 13 and a man named Will Magrit. Do you have any idea where it's at?" Without saying a word, she walked toward the road, stopped and motioned for him to follow her pointing back West. She smiled and said, "It's about ten miles back that away. You'll come to da only road that turns back south." He could not help but watch her walk away hearing the sweet innocence in her voice. The young girl's voice caused him not to clearly hear the directions and he asked her to repeat them. Irritated she said, "I knowed who you wuz talkin' 'bout. He comes in here all da time and gets supplies." Her expression changed as she continued, "Matter a 'fact, he's due here dis afternoon. If'n ya wants ta wait, we ken sit down an' talk awhile." Danny, not really wanting to waste time just sitting around, thought for a minute. He agreed to wait because he really did not want to miss finding Will either.

He walked to his truck when she spoke again, "Where' ya go'in?" He reached into his pocket, retrieved a few dollar bills and followed the girl into the store. Just inside the door, to the left, was a long counter that reminded him of a bar in Okeechobee. He would have to go there occasionally when he was younger to get his uncle on his mother's side of the family. He had even worked in one for a few weeks after he left home.

There were several men drinking at the bar. The men stopped long enough to turn and see who it was walking through the door. Realizing it was just a boy, they returned to their conversation. Danny stepped up to the counter, purchased a soda for himself and offered to buy the girl one. He purchased the few supplies he would need for camping that night if he could not find Mr. Magrit that afternoon. Danny was hungry but did not like to eat in front of strangers.

As he turned back toward the door, he noticed a man and young boy coming through the front door very quietly. Cat-like, the tall stranger moved past Danny into listening range of the conversations taking place at the bar. Danny could see the man's narrow eyes become fixed on the men sitting on the bar stools. The man was tall with sandy blonde hair. His actions were bizarre to Danny. The blond haired man moved into the shadow of the stocked shelves and stealthily moved closer to the unsuspecting men at the bar. Danny remembered their old house cat as it stalked its prey. Without warning, the newcomer grabbed the closest man by the collar, drew back his hand, and punched him as hard as Danny had ever seen a man hit. Before the other men could react and figure out what was happening, the stranger was attacking them. In a matter of just a few moments, three men lay bloody and out cold on the floor. Without saying a word, the aggressor and the boy walked passed where Danny and the girl were standing watching the seemingly unprovoked attack. The child with the stranger stopped where Danny and the girl stood. "Melba, they was talkin bad 'bout daddy." he said in a whisper. With the slightest grin on his face, he turned and followed his older brother out the door. They mounted their horses that were tied out front and rode away. Later that afternoon Danny learned the man's name was Oddy. It was told to Danny that Oddy was actually an otherwise gentle man and only got riled if someone talked bad about his pa.

Danny watched as the three injured men stumbled outside to the porch. He followed them with his eyes, watching as they disappeared in different direction. He was confused about what he had just witnessed and sat on the edge of the porch staring at the three defeated men as they disappeared around a large clump of palmettos.

Danny and the girl talked the rest of the afternoon. Danny could not remember a time when he had enjoyed himself as much. So caught up in their conversation, Danny forgot to formally introduce himself and was thankful the young boy had called her by name earlier. Time did not exist for the two of them. It was getting late when her pa came around the end of the porch and discovered her sitting talking to a stranger and her chores not done. His coarse voice reminded her of the chores needing done and gave Danny a harsh look leaving no doubt about how he felt. She jumped up but before she left, she smiled and asked if he would come again on Sunday and go to Church with her. Danny looked first at her pa with a confused look then asked where a Church would be way out here next to nowhere. She giggled and simply pointed over Danny's shoulder as she turned and bounced off to do her chores.

Danny quickly turned and sure enough right there on the other side of the intersection stood an old wooden Church with a sign that said Pine Grove Baptist Church. Danny smiled as he turned and said to himself, "I just might do that."

Will Magrit never showed up that afternoon and Danny ultimately walked back into the store just before it was to close. After introducing himself to Melba's pa, he asked the man if there was a place close by he could camp for the night. He was not sure if he could find Highway 13 or the Magrit place after dark. The old man stared at him for a moment without saying a word then finally spoke as he led Danny onto the front porch. "You can sleep over there next to the Church. There's a pitcher pump with fresh water and a shelter you can sleep under." He looked square into Danny's eyes pointing his bony finger right in his face and said without any expression. "Don't get no idea you can come sneakin' 'round here tonight. I got a shot-gun loaded and I durn sure will use it." No one had to explain to Danny what the man meant. He did not want to face the old man in the dark or fact of the matter not at all.

Early the next morning Danny returned to the store hoping to see Melba before heading out to find Mr. Magrit's place, but she was nowhere to be found.

After cranking up his old truck and allowing it to warm up, he turned west and accelerated quickly spinning dirt and causing dust to enter the front of the store. This did not set well with Melba's father and Danny heard about it the next time he was in the store. However, when he showed up for Church on Sunday, that changed Melba's father changed his opinion. Especially after the sermon, the preacher gave regarding forgiving your brother and admonishing everyone to be careful because we do not know who our brother might be.

About ten o'clock the next morning, Danny drove up to a broken down wooden gate that barricaded a long winding rutted dirt trail that seemed to lead to nowhere. Stopping to check if it was locked, Danny could hear dogs barking in the distance. With a little effort, he lifted the sagging gate and swung it open wide enough for his truck to pull through. He noticed the thick loose sand just inside the gate as he continued down the trail bordered by large palmetto patches and live oak trees. He came to a place in the road that was covered with grass spotted with dried cow manure. This would keep him from getting his truck stuck. As he had been walking, back to the gate Danny could see that no vehicle had entered the lane since before the last rain. He could also tell that someone had walked through the sand recently. He thought about not driving up the lane but his need to find the illusive man pushed him forward. Cranking the old truck, he let off the clutch causing the back tires to spin as the truck lurched forward. Slowly he maneuvered around the palmettos that protruded out into the lane scraping a long scratch the length of his truck. He feared shifting gears because of the depth of the ruts that could cause the truck to be stuck. Being stuck would have him walking alone up to the house. The sound of many dogs barking wildly caused him to be more cautious. Danny did not want to walk through a pack of strange dogs.

Danny's next obstacle was an old wooden bridge. The bridge crossed a large washout that lead toward a creek swamp nearby. Danny could see evidence of flooding on the land in the past. The landscape was beginning to change as he drove deeper into the creek swamp. Bay trees were blooming with small white flowers that dotted the deep green waxy trees growing among cabbage and cedar trees. Grape vines laced among the trees giving the impression that the trees were one large canopy. Unsure of the safety of the bridge, Danny stopped the truck and examined the structure wondering if it was strong enough to hold his truck. It seemed sound enough so hesitantly he started across holding his breath. It sounded as if the weight of the truck caused the wood to creak and crack as it echoed within the umbrella of huge tree limbs that bordered the narrowing trail.

About a quarter of a mile on the other side of the bridge, it opened up to a large pasture. The road continued across the grass to a large set of cow pens right on the edge of the creek swamp. Moving further down the lane, he entered into the swamp along a well-used path to a clearing. Right in the middle of the pasture was a small house that sat next to the creek. The large live oak trees that sheltered the house shielded the entire area from the hot summer sun and offered abundant shade. The cry of the caddie-did was deafening as the dogs franticly announced the intruders presence. Danny pulled in front of the house and was greeted by a pack of dogs that acted as if they would rip to pieces any trespasser. The truck sat silent as Danny waited for whoever was in the house to have a chance to come out and make it safe for him to leave the security of the truck. He sat there for what seemed to be a lifetime. Over the sound of the dogs, he could hear the rapid beat of his heart. When the front door swung open finally, out walked an old man that stood a strong six-foot tall. Atop his head was an old three-inch brim cowboy hat that had been weathered by many years of exposure to the Florida elements. Walking to the edge of the porch, he let loose a stream of brown spit off the edge of the porch that caused a small cloud of dust to rise. Danny watched the small cloud as a slight breeze blew across the clearing until the small cloud disappeared.

With a robust and clear voice, the old man called out and said, "What ya do' in?" The dogs barked franticly, waiting for their chance to get to the intruder in their world. Danny did not hear the first time the old man spoke. With sharpness in his voice, the command came for the dogs to shut up and let him speak. The dogs quickly cowered down. What little tail they had was tucked away as they ran for cover knowing if they persisted just one more time there would be hell to pay. Danny reluctantly opened the door of his truck and stood on the door jam waiting for an attack from the now coward dogs. He then heard the old man say again "You're either lost or looking' fer me. What ya want?" Nervously, Danny spoke up as he exited the truck. Introducing himself, he could see the harshness in the old man's eyes soften and become inviting when he said, "I knowed the Whaleys. Are you kin to Horace Whaley?" The boy smiled widely while acknowledging the old man by shaking his head. Danny told him his grandfather was Horace Whaley. The young man told the old man about his grandfather's recent death, the reason why he had left the place he had lived his entire life. He explained why he had come here to find the man in the stories his grandfather had told often. Will turned abruptly away and stared for several minutes down the dirt trail that had brought him to this place so many years ago. He remembered fondly the days of his childhood and the many hours he and Horace had spent together. He was truly thankful that his old friend had spoken so highly of him. At that moment, Will made up his mind that he would try hard to see that Horace's only grandson had a safe place to live even though it would be months before the shy boy standing before him would ever know of the kindness to be shown him. Wanting to lighten the mood and in his usual joking manner, Mr. Magrit told the boy not to believe everything he heard and with that, he turned toward the cabin.

Chapter 2

Mr. Magrit invited the boy to sit with him on the porch. His mood and that of the dogs was peaceful because, truth be told, he was glad to have company. The dogs left their hiding places and watched the old man as they sheepishly returned to the front porch one by one. Each would stand for a few moments looking at their master and wanting some sort of attention when he reached out and gave each dog that approached a casual pat on the head. He loved the dogs. Then turning to the boy who sat next to him, wanting the same attention from him but they did not get it.

The old man removed his hat and hung it on the back of the rocking chair causing the hat to move back and forth, as he sat down. Danny recognized the faraway look in the old man's eyes. He had seen that look often in his grandfather's eyes. It spoke of homesickness, a longing for something or someone in his past. Danny hurt for the old man. They sat for a long time just staring out into the shadows of the mighty oaks, bay trees and the flowering magnolia trees without a word.

Dead leaves from past falls covered the ground-concealing baron ground beneath. The young man remembered hearing his grandfather tell of how they use to sweep their yards with brooms made of dog fennels. Danny turned his head quickly toward the old man wanting to ask him about sweeping the yard when he realized that silence was his best action. For the first time in his life, he began to see things he had never noticed before. The birds singing in the trees had been at one time just noise to him but now seemed sweet. The squirrels as they barked, running from one limb to another, began to have purpose. He embraced this new knowledge and finally started to understand how nature survived, a lesson his grandfather had tried teaching him with no success.

All of a sudden, the old man stood to his feet, stomping to free the leg of his dungarees to fall to the top of his worn boots. He looked at Danny, now on his feet as well. He spoke with purpose in his voice. "Well I got chores that need doin'"". He looked down as if he was searching for the words to express what he was feeling and continued with a slight smile. "You gonna stay the night?" He hesitated for a moment and continues to speak more softly, "You're welcome to stay here providing' you ain't afeard of a little work."

Danny took a couple of steps toward the old man still staring out into the yard as the shadows of the day began to fall. He said "No sir, I ain't got to be nowhere in-particular and no sir, I aint afeard of no work." Deep down inside Danny, this was a dream come true. His entire life had been spent longin' to live the life his grandfather had told him about. To live the life of a cowboy was not possible down south because he first needed to be taught. Danny now had his opportunity and would make the best of it all. Beside that, he wanted to know what it would be like to live a life in the wilderness.

Mr. Magrit placed his weathered gray hat, stained by years of sweat, on his head. He had stuck a toothpick behind his ear earlier, a habit Danny would grow to emulate. The old man placed the toothpick back in his mouth, rolling it continuously from side to side. Danny would learn one day that this habit had replaced another habit for the old man, smoking.   Reaching for the handrail, taking one step at a time, he slowly and cautiously descended into the yard. At the bottom step, several dogs met him seeking approval from their master and crowding him almost causing him to fall. All it took was for him to say one word, "Stop!" Again, the dogs retreated for cover. The only dog that did not run was a little yellow ring- neck dog that befriended Danny and looked to him for his attention. The old man noticed the dog's interest in Danny and said, "I had a dog just like him when I was your age". However, the only words Danny heard him say were "You can have 'em if'n you like". The widest smile came across his face as he turned and patted the dog on his head. The dog returned Danny's touch by licking his hand. As it often is, the two of them would become inseparable.

The old man walked up to the weathered barn and swung open the door. What little sunlight left in the day flooded the barn revealing a dust-covered window into the past. The interior was filled with tools and memories for Danny of a time long past. As Danny walked in it was if he walked into a museum. A Model T Ford truck looked brand new. As if it had never been outside the barn. Tucked away to one side was an old wagon the young man believed to be the one from an old photo he had often seen in his grandfathers' house of Jim "Red" Lanier and Willis Nettles in front of the store at Deer Park. He never thought he would see such things. His mind filled with the stories his grandfather had told him as a little boy and could now see clearly the many miles traveled in the wagon.

Danny walked over to the old wagon and in the bed he found the yokes that had been used. He wondered how an ox would even fit in them when he noticed other items that Mr. Magrit identified as hames. He remembered that hames were wooden implements that sit in an indented groove on the collar where the trace chains are secured, a stuffed leather collar that was placed on the neck making it comfortable for the horse or mule to pull a load. There were trace chains used to connect the hames to the implement being pulled. He saw an old implement called a single tree that was a swivel bar with two hooks for the trace chains used to pull the implement equally. There was a bottom plow, a Coleman seeder and a middle buster, which was a double bottom plow, used to break up the middle of a potato hill or between the rows in the fields that no longer had its wooden handles and numerous sweeps that were used to sweep under the surface of the ground exposing the roots. Danny was mesmerized by what he was seeing and was granted permission to one day explore these antiquities further but right now, there was work to do.

The stale odor of manure filled the air almost stifling Danny but what he was experiencing gave him a feeling of satisfaction as he became intoxicated by the moment. The old man brought him back to reality by saying. "You gonna' hep or just stand there lookin stupid?" Danny turned to see him standing in front of a sealed off room called a crib filled with dried cobs of field corn. He watched as the old man picked up one of the cobs and turned it vigorously in his hand. The kernels fell with an echoing clank into a bucket. The silence in the barn was broken by the sound of hogs penned in back of the barn as they began to squeal in anticipation of their evening meal.

With each new discovery, Danny became more excited about what he was allowed to experience. Danny tried to emulate the old man as he watched his hands stripped the dried corn. The two worked together to fill the buckets and casting the cobs into a pile that looked as old as the barn. A portion was to be fed to the hogs but first Danny, to his surprise, was told to climb into the hog pen and clean out the troughs. Reluctantly he did as he was told quickly scurrying back over the rough-cut wooden fence to safety. In his hasty escape, he received a splinter in his right thigh. Mr. Magrit laughed out loud assuring him the hogs would not hurt him and made fun of his saying he thought that it would have taken a little longer for the boy to become a pain in the butt.

After feeding the hogs, they poured a small amount of the kernels into a mill. Danny turned the big stone a few times breaking up the kernels and making it easier for the chickens to eat. Mr. Magrit commented that the chickens would soon stop laying for a while but Danny needed to check for any eggs that might be in the boxes. He told him to leave the big hen on the end alone because she was sitting on a dozen eggs that would soon hatch. Mr. Magrit threw the cracked corn to the chickens in the coop. Next, they fed the rest to the animals including the horses. Danny instantly fell in love with the small roan horse and from that moment on, he wanted to ride him but dared not ask too much too soon.

There was so much for Danny to see and do. It was unbelievable to him that he was here and in just one afternoon all his grandfather had told him came alive. The stories that his grandfather had told him were true and he looked forward to spending as much time with Mr. Magrit as possible.

After feeding all the animals, they returned to the front porch. The old man lowered himself into the old rocking chair. Danny could see the seat was made of dried stretched cowhide. Danny watched as the old man's rocking took on a rhythmic pace that was relaxing just to watch. The old man reached into his shirt pocket and took out a pouch of chewing tobacco. Reaching into the pouch, the old man removed a small amount placing it in his mouth. Danny watched in amazement as the old gentleman swirled the tobacco from side to side in his mouth, spitting a stream of brown juice out into the yard. Mr. Magrit stared out into the yard as the sun's last light retreated behind the horizon.

The colors in the sky were a brilliant amber blanketing the trees and out buildings that spotted the clearing. The color outlined the grayish clouds that could not be concealed by the thick canopy of oak trees. Danny had never experienced such a sight as they sat listening to the last of the daylight sounds began to be overtaken by the night noises like crickets, rain-frogs and the muffled hum of thousands of mosquitoes that seemed to come out of nowhere. Mr. Magrit never once swatted at the pesky biting bugs. It was if the mosquito could not penetrate the leathery tanned skin and if one could, he had become immune to their bite. While the biting was not bad enough to force Danny indoors, their incessant biting was driving him crazy. Danny instantly forgot the nuisance of the stings that burned and itched at the same time when the old man began sharing a part of his life's story. The young man again noticed, as Mr. Magrit began to speak, he seemed to be carried away and spoke as if he was carrying on a conversation with someone not present.

Chapter 3

It was late in October 1886 when Will Everett Magrit turned fifteen years old. He was an ordinary looking young man standing only five feet three inches tall with broad shoulders when he grew to be a man. Many said he was strong for his age and skilled in hunting and the outdoors. Even as young as he was, at his age he earned a good reputation working around the flighty scrub cows. His skills on a horse and the use of a whip were recognized by several of the cattlemen around the area. He learned this by spending hours on horseback hunting cows during the yearly spring gathering when the surrounding families worked together to ride the vast area around the St. Johns River in Central Florida. It seemed he was a natural on a horse and knew what a cow would do even before the cow could react. The skill of mammying, the ability to observe a bunch of cows by their markings and actions and pair up cows to their calf, came. This invaluable skill was essential to the early cowmen due to open range. The skill was not easy to learn but it seemed to be one Will had as a natural talent and, even at his age, many asked for his assistance when they gathered the cattle.

Pa Whaley heard talk about someone taking Will under their tutorage to develop his skills because one day he would be a good cattleman. Will's hair was sandy colored, thick with some curl and if he did not get a regular haircut, it often tended to turn up from under his hat. He remembered one day when they were working cows close to the Near Slough when one of the old timers told him to get a haircut or wear a sign around his neck that said, "Don't crap in the bushes". Mr. Magrit nearly fell out of his rocker with laughter.

He said he came to live with the Whaley's when he was only two years old because his family was killed in a fire started by lightening burning the big scrub near Fort Defiance. His family had settled there right after the war between the States. Pa Whaley's brother, it was said, was traveling down from Georgia when he happened upon a camp of Indians who had found the young white boy near the burned out house wondering around. The Indians gave Will to the first white family they came across. Pa Whaley's brother stayed at the fort near the area where the child was found and he learned the boy's family name was Magrit. Out of respect for the family, they never changed Will's name.

Will had been regularly teased about the fact he did not look like any of the Whaley children. All of their hair was black with dark skin resembling a pine sapling, thin, wirery, and tall. The other children at the school made fun of him because he was different.

Horace Whaley was three years younger than Will and considered himself Will's best friend. He looked up to Will and always wanted to be with him everywhere he went. They spent a lot of their spare time together in the woods fishing on the St. Johns River. Together they developed a deep love for the marsh and spent many hours exploring every inch of the river marshes. When allowed, they would camp near Persimmon Hammock and fish all night. There was nothing more fulfilling, relaxing, or enjoyable than sitting up all night under a clear starry sky and catching big catfish. Their favorite pass time was using the sane net to catch pop gut minnows and fishin at night for the largemouth bass lying beside the lily pads, which grew abundantly along the river's banks.

During the long summer days, when it was too hot to work, they would slip off to where the big creek flowed into the St. John's River and spend lazy afternoons fishing and swimming. When the sun begun to set they would start home but would often get side tracked as they watched the bald eagles dive for fish on Puzzle Lake and dream of what it would be like to fly like the eagles. If time permitted, they would cut a swamp cabbage and proudly march home excited about the meal they had provided for the family. Soon the days turned into years and their fun turned into continual work. Only in their dreams at night could they enjoy the river again or had time to lazily watch their world drift by.

Due to Will being the oldest of all the children, he was not allowed to attend school as often as the others did. The harsh life of the wilderness forced him to work long hard hours to help provide the essentials of life for his adopted and loved family. He did not mind the work because he was the type of boy that liked seeing what he had accomplished and, as far as he was concerned, he could see no profit in having to attend school. To Will, spending a day in school was a waste of time he thought could be spent in the woods after work doing what he really enjoyed. He had no fond memories of going to school. There were, however, some good times spent with the other children proving to them that just because he did not look like the others or have their last name, he was no different from anyone else.

When they were together, they would play a game called "Piggy in the Pigpen Wants a Motion". It was a lot like hide and go seek but the one person that looks for everyone else yells, "piggy in the pigpen wants a motion". That person would watch for someone to wave his or her hand and the chase was on. When the pursuer got a couple of pigs in the pen, the kids would change places. Will liked the game because he was always outside.

As Will grew older, he learned the truth about his family and how he came to be with the Whaleys. Ma Whaley, Will's adopted mother, was a compassionate soul. She was like Will in that she looked different and her personality was in sharp contrast to the others. She was short and round and in complete control of her world, unlike the others that seemed to let every one around run over them. Will believed the reason some of the boys didn't like him was due to the fact they couldn't push him around.

Late on the evening of his fifteenth birthday, when most folks would be close to home or at least looking for a place to settle in for the night, their world was invaded by the sound of a noisy wagon rolling up the trail. Before the wagon could stop, pa's dogs franticly sounded the alarm of something strange invading their domain. Surprised and alarmed by this incursion into the solace of his peaceful clearing, pa rose quickly while grabbing for his old shotgun. With a sharp eye, the old man watched as a cart drawn by two slumbering white-faced oxen carrying two old black men came into sight. Will noticed Pa Whaley's curiosity

19

turn to relief when he recognized them and called out to them, "Get down and come in, suppers almost ready".

Most blacks were not welcome around those parts because of a long held resentment towards them. Just before the War Between the States, most of the folk that lived in those parts owned their own farms in South Georgia. Being private people, they didn't believe in bothering nobody, white or black. The sole reason for the war was to free the slaves. All of those folks were dirt poor and worked hard to survive on their own land and most of the farmers never owned a slave. However, due to them living in the south, they were considered rich slave owners, along with the fact that most of them fought on the side of the South. The attitude was that they deserved to lose everything they owned and they did. Every one of them was affected by this attitude and they lost everything they had ever known for generations and was forced to move to survive. From that grew strong bitterness and, for some, even hatred towards all blacks. Being stubborn and not wanting to change was the main reason why most of the early settlers at least in this part of Florida came. Their desire was to never have anything to do with anyone or anything that reminded them of what they had lost. They were hard working people and just wanted to be left alone.

The two old black men sat and talked to Pa Whaley until ma called from the doorway, "Wash up, supper time". Pa Whaley invited them to come in and eat a hot meal and offered them a dry place in the barn to sleep for the night. They graciously refused and said that they would head back because they wanted to get back as quick as possible. The family watched as they disappeared around a large patch of palmettos and the noise of their wagon faded in the distance.

After supper, Pa Whaley called young Will to the porch and told him that their visitors had come looking for beef. Pa informed him that delivering ten head to the turpentine camp was to be Will's job now that he was fifteen. His pa said, "I was younger den you when I first lef home." He reached out, put his hand on Will's shoulder, and called him a man! Will thought his heart would pound out of his chest. It was not because he feared the task or the trip. The fear was because he was not sure he knew the way and that every decision on the trip would be his. He was unsure of himself. Will had gone several times to the turpentine camp with his pa, but was uncertain if he could find it himself. His hesitation showed on his face because the old man said, "It should take you about two days to drive 'em there. How you plannin' to go?"

Everything was running through his mind when he said, "I dun know. I hadn't really had time to think 'bout it". The old man slowly reached into the box that he kept under his chair and retrieved his pipe. Thoughtlessly, he lit his pipe and began to speak as if he was just talking to himself. "If'in I was goin' to make the trip, I'd go jus south of Orange Mound, cross the river where it's shallowest". He stopped and took a big draw on his pipe. The smoke drifted from between the mustache that covered his face right by the young man. He turned and, with a half smile, said, "You know the crossin' closest to Lake Cane". Withdrawing the pipe from his mouth and using it as a pointer he continued, "…and then I'd take them cow's dat first night to Paw Paw Mound and camp there. By doin' that I'd be sure I'd be at the camp by noon the next day." He turned and looked out into the darkness. "You sleep on it and we'll talk in the morning". He knocked the tobacco out his pipe on the bottom of his old brogans, stood and stretched his body. Before leaving the porch the old man confidently touched Will on the head and said, "Proud of you, son". All Will remembered after that was hearing the door slam shut.

Will couldn't sleep at all that night for thinking about everything that happened that day from getting a new saddle to being given a task reserved only for the men folk of the Whaley family.

The morning he left for the camp was cooler than usual and there were dark clouds building in the north. The time of year meant that a cold front was coming, more than likely rain. Will knew better than to push the cows too fast, but he was sure he didn't want to be caught out on the open marsh during a winter storm. Keeping the cows moving with his whip and the help of his dog, Buck, at a steady pace was what he decided to do. The plan was to get to Paw Paw Mound before dark with the intention of allowing him and the small herd of cattle to get as much rest as possible before he pushed them on to the turpentine camp. Relief engulfed Will when he could finally see his first night's destination in the distance.

Paw Paw Mound was an island of cabbage and cedar trees in the middle of the river marsh. Its foundation is of shell and some have said that the Indians of long ago transported the shell there in canoes. It had been told the mound was once a camp stop for their migration north from the Everglades' then back again.

The cow pens Will was familiar with ranged from Limon Bluff south of Lake Monroe to Moccasin Island close to Lake Washington. Cattlemen and their cow-hunters used the cow camps during the spring and summer round up. The camps were the starting points where they would gather their cows from the surrounding river marsh and big scrub that ran on both sides of the river. Holding pens were built at the camps they would drive the wild ranging cows to. After they had gathered all of their cows, doctored, cut and separated the yearlings, the cowmen would go from pen to pen driving the untamed beasts to a buyer when they needed extra cash. If it were not market time, they would turn the animals loose to return to the grazing range. The Whaley family was mainly concerned with the scrub called Pockataw Flats that bordered the Econlockahatchee River to the west of their homestead. Each particular pen was constructed and maintained by the family it was named for.

The Cox family from over east of Paw Paw Mound built and maintained the set of pens where Will camped that evening. They had built the pens out of long cabbage tree logs cut and drug here and laying them end-to-end. The set of pens where Will camped that evening were constructed big enough to hold about fifty head of cows without having them so crowded they got restless. Will liked this set of pens because instead of having to sleep on the ground, a lean-to was built off the ground because of an incident that happened one cow hunt. One night the entire Cox family had camped at the pens. Aunt Dot, the mother of the whole bunch' woke up early that morning with a big old moccasin asleep with her in her bedroll. It nearly sacred her slap to death and not one of the men present ever heard the last of it. From that day on every time, that story was told the snake got bigger. Not one of the Cox men received any rest until there was proper shelter for the womenfolk at every place they camped. When any of the boys would tell the story they would always add what their pa said, "Ifn I coulda caught that snake dat morning' I'd a kissed it, then beat it to death". The cattle crew were more motivated by what Aunt Dot warned them of, if they didn't do something bout her a sleepin' place. They'd have to cook for themselves, she proclaimed! For the Cox men that just would not do so they quickly built her a lean to out of rough-cut cypress boards and a thatched roof, high off the ground.

Feeling confident he was on schedule Will whistled for Buck as a signal to circle the cows and slow 'em up. The little dog was fearless and would catch anything Will asked him to. The small dog's breed was cur and bulldog mixed.

The old man told of a time when a group of men from Fort Christmas were hog hunting just east of Hat Bill when they jumped a big suttee red boar hog. All the hog dogs could do was bay the big hog. Gathered for the hunt were some of the best hog hunters that Will had ever known. If the dogs would not catch the hog, the men would rope it by cutting a long pole and hanging a rope off the end. They would approach the hog carefully and ease the rope around the hog's head from behind. The minute the rope was pulled back, the hog's attention would be diverted and the dogs would move in for the catch. One of Grandpa Henry's boys was crawling in with a pole and a rope this particular hog when all of a sudden Will turned Buck loose and sir, let me tell you he made short work of that hog and the story was over. That little cur mix became the young man's best friend and gave him a lot of courage to do things that he wouldn't ordinarily do by himself.

There was another time when they were hunting while boiling salt on the coast at a place called Wisconsin Village east of the Banana River near the salt flats. Boiling the salt water provided the families with salt each year. The Tanners, Coxes and Yates rallied several bar hogs in one bunch. When they were able to stop the hogs, they roped one and the hogs broke and run again. Before the end of the day, they were able to catch four bars, which together weighed close to three hundred pounds apiece. Grandpa Henry spoke many times of cutin'em and markin' the ears of them big ole hogs with a crop-split.

It seemed like an eternity until the sun began to sink behind the trees across the river. After great effort, Will was able to get the hardheaded and stubborn cows in the pen, securing the gate and making sure they could not get out. Will rode out onto the marsh were he had seen several rabbits. He figured it would make a good supper, but boy, was he wrong. The rabbit he shot had more worms in it than he'd ever seen before. He settled for cold sweet potatoes and smoked beef

When the sun finally set, it began getting cold. The rain started to fall about an hour after dark and it continued all night and into the next day. That proved to be one of the most miserable nights the young man had ever spent out on the river marsh, but the small lean-to was constructed well and it kept him dry. When sleep finally came, he was comforted by the smell of home that rose from off the old quilt he slept under as it kept the chill of the night out.

Daylight came late the next morning due to the thick cloud cover. With the coming of morning, the young man was taken aback to see that the river had come up and cut him off from his planned route. It was common knowledge that east of Paw Paw Mound was a high savannah leading due south all the way to Possum Bluff but he had never been that way before. He knew at best it would be hit and miss for him, especially driving cows. The only other option would be to turn west cross the river marsh between Blue's Head and Mud Lake around the mouth of Jim's Creek. He knew if the river was out of its banks then the swamp would be flooded as well. However, it was proven to him many times that the shortest distance between two points was the straight one. After a cold breakfast, he faced the task of saddling his horse and getting the stubborn cows movin' in the direction of the swollen river. He was confident he had chosen the trail well when the lead cow turned and headed toward Mud Lake almost as if she had read his mind. Stepping off Paw Paw Mound into the swiftly running water was difficult. At times, his horse had to swim through the water littered with debris. Will was soaked. His dungarees that were a size larger than he normally wore began to chaff him making him very uncomfortable. Will was soon distracted as he watched a flight of egrets circle; their white bodies contrasted against the rapid moving dark gray and white clouds as they tried to find a dry place to land.

As soon as the first egret landed in a stand of dwarf cypress trees, the green tree limbs turned snow white with the birds and appeared to be suspended against the backdrop of the lush green swamp. Amused by their persistence, he was confused as to why they could not see the river marsh covered with water from tree line to tree line or was it just their nature to follow close behind cows for their supper. The cows had finally moved into a single line. They seemed to understand the need to find dry land with a built in trust of the matriarch of the herd to lead them to safety. Will figured it was safe to trust the instincts of the drifters on the marsh and just fell in behind them and allowed nature to take control as they moved around clumps of switch-grass and wax myrtles. Never once did he consider himself in harms way until he passed within a few feet of a cottonmouth swimming toward him. From that moment on, he became more diligent and watched carefully over his charges as well as himself.

Chapter 4

Will finally made it to drier ground where the cows began to eat hungrily on the Johnson grass. Dog fennels grew abundantly along the higher bluff now encircled by the dark floodwaters of south Florida. The small island was a solace for several marsh rabbits that franticly darted from one clump of grass to another trying hard to avoid the continual moving hooves of the grazing cattle. It would take all he had ever learned from watching the old timers in similar situations to maintain control of the cows and keep them from scattering. It is the nature of the wild cows to survive. With continual effort, Will and Buck finally bunched the cows and drove them along the edge of the swamp and across the pinewoods flat until they made it onto open scrub. His anxiety was replaced with a sense of accomplishment. He could now take a deep breath because the hazards of being so close to the water. Alligators could simply reach out and grab a cow would be gone. He knew if the alligator tried and missed, he would lose time and some of the cows. It was a lot easier knowing he was in an area open enough for him to see any source of trouble that might come upon them. His greatest fear was being distracted and loose track of time.

He could tell by the blackened trunks of massive pine trees a wildfire had scorched the area in the summer. The new growth emerging from the burnt palmettos, the abundant growth of needle grass and the thick growth of yellow and violet bloom drew the attention of honeybees. Will rode lazily in and around leaning and fallen trees following the cows. He was sure that Ma Whaley would enjoy seeing the scrub blooming and would spend hours picking the beautiful flowers. A sense of loneliness overcame Will while he saw a slight southern breeze make the yellow bloom blanketing the ground sway. He wished for someone to be with him and share the beauty because its splendor was intoxicating.

The massive virgin pines towered fifty foot in the air and showed little sign of a previous rapid moving fire. Control burning was a practice used by the early cattlemen to avoid fire that could sweep through and destroy everything in its path. He knew the fires also improved the source of feed for their cattle.

The cattle grazed eagerly making it more difficult to drive them on but the dog helped to keep the small bunch of cows moving south. Will's first notion was to use his cow wipe and force them but he thought better about it and decided the best thing to do was to move them slowly and allow them to eat their fill. If he were to scatter these scrawny cows on the scrub, it would take longer to regroup them and time was something he did not have a lot of.

Later in the afternoon, the wind picked up and the only thing he could hear was the whistling sound produced by it whipping through the tops of the trees. He hoped the wind would die down before dark so it would be easy to detect predators. His greatest fears were Indians, rustlers and wolves knowing they could easily slip into camp and wreak havoc if the wind continued to blow beyond sunset. A spooked cow could hurt you when they broke and ran.

Thankfully his clothes had dried. It had not gotten any warm by the time he decided to stop for the night. The weather was changing and soon the spectacular colors on the scrub would turn a dismal brown. Will chose a small cabbage hammock surrounded by a sea of virgin pines that had stood vigil for countless years over this part of the woods. There was no sign that the turpentine industry had discovered these pines nor tapped into the rosin, scaring the land with the deep ruts of their large wagons as he had witnessed in other places. Will wondered who owned these pines or even if anyone other than himself was aware of their existence.

Finding an abundance of liter knots, he built a nice hot fire that was his assurance of staying warm throughout the chilly night. After eating his fill of bacon cooked on a palmetto stick next to the fire and after he cleaned up his mess, he sat staring out into the darkness that surrounded the hammock. The cows finally settled down.

It seemed darker here than on the river marsh. As he rested and watched the light from the fire, his mind began to play tricks on him. Will saw shapes and shadows dancing and darting among the trees. Will wished that he had brought someone with him but found some comfort in his four-legged companion as he held the dog in his lap for warmth. He listened to the lonesome and eerie cries of hoot owls off in the distance. He drifted off to a time when he was younger when Pa Whaley and several other local men took him hunting. Late in the afternoon of the hunt, they heard a hoot owl. "When you hear a hoot owl call out in the middle of the day, it meant the deer, cows and fish are feeding" one of the men said. Will had tried to imagine what the deer looked like the owl was sitting, watching and betraying. He later learned what was really happening. The hoot owls were crying in hope that something would move and they would have supper. He was to learn another wives' tale. He was told you could also discern when the cows are laying down, fish will not bite. Will was sure these tales were true. He had observed them with his own eyes. Watching nature could be an education, just like the school he was not allowed to attend. He felt nature was a better teacher in the long run.

Will's mind was flooded with memories of last year's cattle drive. The older cowmen finished a long day of doctoring cattle and a good hot meal relaxing around the campfire and would begin telling stories. Will recalled one that night that he liked more than any other. It was told when Grandpa Henry guided some fellows out to Horse Hammock not far from Orange Mound on the St. John River to hunt turkey. There was one man that no one really liked too much, but the man did pay well.

Grandpa Henry told him that he had roosted a bunch of turkey next to the river in a high cypress tree. If the man went there first thing in the morning he could take his pick of them turkey and kill as many as he wanted. About three o'clock the next morning the short, bald-headed man left camp and traveled about four miles to the big tree Grandpa Henry had told him about. Sure enough the tree was full of what he thought was turkey. At daylight, all the men in camp heard a gun exploding with many shots. Grandpa Henry found everyone up and told them what he had done. They waited for the old man to return to camp and got a good laugh at his expense. He came back to camp madder than an old wet hen because Grandpa Henry had sent him out to a buzzard rookery. Using all his shells, he kept busy trying to knock buzzards off the roost. Realizing he had been skunked, he joined in on the fun by saying, "Aint as easy as you think to kill a roostin buzzard." Will chuckled out loud as he remembered that story and wished he could be in the company of those men again.

Danny came to a decision that morning around the campfire. He realized that, even without schooling, everything he had heard, seen, and done in his short life had led him to this moment in time. Everything he would see, do, and hear in his future would make him into the man he was to become. Life for him at that moment would become a learning experience to remember as long as he could remember.

Immediately, Will was brought back to reality when an owl lit above his camp, betraying his presence as the owl cried aloud, "He's over here. He's over here".

Out of the corner of Will's smoked filled eyes, he thought he saw a ghostly figure move out of the dark shadows that surrounded his camp, startling him. He could feel his heart pound so hard that it was all he heard over the sound of the night creatures singing their night songs.

The ghostly apparition seemed to be a figure of a man. It looked as if his skin was stretched over bone and scorched by an unforgiving Florida sun. His dark eyes sunk back into his head, his face was covered with a raggedy beard streaked with gray, and he was partially clothed in tattered overalls that barely hung onto bony and dirty shoulders. Red sores could be seen on his chest and arms. No shoes were on his feet that were stained black from walking through the burned scrub and cypress strands scorched from the summer wildfire. When the figure entered the camp, Will could smell a stench from the sores and filth that needed attention. The smell was unlike anything Will had ever experienced before. It was so strong that it almost took his breath and caused him to turn from the figure as he stopped next to the fire. It appeared as if this stranger floated from the shadows and squatted next to the fire. The stranger shivered as the cold wind caused the flames of the fire to sway under its influence, moving the flames and sparks to move this way then the other. The dim light of the fire made the figure to look as if he was death walking.

The intruder caught both Will and his dog by surprise. Buck lowered his head but never barking, his eyes never leaving the man. In the quiet of the night, you could hear Buck's muffled growl protesting this stranger's intrusion of their world. Will reached over and rubbed down the dog's back to calm him. The dog instinctively snapped at Will, but immediately turned his attention back to the trespasser that had caught him napping and not paying attention, as he should have. Will felt every hair bristle down his back as the dog nervously shook with fear.

The abrasive hollow eyes of the figure watched the slightest movements of the stunned boy, especially as his right hand moved from the back of the nervous dog to his saddle where he had foolishly laid his rifle the night before. For some unknown reason to the young man, the initial fear he had felt vanished and he did not feel frightened at the presence of this stranger from the darkness anymore. Will had known what evil men were like. In his short life, he had experienced what they were capable of doing and this man did not have any of the traits possessed by evil. A sense of calm blanketed him as the ghost like man's eyes lifted from watching his movements to finally looking Will directly. His stare revealed loneliness unfamiliar to Will, a sense of longing for something that had long since passed. The old man never said a word but sat shivering beside the campfire. What had seemed like a long time to the frightened boy was actually only a moment in time. He could see that the visitor began to relax as he lifted his face and offered a slight but suspicious smile. The ghostly looking man tensed as Will reached for his wallet. The old man looked like a scared animal that distrusts any movement, ready to take flight like a covey of quail roused from their hiding place.

Will watched as the old man looked out into the darkness then back to the fire. Buck was just as nervous, watchful of the stranger and even though he was very tired, he would not be calm. The dog watched for any movement that was threatening for which he could attack. Then leaning forward Will retrieved an extra tin cup from his wallet and poured it to the brim with hot coffee. Cautiously he reached across the fire to where the man sat and said, "You can have some coffee if'en you'd like". Before he could get all the words from his mouth, the stranger snatched the hot cup of coffee and gulped it down. His quick movement caused the dog to lunge forward and snap wildly at the stranger, which startled Will, causing him to speak harshly to the dog. The display of aggression by the dog did not faze the old man.

Without hesitation or fear of the dog, and without seeking permission, the dirty man reached for the coffee pot that sat next to the fire. With a flourish, he finished the coffee and slowly lowered the cup having now closed his eyes as he sat motionless by the fire. Will could see him relax even more as he seemed to enjoy the warmth of the fire and the hot coffee that had warmed his belly. As suddenly as he appeared, he was gone back into the shadows and the darkness.

Will quickly stood to his feet from a sitting position and walked with trepidation out into the darkness trying hard to see where the old man had disappeared too. He was still shocked and shaken by what had just happened. Walking back to the camp, without thought he reached over and threw several more pieces of littered on the fire. The fire burst to a large blaze. Its light now reached further into the darkness. Will searched the darkness hoping to reveal answers to the questions that now flooded his mind. Quickly he returned to his bedroll and the security it provided. Had what he saw been a haint? He had heard old folk talk about haints before. Had he seen one tonight?

The rest of the night was very quite as he watched the light from the fire dance and sway on the cabbage trees that offered a canopy to protect his camp from the dew that was beginning to fall. The silence of the night was finally broken by the cry of an owl off in the distance. He wondered what would drive someone to be out here in the woods so far from anyone. Why would anyone choose to live and dress as the old man did? Had he chosen that life or had it been forced on him by circumstances. Will's mind was filled with a thousand questions and not one conceivable answer.

The events of this one night would change the young man forever and he vowed to find the answers about the old man one day.

Chapter 5

As the last light of day vanished and darkness invaded the clearing at the Magrit homestead, the old man was forced to come to an end of his story. Caught up in the old man's stories, Danny was unaware of the passing of time. He was unaware of the bugs as they continually bit him. He did not care that his arms were covered with whelps. The bites burned and itched but he had not felt them until the story ended because he was reliving Mr. Magrit's life as it had been. He relived every detail as it unfolded before his eyes. Standing at his rocker, Mr. Magrit moved inside slowly. Danny noticed the effort it took and the anguish on the old man's face.

Danny stood outside the door waiting until the lamp was lit because the interior of the house was unfamiliar to him and he was unable see where he was going. When Mr. Magrit lit the lamb, Danny followed him inside and sat at the kitchen table. He watched every move the old man made, amazed as he stoked the fire in the large hearth. Reaching above the stove where several cast iron skillets hung he placed a frying pan over the open flame. Without turning, he told Danny there was a candle on the table and continued by telling him to light it. He bade Danny to go to the back porch and cut a chunk of the salt pork for their breakfast that was seasoning in a small wooden barrel. "How much should I cut?" the boy asked as he searched for a way to light the candle. "How hungry are ya?" He turned and handed him a large knife. "I'll only eat a few pieces. There are some baked sweet potatoes in the pie safe. We'll eat some of those too." Danny was unsure and did not want to mess up his first assignment, so he cut a piece big enough so both could have their fill. As Danny swung open the door the old man jokingly said, "Cookin'll be one of your chores for a while. I dearly hate cookin' and cleanin' up". Danny knew that he was joking but he was glad because he was not good at that particular task. He remembered getting in trouble as a child at home because of his carelessness in the kitchen.

The two now sat down at the table. Danny noticed the rough-cut cypress planks the table was built from. He drew his hand across the surface and pulled back quick as a splinter stuck in his hand. A small speck of blood oozed out from around the splinter and with one swift jerk, he tossed the small sliver of wood to the floor. The four chairs placed around the table had cowhide dried and stretched across the back and seat. Each chair had a different pattern and color and Danny asked if the hid was real. Mr. Magrit ignored him and Danny thought he did not hear the question he had asked his newfound friend.

They ate their meal without speaking a single word. Danny remembered how his grandfather had taught that speaking at the table was not permitted. That was the way he was raised. To speak without being spoken to was cause to be told to leave the table without finishing the meal. He figured Mr. Magrit had been raised with the same rules. Even though the only thing they had to eat was fried bacon and cold sweet potatoes, Danny had never eaten a better meal. He could not believe he was finally able to meet his grandfather's half-brother, much less have the possibility of living his dream.

After they finished eating the meager meal, Danny filled their cups again with coffee. Mr. Magrit reached for a wooden box sitting in the center of the table. Pulling a corncob pipe from the box and filling it with very strong smelling tobacco, he lit the pipe by leaning toward the candle now previously placed in the middle of the table. The candle cast its light in the dim room. Taking a long drag on the pipe, Mr. Mgrit leaned back in his chair, relaxed and continued telling the story he had started last night.

He began by saying that even though the way to the camp he chose was thicker than he liked, he was able to keep the cows grouped and made good time. He had never been through the Jim Creek swamp by himself, he was assured he was not familiar with the lay of the land. He figured the best plan was to head due south. There was an old tram road leading to the camp in that direction and if he headed as straight as possible, he would eventually cross it. Night in the swamp was scary because he had to deal with wolves spooking the cows and him as well. When wolves howled, the sound filled every inch of the darkness. Just the thought of it caused Will to shiver and with the little light cast by the fire at camp, he would see boogers peaking around every tree. He had to continually remind himself that there was nothing in the dark that was not there during the day.

He wished he had stayed on the east side of the river until he came to Possum Bluff. The area was more open and even in the dark you could make out forms as they approached. He would have much preferred to cross the river further south and be able to head due west to Settlement Slough but he was already committed and to far to turn back. The terrain at Settlement Sough was not as harsh as the trail he traveled now. He would have had an advantage because he had traveled the trail many times with his Pa. It would have been a lot easier, as well, to keep the cows from bolting at the slightest sound.

It was late the second night when the ghostly figure that had invaded his camp the night before showed up. This time Will was not frightened but relieved and welcomed the man's eerie companionship. Just having some one with him made the task of sitting up all night and tending the cows almost bearable. The appearance of the old man was uneventful.

Daylight finally broke in the east and gray clouds out-lined by a brilliant reddish orange were welcomed by Will. He could relax knowing that any unknown danger had passed. As the first light invaded the hammock, the ghostly figure disappeared into the shadows still lingering in the recesses of the swamp.

Early the next morning, Will closed the gate to a set of well used pens that now held his uncle's cows. He was unsure if they would hold the cows but it was the problem of the people in camp now. Filled with a sense of pride that he had successfully delivered the cows entrusted to him, he whistled for Buck. Buck raced to his side wagging his tail as Will took hold of his collar. Will tied the dog to a fence next to the gate with a length of rope Will carried in his pocket. The young man was sure no stranger would be able to get close enough to bother the dog. He turned and walked toward a building that looked like a store.

A large crowd of Negros had formed outside the building. The store reminded him of the one at Hat Bill. By the reaction of the crowd, he guessed it was not often a white person visited these parts, much less a boy. He recognized one of the old Negro men who had come to the house several nights before and contracted with his pa for the beef. Will was relieved as he cautiously walked through the crowd toward the familiar face of the old man he had met before. Before he got too far an enormous man with arms like tree trunks stepped into his path almost knocking him down. With anger in his voice and murder in his eyes, he shouted. "Whuts yo bisness here? Whuts a young white buck like you doin' outs here?" Startled and unable to respond and being just a boy Will knew he could do nothing about this giant standing before him. Will wished he had not tied Buck. He could sure use his old friend. He knew, however, the giant standing in his way probably could have killed the dog with his bare hands.

The old man's voice thundered with tones of retribution, surprising even the aggressor himself. The others in the crowd cowering down as if they had just heard the voice of God Will noticed them trembling. Stunned by what he was witnessing, he could not believe a man of such stature could have this much control over the crowd. Out of the corner of his eye, Will could see the old man with the familiar face. He spoke loudly to the giant in a demanding way and the giant disappeared back into the crowd.

Will was surprised that the giant, who stood two foot taller and outweighed him by fifty pounds, became so submissive at the sound of the old man's voice. Everyone in the crowd took on a child-like submission as the old Negro pushed his way through the mob. He walked up to the giant who had threatened his invited guest and slapped him with an open hand saying, "You's know's bedder". Shamefaced and with deep fear, the giant acknowledged the old man and as he turned he looked at Will. Will knew he needed to be diligent and watchful while at the camp.

Will later learned the old man who had visited their home was the Foreman of the camp. Foremen at the camps were considered the only law in the camp in a world so different from what was considered civilization. The people in the turpentine camps did not care about the law because their's was a world to itself in the camp. The workers and their families lived their entire life unnoticed and uncared for. The desperate need for order was so great in such a lawless place the foreman had to hold a strong grip on a place of such indifference, no matter his size. He had to constantly demand strict obedience from every person in the camp and maintain order by using a strong hand, even taking a life occasionally to keep some semblance of order.

If the foreman could not keep control, the hard life as they knew it would fall apart. The foremen had the power to control every aspect of every person's life from birth to death. When a child was born in turpentine camp there was no official record of either birth or death. Both life and death was frequent and unnoticed. Will learned that life began in great peril and without celebration. The cry of a newborn baby faded as the sun rose and work details were formed. Life ended without sorrow, the only sound that was heard were the shovels being pounded into the hard dirt and the dull thud of the dirt striking the cloth covering body of the dead. No grave was ever marked because there was no time to mourn the loss of a loved one. When the camps moved on there would not be an investigation of the cruelty that had taken place there. Life just happened.

The foreman had the power to arrange marriages. This was an essential part of his job, helping to assure a continual supply of workers. If a person was born in a turpentine camp, they would more than likely die in that turpentine camp. Only a few had ever tried to escape and ever made it to freedom.

Will only heard of two men who had successfully escaped. The cost of their escape had been high. The first one lost his wife and children, along with the sight in his right eye. The foreman and his crew of enforcers had gotten close to finding the man. The crew became so angry that the guards just started shooting into palmetto patches the escaper was hiding in. The man was struck in the right eye loosing the eye as punishment. The other escapee eventually starved to death in the big swamp to the south of Wolf Creek. Will spoke of this time in his life with great sorrow.

The only other person considered important or due any respect was the preacher in the camp. He worked just as hard as everyone else. Sunday was the only day in which their lives were like anyone else. The cruelty and inequality disappeared when they worshipped their God and had church under the same tree used as a place of torture and discipline during the week. The voices during the week were silent due to the oppression of the cruel foremen, and on Sundays, the voices of the enslaved seem to take on a tone of jubilation because their burdensome life was forgotten with the rapture their very souls felt. If but for a few moments their dreams filled with hope of a better time to come.

Will said he learned these stories from an old Negro he had come across in the scrub one day. The old man had not escaped nor was anyone looking for him. He was driven from the turpentine camp because he was no longer a productive worker for the foreman. He was sent out there to die and for the first time in his eighty-eight years, he was free to go as he wished. He spoke of going home soon and seeing his mother. Will understood what he was referring to because the preacher at Pine Grove Baptist Church talked about Heaven and the hope of one day seeing loved-ones who had died. The two men spent the night together when Will had happened across the old man's make shift camp and listened to the stories of the his tortured life.

The old man was born in a turpentine camp in Old Town to a run away slave from South Carolina. All he had ever known was the hard work of gathering, hauling and cooking out pinesap. He'd once married, he said, but the foreman in the camp in Old Town took a-likin" to his bride and took her from him.

He pulled up his right sleeve and revealed a long scar running from his elbow to his wrist. He told how the merciless foreman had been angry and used a large knife to cut his arm wide open in the camp one day. As he lay bleeding, the foreman took that same knife and drove it into the belly of his wife because she was with child. He spoke as if there was no bitterness in his life about the hardship he had lived. He had a desire for it to soon be over so he would "sees my reward". The gentle old man thanked Will for being so friendly.

The next morning Will awakened to find the old man dead. He buried him, marking his grave with some flowers he gathered from the scrub. Will, at such an early age, thought how much a shame it was this was all the old man had for eighty-eight years of life. Standing at the foot of the freshly dug grave Will could not comprehend a human being like that foreman having such power over another person.

Will was shaken by what he was seeing in the midst of the camp that day, he said. Under the same tree used as a place of worship on Sunday, hanging from one of the lower limps was a young man tied, suspended by his hands. He twisted as the northern wind blew and spun his lifeless body revealing the bloody lacerations made by the bullwhip hanging from a nail as a solemn reminder of the consequences of breaking the simple rules of life. Do your work and do not steal.

The old Negro man spoke to Will, bringing him back to reality by saying, "Stealin aint tolerated here." Startled, Will turned and stared at him dumbfounded when he began to speak saying. "Foller me and I'lls pays ya what's due ya." The respect Will once had for the old Negro rapidly dissolved as he tried hard to understand a reason for such callousness and cruelty from any human to another.

Following the man into the store, Will became even more confused by what he now heard. In a large back room of the store, Will could hear men speaking and they were not Negroes. The noise in the room was mixed with the laughter of women. Easing to where he could look into the room, Will saw three white men engaged in what the preacher would call sin. One of the men noticed him staring. The man smiled and said "What da hell you lookin' at, boy! Get out o here fer I kicks your ass." as he stomped his foot on the filthy floor.

Quickly Will turned his attention from the back room and looked around the store. He was not a very good reader but could see the shelves where filled with lots of goods but there were no prices posted. Pa Whaley had told him once about a company store in a turpentine camp in South Georgia where they provided everything that was needed for daily life but at a high price. This was how they could legally enslave the workers. The workers could never pay their heavy debt and the law could not touch the camp owners, even if someone reported them. The longer Will was with the old Negro foreman, the more Will's revulsion grew for him. The young man knew he had to leave this place before his newfound knowledge consumed him. The foreman reluctantly paid Will with cash. A wave of uneasiness came over Will and caused him to wonder if he would get away from the camp with any of the money or even his life.

Will had never seen so many Negros nor had he seen any people living in such filthy condition. Will lived in an open cracker style house having only wood slats over the windows during the winter months. He had gone to bed more times than he could remember without taking a bath, but the filth that he witnessed here was beyond unclean. The ground around the store and the row of cabins was barren of any living plant and the stench that enveloped the area was overwhelming to the point of making Will sick to his stomach. Will felt as if he had visited a land forgotten that he had read about while in school. He wondered why anyone would choose to live like this. How could men, honest men, allow another man to live in this condition? Will had been taught not to stare, but he could not get over what he witnessed in the camp that day.

Startled by the soft-spoken man that stood before him, he asked Will if he wanted to stay the night. He offered entertainment that a young man would find enjoyable, but for a price. It wasn't until later Will learned what the man was talking about. All Will wanted was to get as far away from that place as possible. While walking back to his horse he stopped and watched as one of the Negroes that had been beaten was being taken down from the tree. The dull sound of the young man's lifeless body made when it hit the ground made Will sick.

Placing the money deep in his wallet hanging over the horn of his saddle for safekeeping, he paused for a few moments looking trying to se if anyone had followed him. Aware of the fact that he had never had so much money at one time, he feared loosing it, either on accident or at the hand of evil men. Still thoroughly shaken by what he had witnessed while at the camp, confident he would never visit this place again, he mounted his horse. If he did come again, it would be to help change what he had seen.

He was eager to be back in the saddle and retrace the path he had taken to get to this place which he believed to be hell. Waiting until he had gotten out of the sight of the main gathering area of the camp, he spurred his horse hard, wanting to put as much distance between him and the camp before night fell. He wished that his pa were there to help him put what he had witnessed in some sort of perspective or some sort of reason for the way men treated others that were less fortunate. He hoped he would never have to smell the stench of cooking turpentine or the foul smell of another man's blood again.

Chapter 6

It was late in the day when the old man finished telling Danny the newest part of his story. His voice was sorrowful as he told Danny it was time for him to wash up, pointing to the back porch where he had placed some lye soap in a bowl. A good cold wash would help Danny get a good night's sleep. Their plans were to head to Fort Christmas and the store first thing in the morning to get supplies. He told Danny his intended plan was to meet several men to make final preparations for gathering and working his cows the next week. With that, the old man disappeared into his room and the lantern was snuffed out.

The water Danny used to wash was extremely cold. The water was being drawn directly out of a creek that ran under the back porch. The moon was on the decline and the night was very dark. Looking up in the sky Danny could barely see the stars glimmer against the blackness of the night. Danny shivered. He was unfamiliar with the sounds the night creatures made in the deep swamp. Off in the distance he could hear the hoot of an owl that created an almost musical beat for the doleful cry of a whip-poor-will. The night erupted with squealing from behind the barn. Between squeals from the hogs, he could hear a deep eerie growl of an unidentified predator. The trespasser was not welcome and had to be dealt with. Before the boy had the chance to wake Mr. Magrit, the old man was up and standing in the doorway with a shotgun in his hand. "Follow me and let's sees what's happenin'," he commanded as Danny jumped up quickly from where he was sitting. Still barefoot and with no shirt, Danny courageously followed the old man into the darkness. The dogs had already advanced upon the intruder and had what ever it was bayed up in the palmettos behind the barn. "Sounds like a wolf. I been a seein' sign of 'em lately messin' round here." the old man said with a sharp and keen voice. They quickly moved into the barn. "We needs to be careful cause them critters can be mean if'n they gets cornered". The two of them moved through the old barn toward the hog pen out back. The battle between wolf and dogs was getting severe.

When they reached the hog pen and lit a lamp, one of the hogs was ripped to pieces and the others were huddled in the corner squealin franticly. "Damn it, the dogs ain't letin' up on the critter." Clearing his throat he shouted the command "catch em" and the battle intensified. In just a few moments the ruckus was over. Silence flooded the night and Danny could again hear the owl in the distance still echoing its soulful sound through the swamp. The dogs left the palmetto patch and came within the sphere of the light, covered with blood. Evidence of the fight that took place. Several of the dogs had deep cuts from the animal now dead. Mr. Magrit grabbed some cob webs off the barn walls and placed it over the cuts on the dogs. After cleaning the mess in the hog pen and feeding them a little corn the remaining hogs settled back to normal immediately. Danny and the old man headed for the house. "Aint you curious 'bout what it was?" asked the stumbling boy as he tripped and stumbled on everything between the barn and the house. Mr. Magrit said, "It'll be there in the mornin" as he hurried toward the house. Without another word, the old man washed his hands in the bucket of water on the back porch, returned to his room and closed his door. Danny sat up most of the night trying hard to figure out what had just happened.

Danny was up at daylight and headed toward the barn. Forgetting about the dogs who still thought of him as to an interloper who had invaded their world the night before. Thankfully, he had parked his truck close by and was able to make his getaway into the back of the truck before they got too close. The old man stepped out onto the porch and with a thundering voice causing the aggressors to scatter. From that moment on, Danny was accepted as a part of the family. The old man asked if he had been able to see what the dogs had killed the night before. Danny laughed and told him he was going to do that very thing when the dogs forced him into the back of his truck. "Well, don't bother. Aint much left. It was an old she wolf that was sucklin' pups so we gonna find her den and kill them pups. Let's eat some breakfast and we'll head out." The boy could not believe all that was happening and could not wait for the meal to be over and they were able to leave.

The old man walked with a spring in his step as they headed for a small room inside the barn where he stored his saddles. Two hung from the ceiling by ropes and Danny watched as Mr. Magrit grabbed the larger of the two and pointed to the other, which was a McClellan. He said, "Bring that one with you". Mr. Magrit then pointed towards the small roan horse and told Danny that he could ride him. After saddling the horses, they rode down the dirt lane and crossed the creek then headed south along the creek swamp. The old man mumbled something about seeing sign of wolves close to Cow Pen Branch. The dogs steadily worked the palmetto patches and small cypress heads as they moved further away from the cow pens. Finally, the dogs struck a trail leading them back through the thick underbrush across the creek and into the Pokka-taw Flats. About noon they eventually found the den. It was in a pile of dead treetops left from the time when loggers came through and clear-cut the scrub. Sure enough, several young wolf pups had no chance against the dogs that made short work of them. To make sure that this den would never be used again, Danny was told to go and gather litered knots and stuff the mouth of the den full. The old man used this time to instruct the young in more common sense wisdom. When he sees a rattlesnake go down a hole, he used the same tactic. Stuffed the hole with littered knots, and leave. He would come back in a few days, the old man said, unclog the hole, wait for the hungry rattlesnake to come crawlin' out and that ole snake would be no more.

It took them about an hour and a half to get back to the barn. After unsaddling the horses, Danny brushed them down and gave them some corn. He then walked the horses to the cow pens so they could eat some grass that grew so abundantly.

After their chores were complete, the old man started the old truck that sat in the barn and headed toward Fort Christmas. He was going to meet with the men that had agreed to help gather and work his cows. Standing in front of the store was Emmett Tanner and two of his son's, Little John Nettles and Elbert Yates and his eldest son. As the men talked of where they would meet and what they planned to accomplish, the three boys got acquainted. Danny introduced himself and learned that the Tanner boy was named Junior and the other was Charles. From that moment on there was a strong friendship born, one that would last their entire lifetime. Danny recognized the other Tanner and from his first encounter, there was a deep respect that bordered on fear. It was determined that the Yates would ride through the woods from their place on Tosohatchee Creek and Emmett and Little John would meet at the cow pens and head west, then south, then back up the creek swamp. They shook hands and the deal was done. It seemed like a simpler time when a man was as good as his word. That night, Mr. Magrit went to bed early. Danny could tell that he was tired because his steps were not a spry as they had been earlier that morning.

Several of the Yates men showed up the next morning with the task of repairing the cow pens they were to use on the cow hunt. Danny went with them. Their first task was to cut cypress poles and cypress posts so that the lane leading up to the holding area was long enough not to spook the wild cows that still ranged the open spaces of East Orange County. They decided to stay the night so Charles and Danny saddled the horses and rode out to see if they could kill a deer for fresh meat for the camp. They rode for hours and talked, joked and told embellished tales that made themselves smarter and sharper then they really were. Each was glad that they had just met and did not know fabricated from real.

That night at supper, Mr. Magrit seemed to be in a celebrative mood and continued his story to the group of cowboys who listened.

He began by saying he had ridden several miles from the turpentine camp before he slowed his horse. The confused young man felt sick deep in his stomach because of the brutality that he had seen. Will vowed to himself that he would never treat anyone with such cruelty. His adopted family had taught him by their own actions that a man is worth respect no matter who they were. He quickly cleared his mind of the matter and hoped for another encounter with the ghostly figure that had entered his life and thoughts, complicating his once simple life.

Will felt cool blasts of air as it blew across the open scrub. The clouds to the northwest moved to the wave of some strange force that drove them on. Will watched becoming rapt by the movement of the storm clouds, but instinct pushed him forward, driving him homeward. He was sure he did not want to spend any more time on this side of the river because it was still too close to the turpentine camp.

Will knew the river would still be flooded. His hope was that he would have enough time to cross before the dampness of night caught him. His mind was a long way off because he did not see three riders circling the flag pond from the other direction. Just before he entered into the swamp, Will heard someone holler and turned to recognize the riders as they approached him at full gallop. He was relieved to recognize Bud, Bryant and Willie Yates. After a short greeting, Bud spoke up and told Will that since it was decrease of the moon they were going to camp at Paw Paw Mound and hog hunt. As long as he was there, they wondered if he was interested in going with them. Will really liked to hog hunt and knew the time spent in the woods would be worth any trouble he might get into when he got home. He envied the Yates and their dogs when it came to finding a hog. He wished that he too could have just one trial dog as good as even one of theirs. Most of the hogs in these parts belonged to someone. It was an unwritten law that a man's marked hog was his possession and you didn't mess with another man's marked hogs. Will knew from experience that stealin' hogs was an offence that would not be tolerated.

Pa Whaley had told him of a time when some of the Tuckers caught a man stealin' hogs and the man was beat for his offence and run out of the territory.

The men in the community liked going to the river to hunt hogs because they were always able to find a big boar hog traveling from points unknown, and unmarked. The hogs would give them a good run and fight. This particular night would prove to be a memorial one for Will. After making camp and fixing what they had in way of food, it finally began to get dark enough. Willie took the lead as they rode off to the west into a large cabbage hammock. The hammock ran all the way to Big Prairie just below Persimmon Hammock. To the east was an expansion of river prairie that ran all the way to the coast. Spotted islands of cabbage and cedar trees broke up its landscape. About a mile or so from camp, the young men jumped the trail of a large hog. Familiar with the smell it left behind, everyone knew it was a big boar hog. The hog ran in one big circle and then left the country, stopping for only a moment as the dogs bayed it up. The hog would break and run again. After about an hour, the group of men were finally able to stop the hog in a large patch of palmettos. Will laughed and said that ole hog was givin' them dogs a fit. Dogs and hog fighting and squealing, the dogs barking incessantly. To those who loved to hog hunt, it was the sweetest sound ever heard.

Getting closer the men could hear that old hog popping his teeth even over the sound of the dogs baying. The hog would charge at the dogs, hit 'em and toss 'em into the air and the dogs would be right back on him. One of the dogs came limping out of the palmettos with an enormous gash under his neck. Willie got off his horse and found he needed to sew up the cut or the dog would bleed out. Pulling a hair from his horse's tail, he started sewing the wound. When he was through, he laid the injured dog next to a tree and returned to the action. Things were getting good when all but one of the dogs shut up. They seemed to just disappear. Everyone looked confused when Bud said, "It sounds like old Sally, and she wouldn't give up on a hog. Them other damn dogs wouldn't stay with a hog if'en their lives depended on it. We's lost more hogs 'cause of them dogs." Aggravated, Willie shot back, "If'en she's so good, you go on in dere and get dat dang hog by yer self. I'm taken Hank back to camp." Bud climbed down off his horse and started a cabbage fan on fire. He got on his knees and crawled into the fray. He was gone for a few minutes when they heard the dog yelping. Bud began to cuss and calling that old dog a dumb fool. The old dog come runnin' out just as bewildered as the rest of the young men and followed Willie back to camp. Bud came crawling out of the palmetto patch, streaks of blood running down his cheek from the saw palmetto and told us what had happened. "That dam dog had her eyes closed an' a bayin' a palmetter root." Will began to laugh because in just a few minutes, the best dog in that bunch of ole hounds had turned into the dumbest and neither Bryant nor Will would let Bud forget it.

They decided the hog had not run by them so he had to have turned north. Trailing again, after about a mile they could hear the dogs baying off in the distance. Just as they got to where the dogs had the old hog stopped, they dismounted so they could rope the hog. It was not their habit to shoot the animals. All of a sudden, a yellow streak ran by them and before they knew what happened, all hell broke loose in them myrtles. Will's little dog, Buck, had chewed through his rope and followed them. The dog had caught that old hog. They finally got their hands on the hog and tied it off. Bryant wanted to buy the dog from Will, but no amount of money could have purchased him from Will. They all agreed that since Will's dog caught the hog, Will could cut him and mark him with his mark, only if he bobbed the hog's tail. The Yates liked to bob the tails to make it hard for the next person to catch it.

On their way back to Paw Paw Mound, the dogs jumped a sow and a bunch of shoats. They were fat for this time of year and did not have any one's mark. One fat gilt was shot, and then skinned. The group of tired young men headed back to camp for breakfast. They cut palmetto sticks and pierced the meat, pushing the sticks into the ground next to the roaring fire. The meat sizzled as it dripped fat onto the ground.

Will continued with his stories. It was daylight when the three of them got back to camp. They sat and talked for a couple of hours before Will stood up and told them he had to go. Even though he was tried, he still wanted to see the old man that he had seen a few nights before. The meeting with the ghostly figure never happened. In two days, he entered the lane that ran from the river to his home.

Chapter 7

It was about noon when he reined his horse in front of the barn. It seemed strange because the dogs did not announce his arrival as times before. To the young man's surprise everything was cleaned out of the house; the only things left was the few possessions that he had in this world. Will called out to anyone that could hear him but there was no response. Everything was gone, the chickens, the hogs, the oxen and wagon, even the corncrib was empty. He could not understand what had happened and felt guilty that he was off hog hunting and did not get home as soon as he could. Maybe he could have been here and helped his family out of the ordeal that they found themselves in whatever it was.

Will figured that they had been gone for about a week. He sat on the front steps of the house and wondered if they had known they were going to leave. Was that the reason why Pa sent him to deliver the cattle to the turpentine camp? It wasn't till dark he let himself believe they were gone and would probably never be back. After fixing the last of the bacon and eating a cold biscuit, not because he was hungry but to keep his strength up, he fell asleep. Restless sleep came only because of sheer exhaustion. The dreams of the ghost, the money in his pocket and the disappearance of the family disturbed his sleep.

The next morning he angrily packed his meager possessions. His plan was to ride east to the small settlement on the St. Johns River southeast of Lake Harney at Persimmon Hammock called Hat Bill to inquire about his family. His search began at the general store. A small man by the name of Billy Tyner owned and operated the store. Everyone in the settlement called him Uncle Billy out of respect for his age. Uncle Billy thought it was his life's calling to know every bodies business and if he did not get all the details, he would just make things up.

Pa Whaley told young Will, "If you don't want folks to know your business, keep your mouth shut". Uncle Billy was a short man with black hair who tried real hard to grow a handlebar mustache. The mustache was never more'n a few hairs stuck together and streaked with a little gray. Some people just look strange even if they don't try, Will thought to himself.

Will really liked a good story and he was convinced that Pa Whaley could tell the best ones. His favorite, he said, had to be about a card game that had taken place at the store at Hat Bill that lasted all night. Someone had brought in a jug of fresh pulled shine and Uncle Billy got drunk. In addition, when Billy got drunk, he started runnin' his mouth and sure enough a fight would break out. Will said you could hear him from outside the store hollerin'. He had crawled under the table, closed his eyes and was swingin' a stick wildly in no particular direction. At that point in the story, Pa Whaley would get so tickled he could barely continue with the story and Will remembered nights they all would break out laughin'. They would get to laughin' at each other and the stories would never stop till they became exhausted. Pa Whaley would catch his breath and say, "The man gots to laughin' so hard he plume fergot what he were fightin' bout, the harder the men would laugh, the madder ole Billy would gets and the crazier he swung dat stick". You had to see Pa Whaley tell the story because he closed his eyes and swing wildly with an imaginary stick.

Every time Will saw Uncle Billy, it was plum hard to keep from laughing. Billy Tyner just thought Will was a little off in the head and felt sorry for him 'cause he always had a silly grin on his face.

As he walked up the long steps to the porch that surrounded the entire store, Uncle Billy met him at the door one day and said, "No use com'in in heres. That family o yers done left a few days back on da steamer fer Georgia. They was talkin' sompin' 'bout Ware County, sompin' like dat. Heck, I can't 'member ever thing he said. Ya'll all been a little tetched in the head to me. Your pa heared word they's trouble with his ma and dey just up and left."

Will was stunned by the news and must have shown on his face when the storekeeper said, "Yer pa told me to tell you head for Fort Christmas. He got family there. You to stay with 'em." Will turned and looked out toward the river. He had never felt so alone and fearful. Conscious that his feelings was showing but not wanting anyone to see him cry, he mounted his horse and rode east. The storeowner yelled out, "Your pa said you could have da money and da cows he got's left on da marsh. I got da papers dat says it." The last thing Will heard him say was, "I gots a buyer" as the man's voice just faded away. The confused young man rode away as hard as he could.

Will spent the next two nights back at the homestead wondering where he was going to go. He knew that he did not want to live at Fort Christmas with his pa's brother. If there was one thing he had learned was the man was harsh and curial. Will did not want to be obligated to him for anything and believed that it would be better for him to care for himself. After the second night alone, he went back to Uncle Billy's store and got the paper that showed that the cows with the crop split mark in both ears were his.

Using some of the money from the sale of the cattle at the turpentine camp, he was able to purchase supplies for a trip up the river as he looked for work. Will had heard the Cameron Cattle Company near Melonvillie was hiring. Maybe they could use him for something. At that time, he just wanted to be around people.

After two weeks of unsuccessful searching for work and at the end of his supplies, he rode toward Curryville to visit with the Lane family with no success. He then traveled to Chuluota in hopes of finding some work. The Simmons family were clearing a small piece of land they had just acquired in a trade to plant chuffers for their hogs. Will recalled being told chuffers were a peanut-like bulb that grew naturally and was used as hog feed.

The Simmons family offered Will work for a few days. It was hard work cutting down brush, digging roots and burning stumps, but Will liked the challenge and he especially enjoyed the company.

Just across the creek from the Simmons lived a family that made their living off shine. He had considered that line of work but something inside him kept telling him to keep moving. About a week after he was there, he heard the still had exploded and killed two of the boys. Will believed that God looked out for fools, of which he felt himself one.

Finding work hard to come by, he finally returned to the only home he had ever known. His thought he could make it on his own. He believed that, with the few cows that were left on the marsh with his mark, he was convinced that he could get enough for them in the spring after the calves dropped.

The surprises where not over for young Will. When he got back to the old homestead, he found out that Pa Whaley had sold the place to some stranger he'd met on the steamer trip north. It became apparent to Will that there was now no place for him in this entire world. If he were to survive, it would be entirely up to him. He began to accept why he had to be made to work like he had. The knowledge he had learned made it easier to live on his own. He managed to get a price of twelve dollars a head for the cattle from the man that bought the old place. There were fifty head of cows. Will kept the rights to the mark crop split in both ears. Will felt an overwhelming loss of security and thought he had learned a very important lesson. Money could elevate a man to gain respect and answer all a man's problems. However, much later in life he would learn that was not always true.

During that particular time in his life, he faced many hardships and difficulties that challenged everything he had been taught and believed. Will paused in his story and told Danny he was glad for the foundation his adopted parents had given him. He had considered following his pa's advice and moving to Fort Christmas and to living there with his uncle, but he did not have to consider that possibility long before deciding against it. All he could think about was the time his family had gone over to his uncle's home to butcher hogs. His uncle got so he beat his oldest son, Newton, for no fault of the boy's. He was a drunkard and a wicked man. He had often thought it would not surprise him if one day he heard that someone had killed the old man. A few years after that incident, Will heard that several men from the community visited his home wearing hoods and beat him half to death, warning him not to be abusive towards his wife and kids again. They told him that this was a learnin' lesson and he would learn without them having to come back. It wasn't long after that the drunk found religion and started attending Pine Grove Baptist Church. The preacher baptized him in Savage Creek.

Things after got a little better for his uncle's family but Will feared that it had been too late for some of his boys. It was told they ran away from home and joined the Confederate Army. Both were killed at Olustee during the Civil War.

Mr. Magrit stopped telling his story abruptly at that point. Danny could see a far away look in his eyes. Danny became concerned because of the old man's demeanor changing. Danny watched as his lips moved but no words could be heard. It was as if he were carrying on a conversation with someone that was not there again. Without another word, Mr. Magrit got up from his seat, took off his hat and rubbed his head, seeming to be confused with his surroundings. The old man turned and walked to his room and laid down on his mattress made of moss.

Chapter 8

Early the next morning Danny stood out in the yard as heavy fog lay close to the ground and the air was filled with the sound of frogs croaking. Several days before, a hard rain had fallen and filled the low areas around the clearing. Thousands of frogs now croaked their own melody, competing to be heard.

Danny watched as the cowboys started showing up with their trucks bringing different sized and color horses, along with all types, shapes and sizes of cow dogs. Danny was fascinated by the way the local cattlemen hauled their horses. They used the back of their trucks, training the horses to leap into the beds for transporting. The later the morning got Danny became tremendously eager to get this adventure started. He didn't realize until later in the morning what he thought would be fun was actually hard work. He had never been on a drive before.

After saddling their horses, the crew of men rode off in the direction of the old set of cow pens just south of the main gate on the homestead. It was there everyone would get their assignments for the day. Danny was instructed to pay close attention to how the men, horses and dogs worked the area. The dogs did most of the work keeping order and moving the cattle forward.

They had not gone far before they found the first bunch of cows and calves. Bringing them out of the creek swamp onto the scrub, they drove them toward two younger boys that would hold the small bunch of cows till the others were found. The small crew of cattlemen moved deeper into the creek swamp for the strays that had broke and run. It did not take long for the dogs to stop the lead cow and turn her. Danny could hear the sound of cracking whips and barking dogs. All of a sudden, he saw a small group of cows moving slowly toward him. Mr. Emmett galloped up to him and told him to keep the cows moving toward the others that had already been gathered. Danny admitted to himself he was nervous when given the responsibility of driving twelve head of cows and calves to join up with the two younger riders still holding their charges. Danny was relieved that once the other cows came into view, the task of driving the cattle became a lot easier. Once his group of cows joined the others, Danny had an opportunity to get to know Junior better. He concluded Junior was too serious for his age. The entire conversation was about how much he liked being on a horse and working cows because the chores he had to do at home were hard. Every day he had to tote water from their open thirty foot deep well to the newly planted orange grove. It was also his responsibility to work the family garden, which was the main source of food for the family. He also had to help with the care of his younger brother that was bedridden. As they spoke, Danny never sensed an ounce of bitterness or complaint from Junior. Every family that made their living off the land knew hard work as a burdensome task that had no end and was a necessity for survival, but a task none-the-less.

The boys watched constantly in the direction of the sounds of lowing cows and the crack, crack, crack of the cow whips. The sounds echoed off the large pines and shrubbery. Little John and Mr. Emmett drove the remaining cows out of the thick palmettos that bordered the creek swamp onto the open scrub just west of where the young men held the main herd. Mr. Magrit rode up to the boys and instructed them to begin to move the cows, which numbered about one hundred and twenty head, slowly toward the men waiting to begin their work at the cow pens.

When they joined the others, Little John and Mr. Emmett soon left the herd and headed south to make one more wide sweep in order to gather any stray cows that had escaped. Mr. Magrit spoke with an authoritative voice that would intimidate even a grown man, "We got all day, drive'em slow". When the cow pens came into view, Junior rode ahead and made sure the gates were opened. As Danny rode his horse slowly beside the others, the air became covered with heavy dust produced by the steadily moving cows. The steady lowing of the cattle and the skill demonstrated by Charles and Junior in their use of the sixteen-foot bullwhip captured Danny's full attention. Danny made up his mind that by the next time they worked cows, he would be able to use a whip as well. Mr. Magrit counted the cows as they passed by him. He commented that he was well pleased with the shape his cows were in. There was nothing to do but wait for the others to drive any strays found back to the pen so the three boys were given permission to explore the surrounding area close to the pens. As they walked nearby, they discovered a long concrete pit with a slight ramp on either end. Mr. Magrit explained to them it was a dipping vat used during the Texas tick fever days in the early nineteen twenties. He went on to explain how they would haul water from the creek in wooden barrels, pour an arsenic solution in and then force the affected cattle and making them swim in order to eradicate and kill the ticks. Caution had to be taken, in the process, because if you used too much of the dip or it rained soon after, it would dry on the cow's belly and cause it to split. The process would have to be repeated every fourteen days under the threat of legal action. As he walked to the edge and peered into the vat, he told the boys that the use of the vat and dip caused many of the smaller cattlemen to have to go out of the business. It was during this time, as well, that Florida's fence laws were introduced. The end of an era of free range was over, Mr. Magrit said sorrowfully. He told them that one day he would tell them more of the days when he was a Range Rider, but they had things they had to do as the sound of more cattle touched their ears. Turning back to the pens because they heard the crack of whips and the lowing of cattle, they waited. Mr. Magrit told Danny that Mr. Magrit had ridden with Junior's father as far north as Taylor County in southern Florida when they had both been Range Riders. Junior looked perplexed because he thought that he knew everything about his father. He never knew that his father had such a job. It had to have been before he was born. He made Mr. Magrit promise that he would tell him more some day and the old man agreed with a smile on his face. He then said, "Run ahead and open the gate fer your pa".

Just before dark Elbert and Morris who had been cow hunting the eastern edge of the Magrit property drove the last of the cows' that they had gathered into the holding pen for a total of two hundred and sixty four cows, calves, steers and four old ugly Brahma bulls. The cows were calling for their young as they milled around grazing on what little grass grew in the five-acre holding pen. As the men stood around the pen talking about the day's work and how healthy the cows were this year, Mr. Magrit listened with pride as he silently agreed. The three boys sat on the fence enjoying listening to the old men talk and they all agreed that they were some of the smartest men they knew when it came to cows.

While the men were out gathering the cows, Aunt Daisy and Aunt Julia arrived and took charge of the cook shed for the preparation of the meals for the next few days. When everyone gathered to work each other's cows, the work took on a festive mood. The pens they would use were back at Mr. Magrit's homestead and he insisted the women folk take the house even though the women enjoyed camping out under the stars like the men and they always came prepared to do so. "No" he insisted. They must stay in the house and treat it as their own. It didn't seem right to him for them to have to be outside all night. Danny and Mr. Magrit gathered what they would need for the night and left the house without saying another word. Danny noticed that Mr. Margit seemed very uncomfortable around the women and wondered why it was so awkward for him.

Early the next morning Danny was again surprised by the toughness of those that lived and eeked out a living in the wilderness. Aunt Daisy and Aunt Julia saddled their own mount and joined the men on the next days cow hunt. The women worked as hard as any man on the cow hunts. The women had risen early that day and fixed a meal of fried salt pork, sweet potatoes and biscuits. After the meal, the women had packed the extra salt pork, sweet potatoes and biscuits for the noon meal. They packed the old coffee pot and coffee to be served at the meal. Each cowboy had a tin cup tied to his saddle for water and coffee.

Mr. Margit told Danny he could ride his horse that day. He would not be going because he was not feeling well and would only be a drag on the entire party.

Mr. Emmett led the party north along the creek swamp around and through the thick pinewoods past the Partin and Tanner homesteads. They made their way toward Lake Pickett, then due east to Buncombe Branch in search of any of the Margit cows. The Carters that lived on the southern shore of Lake Pickett had gotten word to Mr. Emmett that they had been seeing the Margit brand in that area. Sure enough, they were able to locate twenty-five head near Rattlesnake Branch and drove them back before nightfall to the Margit homestead. With the new found cows now secure in the holding pen with the rest of the cows, Mr. Emmett called everyone together after supper telling them to get a good night's sleep because they were going to start in the pens first thing in the morning.

Little John had spent the afternoon before mammying the already gathered cows in order that each man would get his pay. It was common practice to pay the workers in calves and the mammying was done so that the right calf would be matched to the right cow. The calves would stay on their mothers until weaned. When they finally started working the cows, Little John and Morris were in charge of working the cows in the pen from atop their horse. Danny thought it was like watching artists at work. The boys were each assigned a gate where the cows would be separated. As the cows moved down the shoot from the holding pens, the two older men would do the doctoring using a medicine called COBOL. COBOL was a green gray liquid that was poured down the throat of the cow using an old coke bottle. If the cow would not swallow, the men would grab the cow's throat and shake it, forcing the bitter liquid down the cow's throat.

The first bunch brought into the working area of the pens set the stage for the rest of the day. Danny, because of his inexperience and overwhelmed with what was happening around him, was not paying attention when a banana horned cow hit his gate, sending him flying into the cows loitering in the pen next to him. The cows began stepping all over him. Danny didn't know there were different kind of cow horns. He quickly learned a banana horned cow was a cow that had horns that look a lot like small bananas hanging off their head. He was hurt, but would not show it or let anyone know how badly. Young man's pride had a lot to do with it.

Morris was knocked from his horse when one of the bulls run into his horse's side causing him to hit the wooden fence, and falling off his horse. As fast as he hit the ground, he was back in the saddle. The only words that came from his mouth are words that cannot be repeated in mixed company. There were women present. Mr. Emmett spoke harshly and Morris never said another word the rest of the day. One of the other men accidentally cut his hand as he marked one of the yearling heifers. Little John kept reminding Will to save the mountain oysters for his supper, and joked with his sister, Aunt Daisy, about frying them for him that night. Just the mention of such a thing caused the boys to look at each other and laugh out loud getting them in trouble. Aunt Daisy reminded everyone that boys would be boys and that when they were young they laughed at the same thing. Everyone agreed and returned to the job at hand.

After the last cow was run through and doctored, the time every came everyone looked forward to. The young boys in the crew got their chance to prove to everyone they were worth their hire. The only thing that remained was the bull calves to be legged, thrown and cut. Mr. Margit explained to Danny that cutting the young bulls made them into steers. Danny stood back and watched as Junior and Charles rushed into the bunch of calves. One of the young men grabbed a back leg of the bellowing wriggling calf while the other would go to its side, reach down, and grab a front leg. Lifting it up, the calf would fall on its side. Then the one that had the back leg would place his foot in the crotch area of the calf that would immobilize the calf. Mr. Margit or Emmett would grab the testicles, or go-nads as the cowboys called them, and with two swipes of their very sharp knife, removed them, and marked the calf's ear. The calf would be loosed and it would return to the herd crying for its mother. Mr. Margit explained to Danny that it did, indeed, hurt the calf for a while but that it was a necessity of life. The steers in the herd were the moneymakers where meat for the market came from. The Margit mark was crop sharp under bit in the right ear and a crop split in the left. Danny soon joined in the melee, got kicked several times but enjoyed every minute of the new experience. Danny saw Mr. Margit relaxed enough to laugh out loud.

When the final calf was cut and marked, Little John rode into the holding pen filled with the doctored cows, opening the gate he drove them away from the pens. The lowing of the fifty-five, two and three year old steers filled the air as the crew kept a watchful eye on the herd. The cattle began to graze and mill about. The cowboys kept circling the herd as they waited patiently for the calves to find their mothers. It was dangerous to the calves if they did not find their mothers. A calf on its own on the marsh would be fair game for their enemies who waiting to capture and eat them. Not only did the cowboys circle the herd, the dogs kept a constant vigil for strays that tried to break and run from the herd. The recently cut steers and young heifers had never seen humans or been separated from their mommas and protested all afternoon until it was determined that all had been reunited and they were driven back toward the marsh.

Danny, Junior and Charles were given permission to go to the creek to wash up. They hurried to their horses and with a chorus of hollers rode toward a deep water hole in the creek away from the women folk. It didn't take Danny long to strip down to bare skin and jump into the cold tannic water causing ripples and bubbles to rush across the surface of the water. Coming up and taking a breath of air, he looked at Junior and Charles standing there with their mouths wide open. Their back woods modesty would not allow them to go skinny-dipping. Danny teased them for their awkwardness .Junior got angry and abandoned his shyness, joining Danny, with a shout, in the cold clear water. Charles was not as sure as the others were and reluctantly yielded to the their constant banter. It was Charles that did not want to leave once he jumped in.

The next morning, Little John agreed to allow the boys to ride along with him as he drove the fifty-five steers in the herd to Wewahoottee to the market. Danny fell in love with the country and the gathering of the herd, the work involved, and the trip to market convinced him he had found his life's work. The friends he made boosted his spirits, as well.

When Danny finally arrived back at the Margit homestead, everyone had gone home. He was relieved to be able to sleep in his own bed. There was a fire burning in the stove, casting an orange glow that danced on the ceiling and walls inside the house. Even though Danny was extremely tired, he hoped that Mr. Margit was feeling better so he would tell Danny a little more of his life's story.

Chapter 9

After the only family Will had ever known had abandoned him, Will moved to Osteen Island just off Lake Cane trying to figure out what he would do next. It didn't take very long for him to get tired of being alone and a limited diet of fish and turtle meat. He knew he could not stay there much longer. He had no shelter but cabbage leaves if the weather were to turn bad. One evening, Will recalled, he was awestruck by the reflection of the full moon glistening off the river that flowed slowly and lazily passed where he was camped. He wondered if his life would pass him by like the river and pondered how much of it had already passed without his even noticing. Something caught his eye as it moved on the river. It floated just above the surface of the water and moved with little effort. Uncertain of what he saw, Will quickly doused the campfire and moved into the cabbage palms along the riverbank hoping that he had not yet been detected. As he crept from one clump of switch-grass to another, inching closer to the river's edge' he made out what he saw was a dugout occupied by two Indians. He had heard from several old-timers that the Nettles family often traded with the Indians, trading salt for furs and other supplies.

Salt was taken with little effort from the beaches at New Smyrna, but the trip took almost a week and involved hauling large kettles in ox drawn wagons. Several of the families from the area would take the yearly trip and camp for days as they drew salt water from the Atlantic Ocean, boiling it for days in the kettle, and drying the salt that had separated from the evaporating water. The salt would be used for household use and for curing their meat. Curing the meat was a necessity to keep it from so that spoiling in the summer heat. Smoke houses were built when their homes were built. Smoke from fires built under the smoke houses, as well as salting the meat down, would preserve the meat for many months. The salt was also used as a type of currency for trade.

There was another way to get salt from the wilderness. Palmetto fronds were burned and as the dew fell, it began to dry. The white crystals that formed was salt. This was only used when they could not travel to the ocean.

Most that knew the history of the Nettles family found it very difficult to understand why the relationship with the Indians was so strong. Years before, it was told that the Indians had killed the grandfather of Crete during the Second Seminole Indian War near Fort Defiance in north central Florida.

For a long time, Will believed that Indians traveling the St. Johns River was only a tale people told around the campfires, but that night Will became a believer.

He hid in the cattails and watched as they moved their craft up to a raised platform, one that he had not seen until now. Will noticed that the night creatures with their sounds filled the air every night since he came to the island. There was complete silence as the creatures, too, seemed to watch and listen to the strange voices that broke the still silence of the night. Without alarm or acknowledgement of Will and his campfire, the two figures in the dugout removed their package, replacing it with something that Will could not make out and moved quickly north. Captivated by the events that had just taken place and after several minutes, Will stood up from his hiding place and stared off into the distance as they disappeared into the darkness. He was not sure which emotion was stronger, fear or curiosity, as he turned to retreat back to the safety of his camp.

He happened to look north one more time, noticed the glow of a campfire at Orange Mound, and wondered if this was the Indian camp. Unsure of what he might find, he thought it best to go there at first light and investigate. It was late into the night before sleep came, but when it did, he dreamed of adventure and conquest over these uninvited invaders of his peaceful existence.

At daylight, Will was already in the saddle and quietly making his way in the direction of the campfire he had seen the night before. Not sure if he wanted to find the camp occupied, his curiosity won out over fear and he pressed on.

The morning was foggy and it seemed to lay low on the ground so he dismounted about a quarter of a mile from Orange Mound and walked slowly and as quietly as possible toward the mound. He would take a few steps, allowing his eyes to adjust to the shadows that were cast by the fading fog as the sun rose. Seeing no movement, he would then take a few more steps and repeat the process. Finally, he entered a clearing determining this to be the campsite, relieved that he must have just missed them because the coals were still smoldering. Truly pleased that he had not found them still there, and really not sure what he would have done if he had surprised them, he paused.

It was on one of his many trips up and down the St. Johns that Crete Nettles befriended several Indian families and told of the platform ritual that Will had watched. If Crete Nettles had learned the secret of the platform ritual, he had not given the secret up.

Mounting his horse and turning toward Osteen Island, Will heard cattle lowing, whips popping, and dogs barking in the distance.

He rode toward the sounds that were familiar to him, knowing that very close, men were gathering cows. He had not ridden a mile before seeing a big herd of cows immerging from the fog and the shadows of the cabbage hammock that many called Bee Tree Log.

Will recognized the silhouette of the lead rider as Henry Tanner. A short man with a gray mustache that covered most of his face, the mustache masked the scar he had received in a knife fight when he was younger.

Not wanting to spook the cows, Will rode far enough ahead of the man to make his presence known. Sure that the sharp eye of Henry Tanner would see his movement and recognize that he was friendly and wanted to talk, he rode closer.

As Will told him about his desperate situation, the old man was responsive and sympathetic, and hired him on the spot. Grandpa Henry told him he could not pay much, but agreed to teach him all he knew about cows, the woods and provided him with food and a dry place to sleep. Agreeing with the terms set before him, Will was pleased to have secured a job and started a new life as a cow hunter. This was a dream of Will's and he made up his mind that this would be his life's work.

Will then smiled at Danny and said he learned a lot from Grandpa Henry as he spent the next two years with the Tanner family on the big creek.

Listening to stories was one of Will's favorite things to do. He especially enjoyed the one of how the Tanners ended up in this part of the country. John Tanner, Grandpa Henry's father, was commissioned by the government and ordered to Fort Gatlin as a Federal scout. His duties required him to scout east of the fort during the Second Seminole Indian War. It was during that time John Tanner fell in love with a place called big creek, but later named Econlochatchee River. The openness of the wilderness offered to him the solitude he wanted and the freedom to raise his family as he saw fit. Vowing to move his family to the big creek as soon as he could, in 1834 the entire family left Coffee County Georgia and headed south. It took them almost three months by ox cart when they finally settled on Lake Apopka, then later in Longwood. When that area started to get crowded, he up and moved further east to the place he really longed to be. Here he was able to clear ten acres and planted an orange grove.

He provided for his family by hunting, fishing and raising cattle. After a while, the Indians became hostile again and John moved his family back to Fort Gatlin. As soon as the Indians quieted down, he returned to the big creek. Due to illness, John and his wife and family moved back to Longwood in 1874 and agreed to sell the homestead and two hundred acres on the creek to Henry Tanner for five hundred dollars. It was here that Henry Tanner raised thirteen children from what he scraped out of the wilderness.

After spending just a few days at the Tanner homestead, Will began to understand why this particular place was chosen. The creek was widest and deepest here and lay less then a quarter mile from the back steps of the cracker style home Henry constructed out of heart pine. The house was built about three feet off the ground and had what was called a dog walk between two big rooms. The dog walk, called that because the dogs walked freely back and forth through it, allowing the breezes to blow under and around the house. Fish and deer were abundant and there always seemed to be a breeze blowing off the creek. The large live oak trees offered shade in the summer and shelter for the young grove in the winter. Will developed a love for orange trees and hunting and it didn't take long to convince him that Grandpa Henry was the best there was in the woods and hoped that one-day he would be just as good.

One of Will's fondest memories was the time when Grandpa Henry's oldest son, Willey, had bears messing with his beehives. Will knew how quickly bears could destroy a beehive and eat all the honey in a very short time. Honey was a needed staple for the homesteaders. The whole Tanner clan of men set out the next morning determined to hunt down the bear and stop him from robbing any more hives. The party turned north from the old place and rode along the creek.

Will had always thought the creek to be beautiful. Its cypress trees were so large that it would take six men with their outstretched arms to encircle one tree, oak trees towering so high you could barely distinguish where the treetops stopped and the sky began. The white sand in the creek looked like small crystals along the creek bed, the pools of water spotted with little clumps of green vegetation yielding only to the swift running tannic water that seemed to always flow even in the deepest holes. It was said that mullet and other salt-water fish found their way into the creek in the old days. The sounds of the water and animals captivated anyone that would stop long enough to listen. The chorus of songbirds and katydids with their deafening shrill cries that rise to a high pitch then soften was present. The sound repeats itself repeatedly through out the day. The bark of a playful squirrel announces the presence of intruders into its domain along with the lonesome call of the chicken hawk circling high above the creek. An occasional tree limb or cabbage fan would fall to the ground adding an exclamation point to the tranquility of this paradise. Will said he enjoyed sitting on the creek bank allowing its busyness to help him relax.

It didn't take them long for the group of men to pick up the trail of the pesky bear as it crossed a flag pond leaving the massive imprints of its paws. Grandpa Henry said it was heading for Bear Branch and it would be quicker if they were to ride straight for the Simmons place, then turn northeast from there. He said, with confidence, "We could probably cut him off and save us a lot of aggravation". An hour later, they caught up with the bear. The bear tried hard to loss the dogs by making wide circles and crossing the creek twice, but the dogs finally bayed it up in an old dead oak tree. The ruckus caused by the bloodthirsty dogs was now at a high pitch so when Willey shot the bear and it fell out of the tree, the instant it hit the ground the dogs ripped it to pieces. Usually Grandpa Henry would not allow that to happen because he could not truly abide cruelty to man or beast. He relented on this occasion did not mind because of damage the bear had caused, and a deep sense of revenge. It was understood by everyone that one bear had robbed them of a year's sweetener. They would have to go through the effort of cutting down a bee tree and robbing the honey. They were reluctant to rob a bee tree since last year's tragic accident. Grandpa Henry stated, without changing his voice, while cutting down a bee tree his youngest son had been killed.

For the next few days after the bear hunt, and with nothing else to do for the men, it was decided that everyone would go hog hunting. Hog hunting was a sport enjoyed by the Tanner men because it tested their skill and bravery against one of the most determined adversaries in Florida's wilderness. A wild hog could hurt a man or dog really bad if you did not respect the hog's fierceness.

Will recalled hearing a story about a man who got his kneecap almost cut off by the sharp tusks of a boar hog. It was said that the local hunters had some of the best trail and catch dogs in the country. The group of men and boys saddled their horses and rode to the creek. Fresh hog sign was spotted instantly and the dogs turned loose to do their work.

A young man named Jim Sweet had been hired on for the cow crew at the Tanners. It was known that Jim thought very highly of himself and didn't mind telling you just how much he knew about everything. Well, that particular day the dogs finally bayed up in a large palmetto patch on the edge of a cabbage hammock. Jim jumped off his horse that was in full gallop. Without missing a step, he ran right off into the palmetto patch. All hell broke loose and the men left behind could hear was a strange scream coming from the direction of the palmetto. It wasn't the dogs or the hog squalling. They all looked at each other and wondered what was going on. All of a sudden, Jim come running out of that palmetto patch and right into a cabbage tree. He fell on his back still screaming bloody murder and before any of the men could say anything to him, he was up again and ran right back into that same tree, knocking himself out cold. Will said he like to have fallen out of his saddle laughin' so hard. Never did find out if'n it was the dogs or the hog that spooked Jim, Will said with a laugh. Grandpa Henry said there was one positive thing come out of Jim's display of show offin'. Jim Sweet never bragged about hisself or anything' no more.

Chapter 10

Come next morning, Danny woke up without anyone having to wake him. After getting the fire started and the coffee going for Mr. Margit, he received permission from Mr. Margit to saddle the horse to cross the creek and check the old man's hog trap. Mr. Margit grabbed his old Winchester rifle and handed it to Danny telling him if he seen the old buck again that morning to shoot him. Mr. Margit, he said, was hungry for fresh meat. Danny bolted from the house, letting the front door slam. The old man thought about calling him back and scolding him for letting the door slam, but just smiled. Realizing it was excitement rather than carelessness, he let the young man scamper off to the barn.

Danny rode out into the scrub turning south toward the cow pens. He wished Junior and Charles could be there with him so they could spend the rest of the day discovering afresh what he had found weeks before. Following the rutted trail past the cow pens down into the creek bottom, he spurred the horse through the water and on to the other side. His first thought was what he would do first, go check the trap or hunt the deer. Soon nature would make the choice for him. Right on the edge of the paint root pond stood a large buck. Surprised, Danny could not understand why the buck paid him no mind. The large buck acted crazy running with his head down to the ground, then tossing it into the air as if it was dancing. He would later learn from the old man what he witnessed was the rut, a time of the year when the buck deer court the does. Only the strongest of the males would breed.

He watched the large buck disappear around a palmetto patch. Danny had lost his only opportunity to get a shot off. A doe ran out from a palmetto patch franticly trying to escape her hotfooted pursuer. The doe noticed Danny but was so preoccupied she did not care that something foreign to her world was in front of her. Danny watched as out jumped the buck and stood broadside looking toward the doe and just inviting Danny to shoot. He raised the old gun to his shoulder, centered the sight just behind the front quarter and pulled the trigger. The explosion and percussion of the gun almost knocked Danny from his saddle. Startled, the horse jumped side way causing him to drop the old gun. Instinct dictated that Danny grab for the horn of the saddle. It took a moment to bring the situation under control but when he finally did, there lying on the ground in front of him was the big buck.

Walking the horse toward a bunch of wax myrtles, he tied it off. As he walked away, he gently patted it to assure him he was pleased. Knelling down, he lifted the buck's head by the horns and admired his prize. In all the excitement, he never considered how he would get the deer home if he actually killed one. Should he head back to the house and get Mr. Margit to come and help him? He decided against it, knowing the old man had not been feeling well lately. Danny realized at that moment he had to learn to do things on his own. He thought the job over and finally decided to pull the large deer over to a low limb. Using a rope, he hoisted the deer up to the limb. He then rode the horse underneath the deer then lowered the deer onto the saddle. Satisfied the horse would not spook, he climbed on back of the saddle behind the deer and turned to begin his trip home. All the way home he rehearsed the story in his mind so he would not miss any detail in recounting it to Mr. Margit.

Mr. Margit was tremendously amazed and very proud of the young man for killing such a fine ten-point buck. The old man told him that his first deer had not been as grand as Danny's but it was a memory that he relived often.

Mr. Margit instructed the boy on how to skin the deer and together they completed the task. Danny had provided a nice piece of meat for the two of them. The old man told Danny to dig a hole and bury the guts so as to not draw scavengers. Mr. Margit did not want an open invitation to any wolf that might still be around to come messing around his place. When he got through with the tasks he had been given, Mr. Margit taught him how to nail the hide to the wall and begin the process of tanning it.

Mr. Margit sliced the back strap that was the tenderest part of the deer. The meat was a dark purplish red and had sort of a musky wild smell to it, but Danny said it had a wonderful flavor. Mr. Margit fried the small strips of meat and served it for supper along with some white potatoes from his garden, and a pot of hot boiling coffee. The two men feasted as kings. Mr. Margit said he felt exceptional and the only thing that would make their food any better was if they were on the scrub camping.

Placing a wad of tobacco in his mouth, he began to tell Danny more of his story.

After two years at the Tanner homestead, Will decided it was time for him to go. He thanked the Tanners for all they had done for him and promised to come back around Christmas time. Will knew better then to leave this time of year, but knew as well he had stayed longer then he had planned to. Life had gone well with the Tanner clan. No problems made it necessary for him to leave' but the older he got the more independent he wanted to be. In his present situation and without feeling prideful, he felt that he had learned as much as he could with them and wanted to try it out on his own.

Entering the pine wood flats, Will stood in the stirrups of his saddle. Turning his body, the wind coming out of the southwest hit him in his face. From what he had learned by experience from past summers living in the wilderness, this time of year brought rains regular like. He had heard thunder for several hours saw flashes of lightening as the summer storm drew closer. Not wanting to get caught out in the tall pines with lightning close by, Will figured it was safer in the creek swamp.

Finding a break in the thick palmettos, he began looking for a dense stand of cabbage trees in hopes of sheltering himself from the storm. Luckily, he came upon a small house that appeared to be abandoned. It had been strangely constructed and was unlike any he had ever seen before. Most crackers houses had high ceilings with two rooms separated by a hall between them called a dog walk. The abandoned house had a porch that ran along the front and back of the house. The ceiling inside was lower then what he was use to. Each window was made of real glass that allowed light from the outside to shine in. It looked to have been white washed at one time but the years of neglect had taken its toll.

Will did not care what it looked like. His main concern was if someone lived there. He hoped that if they were living there, they wouldn't care if he got in out of the rain. Calling from his horse, no one responded to his call. At that moment, it began to rain harder then he could ever remember. Quickly tying his horse to the post in front of the house, Will grabbed his gear and tossed it onto the porch so he could dry what got wet. It would not take him long to leave if the owner suddenly came. In a few minutes, the sky darkened as if it was midnight and let loose a downpour. Will stood on the front porch looking out anxiously as the lightening strikes closer and closer.

He remembered when he was at a funeral for one of the Tanner kids that had died suddenly. As the crowd stood at the gravesite, it began to lightening. Everyone watched the preacher as he began to read from the Bible. He jumped when it struck only yards from the grave and said "Amen". He turned and ran toward the church house. He recalled that everyone just stood there stunned, not believing what had just happened.

Grandpa Henry said he would never ask that preacher to do a funeral again even though it was the least words he'd ever heard a preacher say. Will chuckled as he remembered Grandpa Henry's expressions when he told that story.

The rain began to blow onto the porch drenching him and causing a shiver to run down his back. Cautiously, he pushed the door open not sure of what he would find when he entered the main room. Astonished when the lightening flashed and illuminated the room, he saw that the owners had just up and left every thing. It looked as if they still lived there. Reaching into his satchel, Will retrieved a candle and quickly lit it. Every thing in the room came into clear sight. He was thankful no one was hiding in the darkness.

By next morning, the rain had stopped and Will stepped onto the porch to survey his surroundings. The mosquitoes were thick and bit through his osnaburg long sleeve shirt spun from cotton in coarse linen, forcing Will to hunt for a myrtle bush. He had learned that he could crush the leaves in his hands and rub the paste on his exposed skin, a natural repellent. Above the buzzing of mosquitoes and an occasional deerfly around his ears, Will heard the sound of running water.

Moving toward the back of the house, he discovered that whoever had built the house built a porch over the creek. The porch gave access to running water out the back door. Heart pine was used knowing the tannic water would not cause rot. Curious what he might find next, Will returned to the front of the house and began to look over every foot of the overgrown clearing. He discovered a small barn that housed an ox cart with equipment used for plowing with a mule.

He could still smell the faint odor of manure in the small pen that bordered one side of the barn. He was sure the owners had not been gone long, maybe not even a year. Dust covered several old trunks that were locked.

Will shook the lid of one, hoping the weather had weakened it enough to allow it to open. Unsuccessful with his effort to open the trunks, he decided to continue exploring. However, his curiosity would not be satisfied until he knew what was in the trunks.

Leaving the barn area he found where the garden had been and was shocked to find some vegetables still growing. He recognized wild mustered and sweet potato vines. He really liked both of those vegetables and made up his mind that he would eat well if he could remember how Mrs. Mollie had fixed the mustered. The sweet potatoes would be easy because he would lay them in the ashes of a fire and cook them.

Will walked back toward the house and thought that this would be the perfect place for him to stay for a few weeks, or even for good. Will busied himself with repairing one of the pens so he would have a secure place for his horse. He cleaned as much of the dust he could that had caked on the windows of the house. Even a small amount of cleaning allowed sunlight to reach into the dark corners of the house. His eyes surveyed the interior of the abandoned house watching dust dance into the beams of sunshine, settling into the shadows. Fortunately, Ma Whaley had insisted that Will help her inside the house when he was growing up, warning that he might never find someone to clean for him. This type of work, even though he did not like it, was not foreign or difficult for him.

Late in the afternoon, he heard the rumble of thunder in the southwest again. Growing up in central Florida, he had learned that when a thunderhead built up in the southwest, which the old-timers called "Peter's Mud Hole", it was a sure thing to it rain, hard and early. He gathered some wood from off the front porch and carried it into the kitchen where there was an old cast iron wood burning stove. By the time the first drop of rain fell, Will had settled in for a warm dry night.

The next few days he moved his search further from the house carefully noting every direction he traveled so that if an afternoon storm popped up he could find his way back quickly. While on one of his trips away from the creek, he saw a couple of shoaty hogs and shot one. He cleaned it near the creed and cooked it over the coals along with a pot of wild mustered. It only weighed about twenty pounds and was just enough for him to eat without the food going to waste.

The smell of the cooking pork filled the creek swamp with an aroma that reminded him of when he was younger and still living with the Whaley's. Will had eaten with many families and had tasted some good cooking, but Ma Whaley was the best cook he had ever known and he was convinced she could even make a skunk taste good.

About dark as he sat next to the fire, he heard the back door of the house slam and it startled him. He had left a candle burning on the table and through the window, he could see that someone was inside. Unsure of what to do and knowing that his rifle was inside, he was unprotected if that person meant to hurt him. He was confused by what was happening. He could not understand why the intruder had not seen him sitting at the fire.

He moved quietly to the back porch and removed his boots so that he would not make any noise as he climbed up and peered in the back door. He watched from the shadows as he strained to see around the corner of the kitchen into the main room. He jumped again when he heard the front door open, the hinges squeaking, and then slam shut. Hurrying through the house to where he had laid his gun, without hesitation he opened the door and moved onto the porch only to see the figure of a man sitting next to the fire where he had recently been sitting. Will was relieved when he recognized the intruder, but confused as to why he had not made his presence know by simply walking into the clearing and straight to the fire. Will relaxed as he leaned the gun against the side of the house and joined the old man next to the fire. The old man stayed a couple of hours. They ate together what little there was without speaking one word between them.

Will began to yawn because the chores of the day were beginning to take their toll. The old man saw his yawns. He simply got up and left. Will spoke up just as he started to enter the dark shadows beyond the reach of the fire's light and asked him to stay the night since it was so late. The old man turned around and looked past Will toward the house, waved and disappeared. The misquotes were getting bad so Will retreated inside the house and peered into the dark in the direction the eerie character had disappeared. His thoughts were consumed with questions that had not been answered and he wished the old man would have just spoken to him and told him who he was. He wondered if he would ever see the man again and if his life would be revealed.

A week later, he happened on a small cemetery with five graves.

Each of the graves had fresh wild flowers strewn on them. All but one of the names was faded. Will could barely make the name out. It read "Baby Malby 1867". He was stunned by the reality that someone had been so close to for a week and he had not know, he stared at the name on the grave. He turned and with a sharp eye surveyed his surroundings, hoping to see anything that was out of place that would indicate the presence of the person responsible for the flowers. He would be careful and diligent from that moment on.

A month had passed since he first found the homestead. Will figured it was time for him to move on. He was reluctant to leave for he had grown to love the place. Entering the pine wood flats, Will put the spurs to the flank of his horse hoping to create some distance between him and the creek before the afternoon rains. It was his hope that Mr. Henry, another of Will's new friends, could provide some information about the perplexing discovery he had made and shed some light on the identity of the people that had once lived on the creek.

After an hour of hard riding, the first sound of thunder rumbled in the sky. The wind blew coming whipping strangely first from one direction then another. It was obvious the coming storm would not be like any that had come before. By mid-afternoon, it began to rain and the drops stung like small bee. Within seconds Will was drenched and chilled down to his bones.

Off in the distance he could see a very dense stand of cypress trees. He was relieved when he discovered he could use the exposed roots of the large trees that created a natural shelter from the storm. Large lush ferns grew all around the opening in the roots leading to a bed of leaves and cypress needles. Using a hobble, he secured his horse so it wouldn't run off and leave him stranded in the middle of nowhere. Will found the blown over cypress trees offered him minimal cover and some comfort from the storm. Pulling his hat down over his face and his slicker's collar over his neck, he settled in for a long and soaking ordeal.

The only light that invaded his hiding place was the flash of lightening that rumbled into the early hours of the next morning. Exhaustion from the ordeal finally forced Will into a deep but restless sleep. Will made up his mind that he would not be caught out in the open by another sudden storm again.

The sun broke through the clouds to the east as it did every morning. Everything looked fresh and clean and the sun came up bright. The longer Will sat around the fire he had built, the sleepier he became. He decided he would camp there another night. Searching the flat woods, he gathered more lightered and dried his clothes. Will had always been taught that modesty was important. He was glad there was no one around because he sat buck-naked for almost an hour. He was relieved when he was able to put his britches and boots back on.

The ground hurt his feet which were not as tough as they had been since he started wearing boots every day. He could remember a time when he ran barefoot through sandspurs, briers, and stinging nettles and never felt it, but now he could feel a stick down in his boots. He was getting ringworm due to the damp ground. It would take days to get over the infection and could become infected. He didn't have time for that.

Taking out his pocketknife from his pants pocket, Will cut a few palmettos fronds to use as the bottom layer of his bed. The dampness would not seep through to his bedroll. The palmetto sticks were used to weave pieces of bacon on. He stuck the bacon toward the fire to cook. There is nothing more satisfying for a man then to sit in camp around a lightered fire. The smoke hung in the canopy of limbs above the camp and filled the air with an indescribable smell of home and comfort. A smell he would never forget. The smell of fresh bacon sizzling next to the fire and the satisfaction of good food could not be compared with anything that civilization had to offer Will thought to himself.

Nightfall came without another hint of rain. For Will, that day and night had been one of the most restful times he had in a long time. He wished he could just live this way the rest of his life. Relieved he would get a good night's sleep, he laid on his bedroll staring up into the sky. The hoot owls serenade filled the air, joined by the rain frogs competing for attention and singing in chorus for more rain. That time of evening was Will's favorite. Watching the flames leap and bow under the influence of the wind, he watched as the flames flickered. His mind raced back to the first Christmas he had spent with the Tanners.

The morning started out like any other with their assigned responsibilities at the Tanner homestead. Grandpa Henry acted strangely as if he was preoccupied with something in the barn. The young man watched curiously, wondering what was going on. Finally, Grandpa Henry emerged from the barn sitting in a wagon filled with fishing poles. It was a tradition in the Tanner family to spend every Christmas day down on the creek fishing and having a fish fry. Everyone was festive and as Ms. Mollie would say, "We let our hair down".

Will was deep in thought when without warning the stranger walked into Will's camp, silently moving from the shadows. He knelt by the fire. As he jumped to his feet, Will said out loud, "I wish you would quit doing that. Every time you do that you scare me to death". The old man smiled wide as their eyes met for a brief moment. Will noticed that he was cleaner then the last time they met, probably due to the rain the day before. Proving his desire to be friends, Will offered him what was left from supper.

The first time the two meet the old man left as soon as he had eaten. Will hoped with this meeting he could get some of his questions answered like if he knew who lived at the house next to the creek. However, the old man relaxed next to the fire and fell asleep. Will sat up until late just watching as the old man fought many battles in his dreams. Completely exhausted from the night before and the knowledge that someone besides himself was there, Will did not wake until mid-morning. Had he dreamed about the wraithlike figure the night before or had he actually been there beside the fire? All doubt was gone when one of Will's coffee cups was missing. Aggravated that his kindness had been repaid with an act of thievery, Will made up his mind that the stranger would not be welcome in his camp again.

With that, Mr. Magrit rose from his chair and disappeared into the house returning quickly with a cup of fresh water. Taking a sip, he swirled the cool water around in his mouth and spit it to the ground. He drank what remained in the cup then set it on the ground beside him.

Turning to Danny he asked if he had a chance to check the hog trap. Danny answered no. He turned and walked down the steps into the yard.

Mounting his horse for the second time that day, Danny retraced his earlier path through the creek to the hog trap. The trap door was shut which excited Danny. Getting down from his horse, he tied it to a small scrub oak several yards from the front of the pen and walked briskly to peer over the gate. Danny got the surprise of his life.

Inside the pen were several turkeys that were eating the pieces of corn that had been strewn the day before. He startled them causing them to take flight. The swishing of wings and the dust it produced startled Danny as much as the turkeys. Within just seconds the whole incident was over. Next time he would be more cautious when he walked around to check what was in the pen. There was sign all around the trap where hogs had tried to get to the corn inside but no hogs. He reset the trap, strode more corn vowed to himself to visit earlier tomorrow.

He told Mr. Magrit about the turkeys and he started laughing and said he wished he could have seen it.

Chapter 11

Several months had past with Danny spending a lot time riding out onto the scrub to become more familiar with his surroundings. He started making several trips a month visiting Lockwood Church, spending Sunday afternoons with the Tanners that lived near Fort Christmas. He met a preacher from Plant City that he really liked. The preacher's strong foghorn voice captivated Danny and he enjoyed just talking to him. The man told him his own life's story was like Danny's in many ways. He left Georgia because of an abusive father, hopped a train and woke up in Plant City. Danny felt a companionship with him and looked forward to spending time with him, learning more about the subject he taught.

He became more confident in his ability to survive and began spending long days alone on the Pockataw Flats. There were several deep water holes along the creek where he would catch large catfish. He even started checking the cows just to get familiar with them so he could recognize them when he saw them.

One afternoon he happened to meet Mr. Emmett and Junior as they were passing through the area on their way to gather cows for Magnolia Ranch. They spoke for a few minutes and Danny excitedly told them about his first buck and the hog trap he was working. Mr. Emmett suggested that they meet soon and camp for a couple of nights at Dead Horse Gap. That area produced a lot of turkeys and they were easy to roost. Mr. Emmett told Danny to let Mr. Magrit know that on their way back through, he would stop and check on him and make arrangements for the camping trip. He also promised Danny the next time they worked cows at Magnolia Ranch he could go with them and get more experience.

After saying their good-byes, Danny rode back to the house and told Mr. Magrit of his meeting with the Tanners and told him Mr. Emmett would be by soon. He cleaned the catfish and heated the large twelve-quart Dutch oven that hung several inches over the open fire by a tripod. The hog lard quickly melted and Danny watched as the grease popped and hissed. He lowered the fish fillets dipped in fresh-ground corn meal into the dutch oven. It didn't take long for the fish to cook to a deep brown. He peeled the last of the sweet potatoes to complete their meal.

As they were eating supper Danny asked if he could go to Lockwood Church the following Sunday for services. Danny looked for his approval but there was silence for several minutes. The old man agreed and said that he himself had been thinking about attending as well. Getting up from the table, the old man walked away from the table and stood in the door looking out into the yard. "Have I ever told you how your grandpa ended up down south?" asked Mr. Magrit. Danny spoke up and told him that he had not but would really like to hear the story if he felt like telling it. Pushing open the door with a squeak that echoed out into the silence, he shuffled onto the porch and just before he sat down reached in his back pocket and withdrew a pouch of chewing tobacco. Wadding a mouthful of tobacco and wedging it into his mouth, he lowered himself carefully into his favorite rocking chair.

Clearing his throat, he began to share another of his stories.

Will spent a day and night with the Tanners s often as he could and enjoyed the company of the men and the good cooking of Aunt Mollie. He was unable to find the information he wanted about the possible owners of the house he now lived in. He needed to know if they were alive. Several of the people told him to ride to the land office in Kissimmee. There he could look at the records and find what he wanted to know. One of two things had happened, he was told. Either they were squatters who had gotten discouraged and left or they actually had owned the land. If that was the case, it would be recorded there.

Whichever way his enquiry ended he could get answers and possibly be free to move in and take advantage of any offer from the timber company who managed most of the land in the area.

Before Will left for Kissimmee, he headed for Hodges General Store in Fort Christmas to purchase the needed supplies for the weeklong trip. While there, he overheard several strangers talking about the flood that had ravaged the cattlemen down south around Lake Okeechobee recently. Times were hard and work was difficult to find this time of year. There was a need for experienced cowmen to help drive the cows that had been stranded and were starving off the islands and high hammocks. Will and the other young men in the area thought it would be an adventure to go down south and maybe see Indians.

Ever since Will saw those Indians on the St. John's he had been curious and wanted to see some up close.

Jim Sweet, Horace Whaley and Will left early the next morning. Their plan was to ride straight south the easiest way and take the trail that ran down the east coast.

Jim Sweet may have been put low by the dogs and hogs and gave up on bragging on himself, but there was one thing that everyone knowed about him and that was that Jim loved his hard licker. He plum knowed where ever still was in the surrounding community. The older he got the worse it got. He blamed his old man for treating him and his brothers so bad, but everyone knew that tale was just an excuse. Drinking would prove to be his undoing and it would not be long before Will had the unfortunate responsibility of burying Jim next to a lone cabbage tree on the river marsh. It was a sad time for Will and one that would change Will's life because it was at that time he learned what complete loneliness was.

Horace Whaley had run away from Georgia because he didn't like living away from the open wilderness. He often told Will and Jim that it was too crowded for him up north. The red clay and rolling hills were too much for him so he run away and made his way back down here to be with Will. He was an awkward looking person standing almost six and a half feet tall with pale skin that caused him to look sickly.

He had to wear long sleeve shirts all the time because the sun would blister his skin. His black curly hair was kind of smutty looking like a charred lightered knot and he had a set of ears that stood straight out from the side of his head. People often joked with him about needing them pinned back on his head. There were those that used to joke with him as a boy about using his ears to fly. Due to the constant joking, Horace developed a tolerance for aggravation and it took a lot to make him mad.

But boys, when he got mad no one wanted to be on the receiving end. Jim was the instigator and Horace was the finisher. Will only fought when there was no other way out of a difficulty. He was often accused of having a silver tongue and quick to use it to avoid confrontation. Not one person was fooled by his hesitation and see it as weakness, because he would fight and when he fought he fought to win, fair and square.

The three young men rode south beyond Jim's Creek, a well used trail. The fastest way to Okeechobee was the East General Harney Trail to Fort Pierce with a turn west that headed straight into Okeechobee.

After a week and a half of hard riding, the three young men reached the north shore of the big lake. They had not been there long when they learned that there was no more work. Aggravated they had made the long trip for nothing Horace helped to lighten the frustration by suggesting they look around and do a little fishing. They were disappointed by the news. They had put a lot of their time and what little money they had into the adventure. They knew they would never recover those losses. They talked about how they could have used the extra money they would have made down south. Enough, Jim said, to hold them over until the spring cow hunt.

Jim left them in front of the small store to find the only other place on earth that made him feel like a man, the local drinking establishment. Will wished that he could help Jim but there was no amount of words that would change Jim's ways. Will was content talking to the Man up stairs about it, even though Will sometimes believed his prayers went unheard. Will and Horace turned and walked down to the edge of the big lake. Neither one of them had ever seen so much fresh water in all their life. Horace was awestruck by the fish that struck the surface of the lake. As far as you could see schooling bass worked the top of the water. Will walked along the edge for as far as he could go and watched as the blue herons flapped their wings and took flight. Bullfrogs crocked and jumped into the water making a splash. The large Blue Herons squawked their protest as they took flight moving only yards away to resume their hunt. Fish struck the shoreline chasing after minnows that hid in the shallows. It looked like someone somewhere was throwing stones into the shallow water.

Stopping, Will squatted and touched the warm water with his hands. He remembered the times he and Horace would catch bullfrogs while fishing and swimin' across the St. Johns River. Ma Whaley had enjoyed frying the fish they caught and cleaned, listening to her children laugh as the hot grease popped in the frying pan.

Will learned something about Horace this trip that he probably already knew. Horace loved to fish as much as he loved to eat. Their adventure gave Horace the perfect opportunity to try new ways of fishing. He really liked the big nets the anglers used on the lake. "You can catch a boatload at one time" he said to Will with a sparkle in his eyes. He watched as the fishermen sold their catch to the fish houses and told his companion there was money to be made on that big lake. He figured if a man worked hard enough he could get rich.

Will watched the fishermen and he could not grasp the reason why they would want to catch so many fish at one time. He wondered how many fish a man would need to feed his family for supper. How could anyone eat that many fish before the fish spoiled. Horace tried to explain to Will that the fish caught today would be sold in the big cities to the east.

All of that knowledge was too confusing for Will. He wanted to head back to the creek swamp and the pine flat woods as soon as possible. He knew better then to try it by himself and pushed Horace and Jim to leave but neither wanted to leave what they perceived to be paradise.

Seeing he could not talk Jim or Horace into leaving until they had seen everything there was to see, he began to ask if anyone around him if they would be heading north for him to ride a long with.

While fishing one morning Horace became acquainted with a man who made his living fishing the big lake. His name was Catfish Jim Creech and he was the nicest man you would ever want to meet with a heart of gold. But the thing that convinced Horace to stay in Okeechobee for good and abandon his life long friends was the moment he saw Catfish Jim's daughter. He fell immediately and madly in love. He described it like being drunk and what he was feeling right then was almost as satisfying, but better. He couldn't stop staring at her and it made everyone around him uncomfortable, especially Will. Will could only imagine how it made the girl feel but she didn't seem to mind. Will had to admit she was the prettiest girl he had every seen and real easy to look at. She was thin and deeply tanned by the Okeechobee sun. Her long blonde hair shone in the sun like a newborn calf.

It flowed down her back and stopped just above her shapely hips, which even in the dungarees she always wore. It didn't take much to tell from behind that she was definitely not a man. One of the things that pleased Horace the most was when she smiled which she did all the time. When she smiled, Horace said, her blue eyes sparkled like the lake did at the sun's first light. Will said if you had seen her you would have understood why Horace turned crazy that day. It really didn't have to be said, but Horace changed everything about himself that day. From that day forward Will never put much stock in what Horace had to say because this was the second time Horace had left him high and dry. Horace changed like the wind and no amount of talking could deter him from his thoughts. The last time Will remember knowing about Horace was when him and Sallie was married and soon had a young son by the name of Dan.

The old man stopped talking, looked at Danny, and noticed that he was grinning widely picturing Horace and Sallie haulin 'that youngun around.

Danny had never known his grandmother because she died before he was born and no one talked much about her. He asked Mr. Magrit to tell him more about her. The old man said that what he had told was all he knew because a few days later he left Okeechobee. He assured Danny that if Horace liked her, she must have been a pretty good ole gal.

Chapter 12

Sunday morning came and Danny and the old man got dressed and cranked the old truck. The truck still sounded that familiar rattle as they bounced through the deep sand ruts leading out to old State Road 22, which led them directly into the middle of Ft. Christmas. Turning left, they drove without saying a word for almost thirty minutes. They passed no other vehicles until they got close to the church house.

As they pulled into the yard, the men that were standing out front stared more out of curiosity as to why Will Magrit was coming to church. Before he could get clear of the truck, several men greeted him and expressed their surprise but welcomed him anyway. There was a lone cabbage planted by one of the Hancock men that stood to the right of the front door of the church. Squatting at its base was old Henry Tanner. Now well up in age and unable to go anywhere other then church, he was still vibrant and busied himself in his garden. Mr. Magrit walked over to him and they talked until the preacher called from the doorway that it was time to get started.

Just before the first song started Mr. Magrit whispered to Danny and told him that Grandpa Henry took him in when he was a boy and was very instrumental in him being who he was today. Danny was not as impressed with the new preacher as he had been with the one from Plant City, but as Mr. Magrit would say, "He'd do." After church, they were invited to go home with Emmett Tanner and his family. Even though Mr. Magrit would prefer to go strait home, he graciously accepted their invitation.

Danny and Junior watched his two little sisters by the name of Hannah and Nay Nay playing with a couple of bugs in the front yard. Danny thought it strange for little girls to play with bugs but, living in the woods where there was nothing other than work for the people to do, anything could be cause for joy. The Tanners lived in a large oak hammock; the canopy of trees was so thick that nothing but tea weeds grew under them in the shade. The bugs the girls were playing with were called tumble turd bugs. The tumblebug is like a small beetle that flies around until it finds a fresh pile of manure, lands, and roles up a big ball of it and scoots it along the ground using its back legs, making people laugh and calling 'em "tumble-turd". The girls had made a track in the dirt and they were racing their respective bugs. They didn't mind the bugs rolled around a ball of crap.

Aunt Daisy called from the front door telling the children that they could wash up and come eat. After the men ate, the children were able to go to the table and eat. Then it would be the womenfolk who would partake of the remaining food, which was plentiful. Danny could not believe the spread of food. There were piles of fried venison, collard greens, and black-eyed peas, homemade biscuits and all the fresh butter, jelly and guavas a person could want. Junior and Danny sat and ate until they were about to bust. After helping to clear the table, Danny walked out to the porch where the men had laid down on the porch floor in different spots asleep.

Junior motioned for Danny to follow him. They walked past an old shed constructed out of pecky cypress that was used as their wash shed and out toward the corncrib. Picking up a small can, Junior filled it with whole corn. They then walked through the orange grove. The trees were only about six foot tall and surrounded by broom-sage grass that, in places, was taller than the trees. They entered a pasture area where there was no grass just bare ground. Junior reached into the can and flung a couple of hand fulls out onto the ground. Backing into the tall broom-sage to conceal Danny and him, Junior cleared his throat and clucked and yelped using his throat, then sat silent as he motioned to Danny to do the same. A few minutes later, he did it again and in a few moments a turkey hidden from their view answered him. Junior yelped again and out popped several turkeys that went right to picking up the golden kernels shaking their head and allowing the morsels to move down the long neck, only to repeat the process until the corn was gone. Junior whispered and pointed to one of the smaller turkeys and said, "That's a Jake. A Jake is a young male turkey." Danny nodded to acknowledge that he heard him. They sat there watching the turkeys as they scratched around diligently searching for every speck of food. The first to leave was the old hen and just before she disappeared into the broom-sage, she clucked and the others formed a single file line and followed her. Junior stood and threw the remaining corn onto the ground, turning and walked back to the corncrib.

When they made it back to the house, Mr. Magrit and Mr. Emmett were sitting on the front porch rocking and talking casually. When they saw the boys, the old man stood, stretched and walked to the edge of the porch. He told Danny it was time to go. Mr. Emmett called for Junior to go saddle his horse and load it up in the back of Danny's truck. "You goin' with them. I'll be there in the morning and we'll look at the cows," Mr. Emmett said, surprising the boys. "This'll give you boys more time to spend together", he continued. The boys turned and ran toward the old barn and returned soon ready to go. They did not leave, however, until they had thanked Aunt Daisy for the fine meal and her hospitality that day.

It was late in the afternoon when they made it to the Magrit place. Junior unloaded his horse, and Danny grabbed his wallet that held his clothes for the night. They walked toward the barn.

There was still a couple of hours until dark so Danny asked if they could ride across the creek and check the hog trap. The old man said they could go after Danny completed his chores, which he hurried through. At long last they were riding toward the cow pens at the crossing. It had rained a lot lately so the creek was higher then usual but the horses had no problem making their way down the steep bank and into the swift running water. On the other side, Danny took the lead. He was glad that they had this time together so he could show Junior around. Turning off the trail onto a smaller path, they skirted the old hog rooting into the paint-root pond. They rode side by side talking about anything that came to mind when Junior pulled back on his reins and pointed in the direction of the trap. Danny drew back on his reins and looked only to see the backside of a large bobcat leaping over the side of the trap. The old cat trotted off a distance, stopped, turned in its tracks and stared at the boys. Danny thought about shooting the cat but remembered what Mr. Magrit had taught him about killing only what you could eat. Satisfied that he was safe, the cat trotted off into the palmettos. There was nothing in the trap, so Danny tied up the gate and determined to reset it in a few days.

Junior commented about the flock of buzzards circling off to the west and wanted to ride over to see what had died. Once back on the larger trail they were able to make good time in the direction the buzzards were circling. Before they were able to get close, they smelled rotting flesh.

Junior did not have a very strong stomach when it came to things that stunk so he stayed back while Danny pushed his way through the thick briers laced throughout the high palmettos. The buzzards, feasting on the corpse, flapped their wings and made a swooshing sound as they rose high into the air. The massive wings created a breeze that forced the stench toward Junior. Danny could hear him gagging and puking. He laughed which only made things worse for Junior.

Danny discovered that a large buck had died. His horns were enormous and Danny wanted to take them home. Grabbing hold of the horns, he began to drag them through the palmettos causing the body to pull apart. Danny started laughing harder while dragging the dead carcass, the source of Junior's problems, toward him. Junior threatened Danny with great harm if he continued on his present course, but Danny did not care for he was older and bigger then Junior and felt no threat. Breaking through the bushes and throwing what remains of the stinking corpse at Junior's feet was all it took. The meal Junior had enjoyed earlier came up in waves. Junior could not get far enough away from the smell. He later swore that the smell was in his clothes. Danny had never seen anyone puke as much as Junior and could not stop laughing. Finally Junior reached into the wallet that hung over the horn of his saddle and handed Danny a piece of rope strongly urging him to hang the rotting deer head in a near by tree. He told Danny he could come back in a few weeks and get his prize if he just had to have it. Danny quickly agreed because Junior's vomiting was beginning to affect him.

He finally got the rope tied to the horn of his saddle and climbed up on his horse. After hanging the rotting head of the deer in the tree, he sat there for a moment while Junior gathered himself. Ultimately the waves of nausea faded and he was able to get on his horse. They rode off toward the creek so that Danny could wash his hands and Junior could wash his face. Several times they both would get a whiff of the stench that hung on their clothing and Junior would heave again. Danny thought it was funny but Junior never saw the humor in any of it.

The sun was starting to set in the west, casting long shadows onto the scrub, when they finally rode past the wash out and into the clearing in front of the house. Mr. Magrit could tell that something was wrong with Junior and asked what had happened. Danny began to tell him the story, trying not to laugh. Right in the middle of the story Danny made a gagging noise that started the whole thing again. Junior told him to stop or he was going to hurt him bad. Mr. Magrit started laughing and after a few minutes said that he had not laughed that hard in a long time.

At daylight the next morning Mr. Emmett drove into the front yard of the old house shining the headlights onto the porch were the two boys slept. The dogs barked and carried on as if he had never been there before. A sharp command to shut up came from the large framed man as he crossed in front of the truck and stepped onto the porch. "Get up, boys. We got lots to do before we can ride out." Mr. Emmett opened the front door and greeted the old man as he sat drinking his second cup of coffee. They sat together and discussed the day's plan and what Mr. Magrit wanted accomplished. Danny and Junior passed through the kitchen and washed their faces in the cool water drawn from the creek. Danny returned to the kitchen with fresh water. After pouring themselves a full cup of hot coffee each, they sat and listened to the two men talk. They heard the sound of a second truck enter the clearing and the soft voice of their friend Charles. Setting their cups of coffee down everyone greeted each other and settled in to sharing the plans for the day. Mr. Emmett looked at the three boys and told them they needed to saddle their horses because they were going to ride the west side of the creek to Wewahootee. They would need to take their sleeping gear because it would not be until tomorrow when he would meet them there and give then instructions for the day. He told them their job would be to count the calves that had been born since the last time they worked cows and if they saw any steers two years or older they needed to remember about where they were so it would be easy to gather them if need be. Even the old man could feel the excitement as the boys left the kitchen in anticipation of their first time alone on a trail together. Mr. Magrit rose from his seat and began to put together some food for Danny and the boys to take so they wouldn't go hungry. He then reached above the door and retrieved the old rifle, placed it in a sheath and laid it on the table.

The boys feed and saddled the horses and poured corn into their wallets. The entire time the boys joked and spoke with boldness of the adventure but inside they all hoped the trip would go uneventful. Leading the horses to the front porch, they tied them to the post in the front yard. Danny headed to his room and rolled a shirt and extra pair of jeans in his quilt, tucking it under his arm and walked into the kitchen where everyone was still sitting around the table.

The first thing he noticed was the repeating rifle that lay on the table. The old man gave him instructions and made Danny promise he would be careful and only use the gun if needed. He said, "You may want to kill a deer for your supper". They walked together to his horse and Mr. Magrit showed how to secure the gun to the saddle. Daylight was starting to send slivers of sunshine through the dense canopy of tree limbs erasing the darkness that had covered the clearing just moments before he retreated. Danny shivered in the morning cool and could not wait until they were able to mount up and head out.

The creaking of the dried leather could be heard as they mounted their horses and guiding them toward the narrow lane that lead out onto the open scrub. Silently they rode toward the creek, crossing the swift knee-deep running water. They did not talk until they had passed near the place where the rotting deer head hung in a low scrub oak just off the two rutted roads west. Danny began telling Charles about the previous day's events and how Junior gagged. The boys laughed as Junior just stared ahead until the conversation turned serious between the boys as they followed a well-used cow trail due west. The cows recently bunched were now scattered into smaller bunches of cows. The cows were not as fat now that they had dropped their calves. The animals were skittish and they were not able to get very close before they bolted to a safe distance, turning and watching as they passed.

Entering a low area in the middle of the scrub, they stopped and watched several large gobblers feeding without one care in the world. Junior said that he would like to shoot the lead gobbler but it was a long time til they stopped to camp, so they just rode off. The rest of the afternoon passed without the boys seeing another cow. Riding around large cypress heads and through scrub oaks, they spoke of the cows that might be concealed from their sight.

The sun was starting to set in the west casting red orange streaks around high thunderheads building to the west. By the time they decided to stop for the evening, they had made it back to the creek swamp and found a clearing they could set up camp in. Junior had shot a small doe earlier. He had skinned it and removed the back strap for their supper. They gathered wood for the campfire. The fire burned bright when they cut strips of the fresh meat and weaved it on palmetto sticks. One of the boys stuck the sticks into the dirt next to the fire to sizzle and cook. Each unsaddled their horse and fed them from the feedbags they had brought with them.

The owls started hooting long before it got dark and their cries filled the woods the entire night. They lay with their heads in their saddles close to the fire. Danny told the boys about the ghost Mr. Magrit had been telling him about. The boys secretly watched into the darkness for any movement hoping someone or something did not surprise them.

As daylight broke the horses, snorting and whinnying as the animals looked toward the opposite side of the creek awakened them. Charles placed another piece of wood on the fire and rose to calm the anxious horses when all of a sudden they heard the scream of a panther. Danny was sure that the scream he had just heard sounded just like a woman in distress. None of the boys would admit how scared they were but each was relieved that the others were there.

After a cold breakfast of beef jerky, they saddled up and rode back onto the open scrub. Danny mentioned how thankful he was being away from the dark and damp swamp and in the open so he could see if anything tried to slip up on them. About noon, the cow pens at Wewahoottee came into sight. It took them about an hour to finally ride up and tie their horses to the side of the cow pens.

They spent the rest of the afternoon exploring an old railroad track bed for the spikes discarded by the workers repairing the tracks. Charles found the most and was proud of the discovery of a hammer with a broken handle. The other men they were expecting didn't show up that night so they made camp under one of the sheds behind the cow pens. The horses ate their fill of the tender grass that grew in the pens. The boys had placed the horses in the pens and were relieved that they would not have to watch the horses that night. Another night of embellished stories and restless sleep passed without incident after a good supper of fried venison.

They waited 'till about ten the next morning when Mr. Emmett finally arrived. He told the boys to saddle up and ride east until they found the main road leading to Fort Christmas. He told them they would have to sleep one more night on the scrub. He told them he wanted to meet them at Hodges Store mid-morning the next day so they could gather the cows at Wheeler Ranch. He had to sell about forty head and wanted them to help.

Danny finally rode up to Mr. Margit's front yard late Saturday afternoon. He had been gone from home for a full week and was relieved when he finally sat down to tell Mr. Magrit about his week.

Chapter 13

Long before the sound of the first thunder exploded, Danny had felt the cool air as it swirled in the open field as it came first from the north then from the south. Mr. Magrit commented that he believed it would rain soon and they needed to head back to the house. Immediately after the first clap of lightening, which was deafening, it began to rain softly. The thunder startled the horses and they reacted crazily but where quickly brought under control. There was urgency in the movements of the old man and a grave need to find shelter for them. The solace the old man longed for was the warmth of his house. It was not because the old man feared the storm, which had nothing to do with his insistence, but he had just recently gotten over a lingering sickness and did not want to have a relapse.

Just as they entered the clearing by the house and through a hale of lightening strikes, the old man sighed with relief because he finally made the front porch and out of the cold rain. Danny took the two horses to the barn and tended to them. The smell of the rain as it washed the dust from the trees surrounding the old barn mixed with the strong stench of aged manure in the barn was the motivation that pushed Danny to finish his chores as fast as possible. He grabbed one of the croaker sacks and dried the horses off, then brushed them down and poured a generous amount of whole corn as a reward for the hard work they had done over the last few days. Danny swung open the barn door and watched as the lightening flashed filling the air with electricity. He watched and waited to time his departure from the dry barn between strikes.

When he thought it safe enough, he ran across the yard, which did not keep him from getting soaked to the bone. The rain mixed with the wind as it whipped in and out from under and around the porch. Danny shivered after turning and facing the open yard. Mr. Magrit had thoughtfully laid an old quilt across the back of the rocking chair at the front door. Danny reluctantly removed his drenched clothing and hurriedly wrapped the quilt around his shoulders. He watched as a small wren busied itself probing the spider webs and dirt dauber nest for her allusive supper. The nervous chatter echoed the desperation the wren must had felt looking for a small morsel of food.

Danny remembered the wren that nested on his grandfather's front porch and how his grandfather constantly protected the little birds from his mischievous grandchildren. Holding to one of the posts that held the roof up, he leaned out reaching his hand to feel the rain that steadily poured off the roof and watched it puddle on the ground. He remembered how his cousins and him use to pretend to fish from the porch's edge. Danny was unaware of the old man's presence until he spoke, "Looks as if it's set in to rain for the night." Danny simply responded by looking at him. "Bring your wet boots in by the fire to dry, as damp as it is they'll probably not dry by mornin'", the old man finishing his comment. Without thinking, Danny reached down to pick up his boots causing the quilt to slip from his shoulders almost revealing his bare butt. Righting himself surly saved him humiliation and the jokes he'd more then likely would have to endure from the old man.

Mr. Magrit sat in his rocking chair and stared into the rain. He said, "I can remember when I wus a little boy. We use ta hunt in this kinda weather. I recall it rained so hard I found shelter in the root of a big oak, when all of a sudden 'bout six big old does come marchin' by, reckin they got caught away from their home too." He smiled then said, "All but one made it." At that moment, he seemed to be transported somewhere far away. When Danny went to his room to put on dry clothes, he returned and sat next to the old man watching him until he awoke from his daydream. He began to tell another story of long ago when Danny's grandfather and him traveled south to Okeechobee.

While in Okeechobee they had heard a lot of talk of renewed hostility between the settlers out in the wilderness and a small raiding party of

Indians that forced the army to get involved. The news spread rapidly throughout the small community and caused the settlers to fear for their lives. For that reason, many had to leave their homesteads and live in the fort which proved not to be all that it was supposed to be because the days were long and very hot with nothing to do.

A column of soldiers lead by a young Lieutenant by the name of Baxter was re-supplying their outfit in their pursuit of the renegades responsible for the killing of the homesteaders and burning everything north of the fort. Will really wanted to head back north but knew that it would not be wise to go by himself. He spoke to the young Lieutenant about riding along with them as far as Fort Taylor. The small fort was located on Taylor Creek southeast of Christmas and not far from where Will called home. He was sure that if he could make it that far he would be safe.

Will was hired by the Lieutenant to provide fresh meat for the unit every other day. By what he had learned on his other trips south, the game was plentiful and he was sure he could fulfill the obligation with little danger to himself.

He remembered Pa Whaley telling about Isaac Nettles when he and his family first come to Florida from Georgia. They were living up north of Fort Christmas at Fort Defiance. A band of Chief Osceola's Seminoles forced many settlers to move into the fort for protection and it did not take long for the food to begin to run out. Being independent men, the settlers decided to leave the safety of the fort to secure food for their families. With Isaac leading, the few men in the hunting party got ambushed not far from the fort. As Isaac Nettles turned to flee, he was shot in the heel of his left foot and was not able to run with the other men.

Telling the others to go ahead, he waited there and tried to make his way back to the fort under cover of darkness. Unfortunately, he was captured and everyone in the fort could hear his screams as he was tortured. They were able to see the glow of the Indians' campfire and see the ethereal figures as they moved around the camp. The next morning they found that the Indians had cut out his heart and roasted it over the fire. The story and the brutality of the Indians' cruelty caused Will to be very watchful and use ever skill he had been taught while on his hunting trips in the woods gathering meat.

The army agreed to pay him five dollars a weeks, seven dollars if he engaged the Indians. He was very surprised and content when they issued him one of the repeater carbines. They promised if he fulfilled his obligation, the gun would be his as a bonus.

After securing supplies of dried beans, coffee, salt pork, tobacco and three bushels of potatoes purchased from the store, they placed them into the small covered cook wagon. The soldiers mounted in unison and with a simple wave of the hand from their leader, headed north.

The group of soldiers wandered aimlessly across the open marsh in hopes that their scouts would pick up some sort of sign left by a group of the raiders. Several trails were found but never produced their desired end of finding the raiders and finally putting to rest the rebellion.

Off in the distance a large cabbage hammock came into view and the procession came to a stop. Due to the dry weather, a cloud of choking dust engulfed the men in front of the column. Lieutenant Baxter ordered the cook wagon to go forward to set camp in a hammock ahead. The others would make a big circle in hopes of finding sign. He said, "Mr. Benjamin, we'll eat a half hour before dark. Mr. Magrit, some venison would be nice". Then turning, he faced the open marsh surveying the horizon. He raised his hand and the order "Forward" echoed down the column.

Without another word, the cook wagon lunged forward and at a quicker pace than before moved towards the hammock in the distance. Will watched as the wagon moved away in a small cloud of dust wafting from around the wobbling wheels. After a few moments, he looked around and wondered were he would find a deer out on this open span of marsh. He had never seen such an open plain as this when his eye caught the movement of several objects in the distance. He put the spurs to the flank of his horse and loped off. He kept his eye on the formless shapes as they moved methodically towards a small cypress head that had been hid from their sight by the lay of the land. He checked the wind and knew that he had the advantage as he slipped from the horse and carefully moved into position. At the edge of the cypress trees Will could see a small body of water that reflected the sun as if someone had laid a large mirror down. Will had to shield his eyes. He moved a little to the right and was able to see several deer bedded down and unaware of his presence.

He had not had a chance to prove the new carbine so he used his Winchester Model 1866 lever-action 44-caliber rifle. Picking the animal closest to him, he raised the gun and held it tight to his shoulder taking careful aim. Squeezing the trigger, his target's head fell back and the animal lay lifeless while the others jumped straight up into the air at the sound of the gun. In the blink of an eye, the deer disappeared into the small cypress strand. Will rose to his feet and walked slowly forward to where the deer lay, curious as to where the others had vanished. Just inside the strand the remaining deer ran, seeming to explode in every direction, startling him. He turned and walked back to where his kill lay with its eyes and mouth open. Will drug the carcass over to the water, hastily gutted it and washed his hand in the small pool. The water was extremely cool. Will undressed and washed in the waist deep water because it had been several days since his last bath.

The ride back to camp was satisfying. He was refreshed and had successfully returned with venison for supper. Uncle Benny, a name a lot of the younger soldiers had given to the old cook, made short work of skinning the deer and had it stewing, along with big white onions and potatoes in the two large Dutch ovens over a well stoked fire before Will could stake his horse. They spent the rest of the afternoon getting acquainted.

Will had told him about his life and how he had lost two families in his short lifetime. He began to tell Uncle Benny about the strange man he had first met while camping one night. The cook watched with fascination and intrigue as the young man described his encounter with the eerie figure that seemed to move without being detected. How, with such speed and stealth, he moved from the darkness into the light, and how lonesome and empty his eyes looked. Will seemed to have drifted back to that very moment and again watched closely every move he made in hopes he would see something that he had not seen before. He didn't see Uncle Benny get up, move his hefty frame toward the boiling pots, return to his stool with a grunt, and sit back down.

Will did not know how long he just rambled but it did him good to just talk to someone that would not judge him harshly. Uncle Benny and Will began a friendship that lasted for several years.

The sunset was brilliant with colors of orange, red, and gray. Will thought it was as if God himself had taken a brush in hand and indescribably blended the colors together causing everyone in camp to pause and stare in silence. Small talk was made at supper and the camp took on a sort of cheerful feel.

Supper was over and all the chores of the day complete as the men sat around the camp file and waited for Uncle Benny to begin telling his story. The glow of the fire flickered as its light danced on the faces of those that had gathered to hear the tales. Each had a look of suspense on their face as if they were waiting for something to happen. All of a sudden, Uncle Benny stood up and walked to the wagon to retrieve a bottle of whiskey he had for cooking purposes and returned to his place by the fire. He cleared his throat, took a big swig, and began to speak. His words spoken like he was reading from a book.

"Tonight's sunset reminded me of when I first enlisted in the army. It was during the Second Seminole Indian War, I believe, if I can remember right. It was around 56. My first assignment was to track and capture a deserter from our outfit. I was stationed at Fort Meade over west of here." The old man spoke as if he was well educated. Will later learned that he once held the office of Major, but because he killed a man out of jealousy, he was demoted and spent the last thirty years as an army cook.

"We tracked that rascal fer three days. He musta' been part injun 'cause he took us through ever bad place there was tryin' to loose us. We found sign where he joined up with some bad men who left a trail of destruction ever where they went. Understand we weren't interested in the others until we seed the devilment they did but we knowed when we found him there was probably gunna be a fight. It was open marsh like this, when on the forth afternoon we noticed buzzards circling' in the distance and high tailed in that direction. We was curious to see who was dead now." Uncle Benny stopped and reached into his satchel and withdrew a new bottle of whiskey and took a long draw that took his breath. "That's good stuff. Now where was I? Oh yea, boyz we was surprised we found six men brutally murdered and stripped naked. A pure dreadful sight" He reached out and picked up his poker, jabbed at the fire to stir the coals and sending embers high into the still night air. Like everyone else, Will was distracted as he watched the sparks disappear into the darkness when his words cut through the suspense and brought them back to the story.

"You guessed it; our deserter was one of them. Ever time I tells this story I gets so thursty." He took another long drink from his bottle, replaced the cork stopper and set it on the ground next to him. Looking each man in the eye that sat watching him he said, "It was a massacre and looked to be only a day old." As the words drug out, the old man busily tugged off his cap again and turned the bottle up. The others had heard the story before and the delays when he took a drink didn't bother them. But for Will it was maddening.

"The tracker left us so we could bury those rascals and after lookin' 'round he returned and said that if we push we could catch 'em before dark. We buried the poor bastards and I ordered the men to keep a sharp eye and a keen ear. As luck would have it, we didn't catch' em that night. We spent a miserable night, and by mid-morning the next day we happened on an oak hammock where we found two wood boxes above ground and they was fresh. That's the way they say Injuns bury their dead. First time I see'd some' like that, it were plum frightful but peaceful. We figured they died 'cause of the fight."

He stopped speaking, stared out into the darkness with such a distant look in his eyes, and said. "I ain't see'd death afore that meant so much. Carelessly and without thought we buried those six damn fools the day afore and rode off. It didn't mean nothing' to us, but to Injuns it meant something'." He slowly got up from where he was sitting and took a few steps.

At that point the men who had had been listening casually now watched with curiosity. Uncle Benny had told the story a thousand times and it had not affected him like it did tonight. Slowly he turned and looked right into Will's eyes and said. "When I dies, and if you 'round, bury me with that much meanin'. Wouldn't you do that fer an ole man?" When his last word faded, he turned and disappeared into the shadows. Everyone sat by the fire stunned, eventually getting up and finding a place to fall asleep.

Early the next morning Will woke to the sound of pots and pans clanking together. Ashamed that he had sleep so soundly while others shared guard duty, he was glad that he was not on the marsh all a lone. Will hurried and saddled his horse and vowed that daybreak would not catch him sleeping again. The old man never mentioned the night before or his request again and seemed to be back to normal. He never again told another story the rest of the trip. To Will the evenings were not the same without entertainment from the old man.

Will was relieved when Fort Taylor came into view. They had traveled the entire distance without seeing one Indian. There was sign everywhere but whoever had left the signs seemed to just vanish into thin air. There were a couple of times he thought they would engage the Indians but then nothing. The scouts would say they could feel them close but it was as if they were nothing more than ghosts. It was their land and they knew it well.

The final few miles of the trip north with Lieutenant Baxter and the soldiers was easier because they had made their way to the east General Harney Trail. A small but well traveled trail cut through palmetto flats and around cypress heads that dotted the countryside easily concealing even the large column of troops. Will was relieved as he began to recognize the area around Taylor Creek and as soon as they entered the clearing of the fort, Will set about to resupply what he had used during the month long trip. He purchased new cartridges for both the army carbine and his Winchester. The last thing that he did right after he had said his good-byes was a trip to the well to fill his canteen.

Chapter 14

Mr. Magrit woke that morning feeling good and wanting to ride out and look at his cows, so they saddled the horses and headed down the dirt trail toward the cow pens. From here, they could head in any direction but this morning there seemed to be a specific purpose for the ride. From a distance, they could see the first bunch of cows off next to a rather large cypress head, but the old man turned due south and headed as if he was going somewhere special. They passed still another bunch of cows without even hesitating or slowing up. It wasn't until they rode up to a lone large spooky looking oak tree that they slowed their pace. In the middle of the scrub, it was at this point that Mr. Magrit turned due east and picked up the pace quickly leaving the oak tree behind. The old man pointed to a cypress strand where several of the big trees had fallen and made a natural shelter. As they approached the strand, they dismounted and walked over to the fallen trees. They stared into the darkness of an earthen cave made from the tree roots. Danny followed and peered into the hole wanting to venture in but was stopped short by the spider webs that hung across the opening.

The old man turned and looked toward the open scrub as if he was looking for something or someone to appear. He stood for another minute without saying a word then turned back to the fallen trees before walking back to where he had tied his horse. Danny thought that he may be having a relapse of his sickness and hurried to his side only to see the hand motion by the old man to stop. He turned and looked at Danny with a smile on his face that the boy had seen only a few times before. Then he said to Danny that it was here that he had made a strange discovery several years ago. He had to share it with him in order for Danny to fully understand what he would tell him about the lone eerie oak they had seen in the scrub. Danny sat on the ground as the old man knelt next to the tree and began to speak.

A week before he had to meet the Tanners at the Boar's Nest in Fort Christmas he decided to ride over to the small house he had found on the big creek. Will didn't like the idea of it but realized that he would have to spend the night out in the open one more night. The place he chose to camp was the cypress head where he had camped several months before during a bad rain storm. After hobbling his horse and gathering lightered, he busied himself with preparing his supper. He had just sat down when he heard something rustling around in the palmetto patch behind him. All he could think about was the bear they had bayed up that time they were hog hunting. It sounded like a bull busting through the palmettos but it was too low to the ground.

Without warning a strange creature emerged from the palmettos, a creature Will had never seen before. It wasn't very big for the noise it was making. It looked as if it had a shell of armor from the tip of its nose to the end of its tail. Will was relieved that it was not as big as it sounded. Curiously he watched it as it rooted around until it was too dark to see. Every once in a while it would stand on its back legs and taste the air, unafraid of Will and busy about it's business. If he would have been heading home to see Grandpa Henry he would have shot it to show him and ask what the strange creature was. He planned on swinging back by here on his return trip and if it was still in the area, he would shoot it and take it to grandpa. Later Grandpa Henry would tell him the harmless but destructive armored beast was an armadillo that was not native to the area but had been brought in by some men from Texas earlier on, he didn't know when.

Just before retiring for the night Will tossed a few more pieces of lightered on the fire and checked his horse. Moments later, he could feel himself drifting off to sleep. As he drifted off, he heard the rustling of the leaves again. He was not alarmed because he figured it was that strange little animal returning to its home, but it wasn't.

From out of the darkness, a ghostly figure appeared carrying a tattered blanket and, without a word, unrolled it and lay down next to the fire. Will really wished that he would announce his coming or something because every time he appeared suddenly like that it made Will's heart jump.

Taking the opportunity presented him, Will began a conversation with the old man who seemed to ignore the boy. "I saw the strangest thing this evening". Will paused and watched to see if the old man would acknowledge him and he didn't. "A small armored creator, the strange thing rooted around and stood on its back two feet. You know what it's called?" With a very faint response muffled by his head being buried under the dirty blank, he said, "Don't know, but sure good to eat." And, with that remark, he lay silent.

Will woke up at daylight and as usual and the old man was gone. Wanting to get started as soon as possible Will did not stoke the fire to heat his breakfast. He settled for a cold sweet potato as he headed east toward the big creek. He had ridden about five miles when he saw the old man standing out in the open. Will had never seen him in daylight and had really wondered if he had not dreamed all his encounters. Turning in the direction in which the old man was standing, he spurred his horse to a safe gallop and quickly closed the gap between the two.

Before Will could get close, he heard a gun-shot and immediately pulled his horse up. Will saw the coward responsible for the ambush just as he mounted his horse to run. Stunned by what had just happened, and before Will himself could react, the old man appeared where he was, reached up to Will's Winchester, grabbed it out of its sheath and empted the gun in the direction of the shooter. It took a few minutes for Will to grasp what was happening as the horse spun in circles. Will realized he was pulling too hard back on the reins. The old man grabbed the reins and shouted "Woe, woe there". The sound of his clear strong voice brought Will back to reality and back in control of his horse.

Will was taken aback, not only by the shooting but also by the old man's ability to talk. Gathering his wits and climbing down from the horse Will stretched out his hand and said, "Thanks, Mister. My name's Will Magrit." Looking in the direction from which the shot came, Will spoke again, "Thanks for your help. If you hadn't been here I fear something bad might'a happened." Handing him back the rifle, the old man simple turned and walked away.

Stunned by what had just happened Will knew that he had to do something about the dirty rotten bastard who, for unknown reasons, took a shot at an unsuspecting traveler and might not miss the next time he tried. Getting back into the saddle and cradling his rifle on his lap, he turned and headed for the Tanners.

Grandpa Henry and the boys were saddling their horses when Will rode up into the clearing. There were several other men there he did not recognize but by the way they were acting he suspected that one or all of them had already had a run in with the man that had shot at Will earlier. Will dismounted and told Grandpa Henry and the others what had happened and said it had not been more than an hour since he last saw him and what direction he was heading. One of the strangers spoke up and asked Will if he could take them to where he last saw the shooter and Will shook his head yes.

Eleven determined riders all left the Tanner's homestead, three Partins, four Tanners, a Simmons, Will and the two strangers. No words were spoken. The men knew what their mission was. Will carefully retraced his earlier trip and when they finally entered Scrub Ford he lead them right to the spot where the shooting had taken place. Both strangers dismounted and walk around looking at the sign left from that morning. Turning to Will the tallest of the two said, "We find evidence there was only two men. Six empty cartridges are here. Over there someone stood by that tree yonder. There's one cartridge and blood there. But I thought you said there was three of them?" Will retold the story, not leaving out any of the details. The shortest of the men spoke with a laugh and told Will as he mounted his horse "You must'a seen a haint".

Chapter 15

Mr. Magrit had a good laugh about the armadillo and without another word he untied his horse, mounted and motioned for Danny to follow. They were not rushed or felt any need to be anywhere anytime soon. As they rode down the cow trail leading through the high palmettos out again onto the big scrub they talked quietly as Mr. Magrit pointed out different places he used to camp as a boy and told Danny the names that had been given to the campsites. They first passed Hell's Bay. The old man told of the reason for its name. It was filled with gator caves and thick with the creatures. He never remembered seeing deer or hogs near the place. He recalled one day as they were working cows just to the south of Hell's Bay, a scrawny old bull broke from several cows being pushed hard toward the pens. Instead of running for the open scrub, he turned and headed straight for the bay and disappeared. Will said he had never lost an animal so he reined his horse and started following the old bull when he heard Isaac Nettles holler for him to stop. Will could hear him but did not understand why he wanted him to stop. Isaac rode up in a trot next to him and popped his cow whip nipping him on the shoulder. Will immediately pulled up on his reigns and stopped his horse just short of entering the bay. He couldn't understand why Isaac had hit him with the whip. He had never felt such a fiery sting like it and it aggravated him and caused him to speak disrespectful to Isaac.

He stopped short of entering the deep bay, apologizing to Isaac Nettles for his insolence and was met with a harsh scolding. The old timers lived hard but they lived by what the Bible said, "…Respect your elders". That was the reason Danny did not call Mr. Magrit by his first name.

He had not been given permission to do so and even if he had a been, he wouldn't have. No sir. No first names for the older people, man or woman. He then learned that Isaac's actions were only out of concern because he did not want the boy to get hurt. Willis Nettles told Will that sometimes you have to let young men make mistakes so they can learn from them but this was a mistake that no one should make. The old man told Will to get down from his horse and he would show him why he had to do what he did. They hadn't walked twenty steps when he learned the fate of the stray bull and what Isaac had saved him from. The gators were huge and very aggressive and very many in the small pond in the middle of nowhere on the marsh.

Next Mr. Magrit took him to Green Bay, named that he said because it stayed green even when it was dry. Some said there was a natural spring that bubbled up through the coquina rock while others said it had not always been like. It was told a man by the name of Willie Morrison drilled a flow well in the middle at one time. Mr. Magrit pulled up on the reins and said, "But I ain't never seed it."

As they continued across the pine wood flat that had long been stripped of the large pines that once grew so royally, the only thing that proved they had once been there were the massive stumps left behind. The only other sign of man's intrusion were the scars left on the remaining trees from the men who once worked turpentine. Deep ruts left by the large wagons used by the loggers when they ravaged the scrub were visible. The horses were the first to sensed intruders. Two riders appeared which caused Mr. Magrit to stop talking and turn his attention in their direction. It was Little John and Clarence. They were out looking for a few missing cows. Their concern was that someone might have stolen them because there had been some cows stolen just recently south of the area. Before chasing cattle thieves, the men wanted to first make sure that the animals had not wondered off on their own. Tied to the horn of Little John's saddle was a couple of gopher turtles. Selling gophers to the loggers was one of the ways he made a little extra money to feed his large family. The loggers would buy them from him for a dollar a piece, which was good money.

Mr. Magrit told the boy that they were good eating if fixed right. Clarence spoke up and asked if he had seen a couple a motley-faced cows with calves that looked just like their mommas. Mr. Magrit answered no, but assured him he would be looking and would notify him if they he saw the missing cows.

Just before they turned to leave, Little John let Mr. Magrit know his father was fixing to smoke some meat on Thursday of next week. He said they would be having a gathering at the old place and he was welcome if he wanted to take part. Mr. Magrit answered favorably and told him that he would butcher one of his bars so Isaac could smoke it for him. They shook hands and the two men rode off to continue their hunt.

Mr. Magrit and Danny traveled another mile or two when they turned north and headed toward a large oak tree that stood by itself in the middle of the scrub. Stopping before they got there, Mr. Magrit told Danny that this place was called Hangman's Slough he said in an almost reverent way. Danny was sure he saw the old man shiver and noticed a faraway look in his eyes. Danny heard the creaking of the saddle leather as Mr. Magrit shifted atop his horse. Clearing his throat again, the old man continued his tale of the lone gunman.

Late in the afternoon, Grandpa Henry suggested that everyone ride back to their respective homes and gather enough supplies for a four or five day search. His intention was to hunt these fellows down and issue his own kind of justice. Grandpa Henry was a just man but very fair. He was brought up when times were hard and it made the people hard.

Will especially remembered meal time at the Tanner home. Grandpa Henry would put the food on your plate what he thought you should eat and you could not leave the table until you had finished it. There was absolutely no talking at his table and if you did happen to speak you would quickly be dismissed and not able to finish. Even though he was small in stature, he still commanded his own domain with a strong hand.

There was something about dishonesty and meanness that the early settlers of this area did not tolerate, Mr. Magrit said. A lot of stories were not repeated because they were personal and at times embarrassing when it came to handling thievery and cheating, especially abuse against a child or woman. Usually evidence of the punishment for such acts was visible but other times that someone would just disappeared.

Will recalled hearing about a disagreement between two men. It was said that one of the men had been taken into a swamp, killed and stuffed down a gator cave. He also remembered hearing about three brothers who would visit the turpentine camps in the day after all the men folk would leave for the day. The three brothers would take advantage of the women left alone in camp, which was forbidden and dealt with very harshly if discovered. Their pa and uncles heard about their moral and physical sins and because of the embarrassment of the facts well known to all, their pa and his brothers beat the three young men to a bloody pulp with their bullwhips. It was said there were no more visits to the camp for a while.

The early settlers did not tolerate that particular sin, but you have to understand that sin was defined differently according to who committed it. The greatest sin against any family was humiliation, the old man said matter of fact-ly.

Will later learned the identity of the two strangers that questioned him as the Roberts brother. The brothers had appointed themselves to be some kind of self-appointed law in those parts. During the War Between the States, their pa had been left at home as a part of the Home Guard when a band of Confederate deserters and a runaway slave began to pillage the homesteads just north of here near Longwood.

While trying to stop the marauders, their father was caught by the deserters and hung as an example of their cruelty and what would happen to a man who tried to stop them. The lynching of their father never set well with the boys and ever since, Gator, eighteen years old, and Rabbit, sixteen, took it upon themselves to issue out justice as they saw it. It seemed they were good at dealing out their justice. If not they set out to get somebody, they would get 'em it was told.

Will never changed his mind regarding his plans to return to the house he found abandoned on the big creek. He did not want these men to ever find it because they would not be welcome. He told the men he was going off on his own for the night and he watched as the others rode out of sight and headed due west.

Finding the break in the high palmettos that concealed the trail to the house, Will slowly approached the front porch. Things were different from the last time he was there. Everything seemed to be in disarray as if someone had found the old house and looted its contents. This angered Will and he kicked the dirt in disgust as he said out load, "Damn thieves. If I'd a caught 'em, damn thieves." Time was not on his side on this trip. Will knew that he had to get some rest before having to be up early and back at the meeting spot on time or he would surely be left. If the man that shot at him was the one that did this meanness, he surely wanted to be there when justice was meted out.

After he had secured his horse and made sure that it was feed and watered, Will quickly went about the task of checking to see what other damage had been done. Relieved that they had not found the small graves, he turned his attention to the trunks in the barn. Sure enough, they had managed to open one. If there had been anything of value in the trunk, it was gone. Strewn all around the trunks were papers that, upon inspection included deeds to several pieces of property, birth records, a family Bible and personal unopened letters. The papers had no meaning to anyone other than the actual owner of the property. Will was extremely angered at what he found and respectfully gathered the papers from off the ground and returned them to the trunk, closing the lid as he left the barn.

The sun was beginning to set and Will was too aggravated to go right to bed. He had been taught all of his life that what belonged to a person was private and what belonged to someone else should never be touched by anyone, especially in meanness.

Morning came quicker than Will would have liked, but keeping his word and motivated by what he had found at the house the day before, Will saddled up his horse and rode to meet the group of men. He was the first one at the meeting place and waited patiently for the others to arrive. The next to show up were the Robert brothers who never spoke and watched Will suspiciously. He learned only after Grandpa Henry showed up that they had spent the afternoon before trailing the man that had done the shooting. They were able to locate him about three miles from where they were standing and the man was dead. They said that he was already gut shot and looked as if he had died slow. Gator's expression did not change as he said, "I'm glad you got him. One less bastard we have to worry 'bout."

Will spoke up and told them again that he had not done the shooting. It was the old man he had met on the scrub. "Anyhow! We got ta spilt up 'cause we found sign goin' dat way and found the camp of two other rascals 'bout ten miles yonder." They pointed in the direction of where Will had last seen the old man.

"Dad gum it, I told you the old man was the one doin' the shootin'. Last time I seed, him he was goin' that way. He ain't gunna hurt ya" Will said. "Those others is the ones we need to be after," Will said. Grandpa Henry interrupted Will and told him to calm down because he wasn't makin' sense. All any of'em was trying to do was catch and stop the bushwhackers and keep 'em from hurtin' anyone else.

Will explained the whole story again when Gator spoke up and said that they needed to get going and take care of the other two suspicious characters before they run out of daylight. They all agreed they would sort out the other mess then. With everyone in agreement, they turned and followed him to the camp.

The Roberts brothers rode off on their own. It was later told that the Roberts brothers rode into a camp about five miles away, finding the strangers, and hanging the men in cold-blood without asking any questions. Grandpa Henry was shocked and annoyed by the whole incident and told Gator and Rabbit that he didn't agree with what the scoundrels had done. He didn't like what the brothers had just done and told them he would have no more to do with this hunt of humans. He also told both brothers that they were no longer welcome in his territory. Rabbit rode up to Grandpa Henry as he turned to leave and said that he understood his feelin' the way he did, but those kind of men could not be reasoned with. He spoke without shame and said they done ever one in the community a favor, even the two men that hung dead from the tree.

All the way back to Grandpa Henry's place the group of men didn't say a word. All of them could not believe what they had just witnessed but felt in their hearts that the Roberts brothers were right. Grandpa Henry dismissed the other riders to go and get packed to leave for the Boar's Nest the next day. Will and him was going to find the other man they had seen sign of and deal with him in the proper way.

On the trail to the camp, Will asked if he could show him something and maybe a lot of his questions could be answered.

Will turned toward the hidden path through the palmettos as Grandpa Henry followed close behind. Surprised by what Will showed him and convinced that the third man was not going to harm anyone, he turned to the young man and said, "After round up you need to go to Kissimmee and find out who this place belongs to and if'in you can secure it fer yur self".

Danny and Mr. Magrit rode silently for several hours after the horrible stories just told. They rode up on an orange grove. The old man smiled with satisfaction for the first time that day as he inspected the fruit and determined that they were getting ripe. Mr. Magrit had been saying that he was hungry for one. As they rode through the grove, Mr. Magrit began to tell Danny that the trees were about forty years old. He said that it seemed like yesterday when he had contracted with Charles Hatch to purchase the seedlings in Melonville and have them delivered to Lake Cane Landing. He arranged to have them delivered to his place where he would make it worth the man's time.

After the trees were delivered it took about two weeks to set the trees. "I'd take the wagon to the big scrub, gather cow crap for fertilizer, and haul barrels of water from the creek to make sure they would live", said the old man with a smile that showed his approval of all his past efforts. Riding up to one of the trees Mr. Magrit reached out and picked one of the round orbs, peeled it with his pocketknife and eagerly ate the whole thing in just a few bites. He looked at Danny and asked him if he had a pocketknife and Danny said "No sir". "We'll have to remedy that next time we go to Fort Christmas" answered the old man. Picking several more fruit and putting them in his wallet for later, he turned the horse's head and moved away from the grove.

Chapter 16

It was later in the day when Mr. Magrit continued his story.

Mr. Emmett pulled his old truck in front of Will's house. Getting out, he made a comment on how the old bridge crossing the washout needed to be repaired. He went on to say that next time he saw Grandpa Farron he would ask him to come and look at it. He would give Will a good price on the repairs he commented. Mr. Magrit shook his head in agreement and said, "Whatever you think needs to be done". There was small talk for a few minutes and Mr. Emmett invited him and Danny to join them in the morning at the camp near Wehwahoottee. He said they were going to camp for a few days in a few days. The old man's eyes lit up and he said he believed the trip would be good for both of them as he reached out placing his immense hand on Danny's shoulder and squeezed.

The arrangements were made and Mr. Emmett got in his truck and drove away without another word. Danny was hoping that Junior would be there and could not wait until the appointed day.

It seemed like the next few days passed slowly by and finally the night before they were to go final preparations had been made. Mr. Magrit sat down on the front porch that evening slowly rocking in his rocking chair. Danny sat staring out into the darkness, longing for dawn to break when he said, "I wish it was morning already." Clearing his throat the old man said, "You best quit wishin' your life away. It'll come soon nuff." Danny would not fully understand what the old man had said until later on in his life. Mr. Magrit broke the silence with a question.

"Did I tell ya the one bout da first cow hunt I ever went on?" Danny shook his head no and the old man rocked a little slower.

He began another tale. After the cow hunt the year before, it was agreed upon by all of the men folk of the area to meet on a certain date next year. Most of the families only saw each other at round up time or if there was a wedding or funeral. Without daily meetings and conversations, there was no opportunity to remind each other of s date or occasion in the future. Their words was enough. A man was only as good as his word and he valued it far more than anything that could be bought with money.

Like clockwork, the Yates, Nettles, Coxs, Tanners, Tucker's, Partins, Osteens, Hodges, Simmons and Lanes all began to show up a few hours after daylight. Wagons of every shape and size came rolling down the rutted road to the meeting place called the Boar's Nest located at the Cox homestead. Those Coxs were different from the ones talked about earlier, Mr. Magrit said, even though they were all kin. Will had never seen so many horses and dogs before and was fascinated by the different types of dress.

Some wore brogan boots and home spun and sown britches. Some sported knee high lace up boots and store bought dungarees, and other wore overalls with slip on boots. There was every type of hat from a three-inch brim style to homemade straw hats. Will remembered his first hat given to him as a gift by Aunt Hattie Kilpatrick. Some wore store bought clothes while all the other wore homespun clothes, dyed a dark blue gray unless the sun had faded them. All the youngins came barefoot and in tattered overalls.

The boys and girls knew that while the men was away the children would have long hours of runnin' and playin' in the sun. The meeting was a special time for the next few days with as many regular chores suspended. A few of each family had to stay home to tend the homesteads. The gathering of friends and kin took on a festive feel. Will watched as several of the boys gathered in a group and he remembered when he was younger the mischief they would get into. Not having a family he could call his own, he watched with a longing to belong. He hoped that one day he would get married and his family would be invited to come and join this opportunity at being a part of a community.

The daily cares of life faded as they focused on the present task with each man knowing the importance of what they were about to do. For some the sale of the gathered cattle would mean an opportunity to pay their debts. To others it would bring satisfaction because of their long and hard labor to survive. The Boar's Nest had been named by a bunch of men who stayed at the camp during round up.

Each family had their particular area where they pastured their cattle even though it was open range and the cattle could go anywhere they roamed. Because of the open range, everyone gathered in one place and went into the woods to gather any and all cows that they come upon. Working together guaranteed each family's interests were protected. Understand that Dishonesty and thievery was not tolerated and dealt with very harshly. Gathering the cattle as one gave them a chance to spend time together and lighten the workload. Each man knew his own cows. There was no fear that they would cheat one another. Little John was considered one of the best at mammien calves, a skill that was in great demand making him a valuable part of any cattle operation. He would ride or walk through a bunch of cows and by observing the animals established which calf went with what cow. His mistakes were few. When it came time to brand and mark the new calves, everyone got their own calf.

Will remembers hearing a story about a man that was in partnership with his wife who will remained unnamed. When they gathered their cows, he would see a calf that he knew belonged to his wife and not allow it to be marked. The next year when they would work their cows again he would put his mark on the cow claiming it as his own. He increased his herd through dishonesty and ever one knew it. It got to a place where he could not get anyone to work his cows just for that reason.

Having a herd of cattle out in the woods was like having money in the mattress. They would cut the steers, mark them and turn them loose on the marsh. The steers would only be sold when they needed money for their daily living. It was common to see six and seven year old steers in a herd. They never sold the old cows or cut them out of the herd because they would bring new calves to the owners. The heifers would just naturally die off.

Will had the opportunity to ride with the Yates the first morning. The Yates family lived on Toshatchee Creek and their closest set of cow pens was Doyle Pond. There were several big sets of pens within range where the families grazed cattle. The Tanners had a set close to their homestead on the Pock-a-taw Flats. The Hodges and Coxes had a set at Happy Scrub not far from Jim Creek and the Simmons and Lanes used a set on the Big Prairie called Inna's Barn. Everyone used the set of pens called Snake Pens south of Kissimmee and St. Cloud at one time or another.

Any of the pens could be used by anyone, but it was common knowledge that boundaries did exist.

That particular morning, after several hours of riding, they happened upon a big bunch of cows that had several different brands. Everyone began doing their part, with Mr. Yates taking the lead. Will watched as the cow dogs worked the cows. Any animal that tried to break away was instantly brought back into the bunch. It did not take long for the cows to be bunched up and ready to drive back to Doyle Pond. One of the Yates boys looked around and noticed that one of his dogs was missing. He and Will circled back to see if they could find him. Way off in the distance they could hear the old dog baying and rode to him. They found him busy with an old bull off in a thick cypress head. The cypress head had standing water that made it difficult to get close to so Evert got off his horse and walked in on foot carrying his twenty-two rifle. Will didn't know exactly what Evert was doing so he just sat back in his saddle and watched. All of a sudden Will heard shooting. Confused at what was going on, Will slipped in and saw Evert shoot at one of the bulls' horns. The bull would toss its head back and forth at the sound of the bullet. The old bull would stop long enough to look at Evert. Evert would shoot at the hollow horn again and before long the bull and Evert walked out of the cypress head together as pretty as you please. Evert got back on his horse and began cracking his whip, working the old bull right out into the open. The two of them were able to drive him to the rest of the cows and never had any more trouble out of him. The only thing Will could figure was that bull associated the sound of that rifle shot to its hollow horn and how much it pestered him to that whip cracking in Elbert's hand and didn't want anything to do with it.

About two o'clock that afternoon all the cows had been gathered and they were able to start doctoring' them. After Little John mammyed the calves, they cut the yearling bulls and marked the young calves with their owner's marks and turned them loose to grow another year. About dark, everyone met back at the Boar's Nest for a good night's rest. Camp was a welcomed sight to the cowmen. Way before he got to camp Will could see the smoke from the cook fires drift through the large oak trees that surrounded the camp, which meant a hot meal. Dovie Nettles had taken the lead role as head cook directing the other women in preparing the meal. Will knew that it would not be long before he would be able to lay down for a well-deserved rest.

The mosquitoes were extremely bad and the younger boys would make a game out of gathering dried cow manure to burn in the fire as a repellant while ridding their dog fennel horses around camp. No stories were told that night or could you hear laughter in the camp because everyone was bone tired.

Will laid out his bedroll close to the fire and stared through the thick canopy of live oak trees. He thought of the first time he was allowed to go on a hunting trip with the men. It was cold the first night and he nearly froze so the next night he shared quilts with one of the Hancock boys. They talked for a long time before Tom said he needed to put his head under the covers because he was fixing to spit while clearing his throat. Will didn't want to be spit on so he quickly stuck his head under the cover but to Will's surprise Tom had only broke wind under the cover and it really stunk. Tom laughed and said "Too many sweet taters tonight." Will would rather have froze than smell that again. Somewhere between his thoughts Will slipped off to sleep.

The next morning the previous day's activities would be repeated until all the cows had been gathered and worked for every family in camp. Down at the Inna's Pens they were told about a little speckle heifer that had ripped the nose off a fella' by the name of Kilby. Mr. Henry and Mr. Tucker had warned him to quit messing with her because she was mean and looking for someone to hurt. Sure enough she got him down and he was lucky that she hadn't hooked him a little lower in the neck. Fortunately, someone knew to go to the barn and retrieve a hand full of spider webs that they used to stop the bleeding. The only sign of that day's battle was the old fellow who had a hole in his nose that never healed.

If one of the families had need of money, after the cows were gathered, they would pen what they needed and drive what they needed to pay their debts to a buyer in Mellonville or sell them to one of the cattlemen in camp. Will was pleased with his pay for two weeks of hard but satisfying work. Seven fine heifers that now bore his mark of crop spilt in both ears were his. He studied his cows so that he could recognize them when he saw them again next year. He hoped was they would breed with the old bull him and Everett drove out of the cypress head because he believed the old bull would throw good strong calves.

After spending several weeks riding the range Will and several other cow hunters headed south to join up with the Bass and Crab Grass Yates crews so that they could help gather and work their cows.

After getting what supplies they needed at Fort Christmas they traveled the Fort Capron Trail southwest to where it intersected with the General Harney Trail. They then headed due south to Whittier. The terrain was slightly different than what Will was accustom to due to the wide open prairie even though there were pine woods and low bushed acorn trees mingled with palmettos and spotted with huge cypress heads that were larger than any he had ever seen before. They spent about a month down there, but did not work the whole time. They had a lot of time that was spent fishing and hunting.

Fire had swept through the Snake Pens and destroyed them. Lightered pine posts had to be cut, each one with an ax. Every time you would strike one of those pieces of lightered, you could see sparks fly. Lumber had to be hauled from the saw-mill in Kissimmee. The only things that could be used from the previous pens were the hinges and spike nails. It was hard work and Will would be glad when he could get back on his horse and gather cows.

First, they gathered horses that ranged in the prairie. Everyone had a small herd of horses but was sufficient for their need. Working horses were a lot different for Will. Cows were dumb and predictable. He knew a cow could hurt him but a horse seemed to learn from mistakes made by a cowboy and they were very unforgiving to stupidity. Will really liked the small cracker horses and traded his labor on the pens for a pick of the two year olds.

Bertram Bass owned about thirty head and Will picked a little blaze faced bay filly that he immediately fell in love with and named Mollie. He couldn't wait to get her back to the Tanners so he could begin breaking her.

By the time they were through with gathering all the cows and horses it was getting hot. By mid-afternoon, the sun was blistering and it was hard to keep the younger workers out of the creek. While the older men looked forward to taking a nap the younger ones looked forward to a long skinny-dip. Will enjoyed working cows here because there always seemed to be more of a festive mood when dark came.

Homemade whiskey flowed free down there and it took some convincing Will to take even a small nip. He liked how it made him feel but he definitely didn't like the after effects. Every time he would take a sip he remembered what the preacher said one Sunday when he visited Lockwood Baptist Church close to the Tanners homestead. "It makes a fool out of you". The taste and those words were enough to keep him from partaking anymore. He thought it was funny to watch how the other cowmen acted while influenced by it.

One time in particular they were out hog hunting and happened to bay up a wildcat in a small pond. A boy named Tom figured he would go in after the hog. You never heard such cussin' and fussin' when that one hundred and forty pound boy met his better in a twenty-five pound wildcat. Tom begged for someone to get a lightered knot and throw it to him because when he finally got a hold of that cat, there was no way of letting it go. Needless to say Tom didn't win that fight and that incident sobered him up until the next time.

The last night of the spring cow hunt was festive and the men were in a good mood. New friendships were forged, rivalries developed and characters strengthened as the young cow hunters worked with the more experienced cattlemen. Each of the men present seemed satisfied with the year's calves and the health of the cows heading into possibly a dry summer.

The conversations quickly turned to plans for the winter hunt. It had become a tradition over the past several years to set a date for a particular event months in advance. Most people lived in the wilderness and only saw their neighbors during cow hunts, weddings or funerals. Most people believed the need for winter hunts were not necessary after this year because most families would depend on their stores of goods they produced in their gardens and the hogs and beef slaughtered and smoked to hold them through the winter. For some it had become a ritual that was hard to let die. The Partins and Tanners agreed to meet at Homer's place the morning after the first frost.

Chapter 17

The cowboys finished working their cows and driving them from the pens back to good pasture. Will did not want to be away from the creek any longer than he had to, so he put a lead on his new horse, dallied her off to the horn of his saddle and told Mr. Bass that he was going to head back home. He was exceedingly satisfied with his pay of three shiny gold doubloons that was the common pay for cow hunter.

Will was beginning to establish a reputation with his knowledge of cows, his skill with horses and his use of a whip. The most important thing of all was his reputation as being an honest man. He was told everyone was very satisfied with his work and he had been invited back next year. Will agreed and turned north toward home.

Since Will was going through Kissimmee, he would visit the land office and inquire about the property on the big creek which would save him an extra trip. He hoped the landmarks would be clear enough on the map so he could give the right information to the land agent. It took him about a day and a half to make it to Kissimmee and the land office. He had never seen such beautiful land. The grass grew belly deep to his horse. Now he understood why cattlemen liked the Kissimmee River Valley as pasture for their cattle. You could see for miles on the flat marsh which was a good thing.

The first night he had found a high hammock to camp in and just before dark, he watched as a large flight of egrets glided overhead in concert as they made their way to the roost. The whippoorwills cried their forsaken cry as if it were a desperate call for someone to answer. It was nights like that Will remembered his aloneness and lack of any family ties. He wanted to be angry for what they had done but realized that if they had not gone away he would not be where he was that day.

Off in the distance he could see the glow of another campfire and watched until his eyes blurred. Sound traveled a long way on the open marsh and when the wind would die down, he could hear talking even though their voices were not audible. Even though their camps could be a mile apart, he felt some relief in having someone close by.

Awake at daylight and back in the saddle, the fog lay close to the ground and concealed his closest neighbors. Retrieving his light jacket from his pack and pulling the collar up around his neck, he headed for Kissimmee. It didn't take very long before he tied his horse to the front of the general store that housed the land office and making especially sure that the little filly was secure. Walking up the steps, he entered the front door. No one seemed to notice he was there as they busied themselves with stocking shelves and filling orders for other customers. Will patiently waited his turn. Stepping up to the counter he told the clerk his reason for coming. The owner of the place was a slender small-framed man. He reminded Will of Grandpa Henry because he wore a long sleeved white shirt with a garter on his upper arm. His hair was black with whisps of gray. He chewed tobacco and spit through the cracks in the floor when he hesitated between every other word.

Will explained to him what he wanted and described the area he needed the information about. He was directed to a large map that had section marks and Will could see that others must have been thinking like him because folks were buying up the land all around Kissimmee and Orlando. He found out very quickly a man already owned the particular piece of property he was interested in. The name was Malby. According to the records, taxes had not been paid in several years and the land could be purchased as a tax deed, the clerk told Will. "There are two ways to get land," the clerk continued. "A tax deed was one and squatting on the land was another." State law had forced timber companies to deed over forty acre plots to families that had moved on the land and made any improvements. The timber companies would then purchase the timber on the land, a source of income and help for struggling families.

Will found out he could purchase two ninety-acre tracks for seventy-four dollars. Will reached into his pocket, laid the three shiny gold coins on the counter, and asked if they would be enough. The store owner told him that the three coins was only worth fifty-four dollars and if he wanted to buy the land now he would have to come up with twenty dollars more.   Disappointed, Will walked out the door and looked at the little filly tied off to the horse he was riding. He knew the minute he laid his eyes on that filly that he could never part with her. Determined he turned and walked back into the store and asked if there was any way for him to pay the fifty-four dollars now and in one month pay the balance. The storekeeper studied the young man for a few moments, stuck out his hand and said; "It's a deal". Will quickly reached out his hand, offering it to the man in agreement but the merchant said, "No! Give me the money and I'll give you a receipt. When you bring the rest of the money, you'll get the deed. Now understand these taxes are due every year and if you don't pay someone will get it out from under you like you're getting' it from the present owner".

Will left Kissimmee with one thing on his mind and that was he needed to make twenty dollars in the next thirty days so he could pay for the property. He would seek the advice of Grandpa Henry on how he could make the money needed to secure the land that he had fallen in love with. It would be easy to just sell the new filly but he knew also that if he could break the colt he would be able to build a good herd of horses for himself.

Grandpa Henry told him he had two options. He could hire out cutting' railroad ties or he could trap coons for their skin, which he could sell at a dollar apiece." Will spent the next few days cutting railroad ties. He soon realized cutting railroad ties was hard work for nothing. He gave the man that hired him a week's work, which they agreed to. He happily returned to the creek to trap coons. It would be too expensive to shot them so he set traps along the creek around his place.

The first morning after returning from Hodges Store at Fort Christmas with the traps, he walked down where he had seen coon sign and set several traps there. He found a bee tree not far from the clearing. He would rob when it got a little cooler and have a good supply for the next year. He had been with Pa Whaley when they robbed a bee tree several years before when he was a small boy.

Devoting the next few weeks to trapping coons, skinning and tacking the pelts to the side of the house to cure them, he hoped they would dry enough so as not to ruin. Will was proud he had caught fifteen coons and had found three grown otters he finally was able kill and skin.

At the beginning of the third week, he carried all the hides to Fort Christmas and sold them for twelve dollars. Disappointed that they did not bring any more than what they did, he had to figure out how to get the rest of the money he needed. Running out of time, he went to see Grandpa Henry to ask his advice. Grandpa Henry offered to purchase one of the heifers he had received as pay for working the cows. He explained to Will buyin' those cows from him was a way to increase the cattle herd he already had. Will sold one of his heifers back to Grandpa Henry and received ten dollars.

Two days before Will was to make the last payment for his property he finally had enough. Without returning to his place, Will headed for Kissimmee to make the payment and pick up his deed. The storeowner recognized Will as he walked through the door. After all the paper work was done, the two men sat down for a cup of coffee and made causal conversation.

Will enquired as to the price of the land and the name of the timber company that owned the land around his. The storekeeper was not sure but told Will he would find out fir Will next time he saw him.

Having the deed to his own land in his hand gave him a since of pride that he had not known before. He would sleep well knowing that he finally had a place he could call home. The man at the land office told him that as far as he knew the taxes would only be twenty-five dollars a year unless something happened that would cause them to go up.

It was late August of 1904 when he began realizing his dream of owning his own place and the start of his own herd of cows.

In late October, the nights began to be cooler and Will knew that winter would soon be upon him. There was so much that needed to be done.

He continued to run his traps and accumulated several coon hides simply because he enjoyed the time spent in the woods.

Late one evening he saw the ghostly figure enter the clearing again. Will was surprised to see the old man because he had not seen him for several months. Will had just closed the door to the smokehouse, checking the pork that he had been smoking in preparation for winter, when the old man sat down next to the fire. Will joined him and was glad to see him. It were really lonesome out there when a body was by their self. Will looked forward to the times he would visit with the Tanners and Partins, but those times had been few and far between lately.

It seemed as if the old man wanted to say something but the words just would not come. Each time Will had encountered the stranger it only fostered more questions with no answers. Will sat next to him and told him what he had done and let him know that he was welcome to live with him so he would not have to sleep out in the cold any more. Will wanted someone around.

The night was dark and cold making Will seek the warmth of the house early. Stoking the fire in the stove and moving the kettle closer to the flame, he could enjoy a cup of coffee. The ghost walked to the porch and timidly entered the front room that was illuminated by a candle given to Will by Ms. Mollie the last time he visited the Tanners. Will was seated at the table in the center of the room when the old man reluctantly joined him. Will was tired but felt the need to make his guest feel welcome so he sat up longer than he usually did.

The stranger looked toward the door as if he was about to bolt. Will walked to the corner of the room and pulled out a mattress stuffed with moss and two quilts from one of the trunks that he had brought from the barn. He placed them next to the hearth, turned away, walked to where he slept blowing out the candle, and crawled into bed.

Will lay awake in bed and listened to his guest wrestle his many adversaries in his dreams. He felt sorry for the man and truly hoped that he could help him recover some of the dignity he had lost while living as a wild animal in the wilderness.

The next few days passed without much change. The outsider would spend his days somewhere beyond the boundaries of the clearing and at night, he would return to his mattress in front of the hearth.

Chapter 18

Danny awoke early. He did not hear the familiar sounds coming from the kitchen. Concerned, he pulled on his britches and walked into the kitchen. He didn't find Mr. Magrit. He quickly turned and walked into the old man's bedroom. It was unusual but he found him still asleep. Danny quietly closed the door to the bedroom and returned to the kitchen. He stoked the fire in the hearth then went to the back porch that extended out over the creek. He got the water bucket and filled it with water for cooking. With the bucket still in his hand he looked to his left then back to his right amazed at the beauty that lay around him. He especially loved the large oak trees that swayed gently in the soft morning breeze. He heard the nervous chatter of a pair of wrens that flew from one cabbage tree to another, exploring every hole under each cabbage fans. The sound of the cabbage fans' movement by the breezes mingled with the constant barking of the squirrels as they sounded an alarm of an intruder into their world. Playfully racing up, down and around the branches of the oaks Danny laughed out loud as one jumped for a limb and missed. Falling quit a distance to the ground and stunned by its sudden stop it franticly scurried back up the tree ignoring his partner in play for a safe place to wonder what had just happened.

Just as Danny was about to turn and go back inside, he heard hogs squealing across the creek. Curious, he set the bucket on the bench and walked down the porch steps on the opposite side of the house. He headed in the direction of the noise. He found where a cabbage tree had recently fallen and made a natural bridge across a narrow deep portion of the creek. Unsure of his balance, Danny sat down and scooted across on his bottom. He quickly learned it was not a good idea because the small fibers from the tree stuck him and made his trip very painful. He found himself in a predicament. He had to continue or fall into the deep creek. Committed to the task, no matter the pain, he had to finish.

Once on the other side he continued to hear the hogs squeal. The hogs were a lot closer. With no gun and unsure of what he would do if it were a big boar hog his curiosity pushed him on. Taking a more open route so as to make as little noise as possible he walked through an open switch grass pond. He had not walked another fifty feet when he saw what was doing the squealing. A large sow was being tormented by a persistent boar hog wanting to fulfill nature's most basic need, but she was having nothing to do with it and was voicing her objection. His persistence finally paid off. Danny decided since he was already on the other side of the creek and Mr. Magrit was still in bed he would satisfy his curiosity by exploring the nearby woods. Hogs had rooted up the entire area in search of paint-root. Hogs loved the plant that grown in low areas on the marshes. The orange colored root the hogs ate turned the body fat of the hog yeller. It was said the root could cause hogs to go blind.

Off to one side of a low area surrounded by broom sage and grape vines stood an old hog trap. It had been constructed out of heavy-duty wire and had a trap door on one end tied with a rope used as the trigger. Danny figured out the way it worked. Two thick sticks were pushed down at an angel into the dirt side by side in the center of the pen. The trigger, made with another piece of wood, was tied with a piece of rope and was placed under them. The trigger was attached to the gate and the weight of the gate held it in place.

Danny headed back to the corncrib to get the whole corn in a small bucket and set the trap. Danny strewed the corn around the trigger. When the hogs began to eat the corn later, the hog would lift the trigger with its nose causing the gate to fall.

Turning south, he walked along a high break which was well defined and lay between the pine wood flats and the creek swamp. The landscape allowed him to traverse the break by dodging the palmetto patches as he walked along a well-defined used footpath. The wiregrass brushed against his pants legs causing them to become soaked by the heavy dew that had settled. The myrtles were thick along the edge and covered with dew soaked spider webs that seemed to sparkle in the morning sun. Danny began to see sign of where a buck had rubbed his horns on a small tree. Stopping Danny touched the rub then looked around hoping to see the buck. He began to walk again following a trial that showed fresh sign that the deer had been there earlier that morning.

Cautiously he took a few steps, and then stopped to scan the openings between the myrtles and small pine saplings. Taking just a few more steps, he finally saw the buck laying in the sun with its back to Danny chewing its cud. Danny could see that his massive horns were an orange brown color and shined brightly in the sun. Danny watched as the deer finally stood up, stretched its back by arching it. The deer shook the dampness from his dark tanned skin. He stood majestically aware of its surroundings when all of a sudden the buck seemed to sense something was not as it should be. Standing very still, the deer seemed unable to determine what it was so he lifted his front foot and stomped it several times, pawing the ground each time he stomped.

Danny did not move but his heart felt as if it would pound out of his chest. The buck sensed something in his path as it took several steps toward where Danny stood sniffing the air with its nose. Danny smiled and slightly shifted his weight from one foot to the other. The buck snorted and took two bounces. The big buck was gone.

Danny stood for several minutes trying to move because it seemed as if all the blood had rushed from his legs making it difficult to stand, much less walk. He marveled at what he had just witnessed wishing he had brought his gun with him. He walked south and came upon an old two rutted trail leading down toward the creek. The creek was shallow but swift running. He waded across the creek stopping in the middle to take a long cool drink of the refreshing water. The tannic water was sweet to him and tasted a lot different than the sulfur, rotten egg smelling water he was raised on in south Florida. The cool water relieved the itch of the mosquito bites that covered the back of his hands and the scratches from the briar bushes covering the myrtle trees. Walking in the knee-deep water caused a wake to form in front of him. The small waves washed on the sandy shore making minnows to dart in the opposite direction. He watched the minnows, remembering wading along the edge of Lake Okeechobee where hundreds of the little creatures played at his feet. His grandmother would use an old pair of stockings and make him a small net for him to scoop up minnows with. Oh, how he missed his family, especially his grandfather. How he wished his grandfather could have been with him to see the hogs and the big buck. He wished they could have seen him on his horse and working cows. He knew they would have been proud of him. His recalling of the fond memories seemed to satisfy his loneliness for now.

Danny stepped from the water and sat on the bank of the creek watching as leaves steadily fell down from the trees that shaded the creek. The leaves drifted slowly down the current and immediately were swept away from his sight. He listened to the crows as they flew above the canopy of trees announcing the dawning of a new day. Each thing he heard and saw caused him to remember things about his family. He loved the beauty of the creek but he knew he had to leave the haven of peace because he did not like the feelings that constantly overwhelmed him.

Following the trail out of the creek swamp Danny came out at the set of cow pens where he and the cattle crew had worked cows before. Stopping and looking around he took in the changes in the land around him. The transition between the foliage of the deep creek swamp and the high dry sand hills was striking to the naked eye of man. Large palmetto patches, pines and sporadic cypress heads intermingled with many types of trees and shrubs. Each day and each step he took brought new discoveries to the young man.

He had been at the cow pens on several occasions. He noticed a path leading around some wax myrtles that was shaded by a grove of large oak trees. Under the umbrella of limbs, Danny found a small cemetery. The fence surrounding the graves had all but disappeared. Danny figured many years had passed since the fence was first built. The graves had not been cared for. Weeds and small trees grew around the headstones. A green moss like growth covered the stones. The small wooden crosses leaned and sagged

Carefully stepping over the dilapidated gate at the entrance, Danny passed into another mysterious part of the old man's past. Nine headstones were stile standing but only four were legible enough to read. One of the headstones had the name Ben Franklin carved into a single piece of board. Another headstone had The Ghost written upon it.

Danny's heart skipped a beat. Could this be the ghost that Mr. Magrit had mentioned several times already? Danny's imagination ran wild with him and he wished Mr. Magrit were here to tell him what all of this meant. The other two headstones created the greatest curiosity for Danny. One read Sarah-beloved wife and the other just said baby. The dates etched on the markers indicated they both had died on the same day.

Danny sat on the ground nest to the tiny headstone and tried to envision what had happened many years ago. The only thing he could figure was that Mr. Magrit was once married and his young wife had died in childbirth. Danny felt a kinship with the old man. He felt and unspoken closeness because knew Mr. Magrit too had lost someone he loved, just as Danny had. Quietly walking away, he left the small cemetery determined to return soon and repair what time and neglect had almost destroyed. Danny noticed some wild honeysuckle growing and picked a handful, which he gently placed on the baby's grave. He left without another thought.

When Danny returned to the homestead, he saw Mr. Magrit sitting on the front porch. Danny sat next to him and told him about what he had been doing all morning while the old man slept. He could not bring himself to tell about his discovery of the graves. Mr. Magrit listened with great interest while Danny told of the buck he had watched and finding the old hog trap. He had set the trap, he said. Mr. Magrit rubbed the sleep from his eyes using both of his aged spotted hands. He looked off in the woods as if looking for something he had lost and began to speak.

Chapter 19

The morning the Tanners were supposed to meet and leave for the camping finally arrived. During the long days of waiting, Danny built side panels for his truck and he had taught his horse to load on command. Mr. Magrit watched with pride as the boy worked diligently preparing for their adventure. After everyone arrived and the truck was loaded with supplies and horses, they began their journey down the dirt roads toward the camp. The truck jumped and rocked due to the extra weight of the horses. The old truck did not rattle as much with the extra weight it hauled. Driving past an orange grove Danny stopped and picked a sack full of oranges to share with the others while they sat around the fire at night and listened to the stories that would be told by the old cattlemen.

The terrain had changed and Danny no longer saw the palmetto patches and pastures that surrounded their place. Mr. Magrit called it improved pasture. For miles, there was nothing but grass and hundreds of cows dotting the horizon. The cows looked a lot healthier than the ones that Mr. Magrit owned.

The old man pointed to a set of double gates telling Danny to pull in and he would open them. He seemed to have a little difficulty opening the gates but refused any help from Danny who was told to get back in the truck and drive. Embarrassed and a little aggravated Danny did as he was told and the rest of the way the only words spoken were directions to the campsite. In the distance, Danny could see a set of cow pens under some oak trees. A column of smoke rose from a fire that was centered by several large canvas tents that surrounded it. He could see several men moving around in the camp and the anticipation and excitement began to grow even stronger for Danny. The silence was broken when the old man finally said, "We needs to get us one of dem tents". Danny simply shook his head to acknowledge the old man's words then respectfully said, "Yes sir".

The rest of the morning was spent setting up camp and being introduced to the other hunters. Danny meet Mr. Penny who owned a ranch to the south, John Henson and several of his nephews who operated a several hundred acres ranch on Lake Hart.

One of the funniest things to happen on this trip was when the older men gave the younger ones permission to go and shot a hog. Well the Henson boys didn't hear the words "a hog". They heard shoot hogs. As Mr. Magrit described it, the young men had not gotten far from the camp when "all hell broke loose." The men in the camp heard shooting and hogs squealing. By the time some of the older men had caught up with the boys, and the chaos was all over they had killed eleven hogs. It took them the rest of the day and late into the night to butcher the hogs. One of the men from Orlando had started drinking early that morning and by the time they had finished butchering the hogs he had cut his hands several times. He held his hands out and complained about injuries when one of the Henson's poured raw whiskey on his hands, which made him cuss out loud. The cussing brought harsh words from Mr. Magrit telling him it weren't permissible to talk like that in his camp. The old man started laughing, the mood lightened and by morning the drunk had forgotten the confrontation.

During the afternoon hunt several of the men successfully killed large gobblers. Junior and Danny were given permission to shoot a doe for camp meat so they rode off in the early afternoon and talked quietly between them the rest of the day. As they crossed one of the pastures Junior spotted several forms moving from one cypress head to another and motioned for Danny to follow him. Riding into the wind, they were able to get close enough for Danny to get a clean shot on the lead doe as she emerged out of the opposite side of the cypress head.

The camp cook, an old Negro man from Orlando, fixed a meal of fried venison and turkey breast, a big pot of black-eyed peas and biscuits. There was cane syrup and guava jelly to put on the biscuits for a sweet treat. As was the custom in any camp after dark and a good meal, story time began. The botched hog hunt earlier in the day struck the theme and it was hunting tails. Mr. Magrit recalled a story from when he was younger. The men enjoyed Mr. Magrit's stories. The tales seemed to come alive with his words.

As daylight broke on the creek, Mr. Magrit said, Will woke to an early chill in the air. Instantly Will remembered the agreement reached the last night of the roundup. He jumped quickly from his bed, hurriedly grabbed his britches and pulled them on. Quickly he moved toward the stove to punch up the fire, adding a few pieces of wood that ignited quickly and produced a steady flame. It did not take long for the chill in the living area to be replaced by its warmth. Life returned to the lonely house.

Over the last few weeks, the Ghost had become comfortable with spending time at the house during the daylight hours. He had even begun to take part in the daily chores as Will began to depend on him.

The smell of coffee filled the air and Will walked to the smokehouse returning with a slab of smoked bacon. He liked his bacon sliced thick and hardly cooked all the way, while his visitor liked his fried crisp. They ate their fill of bacon and fried sweet potatoes and enjoyed the companionship of each other, but still not a word from the stranger. While they sat and ate, Will spoke of his plans for the next few weeks and asked if the old man wanted to join them. He abruptly said no and his response took Will by surprise. Will then ask him he if he would stay and keep an eye on the place; which he agreed to which Will added. "Treat it like your own and feed and water the young filly". An understanding was reached with the man even though he spoke no words. Will busied himself with the preparation for his trip. Packing double blankets, along with a dry set of clothes was important because the winters could be harsh on the river marsh. Next, he went to the dry safe, picked up two boxes of Winchester cartridges, some salt, fishing line, hooks and a small Crocker sack that was used to hold his supplies.

He went to the barn and scratched out a few sweet potatoes that had been placed in storage. He had dug a hole, placed pine straw in the bottom, and put the sweet potatoes into the hole. He then covered the sweet potatoes with pine straw and covered them with dirt. Going to the smoke house, he took one of the hams off a hook and a slab of bacon he had smoked earlier in the year. The last thing he did was to cut some wild mustard from around the pasture figuring the cold had sweetened them up. He had wanted some fresh greens and knew that Ms. Mollie would be on their trip. The remaining chores just seemed like a delay but Will knew they needed doing before he could leave for such a long trip.

After his noon meal, he saddled his horse and secured the supplies behind the saddle. Just before leaving, he turned to the old man that now called the creek house his home and asked once again if he wanted to go. His curt response was the same as earlier and with that he turned and left the clearing.

Will knew that he would be early at the Partin's but Uncle Homer told him he had an open invitation anytime. All the way there Will daydreamed about past hunts he had been on and hoped this one would be just as enjoyable.

Along the way Will shot a young doe for their supper and could not wait until he was able to skin it and get his fill of fried venison and fresh wild mustard greens. It took him about two hours to make it to the Parting's' homestead. He found them busy with preparations for the trip on the winter hunt. Will lent them a hand. The mood was like that of Christmas morning with laughter and excitement. The chores that were burdensome now seemed pleasurable. Night finally came and it was difficult for Will to fall asleep yet sleep ultimately came. He dreamed of killing a big buck and catching lots of fish.

They were served a light breakfast by the Partin women because much had to be accomplished before they were able ride out. Two large wagons were loaded with moss mattresses, blankets and cooking pots. Aunt Kittie loved to fish and shouted orders not to forget her fishing poles and net. Even the dogs joined in the excitement as they ran around barking, watching everything that was going on as if the could understand the words that were being tossed about lightly.

By mid-morning, the Tanners arrived with their team of lazy oxen pulling a large cart filled to its capacity with essentials. Mr. Henry had invited two fellows to tag along. Will did not recognize the men but later learned they had paid Mr. Partin for the opportunity to kill a deer and an alligator. Finally, it was time to leave with Uncle Homer and Mr. Henry in the lead.

The eldest of the two strangers was very tall and as skinny as a rail and sat atop the biggest red mule Will had ever seen. By the end of the first day, he was cussing the previous owner that he had bought the ass from, he said. The city feller had to be harshly corrected several times by Uncle Homer about his uptown language. The other man was as tall but a hundred pounds heavier and walked as if it hurt him to take each step. Will liked the heavier man because he was jolly and very friendly. Everyone knew that this would be an enjoyable trip because of how the two men entertained them by just getting off their rides.

The Partins had cleared a trail across the big creek. The trail would be easier to ford the river at high water for their weekly trips to Fort Gatlin and Orlando delivering beef to the meat markets.

One of Uncle Homer's boys named Dallas drove one of the wagons and Houston his youngest drove the other. They argued amongst themselves so not to be heard by anyone but themselves because even though they were full-grown their pa would whip them both for disrespecting their ma, neither one wanted Aunt Jess riding with them. There would be no peace for the driver of the team their ma rode in. She fussed at everything and they both knew if ma weren't happy, no one else would be happy. Dallas and Houston were relieved when she decided to ride her horse for the trip. It made a good trip an' some good laughs as long as ma weren't looking.

The first night they camped where the little creek met the big creek. This was a favorite place because the fishing was good. The Simmons clan came for the supper meal. There was a good time in camp that night. Aunt Kittie lit off her horse while Aunt Mollie grabbed their fishing poles. They headed to the creek. They took their nets made of old stockings and busily caught grass shrimp to bait their hooks with. They could be heared talkin', laughin', and hollerin' the rest of the afternoon while the men and children set up a temporary camp for the evening.

Just before dark the two ladies came waddling' into camp and threw down a string of fish. The women were quick to tell everyone they had worked hard catchin' the fish and ordered anyone in the sound of their voice to clean 'em. The women assured the campers they would fry 'em for breakfast the next morning.

The fire in the midst of the camp sent sparks high into the air as they celebrated the events of the year and the start of winter. It was pleasant sleeping under the canopy of large oaks at the edge of the big creek without the sound of mosquitoes. The cool breeze had blown them south and it made for good sleeping. The families slept apart in separate areas of the camp. Will and the two fellows that Mr. Henry had invited slept next to the fire. Will didn't care where he slept as long as he could be in the middle of everything that was happening. He lay under his quilt propped up on his saddle listening to Uncle Homer and Mr. Henry telling stories until he finally drifted off to sleep.

Bright and early the next morning the two ladies were up frying fish, fixing grits and boiling coffee. The smell of the food and coffee filled the camp and even though it was still early, the mood was festive. Mr. Henry spoke up and said, "I jus' wush you was dis happy at home when I asks ya to fix breakfast." Aunt Mollie rose from her stooped position, put her hands on her hips and said, "Henry, you best tells these peoples the truth. I don't fuss much at home". Everyone got a big laugh from the old couples' exchange of words and foolishness. It was not often people out side the family got to see that side of Grandpa Henry and Aunt Mollie. They, like most of the homesteaders, were very private people. The women had been taught from childhood the Bible verses that made the man the head of the house, no questions asked.

After breakfast, the taller of the two guests asked Grandpa Henry when he was going to get to shoot a 'gator. "As soon as we gets to Lake Jessup and set up camp you'll get your chance" was his answer.

Everyone worked together to break camp and said goodbye to the Simmons. Crossing the creek was difficult but the oxen with their steady pace made it easy and uneventful. The trail through the scrub had grown over and made it a tight fit for the wagons however. Their progress was slower than they had expected. They had to spend the night on the open scrub and it seemed colder than the night before. Will was glad he had to sleep next to the fire.

The mood in camp was not as merry as the night before because everyone was tired from the day's work removing trees that had fallen across the trail and cutting brush to make the passage easier.

By noon the next day, they stopped in a large cabbage hammock on the west side of Lake Jessup. The ladies were quickly off for an afternoon of fishing and catching up on a year of news. Their duties had been fulfilled when they had cooked enough food in the morning for the noon meal, cold as it was. It was the men's job to fix supper. Will had shot a young gilt, dressed it, and cut the meat in strips so it would be easier to cook on palmetto stakes next to the fire. Some one had cut several swamp cabbages and it was cooking in a large pot next to the fire along with sweet potatoes shoved under some coals.

Everyone was excited because they knew the next morning the men would leave for the first big deer hunt of the year.

When it came time to eat the talk was about the plans for the next several days. One and all agreed that it would be nice if it stayed cool, but it seemed the weather had begun to warm up earlier every day. There was plenty to eat and each person got their fill. Again, a large fire was stoked and the yarns began to be woven. The younguns sat in awe as the men and boys told them about adventures they one day hoped to experience.

Grandpa Henry told of an old gal friend he used to court when he was a young man. "She weren't much to look at". Aunt Mollie spoke up and said "She was downright homely, ugliest woman I ever seed as I recall. Don't speak well of his taste." The crowd roared with laughter. "You knows I aint got good taste at that, do I's Ma? I wed you.," said Grandpa Henry with a half smile on his face. The crowd erupted in laughter again when Aunt Mollie realized what she had said. She kept silent after that.

"Well anyhow, this gal wrote poems and I'll never ferget how that one went that was dedicated to me.". He continued in a high-pitched voice that mocked the young woman, "I wish I was a little fly in your cup of tea and ever time you took a sip, you'd give a kiss to me."

Everyone roared with laughter, slapping each other on the back and tried hard to get Grandpa Henry to tell them just who his admirer was. That was a secret knowed only by him and Aunt Mollie, he said.

Uncle Homer told of the time when him and several of his brothers went hunting down at Crab Grass. The youngest of the boys was deathly afraid of rattlesnakes and if he ever saw one in the woods he would see one next to every tree and under every bush. Well, he continued, they happened to run up on a big rattler stretched out sunning. Not wanting to waste a shot, they picked up a stick to beat it to death. Before they could get close, snake coiled and sang its rattles. The hunt was over for Edger. He wanted to go home so he started walking. He had not been away from the others long when his pants got caught in some briers and cut his leg. He looked down and saw blood. It was later said he had convinced his self he had been snake bit. He sat next to a pine tree, prayin' to get to Heaven and waited to die. About dark that night the other brothers made it back to the homestead and found that Edger was not there. It took them all the next day and into the following morning before they found him still sitting by the pine tree waiting to die. No one could convince him that he had not been snakebite until he started realized how hungry he was.

Everybody around the fire laughed as Uncle Homer told the story so well. The night was far spent when they realized how late it was getting. The fire burned low as each family retired to their respective sleeping areas.

Will had not noticed how beautiful Uncle Homer's oldest daughter was until tonight as she was silhouetted in the fire's light. All night long, she was all he could think of. He felt awkward when he thought of speaking to her. He had never even thought of girls in that way much less have feelins for any of them. He wondered how he could get to know her.

The next morning as the sun came up it got hotter. The mosquitoes started aggravating everyone early and the longer the day went the hotter it got. There was talk of packing up and heading home but they had lived through worse they all agreed. Sarah, Uncle Homer's daughter, volunteered for her and Will to gather dried cow chips to burn as a repellent for the evening's campfire. Aunt Kittie smiled and said it would be a good idea and encouraged Will to make sure they got plenty of chips to last the night. She encouraged the two young people to take as long as they needed. Uncle Homer wanted to protest but thought better of it when Aunt Kittie gave him a look out of the corner of her eye. It was clear to everyone but Will what was going on.

Chapter 20

Just after the noon meal, Uncle Homer and Grandpa Henry called for the taller of the two guests, the one that wanted to kill an alligator. The two men were getting tired of listening to him brag on himself about how good a hunter he was. They wondered aloud if they had wasted their time and money on this uneventful trip. Sitting around the cook fire, the oldest would brag openly to the womenfolk while they were cooking, how good a shot he was and how he considered himself to be a good woodsman. Although everyone there was getting used to his bragin' the women was getting sick and tired of his constant talk. The womenfolk were demanding something be done or they would take care of it themselves. Uncle Homer told them all to be patient because he had a plan that was sure to cure the man's arrogance.

The next morning the men saddled their horses and headed toward a small pond not far from where they were camping. Anyone that knew the area knew about the pond and didn't like going there because of the mean sow gator that called it her home, a secluded place to raise her young undisturbed year after year. During the spring round up one of the Kilby cow hunters discovered a dead calf there and it was decided to kill any gator, big or small, found in the hole to stop the gators from eating any more cows. It was the only water for several miles.

The bragger continually questioned the two older men as to where they were headed. Uncle Homer led the party around thick switch grass and even passed saw grass that brought waves of complaints from the so-called hearty woodsmen. The mosquitoes were relentless in their feasting on the men as they rode toward the pond. The mosquitoes did not affect the hardened cattlemen but caused the bragger to be tormented, cussing loudly at every slap.

The men eased up to the edge of the pond and Uncle Homer began gruntin' for the 'gator. It didn't take long for the big sow to surface. They watched her move effortlessly, her eyes searching the bank of the small pond for the source of the grunting. Grandpa Henry spoke in a low voice. "Be plum quite now so's she don't hear ya. We gonna try to get her closer so's you can get a good shot." Shifting his toothpick to the other side of his mouth, he reached up with his free hand and placed it behind his ear. He grunted again. Instantly the she gator turned toward the sound and began her slow advance making little ripples in the otherwise calm pond.

The fellow was beginning to show a little excitement as he shifted from one leg to the other while crouched down between the two old men. Nervously he stroked his rifle when Uncle Homer made him jump when he said, "Get ready and shoot just behind da eyes when I tell ya." The two men grinned at each other as one grunted once more and the other said, "Shoot".

"Bah-boom" echoed the shot as the water before them exploded causing water to spray over the three men. All three stood up quickly still shocked by the blast of the rifle. The water returned to its former stillness and Uncle Homer reached for the rifle causing the shooter to jump. He said, "Why you so jumpy? Take off yourn boots and get in there and get er. Ya got your 'gator. Now ya gotta skin it. "

The man looked shocked and dumbfounded at the order. After just a few words of praise about how good the shot was from Grandpa Henry his confidence and cockiness overcame his fear. Sitting down by the edge of the pond, he mumbled as he reluctantly did as he was told. Turning his body to the pond, he slipped into the water realizing it to be only about four feet deep, which only came to his waist.

When he got to where he thought the 'gator had disappeared, he turned and asked, "What am I suppose to do now?" Uncle Homer told him to use his feet and feel around on the bottom until he located the dead gator. He continued telling the man to reach down, get a holt of her, and pull her to shore. Grandpa Henry assured him that was how it was done and he himself had done it countless times without harm. Uncle Homer looked puzzled at Grandpa Henry and said loud enough for the stranger to hear, "Didn't dat 'gator last year near drowned ya?" "Come to think of it, you plum right." Grandpa Henry turned to the man that was standing in the knee-deep water, "I didn't kill er with my first shot."

With much hesitation, he began working the bottom of the pond with his feet and every once in a while he would almost jump out of the water. You could tell he was uncomfortable and after a few minutes, he turned and said, "She ani't here". "Keep lookin'. I'll come in and hep ya" said Grandpa Henry as he slipped into the edge of the pond holding a large stick that he planned to use to teach this braggart a lesson for life.

His goal was to successfully conceal the stick from the shooter. It worked perfect because the shooter felt something move on the bottom of the pond that made him jump again drawing his attention away from the man that approached him.

Just as Grandpa Henry got to the man that was already in the water, the she gator popped up between them making a splash, which surprised them both. Startled and willing to sacrifice the stranger, Grandpa Henry pushed the stick he had in his hand towards the gator in self-defense as he backed fast away from the situation. This caused the stick to shoot right between the other man's legs. Uncle Homer recalls hearing a panther scream and it had nothing on the scream that came out of the man.

The two brave men and the she gator went in different directions trying to get away from each other. As the gator turned, its tail touched the back of the man's leg and he let out another death-curdling scream. He jumped clear out of the water.

Uncle Homer was laughing so hard that he fell down and rolled right into the pond on top of Grandpa Henry. The other man looked like a coot running across the top of the water. When he got to the other side, he collapsed and lay on the ground passed out.

Grandpa Henry and Uncle Homer could not have planned it any better if they had planned it themselves. Even though the gator almost caught Grandpa Henry, which was not a part of their plan. It took nearly an hour to revive the great hunter because the two old men couldn't stop laughin'. The whole way back to camp they kept yellin' "gator" and pointing' like two younguns. Story time for the next few nights was a repeat of that trip with embellishments of each the day's events.

Uncle Homer was convinced that this was the most entertaining huntin' trip he had ever been on. He made the comment several times the they were guiding should have been paid money for the entertainment they provided rather than the men getting paid for guiding them.

The day after the gator-hunt Grandpa Henry was sore. He tried to convince everyone that it was because he had laughed so hard but no one believed him. He stayed in camp to help prepare meals for the day. So Uncle Homer agreed to take the now meek older man out and give him a chance to kill a nice buck.

Everyone agreed they had never seen anyone as excited as the visitin' man. He sat up next to the fire the night before because he said he couldn't sleep. By the next morning he looked as if someone had beat him and left him for dead after being on a three day drunk, but he was ready to go when Uncle Homer called about four o'clock the next morning. He stumbled around in the dark as he gathered his looking glass and face paint to camouflage his face when he stalked the deer. Everyone that was awake in the camp just gave him a strange look as they turned over in their bedrolls, some risen' and busying themselves with the morning chores.

The hunters backtracked to where they had seen good sign when they first come to Lake Jessup. Daylight was just breaking when they saw a large buck standing broad side forty yards away in the edge of some myrtles. The buck's attention was fixed on a doe he was chasing and it did not even see the fat man as he dismounted his horse, almost falling down and making all sorts of noise. The buck finally saw him as the man lifted his gun and pulled the trigger. Just seconds before the blast the deer had already turned and in one quick jump was gone into a large palmetto patch that bordered the road.   Uncle Henry said you should a seen that man run. Uncle Homer said he thinks he passed the bullet. He returned to where the horses were with a confused look on his face, wondering how he could have missed the deer that close and with such a clear shot.

Uncle Homer had been amused and tried not to laugh out loud as he watched him climb back into the saddle still speechless by what had just happened. Uncle Homer tried hard to console him but nothing he tried, helped until they rounded the next bend in the trail and there standing in the middle of the road was a large spike buck. Believing the noise he made getting off the horse contributed to him missing the last deer, the hunter named Lawrence threw up his gun and pulled the trigger. Click. Nothing. He realized he had forgot to reload after his last shot. Immediately he reloaded and pointed his gun and pulled the trigger. The deer fell down and lay still in the middle of the trail. The next sound Uncle Homer heard was the dull sound of the big-butted man hitting the ground next to his horse causing Uncle Homer's horse to bolt.

Lawrence forgot to let go of the reins and was pulled down on his back. Uncle Homer said he looked like a gopher turtle tryin' to turn itself over and he got so tickled he couldn't even look in the man's direction. He promptly got Lawrence's attention when he yelled, "You got this un". The fat man jumped up and landed on his knees staring in the direction of the lifeless animal that lay silenced in the lane. Before Uncle Homer could say anything, he ran over and grabbed what he thought to be a dead deer when all of a sudden it came to life. The battle that ensued was horrific when the deer began to fight with its captor. Out of self-defense, the deer rose up on its hind legs and kicked at his aggressor. The fat man was flabbergasted and knew he was in a battle for his life.

He was thankfully wearing a thick jacket. The deer shredded it in a matter of minutes. They rolled all over the ground while Uncle Homer got so tickled at what he was watching he almost fell off his horse. You could hear the desperation in the fat man's voice but there was nothing anyone could do. When they had fought for several minutes the deer and the fat man both fell back in shear exhaustion. All at once, they righted themselves landing eye to eye, a regular Mexican standoff.

In that instant the fat man jumped to his feet as best he could which startled the deer causing it to lunge forward. Once again and with their second winds, they were locked in a battle for freedom. When the dust finally cleared, there lying in the middle of the dirt lane was the fat man and he looked as if he was not breathing. Uncle Homer started to move toward him when gradually he rolled onto his back and then into a sitting position. With blood running down his face and a look of disbelief and confusion, he tried to speak but nothing came out.

Uncle Homer didn't help matters any when he busted out into a laughter that could be heard over the entire scrub. The injured man began to chuckle and he burst into laughter himself. When he laughed his whole body shook and his laughter was extremely contagious. For the next several nights, everyone had to relive the tale of the battle between man and beast.

A cold front moved in fast that afternoon and it rained late into the night. By the next morning, it was clear and cold. The fire felt good as the sun rose in the eastern sky with its brilliant colors. The smoke from the lightered fire wafted up into the canopy of live oaks, along with the smell of breakfast cooking. Even with the change in the weather, everyone was in a very festive mood. The men decided to allow that women folk a day off from their usual camp chores for a day of fishing.

A grill was fashioned using several rods brought from home that would cook the fat shoat that were killed the day before. Uncle Homer called Lawrence and asked if he wanted to go see if he could wrestle another deer so it could be cooked too. The joke that morning did not go over as well as it was meant due to the fat man's soreness and the effect of the moonshine he had consumed to forget his embarrassment the day before. Several of the younger men cut swamp cabbages which were cooked along with some wild mustard they found next to the river. They had laid the last of the sweet potatoes in the coals to cook slowly for the afternoon meal. Everyone hoped that there would be fresh fish as well.

The children spent the morning catching grasshoppers and minnows for bait because the specks were really biting. The women could be heard all over the marsh as they spent time talking and catching up on all the gossip. It had been almost a year since they had been able to sit down and just visit. Each other's ailments were compared to the others as bobbers disappeared. Taking fish after fish off the hooks and having to bait their hooks frequently diverted their attention from the hardships of life they experienced. Many conversations were started and interrupted by fish they would call pests, and openly admitted loving the interruptions.

The women were so enthralled in what they were doing Aunt Mollie had not noticed she was sitting in a gator crawl. As the sun rose higher in the sky, the heat chased the cool of the morning away. As fate would have it, the gator that made the last marks in the sand in the gator crawl wanted to sun again. It stayed submerged until it got to the bank when it started to emerge out of the water and got its first sight of Aunt Mollie. The gator swirled and splashed water all the hysterical woman in front of it. Aunt Mollie could not move because of her size and her fear. She screamed and everyone came running. Aunt Kittie said she looked like a crawfish tryin' to scoot on her butt up the bank. Her feet got tangled in her long dress. The material wrapped around her feet slowed her escape. All the while she never let go of her fishin' pole. She hollered, "Pa, Pa hep me" then screamed to the top of her voice. Grandpa Henry recognized the scream, turned and ran in her direction saying, "I' m a comin'. I plum recognize dat scream".

Confusion filled the camp as the people scattered. Uncle Homer took control of the cook fire and said, "Sit still, people". Grandpa Henry soon returned red faced and giggling', trying hard not to laugh out loud but he knew better than to draw any more attention toward the river than need be. He searched through their personal belongings in the wagon and returned to where Aunt Mollie was. He had a bundle of clothes in his hand.

Everyone was still frantic to know what had just happened. There were a few in camp brave enough to rush to Grandpa Henry's side as he returned to the camp fire the second time. The only thing he said with a giggle in his voice was, "No more swimin' in da river today" as he busted into laughter. Everyone was confused until Aunt Mollie came walking back to camp in a different dress and a look on her face that warned everyone to not ask any question. It wasn't until the next evening' around the camp fire that the truth was told about the gator crawl. In Aunt Mollie's own words she said "I messed on myself".

Chapter 21

The end of the hunt finally came that winter. As they traveled back to their own homesteads, Sarah and Will rode well behind the wagons on their horses, so they could talk and get to know one another. The two young people had found themselves drawn together around the campfires the last few nights. The young couple were careful not to draw attention to themselves. Nothing at all was going to happen. Will felt uncomfortable around females and felt awkward. It had been different the first time he had talked with Sarah. When they stopped for the last night on the hunting trip, Uncle Homer walked up to Will and told him he wanted to talk.

Nervously Will rode off with Sarah's father. A short distance from camp, the two reined in their horses. Uncle Homer looked into Will's eyes and said, "Sarah's my onliest girl and I wants you to be honorable in your actions and intentions. I don't mind you a courting' or going' to church with her or coming' over to the house, but I'll be watchin' you close so don't give me no reason to worry." He could only whisper "Yes sir".

The rest of the trip was awkward for Will. He didn't want any of his actions to be thought of by anyone as brash or disrespectful. Sarah could not understand Will's hesitation and thought that he didn't like her. It was a long ride back to the Partin house and Will noticed the coolness in Sarah's attitude which he could not figure out. He was only doing what her father had wanted. Sarah disappeared into the house as soon as they arrived. Will began to say his goodbyes and headin' back to his place.

Before he got out of sight he turned in his saddle and smiled when he saw Sarah standing next to Aunt Kittie on the porch. Both women smiled at him and he saw Sarah turn and skip off to do her chores.

Everyone noticed there was something different about Sarah. Several comments were made among the women about but Aunt Kittie dismissed the talk as nonsense. Sarah had talked to her Aunt Kittie about what was happening between her and Will. Every one of the men, except Sarah's dad, did not see the difference in the two young people.

When Will got back to his place, he unsaddled his horse, brushed it down and gave it some corn. The entire time he was caring for the horse his mind was back at the Partins and he wondered what Sarah was doing. He shook his head to clear his mind and wondered if what he thought was normal or not. He wished that he could talk to Grandpa Henry because he knew that he would be honest and not joke with him about his feelings.   Turning to survey the clearing, he was still confused as to why the old man was not present. Will wished that he had been able to find out the old man's name but they never got close enough. He excused his inaction as normal; he figured his guest was off in the woods doing whatever he did.

Darkness finally came as the full moon shone bright and high in the sky. Even though Will missed, the company of those he had spent the last several weeks with, he relished the quite he now enjoyed. The only sound he heard was the steady buzz of the mosquitoes that ultimately drove him inside. The colder it got the less the mosquitoes would bother him and he could not wait until the pesky bugs were gone.

The next morning Will faced the tasks of everyday life. He complained even though there was no one around to hear, aggravated he had to tend to things that had been neglected by his visitor's absence. After completing his chores, he grabbed his gun and walked toward the creek in hopes of seeing the otters that had left clear sign of their presence several weeks before. He had not walked far before he began to hear a constant hum that caused him to halt his advance. He looked inquisitively in all directions, and then he spotted a beehive about fifteen feet up a water oak tree. He recalled when he was a little boy they discovered a bee tree at Little Prairie. The tree was close to a small running creek that offered a place of retreat for the children present in the crowd. From the moment the first ax hit the base of the tree the bees became hostile and stung the men that did the chopping. You could see bees everywhere. The girls would screamed and cried if a bee came close to them and the boys would run for the creek splashin' around in the water to keep the bees away. A small fire was started and green moss was gathered and tossed onto the fire for smoke that would paralyze the bees the moment the tree hit the ground.

A loud crashing noise echoed throughout the cabbage hammock when the tree finally yielded to the ax. Instantly a cloud of stinging bees rose from the ground and swarmed in all directions. Pa Whaley stirred the fire and placed more green moss on it causing more smoke that immediately tamed the angry honeybees. Once the bees were under control, the men cut away the area around the opening of the hive and retrieved the cone hidden within the tree. It was a good harvest of forty pounds of cone and honey both of which would be preserved for use in their homes all year round.

Carefully making a mental note of the location of the bee tree, Will began to walk toward the creek and continued his original mission. He had already cured eighteen otter hides and twenty-four coonskins. He wanted to add a few more skins before making the trip to Fort Christmas to sell them to Mr. Tucker. Even though he sat still by the creek the entire day, late in the afternoon he was unable to see any otters. Disappointed but he was resolved to the fact when a man went hunting it is more luck than actual skill. As he walked back to the house, he stopped to watch the bees as they actively entered and exited the tree hive. He shook his head with his thoughts and said out loud, "That's what I'll do".

The next morning he loaded the skins on the back of the young filly and headed to Fort Christmas. After receiving payment for the skins, Will asked Mr. Tucker about purchasing cows and how he would go about it. Mr. Tucker told him of a small herd south on the Kissimmee Prairie and the owner wanted to sell the herd for ten dollars a head.

Will contracted with Mr. Tucker for thirty cows and paid one hundred and fifty dollars right there. He promised to have the rest in sixty days.

Arrangements were made to have the cows delivered the next week and they shook on the deal. Will was beginning to accumulate a sizable herd and planned one-day he would be able to make his livin' off the cattle.

He camped that night between Fort Christmas and the big creek where Sarah lived.

Will enjoyed the moonlight as it flooded the open scrub. Just as he was about to go to sleep he heard the crack of a cabbage fan just beyond the reach of the light from the fire. Looking toward the area where the sound came from, he hoped it was the ghost that use to visit his camp. He could see the image of a man pass between the trees emerging into the light only for a moment then disappear. Whatever it was, who ever it was it never stopped long enough for Will to identify it. The intruder turned and ran away as it made a loud crashing noise. He watched the fire and wondered what Sarah was doing. He finally fell asleep. At some time during the night, he was waked up by the sound of his dog bayin' in the distance. Without a thought Will jumped up, saddled his horse and headed in the direction of the dog's baying.

The moon was still bright enough for Will to see where he was going. He thought of the man that had shot at him. He pulled up on the reigns and thought about what he was doing. He did not want to ride into a trap or rouse men that were not friendly. Buck was still barking franticly as Will slipped from his horse, tied him to a small myrtle tree and carefully moved toward the dog and whatever he was baying. Will was shocked at what he saw laying there on the ground. It was the old man and he lay on the ground struggling to breath. Will set his gun down and asked what was wrong. The old man could not answer. Through the break in the cabbages, the moon illuminated his face and Will could see blood coming from his mouth. As the old man labored for breath Will could hear him gurgles he struggled to breath. With the next deep breath, he was gone.

Will fell back in disbelief wondering just what had happened. Alone in the middle of the scrub, fear filled his heart. He felt the loneliness he had felt when he realized his family had left him to fend for himself. No one had ever seen Will cry but his emotions were so strong that he could not help himself. He wondered why he cried for this stranger or was he crying for himself? He stood up and walked toward his horse. He stumbled as he walked with tear-filled eyes, catching himself on a tree. His movement spooked the horse. He picked up the dead body and laid it across his saddle. He led the horse with the dead man's body back to the creek. It took him most of the night to make the trip. By the time he entered the clearing at his place he was extremely tired.

He placed the body on the porch, picked up his shovel and headed to the cemetery he had found. He thought to himself another grave, another loss. Just a few months before the cook he had befriended several years before had found him within days of his own death. Will was getting tired of death and tired of digging graves.

All of a sudden, it hit him. Who would bury him when he was gone? He dismissed the thought and went about the task of digging the grave and burying his friend.

Chapter 22

The moon was full and it illuminated the scrub as Will rode from the shadows of the creek swamp. His purpose for being out so late was to meet Grandpa Henry, Uncle Homer and several other men from the surrounding homesteads to look for the rascals responsible for killing steers on the marsh. Most of the cattlemen accepted the occasional killing of beef in order to feed a hungry family. These killings were different. Whoever was killing these cows was just taking the hindquarters and leaving the rest to rot. Twenty-five steers had been found over the last three months and at this rate, it could affect the livelihood of any one of them. The killing of the steers could not go unpunished.

Everyone knew that the people responsible for this meanness could be anywhere. The last steer found was on the big prairie just west of Titusville. The intention of the men that gathered was to ride at night and sleep as much as possible during the day until they caught and captured the violators. They also hoped their presence on the marsh would be a deterrent.

The first two nights went without incident. It wasn't until the third night that they spotted the glow of a fire in a small cedar hammock on the far eastern edge of the prairie next to Fox Lake. The men could hear the occasional bellow of a lone cow. Cautiously Will and the other men eased toward the hammock. Due to the openness of the marsh, they could see a good distance. Several cattle were milling around the hammock.

The closer they got to their destination the clearer they could make out the voices of three men talking. To keep from spooking the cows they dismounted and removed their rifles from the sheaths and slowly moved toward the glow of the fire. The moon was still full even though it had begun its decline, which made it difficult to approach undetected.

The sound of a dog barking caused the men to freeze. The dog barked a few more times. They saw a man stand up and kick at the dog causing the dog to run out into the darkness, then returning and laying beside his master. The man turned and looked in Will's direction trying hard to see what had caught the dog's attention. Satisfied that the dog was just crazy he sat down and returned to his conversation with the men. One of the young men with Will walked up beside him and whispered; "I thinks I recognize the voice of one of the men as a Tucker boy".

The men decided to return to their horses and wait for daylight so no mistake would be made. The night was chilly and it got colder the nearer sunrise was. Will had the last watch of the night and could see the sun break the sky over the horizon. Flights of egrets passed overhead leaving their rookery somewhere south of where they were camped. He could see the smoke as it rose straight into the sky indicating the stillness of the morning. Will woke the others and they discussed their plan of action.

They all agreed that something had to happen soon because they could not conceal their presence once the sun was fully up. The stillness of the morning was broken when all of a sudden a rider emerged from the hammock on horseback riding at a steady pace north. The rider was one of the young Tucker boys and Will was relieved because he had questioned himself all night whether he could shoot at another man. He had also thought of the Roberts brothers and what they would have done last night when they first came upon the camp. He was convinced that they would have gone in shooting and then asked questions. The men mounted their horses and rode up to the camp, calling out and identifying themselves as friendly. They were welcomed in the camp and enjoyed civil conversation and a hot cup of coffee. They learned that the cows the young men were driving north had been sold but the man that had purchased them had not paid for them. The young men had been sent to reclaim the herd for their pa. They also spoke briefly about the rustling that had been plaguing the area. Every man that had cattle in the area voiced their concerns, the young men said.

Will and the group of men that was with him decided to stay at the camp until later in the afternoon. They would then ride back to Lake Cane, cross the river and head back home. They all knew that it would be early the next morning before they would get back to the creek. The delay would allow them to ride again at night in hopes of coming upon the scoundrels committing the cruel acts of waste.

It was late afternoon when the last rider crossed the St. Johns River. Their plans were to head to Thomas Cox's through Horse Hammock. They enjoyed a hot meal there while they allowed their horses to rest. Mr. Wood had been by earlier in the day and left word for Thomas that last night the rustlers had killed a calf close to Lake Drawdy.

About eight o'clock in the evening they saddled their horses again and continued west. Everyone involved was extremely tired but was committed to the task at hand. The moon that had been so bright the night before was concealed by low fast moving clouds that warned of a drastic change in the weather. It was still cold but the importance of their mission pushed them on. Everyone, including Will, was ready for the task to be over and if tonight were the night they would face it with determination.

When they heard a gun in the distance, they stopped and waited in hopes that who ever had shot would do it again so that they could course it. They did not have to wait long before they heard the next shot and the bellowing of a dieing cow that gave them the direction and determine the distance they needed to travel. Will, with his youthful inexperience, wanted to rush forward, but was slowed by the wisdom of Homer Partin and Henry Tanner. Breaking up into two groups, one headed west to the old Chuluota Road and the other headed south towards Lake Pickett and the Harrell place. Both roads were well traveled and it was their hope that the shooter would use one of the roads to escape if discovered. The group that Will was a part of came out of the high palmettos to see a flaming torch being held by a young boy as two other men skinned the dead beef that lay on the ground. The boy was the first to see the riders approaching. He dropped the torch and reached for a rifle leaning against a tree. He wheeled as he lifted the rifle to his shoulder and pointed at the closest man but before he could fire Will heard the explosion of the shotgun Uncle Homer carried. The impact of the shot drove the boy back as he rolled across the ground.

Before them lay a boy that had to die for no reason. The look on the faces of the other two men was astonishment and disbelief. Before they could retreat to their horses, Will and the others had surrounded them and quickly subdued them. By the time Uncle Homer had gotten to the men they were tied and they cursing because their wrists were tied too tight.

One of the men in Will's group walked to the closest man and grabbed him by the collar. While shaking him, the man asked, "Who was he? Who did the boy belong to?" Between the cursing and complaints about the tightness of the ropes, one of the rustlers shouted, "He's my son. What's it to you?"

No one could believe that a father would be so hard and heartless. The thief was worried more about his own pain than his dead son. His actions enraged Uncle Homer and he drew his fist back and hit the man with such force he rolled across the ground. Uncle Homer leaped towards him and lifted him again only to send him tumbling again. No one noticed Grandpa Henry and Thomas Cox ride up and dismount, grabbing Uncle Homer and shouting, "What's goin' on here?" Will explained what had happened and knowing there was no established law around they would have to deal with the violators.

After they hung the men and because of Uncle Homer's faithfulness to what he believed, they stopped, prayed over the boy and buried the three thieves on the spot. The deeds done by the men were grave. Uncle Homer walked to his two sons and placed his hand on their shoulder. This action spoke volumes to everyone that was there. It was agreed that what happened there on the scrub would stay on the scrub.

Late the next morning Will reined his horse in front of the barn at his home. Soberly he went about his morning chores still stunned by the callused actions of evil men and the vision of the lifeless body of a young boy who had lived and died obeying the instruction of his pa.

After caring for his horse, he laid down on the fresh hay in the barn and fell fast asleep. He slept the entire day and night without dreaming anything.

The next morning he was wakened by the sound of a wagon stopping in front of the door of the barn. He reached for his rifle and eased toward the door so he could get a look at who had come to his home that early without being seen. To his surprise, the first person he saw was Sarah.

Others were milling around the clearing when he finally emerged from the barn still wearing the same clothes as the day before. Sarah saw him coming from the barn, raced toward him, and threw her arms around him. She said, "I am so sorry." Will was confused by her words and gently pushed her away and looked at Aunt Kittie and Uncle Homer. Aunt Kittie told Will that she was concerned for him and asked if the family could visit and maybe fish in his creek. It would be fun to have a fish fry she said. Will told them of a deep hole to the south. He told them he would saddle his horse and they could go and see if the fish were biting.

Sarah turned to her father and asked if she could ride a horse with Will. She was told she should have asked earlier because he didn't have a horse in his pocket. Will interrupted and said she could ride his old horse because he wanted to ride the young filly and see how she would do out on the scrub. Her father agreed. Sarah ran from the wagon to the front porch and disappeared into the house. Will looked at everyone confused and turned to catch the horse when he heard the familiar sound of the front door opening. He turned to see Sarah standing on the front porch wearing an altered pair of her brother's britches that revealed that Miss Sarah was truly a woman.

Will liked what he saw and could not wait to get her alone at the creek so he could tell her how pretty she was. She slowly walked to the wagon and placed the rolled up dress into the bottom of the wagon. She walked past Will and entered the barn. Like a puppy not aware of his actions, Will quickly followed. He asked if she needed help saddling her horse and she said "I might need some later" but she had everything under control. After getting the saddle on the back of the large horse, she called for Will to show her how to cinch the saddle. Her father started to say something about the many times she had saddle her own horse when she gave her father the same look her mother did when he had said too much. He turned and left the barn before Will saw the smile on his face.

Will walked up behind her and while reaching around her to show her how it was done he became intoxicated by the smell of lavender in her hair. She turned and Will found himself face to face with what he thought to be the most feared creature on earth. Their eyes met and they looked deep into each other's eyes. He was trapped. Will drew Sarah Partin close to him and kissed her.

Mr. Magrit moved to the front of the rocking chair he was sitting on. Placing his hands on both arms of the chair lifting his self up and stands staring out into the darkness. He walks to the edge of the porch spits a stream of tobacco juice out into the yard, clears his throat. He turns and tells Danny he was through talking for a while. Shuffling to the front door he reminds him that they have a long day tomorrow and they both needed their rest. With that Mr. Magrit disappeared into the darkness in the direction of the old barn.

Chapter 23

The sun breaks through the clouds that formed thunderheads far to the east in a brilliant explosion of orange-gray. Streaks of sunlight burst forth forming windows into the heavens. Fog lay as if suspended by some great power over the spotted grass ponds dotting the scrub. Huge pine trees tower over thickets of gull-berries and huckel-berries. Large palmettos patch's bordering the hammock of large oaks laden with Spanish moss hanging almost to the ground swaying in the gentle morning breeze. This hammock along with others between the Econlockhatchee River and the St. Johns River has been used for almost seventy-five years as the base camps for the late spring cow hunt. Weathered cow pens that had seen better days but are still function stand as testaments to the hard work and cherished lives of the pioneer families. Each corner post hand cut stand as solid as the day they were cut and planted. The lightered boards may sag but their rigid form has saved a many escaping cowboy from the sharp horn of an angry cow. The myrtles have been cut away from in front of the gates. Oil splashed on the old hinges that squeak with age but still perform as the first day installed. Each gate tested by the older cowmen nodding their head in approval as they pass through each part of the pen making note of every stub or obstacle so as not to be embarrassed later in the day. The fire is checked and the branding irons are placed in order so as to not delay their retrieval when needed. Each thinking the day could not start without first their approval.

Two large thunder heads collided and looked as if someone was churning a bucket of milk. The clouds take on the illusion of someone tossing that bucket of milk high in the sky rising faster than the sun. A few of the old men still seated around the fire watch as others emerged sleepily from the canvas tents. They all now patiently waited to fill their near empty stomachs with fresh biscuits cooked in large Dutch oven's, cold leftover sweet potatoes from the night before, corn grits ground at the local grit's mill and white salt bacon cut thick cooking on a sick next to the fire. They talked of the need for rain. It had been several weeks since the last fast moving cold front produced any rain. The ground now dry and just the simplest of task of walking produced whiffs of dust to rise under a man's feet. The heat had come early and was almost stifling. "I gonna sweat just standing and watching you'll work today" spoke one of the men seated next to Henry Tanner. Who cleared his throat as he looked at the man in disbelief and agitation and spoke as if everyone was paying attention to what he had to say. "When the wind blows straight from the east, you most likely would see rain." Turning to the west and pointing he continued. "The wind needs to come from the south west or what my daddy called "Peter's mud-hole. It ain't till then we got any chance of rain this time of the year". Danny looked in the direction Mr. Henry had pointed then back and could see the stained hats atop the gray heads of those gathered nodding in agreement. Most returned to their previous conversation; when off in the distance the lowing of cattle and creaking of whips came into hearing. This caused the men to quicken their pace eating their meal. Standing the scattered in different direction some to relieve themselves of the several cups of hot black coffee consumed since before daylight. Other wanted to ride out and help bring the cattle into the pen. Many believing the task could not be done without their help. The younger cattlemen out of respect yield to their teachers and allow them to shout of the orders.

The final day working the Magrit cows had at long last arrived. The addition of the hearty Brahma bulls had begun to pay off and the size of this year's replacement heifers are impressive. Danny climbs the fence far enough away from the gate so as to not spook the cows and watches as the cowboys easy the large bunch of cows and calves closer to the gate. Twisting and turning looking for the smallest avenue of escape. Danny admires the wide horns, amazed that another cow is not injured by the sea of sharp tips. Finally the first cow reluctantly runs through the open gate thinking she was finally free only to lead the whole bunch franticly pushing into the first of several pens. Each section of the pen has its purpose allowing the men to divide the wild cows into small manageable bunches.

Due to limited resources it was common practice that the surrounding cowmen pitched in and help each other gather and work their cows. When the Texas Tick invaded the flat lands of Florida banding together was the only way to survive. They would never mix their herds but in order for some of the smaller cowmen to continue to exist they would recruit the help of their neighbors. Watching for screwworms called for everyone to watch out for each other as well. Spring gathering was a time when families could get together and this time was enjoyed by all.

One thing Danny quickly grew to enjoy was just sitting and listing to the older men talk. This practice sometimes caused him to lose track of time and forget what he was told to do; which often got him into trouble. When the others began to leave the fire Danny looked around and noticed Mr. Magrit was no longer sitting in his place. He could hear the faint blunt sound of an ax in the direction of the cow pens striking hardened petrified pine wood called "lightered". He now remembers he was given the responsibility of starting the fire for branding. He places his putter plate in the bucket of steaming water next to the back of the old wagon and hurries toward the sound of chopping. Here he discovered Mr. Magrit with an ax in his hand chopping the lightered. Danny quickly climbed over the fence to his side, apologizing and tried to take the ax from his hand. His effort was met by strong resistance. The old man spoke when Danny noticed the usual irritation was not present in his voice. He instructed Danny to go back to camp and saddle his horse. The old man could see the confusion on his face and shared with him he figured it was time he got some experience working around cows. With great effort Mr. Magrit straighten from his task and said with firmness, "listen to what they tell ya, you can learn a lot from those men". Danny smiled a mile wide smile and got sort of lost in his words when the old man barked, "go". The fire inside the pens now burned hot as Mr. Magrit walked up to Danny saddling his horse. Placing his large hand on his shoulder giving him a gentle shake and reminded him again to watch and listen to what the older cowmen had to say.

As the cows entered the large set of pens Will Magrit was the first to recognize there were cows in this bunch that were not his. He was about to say something about it when Emmett Tanner rode up next to the fence where he was and told him he had noticed cows that were not his. He commented that there was no brand or mark on any of them. He also went on by say most of them are four or five hundred pound bulls. The older cowmen gathered and the new found cows were the topic. No one laid claim on them and since they were found on Magrit property they would carry the Magrit brand from this day forward. Emmett Tanner tied his whip to the saddle and undone his rope. Making a large loop he tossed it catching the first of sixteen bulls. As soon as the rope was tight several of the younger men took hold of the tail and in a split second were kicked loose as the bull ran to the end of the rope flipping its self. As quick as it hit the ground he was up again. Evert Yates flung his rope around the back legs causing the bull to hit the ground and two of the younger men were on top tying the legs. Little John pulled his pocket knife and made short work of the manhood of the bull. He cut a crop split mark in both ears. The legs were untied and the stunned animal stood up wondering what had just happened. The plans were to de-nut the sixteen bulls first so they would not be trouble. Once this was accomplished they began to run the other cows through the long shot while the younger men took turns heading the cows and pouring green-gray liquid called cobalt down the throat of the cows. This was to worm the cows.

Danny along with the other boys spent the last few hours catching the young calves by the head and back legs as they tried to escape from the wooden shoots than holding them on the ground for one of the cowmen to administer the green-gray medicine and castrating the young bulls. Just before they were turned loose another man would mark the ear. This is a way of identifying their cattle while on the open range and a good cowman knew the mark of his neighbor.

Mr. Magrit 's mark was crop split in both ears and he stood there in the heat of the day supervised as the man marking his calves did his part and out of respect for his age did as he was told even though this was second nature to him. When there were only about twenty-five more calves he instructed him to crop split the left ear and just crop the right of every other calf. He turned and called Danny telling him this would now be his mark. His smiles was not as enthusiastic as before as he sat in the shade of a large live oak tree trying hard to recover from the physical beating he had received from the larger bull yearlings and vowed privately to himself he would never allow his calves to get so big before taking care of the issue.

Emmett Tanner had been hired by Mr. Magrit to mange his operation and the other calves would bear the Tanner mark as pay for his help. Emmett Tanner and his two oldest boys would return in the fall and drive his calves to his range near Horse Hammock.

It was a little past three in the afternoon, the sun was high in the sky and it was extremely hot. You could actually see the heat waves rise causing the horizon to fade in and out of view. The last of the calves were finally turned lose. The strong aroma of the lightered fire burning to the last embers glowing orange covered gray mixed with the stench of singed hair burnt on the hind quarter of the young calves and the stale stench of blood from cutting and marking hung heavy in the air. The end of a tiring day was now at hand and everyone busied themselves with the chore of gathering the different tools used while working cows. Another day of hard work for the older men had come to an end when the younger riders open the main gate to the one acre holding pen allowing the cows who had been separated from their calves to locate them. Then they drove them back to their respective pastures.

Most present knew that this life style they had lived and enjoyed for generations would soon be gone. The time of open range was coming upon them rapidly. Many would not be able to maintain their large free roaming herds much longer. Already large tracks of land once open range are now being fenced and closed to them forever. For many this would be their last spring roundup.

The ending of this era was good in one since. There was good money to be made for those willing to cut cypress post. Thousands are cut weekly and delivered to the local general stores where they would be picked up in huge ox drawn wagons and converted cattle trucks then delivered to the large cattle ranches to the south. This was the way of the Florida pioneer, instead of giving up and quieting when things turned bad they learned to adapt and profit from it. The Cattleman was industrious and a survivor. Many knew nothing but cattle and cursed the invasion of foreigners into their lives. But realized common sense would help them to surive.

Danny finds some satisfaction in the fact it had been a long time since he had seen Mr. Magrit smile much less mingle with other cowmen. For the past few months Mr. Magrit had not been feeling well. Danny could see the affects of his age slowing him down but today there seemed to be a bounce in his step. Danny could not hear the conversation but every once in a while he could hear the thunderous laughter and a hefty slap on the back.

Today the Magrit and some of the Yates cows were worked. Plans were being made to move next to Cow-pen Branch where the Partin's cows are centralized. Then they would gather at Possum Bluff to the south of Paw Paw Mound on the St Johns River to work the cows belonging to the Cox's. The last cows to be gathered and worked would be the Tanner and Simmons cows on Big Prairie. By this time the Tuckers would join them and drive their cows that had wonder south back north to Flagler County.

Every day would be the same, starting with saddling horses and spend countless hours roaming the open scrub, marsh's and swamps along the St. Johns River and the Econlockhatchee River than driving the gathered cows toward an appointed set of cow pens. One particular bunch of cows would not be driven from their scrub so everyone of them had to be roped and tied to a tree until they could be loaded into a large cattle truck and hauled to the pens. Danny tried one time to rope a rank cow causing him to thrown from his horse. The cow almost caught him but luckily Emmett Tanner was close enough to him and was able to rope the cow just before she caught the scrambling boy. That night Danny had to endure the harassment but assured if that was his only mistake he would be lucky.

Danny loved camping and seeing the places Mr. Magrit and his grandfather had told him about and hope he could experience just a part of what they had as young men. Even though the glory in which they had described these places could not compare with what he actually saw there is a beauty beyond words. From the large live oak hammocks on the Pok-a-taw Flats surrounded by towering pine trees, to the cabbage islands amidst the switch grass prairies on the St. Johns River marsh. All of these areas held a beauty that cannot be described by song, poem or brush.

Danny looked forward to hunting for the illusory phantom that runs like a deer. They can hide in the smallest of palmetto patches, blending into its surroundings, stubborn and mean. Danny watched with fascination the skills of Evert Yates and Emmett Tanner with the long whips and stiff ropes. Every time he saw them use the tools of their trade he thought of the only true memory he had of his mother. The story she would tell of an artist using a brush and paint. When Emmett Tanner roped an obstinate cow or stubborn bull the large black horse he rode easily won the tug-a-war and the bolshie beast submitted to the constant pull.

For generations these pioneer families used the same sets of cow pens which were built ten to fifteen miles apart and served as base camp for as long as needed. There they would work together to doctor all the cows, brand, cut and mark the calves. The spring round up lasted for almost four months and was one of the only times of the year the local families could spend time together. It was common practice of the day to allow the steers to roam and grow feeding on the marsh grasses and scrubs until their owner needed extra money. At that time no matter the time for the year they would be gathered again and driven to where ever the new owners wanted.

Before night fell everyone had taken their turn in washing up in the creek refreshing and reviving the weary body. Awkwardly the young boys would disrobe rushing into the dark fast running water hoping not to be the butt of any joke. Because Danny grew up in Okeechobee and spent hours skinny dipping he had no modest bone in his body to hear Charles Yates tell it.

Several of the cowmen's wives had come to spend the last night in camp. Working together to prepare a feast that would be enjoyed by all. There was an unspoken competition among the women but not one of the hungry men cared because the food could be served on a dry cow patty after a hot day working cows and they would eat it. Danny always enjoyed this part of working cows more than any other.

Before he could eat Danny took care of the horses making sure they had plenty of water and feed; which the horses deserved after a long hot day. A good cow horse was worth much more than just money to its owner. Just like a hammer is important to a carpenter or a brush to the artist a good horse is important to the cowmen. The horse was a companion depended upon. Any man worth his salt took care of his horse before he would seek food and rest for himself.

As the shadows of the passing day began to invade the camp signifying the coming of much needed rest Danny noticed three strangers drive up to camp. By the way they were welcomed specially by Mr. Magrit the older man he was a friend. Danny became curious and wanted to know, the how. Accompanying him was a man who looked to be about thirty or forty years old and a boy his own age. Danny was tired and had initially planned to eat than go straight to bed. The longer he sat the sorer he felt and again secretly cussed the old banana horn cow that knocked him to the ground and stomped him leaving burses over his back. At the time his pride was more hurt than anything but now he felt as if every bone in his body ached and could not wait until he could finally lie down.

By the way these strangers were welcomed Danny inquisitively approached the fire sitting next to where Mr. Magrit was sitting. Soon he forgot his pain while listening attentively to their conversation. The first thing he learned was the older man's name, Rabbit Roberts. He introduced the other two as Crete his nephew and his son Willie.

Supper was announced and Mr. Magrit insisted they stay and eat with them. Henry Tanner assured them that there was plenty and the women would truly be offended if they did not eat. Reluctantly they agreed and everyone ate hungrily the bounty laid out on the wooden tables brought from the Tanner's homestead. There were heaping piles of pork and beef fired crispy brown smothered in thick brown gravy, a steaming kettle of wild rice, swamp cabbage cooked to perfection and what looked to be hundreds of hot biscuits sitting next to home churned butter and cane syrup. Fresh buckets of creek water cooled by the shade of the trees towering over the brown tannic water sit just under the back edge of one of the wagons and two steaming pots of black coffee sent it's aroma throughout the camp.

The fire now shone the only light upon the faces of those gathered around the lightered fire. The embers burned a bright amber color with streaks of blue and green. Every once in a while the wood would pop sending skyward small pieces of orange ash into the air. Danny relished this time of the night sitting next to the fire as he watches the shadows dance ghost like on the limps above his head. But the main reason he enjoyed this time was the story telling that took place. Some of the older men could tell stories so vividly he felt as if he was sitting right there experiencing what they were saying. Between stories Henry Tanner asked Rabbit what ever happened to his brother. A solemn look crossed his face as he said he had not heard from him in almost thirty-five years. Staring into the fire Rabbit for a moment then looked toward Henry Tanner. He said he had done some things he was not proud of wishing he could take back the bad things he had been a part of. Henry a matter of fact-ly assured him there was not one man listening who had not sinned. He continued by saying he did not have to say another word if he did not want. Rabbit then said, "No, I need to get this off my chest". He began to tell what lead up to his leaving.

Chapter 24

"I will never forget the morning I stepped onto the front porch of a small abandoned house down on the creek". The small one room house in the middle of a clearing, just off to one side was a corn crib built out of pecky cypress, faded to a dull gray due to the weather and was located on the central region of the Econlockhactee River.

"Taking a few steps just outside the door, I took a deep breath to calm my nerves". Standing only five feet, ten inches tall with broad shoulders, he placed his hat on his head and the massive muscles of his upper arm stretched the gingham fabric of the short sleeve shirt even tighter than before. His three day old beard cast a dark shadow and made him look a lot older than he actually was. He stares out into the clearing and beyond into the thicket surrounding the house, alert to every movement and for anything out of place. Reaching down he straightened the gun belt setting high on his right hip. Pulling the forty-five-caliber pistol from its holster and spinning the cylinder making sure he had loaded it with the six cartridges necessary for the day's activities. Nervously he feels his pocket making sure he had not forgotten to bring extra ammo. He reached into the saddle wallet he always carried on his saddle for the box of extra ammo as well. The anxiety he felt quickly subsides when his older brother swings open the old screen door. The noise of the door breaks the silence and even though Rabbit knew he was there he was still startled by the sudden movement.

"Gator stands about a foot taller than I did. He is thin but nature had blessed him with unusual strength. He was the spitting image of our father. He too carried a pistol but prefers to use the double-barreled shotgun one of the only items left to him; which belonged to father".

Both of the boys were born in a small settlement called Gridersville (a small settlement close to present day Narcoossee). Their fondest memories were the times spent fishing and trapping along the shores of the three lakes positioned about a half mile to the northeast. These lakes are presently named Lake Hart, Lake Whippoorwill and Lake Mary Jane. Their father taught them to track and hunt bear and hogs throughout the flat woods and swamps surrounding the only home they had ever known until now. He also taught them about the wild cattle freely roaming the scrubs, marshes and swamps inter-laced throughout the area between the St. Johns River to the east and the large prairies to the south along the Kissimmee River valley.

Crete Roberts earned an auspicious reputation among his peers with regard to hunting and gathering the illusive cattle and took pride in passing these skills to his two sons.

"Our parents left their generational home in Alabama in the mid 1800's in search of a new life. It took them over five months traveling by ox cart to finally find the home Gator and I was born. The fortune their grandfather had often spoke about enthusiastically. Father, longed his entire life for the open spaces of a new territory to escape the boredom and servitude he felt spending, living and working a farm belonging to someone else. He often referred to himself as a frontiersman. When he finally found the place of his dreams, he faced the many challenges of hacking out a big enough place to build a house and land to provide food and a safe place for his growing family. As my parents passed the great prairie north of Fort Defiance, they befriended an Indian family by the name of Youngblood. They helped them to learn how to survive the harsh tropical climate and the many mysteries of this strange land. It was than my mother learned what plant was good for the different aliments coming as a result of the different possible harms. Gator remembered as a young boy the Youngblood's visiting and camping next to Lake Hart at Bear Island (present day an Orange County Park). While living at Fort Defiance, Mollie, our older sister, was born. Both Gator and I was born several years later in the newly built home in Gridersville and by the time the both of us were old enough to begin to contribute to the family enterprise. Father had already gathered a sizable herd of scrub cows and hogs bearing his mark. He, along with others in the area, wanted to be left alone to raise their families and seek the fortune forcing them to leave their homes and come here".

Their world was turned upside down when the War Between the States broke out. It was common knowledge, everyone knew that the reason they left Georgia and Alabama was to find a new way of life still committed to the Confederacy. Vowing to support the cause under one condition they did not want to be far from home. Many of those living within the vicinity volunteered for the Cattle Calvary; which had many responsibilities including protecting all the families, whose men have went to war and the Confederacy's interest. Florida had risen to the largest supplier of beef for the hungry troops and the south.

"Father and the other men in his regiment began to gather the scrawny scrub cows left behind by the Spaniards when they first came to Florida in the 1500's. After the cattle were gathered they drove them north to the Orlando area by the West General Harney Trail".

He looked at Henry and asked if he remembered the old trail, he said. "You remember the major travel road from the Kissimmee River Valley to Fort Gatlin and beyond to Fort Reed and Lane". Another trail often used as quick transport of cattle from the St. Johns River prairies was the Hilliard Island Trail from Kissimmee to Fort Christmas. "These trails had to be abandoned when Federal Troops and Federal sympathizers learned of these shipments, forcing the locals who had the advantage to seek Indian trails that were more direct and better concealed. Large holding pens were built around Lake Holden for shipment to the port of Tampa or and shipping points at Mellonville (present day Sanford) on the St. John's River.

The greatest challenge they faced was not the harsh elements nor the federal harassment nor the four-legged varmints like bears, wolves and panthers following the cattle in search of an easy meal, but the two-legged rascals who had deserted from either the Federal or Confederate armies. They found it easy to profit in stealing cattle and selling them to buyers from the north". It seemed to those involved with the Cattle Calvary a lot of their time was spent gathering cattle, driving them, getting them stolen and then having to retake the stolen cattle. They spent much of their free time having unexpected skirmishes with outlaw's who chose the cowardly ambush as their means of fighting.

"Many of the men who rode with my father got tired of this aggravation and started shooting the deserters on sight. Those bastards were ruthless and evil men, they stopped at nothing to deliver their next ill-gotten booty. It did not matter if it was a large or small herd or the loss of life. They'd just sell their plunder for as much gold being paid at that particular time. I just cannot believe that a man would rather kill than go out and get their own damn cows, there were so many just for the taking. I believe they did their evil just because they were mean and hatful men. When they were finally able to catch one of the thieves, the captive would claim he was doing his part in the war when everyone knew their thievery was only motivated by their own welfare. Father was a determined man and very vocal about his opposition to those men's pilfering. Many who knew my father as a man not to be pushed too far or he would take matters into his own hands. Often I would hear call my mother trying privately to get him to back off a little for the children's sake, but the more she pushed the issue the more resolved he become. He told her it was for the children and everyone's children he must deal decisively with the evil men or there would be no peace for anyone. Many who knew my father believed Gator and I inherited our stubbornness and resilience from him and was the only reason we did what we had to do. Father, was a natural leader and motivated men to stand. His passion and his persistence in pursuing the outlaws and right were the only things standing between this band of roughnecks and a livelihood for the locales.

The dirty rotten rascal who appointed himself to lead the bunch of deserters was named Ben Reynolds". At that very moment you could see his expression change as he stared into the bright burning lightered fire. Rabbit Roberts was a gentle and soft spoken man. Those sitting around looked at each other, wondering why he had stopped sharing his story and could not understand why he was sharing in such detail this story. The silence was broken when Henry Tanner spoke up and asked Rabbit if he wanted another cup of coffee. His response was surprise, as if he awakened from a long sleep. He looked as if he had no idea of where he was, than he began again by saying.

After taking a long cautious sip of the coal black liquid he said. "He named his band of roughnecks "The Reynolds Raiders", living and acting the part of some kind of colonel". Ben Reynolds was exceptionally private person and rarely wanted to be seen on any of the raids."The coward wanted his identity secret. I never got to see him but some described him as being short with a stocky frame. Flaming red hair hung down his back sticking out from underneath his homemade straw hat. I don't know anyone who actually saw him" he repeated. "Many were unsure of what he looked like. One thing I do know is he was as good with a knife as he was with the pistol that hung from a shoulder holster".

It was common knowledge that Ben Reynolds hated Crete Roberts with a passion and was convinced that if he could get rid of him a fortune could be made from the opportunity afforded them by this time of war. "They hid like the cowardly bastards they were by setting an ambush along a trail about thirteen miles east of the West General Harney Trail". He looked at Henry then across the fire to Will Magrit and his expression was one looking for acceptance when he said. "You know the one I'm talken of, the one leading from Kissimmee to Orlando. They received word the Munnerlyn's Calvary was trailing a small bunch of cows north along this trail and lie in wait. They say they waited for two days and nights for the herd, almost ready to give up when the first drover came into view". Reynolds was consumed with hatred and could think of nothing more than to deal with his nemesis, the only man standing in his way. Their plan was to stampede the herd in hopes the mayhem would result in the death of several men including Crete Roberts. If it did not work, their objective was to separate him from the others so they could take care of him. "Father was a smart man and could tell what a cow would do even before the cow knew and just before the first cow broke and run, he anticipated the action and was prepared. They tell me he turned west riding along a small myrtle bed. He always rode a sure footed horse and fast, he easily circling the lead cow. Using his whip he was able to stop her before she made it to the thick hard wood swamp. He knew if he didn't their entire work would be scattered over the scrub. Unaware of the riders slipping toward him on the opposite side of the myrtle bed and in the confusion he had become separated from the others and very vulnerable. What we have gathered from a man involved that just before he could crack his whip indicating his whereabouts, he felt the rope strike the side of his head, knocking off his hat. In an instant he was stanched from his horse. The pain he felt as he hit the ground was quickly eclipsed by the upward thrust of his body as the rope tightened around his neck blocking his ability to breath. In one movement he was jerked high into the limbs of a live oak tree and at that same moment he lost consciousness". There was a roar of laughter and cursing could be heard throughout the scrub as Crete's body spun first in one direction then in another, until he twitched for the last time.

Those riding with him searched the rest of the afternoon for their companion but were not able to locate him before the dark. As they gathered the cows everyone was confused as to why the men who had ambushed them had not taken the cattle but continued with their charged responsibility of delivering the badly needed beef. Confident, Crete would find his way home and knew he would understand their having to leave him alone. Several days later the cow hunters were out trying to gather other cows when they happened across Crete's horse, hung up and close to starving. They searched for several days and the only evidence of what had happened was a rope hanging from a tall oak tree and Crete Roberts hat. His disappearance caused stiff anger and his commanding officer vowed to hunt down the dogs that were responsible for Crete's demise and bring them to justice. Secretly so did his two sons and for them, no matter how long it took, they would bring retribution to those responsible.

"It took one month from the day they found my father's hat the first of the fifteen men to be captured and he was being held in a make shift jail while they questioned him about those that took part in such a useless crime. Gator was so consumed by father's death. He left the house and was gone for several days. Even today no one knows where he went or what he done during that time he stayed in the wilderness. Some believe he went in search of his father's grave but I believe it was Gator that killed the man held in jail".

Mysteriously one morning at the change of guards they found the captive dying, calling out one name; which was Reynolds and then he died. Only one person in the entire world knows who killed him and that was the man who actually did it. He lay in a pool of his own blood on the sand floor of the jail. There was no sign of struggle so who ever killed him slipped in killed him and was gone.

Very seldom did the boys leave the home place because of their commitment to their mother until after she died. Their mother was short and round and loved a good joke. She was a practical joker; which was uncommon for a woman of this time. Neither of the boys ever met their mother's parents but she would sit and talk of them for hours and they are sure that her personality was from her father. Her easygoing traits made life enjoyable and her contagious smile made even the toughest of task enjoyable. Living in the wilderness was not an easy life every day was hard work in providing for the basic needs of life. In order to maintain the proper supply of salt they would have to cut palmetto roots, pile them and burn them on a hot fire and allow the dew to fall on it over night and the white crystals would be scraped off boiled and the salt separated. This was hard work for anyone much less young boys. They would also dig out the bottom of their smokehouse where they would cure their hams for the winter. They would haul water and pour it over the dirt, boil it to separate the salt that had fallen to the ground. Rabbit was a lot like his mother and her compassion was well placed in him. "After we buried mother Gator vowed to hunt down the men he blamed for father's and mother's death, because he always believed that mother ultimately died of a broken heart.

We drifted from one settlement to another, asking questions and we never caused anyone to become suspicious. After selling the last of our fathers herd to a man who bought cattle and his name was Summerland. We took the cash from the sale of the cattle and purchased two good horses and the guns that hung on our hips". Rabbit stopped and reached for the small kettle next to the fire and poured a heaping cup of steaming coffee. Setting the cup aside he lean forward and pulled a brown pouch from his back pocket. The young men leaned forward entranced by the story and looking intently at what he was taking from his hip pocket. All of a sudden Little John Nettles spoke up and said, "Hell, Rabbit stop

this foolishness and get on with the story. I's getten tired and need to hit the hay soon." Rabbit smiles and asked where he was when Danny spoke up breaking the silence reminding him about buying the guns. Rabbit wadded a chew of tobacco placing it in his mouth he said.

"Gator cleared his throat and spit on the porch next to me, patting me on my shoulder; which is a demonstration everything is ok". Rabbit took another deep breath to clear his mind and smiled the slightest of smiles remembering this was the way their father would always assure them he was proud of their work. The silence was broken when Gator asked, "How'd you sleep"? Without saying a word Rabbit nodded his head and this acknowledgment was all Gator needed to see he was ready for what was going to happen during that day. "Gator was well aware of how I felt about what we were fixing to do. In a way I truly believe Gator wished neither of us had to travel this path we were convinced was thrust upon us. But as father had always said, "These are the cards you are dealt, play them well."

Rabbit hesitated for a moment allowing Little John to stand and bark "you boys need to get your rest, tomorrows gun'na be long". With that everyone stood said their goodnights and headed for their beds. Before Henry and Will headed to their respected tents they assured Rabbit he would have a chance to continue his story. Rabbit simple responded with a smile and a nod. He took a long gulp of steaming hot coffee and stared into the fire.

Chapter 25

Danny listened to the crickets and the faint oot of a distant owl. Sleep came with little effort and his night was filled with dreams retracing the miles of the day. He vividly relived parts of Rabbit's story seeing every detail. He was startled awake by the rushing of the old cow as she turned toward him knocking him to the ground. From that moment on he could no longer sleep. He turned and noticed Rabbit still sitting alone at the fire a few hours before day light. It was as if he never went to bed. Slipping from his bedroll, fumbling in the darkness he struggles to pull on his boots feeling every muscle in his body aching. He stood in the shadows staring at the figure that seemed so unreal. Mesmerized by the story so far and the fact he was actual standing within just feet of a man who had experienced such things. For some reason he envied him and wanted to hear more. Drawing what courage he could he walked from the shadows and joins and greeted him with a curious smile. They sat in silence staring at the fire.

They talk for a few minutes about nothing in particular when Danny spoke up telling him he was really interested in the story he was telling the night before and would like for him to continue at some time. Without much prompting Rabbit settled in and said.

"A mile northwest of where we had been staying for several weeks, we located a hideout we believed to be used by some of the men involved in the hanging of our father". The night before we were to head for the hideout we considered every possible scenario. "We careful planned and thought of everything that could take place and detailed our individual responsibilities when we finally arrive".

The men they were after operated the largest of three moonshine stills where the Little Econ River met the Econlockhatchee River. The high banks covered with the moss draped live oak trees situated in high blue palmettos along the two rivers offered an excellent and defendable setting for their hide out. The location of the moon-shine stills presented only one way in and one way out and their operation was a well-fortified compound". The night that Gator spent watching the men's activities gave him doubt of the success of this undertaking but he would never reveal this doubt with Rabbit.

"I recall stepping into the dirt yard as if it were yesterday", he saddled his horse without saying another word. Rabbit prepared for the day by not speaking and remained that way until the task was over Knowing if he were to speak or someone was to speak to him he would find a way out of what they had to do. Gator was just the opposite; he became very loquacious and grew agitated by the silence of his brother. "I remember pulling my pistol from its holster again opening the chamber to make sure for the tenth time it was still loaded. I want you to know that I was nervous and what we did never got easy for me. I then loaded 45-repeating rifle then re-placed it in its sheath. Getting on my horse as I brought him under control I spoke for the first and last time. "If we's gonna do this, let's go". We had been in the saddle only an hour when we turned due west using a well defined trail leading to a shallow ford in the creek. As I recall it was the only one for miles".

The information they had received indicated that just across the creek they would find a concealed trail; which could be found by locating a burned out oak tree off the trail. "After finally finding the trail we traveled north until we could see the hammock where the still was located. We were able to identify it by the column of black smoke rising from the hammock. The hammock protruded out from the creek swamp about a quarter mile into the scrub. Those working the still put forth no effort to conceal its whereabouts and their arrogance would soon prove to be their downfall. If I was to call their name most would know who I am talking about but several families in the area struggles making their living by making moonshine. They were very discreet and only cook out a batch when no one was around and they needed a little extra money".

Danny turns and watched as the camp come alive with the daily chores of preparing a hearty meal for the cow hunters who would soon be breaking this camp for the next one. Early pioneers helped each other gather their cows from far and near to a particular set of cow pens. Each family leader had their assigned responsibility. The day began early for the ladies that would abandon their meager homestead for life on the open scrub for up to eight weeks at a time. They would pack essentials into ox drawn wagons along with their many children and follow their men-folk preparing meals and assisting in the gathering of cows when needed. I remember one particular woman by the name of Daisy "Nettles" Tanner who could take just a few potatoes and a little meat and prepare a meal fit for royalty but climb on a horse and work in the scrubs, marches and swamps as hard and long as any man. She possessed a gentleness everyone loved and she smiled a contagious smile. She cared for her husband and children with conviction but did not fear getting her fingers nails dirty. One day you would see her wearing a dress and apron and the next a pair of altered britches and atop her favorite pony called "Maude". She could creak a whip as good as any man but never boasted of her skills.

Rabbit and Danny watches as she climbs down from the open wagon and busies herself with preparation of the morning meal. No fanfare, no extra recognition, sometimes no compliments but ever so faithful. Rabbit smiles and slips away to another time and continues his story.

"Those men feared no one, not even the occasional lawman that might happen by. No one dare challenge them for fear of retaliation that would fall on them if they did.

Revenge causes men to abandon common since and it makes men braver then they really are. We tied our horses quite a ways from the still and carefully made our way through the fallen cabbage fans that were extremely dry due to the drought making it next to impossible to be quiet. A woodcock took flight over head sending a shrill alarm that echoed throughout the dense undergrowth and towering oak and bay trees". Other then the woodcock they took into account there were no other birds singing and even the kaddie-dids were silent. It was as if the entire area was dead, other than the sound of the ax occasional chopping into the harden heart of the pine for fuel for the still that produced nothing but trouble. Finally they were able to get close enough to hear the men talking to one another. "I was so nerves when I separated from Gator, I held tight to my pistol as I skirted the clearing to the east when I heard the first blast from the old shotgun followed by a blood curdling scream from those poor bastards on the receiving end of the shot. I ran forward in the direction of the screams when I stopped in my tracks when I heard the second then a third shot, then silence". Rabbit rises from his seat and tosses another piece of lightered on the fire causing the amber embers to rise into the canopy and disappear into the coming dawn. The gentle coo of the morning dove greeted the coming morning as the muffled crock of the rain frog called for the much needed rain. Danny watches with anticipation the old man as he reaches for the coffee pot blackened by the burning pine, pouring another scalding hot cup of coffee. He settles back onto the block of wood, turns to Danny and continues.

"One of the scariest things I have ever heard, up to that point, was a panther screaming in the dark. That did not unsettle me as much as the screams of those dieing men. Stopping at the corner of the shed, I peered from my hiding place and there standing over the lifeless bloody bodies of the two old men we had watched from a distance was my brother still holding a smoking gun". Later the Roberts brother learned that the men lying dead at Gator's feet had severed ties with the Reynolds Raiders many years before but this did not matter to him. They were still a responsible part of the boys' father's death. Rabbit did not say a single word as he turned and headed toward the small set of cow pens holding twenty-five head of poor cows. Each of the cows wore different brands and many were recognized by Rabbit. The squeaking of the hinges broke the silence as Rabbit opened the gate swinging it wide. He walked in staying close to the fence and around the cows driving them out into the scrub. He watched as the cow rushing from their confinement and straight away began eating the tall Johnson grass bordering the clearing. Rabbit knew the cows had to starving because Johnson grass is not a cow's first choice for something to eat. After watching the cows for a few minutes he walked toward the old cracker house that shows signs of neglect when he heard his brother call for him. Still quite irritated, Rabbit ignored him and continued up the steps onto the sagging front porch and looked inside for some evidence they had not made a mistake in taking the lives of these men. Carefully searching the contents of the house and finding none, he steps back to the porch, reaches for an oil-burning lamp atop a wooden barrel next to the front door, lights the lamp and tosses it inside. The flame quickly spread and consumes the entire house erasing any reminder of their presence and a life spent as an outlaw. This will be a warning to any who might chose to follow this ill-fated path. He watches still in unbelief as the smoke swirls high in the sky shielding the early morning sun. In a way he feels his guilt leave him and for the first time in this place he hears the comforting song of the mockingbird. There still remained a sick feeling deep in his gut and wonders if he was too far into this thing to leave. He turns and stares at the deep running water of the creek and tries to convince himself his action to be justified.

"I was brought back to reality when two more blast from the shotgun was followed by a loud explosion. From where I was standing I could feel the percussion as the still blew into a million pieces. The white steam mixed with the black smoke from the lightered fire and blanketed the entire area. As I walked across the clearing I passed by the cooking shed when I stopped dead in my tracks because there I happened to notice several chairs and each one had cow hid stretched across the seat bearing a different brand and one was his father's". Finally the proof he had been searching for. This discovery helped him to absolutely justify the killings he had just taken part of. Further proof came when Gator revealed to Rabbit the reason he was hollering so, extending his hand he dropped their father's pocket watch into his hand and told him he found it in the pocket of one of the men.

That night Rabbit's sleep was tormented by the images of the two men lying in their own blood. Something deep inside of him told him what they had done was wrong but from what he could remember of the stories his mother had told them as children, "an eye for an eye", still the sickening feeling would not subside. His mind turned to the men, who were they? Where did they come from? They were not as bad as he had pictured and not as immortal as they thought. The screams were as real and audible in the darkness of the dusty room where he laid out his bedroll as these memories haunted his dreams. He breathes a simple prayer for forgiveness as sleep came with little effort.

The two sat next to the fire for several hours as Rabbit unfolds his entire lives story. To Danny his story was sad and at time unbelievable filled with adventure Danny had only read about in books while in school. Two weeks to the day Rabbit Roberts had chest pains that he ignored and his nephew found him dead the next morning. At the funeral Crete told Danny it was as if he had found some peace somewhere. He had spoken often of how much he admired the young man who lived with Will Magrit and was glad he was able to know him. Danny was so glad he had taken the time to listen to the old man's story and hopes others would be just as interested and find his life, even though it was controversial and exciting tale.

Chapter 26

It would be several years until electricity would come to the Magrit Hammock. Until then nightly Danny would sit at the large eagle claw table, trim the oil lamp and put pin to paper hoping to capture just a portion of Rabbit Roberts story.

The next several weeks passed slowly and uneventful for the Roberts brother as they lazily hunted and fished along the deep creek. Late one afternoon Rabbit decided to take his young newly broke gelding out on the scrub for the afternoon ride. He crosses the creek with ease. Rabbit is impressed by the stamina of the little gelding. Pressing effortlessly through the tall palmettos until they entered a open broom–sage pond. He stops and takes a deep breath becoming intoxicated by the sweet smell of the scrub. He turned north and rode watchful for anything that seemed out of place allowing him to spot deer feeding way before they caught sight of him. Game was so abundant and Rabbit pulled his rifle from its sheath readying his self for the right shot to provide fresh meat for the table.

Mean while Gator watches several otters playing along the edge of a deep hole next to a high sandy bluff topped with a huge blue palmetto patch on the west bank. The creek swamp was so tranquil a person could get lost in the beauty and the peacefulness. The otters scamper up the bank oblivious to Gator's presence, nipping and biting at each other. Rolling in the dirt and sliding back into the dark water making small ripples. He watched bubbles move along with the swift current trying to anticipate where they might surface. The young otters play openly without a care in the world until the adult of the group spots Gator leaning next to a large bald cypress tree towering high in the sky. She whistles and instantaneously the younger otters darted than disappeared into the dark water. With one last glance at Gator the adult otter vanished under the water without making a single ripple. Gator stands up and strained his eyes hoping to see if any of the otters would find a hiding place among the willows hanging into and along the bank disappointed he was unable to locate them. He reached down and picked up the two fox squirrels he killed for their supper and walked slowly down an old trail through and around the sparsely spotted palmettos occasional having to step over fox grape vines hanging from bay trees competing for the sun shining in small rays through the thick covering of the hard wood trees of the creek swamp.

It will soon be Christmas time when the boys will finally get to visit their sister and her family living near Kissimmee. Both of them begun to relax but still were a little nerves about drawing too much attention to their sister's family. It had been several years since they last spent anytime with her. They had heard she had three children but neither had seen any of the children and was not really sure if the news they had received was true. Her name was Mollie and she married at the age of fifteen to get away from their childhood home. Mollie and their mother were so much alike and could not get along. Rabbit recalls hearing his father often say he feared Mollie would leave or there would be a killing. Well, she met a good man from up north and he was able to find a job that paid well enough to support a family in the lumber mill in Kissimmee. He was able to build a small house on one hundred and sixty acres he received from the Armed Occupation Act after the war. Mollie had taken the place of Gator and Rabbit's mother after her death and the boys look forward to spending a few days with them.

Rabbit was troubled by what they had done and slowly came to grips with what they had to do and finally found justification for their actions when he saw again the watch taken from one of the men accused of killing his father sitting on the table. He was thankful for this feeling because he knew there were still a dozen men that needed dealing with.

Gator took the lead as they approached the small trail leading through the switch-grass pond. Rabbit still had traits of immaturity and could not wait to see his sister, his actions irritated his older brother but he kept quiet to not get into an argument. He was excited about seeing her reaction to the chair they had brought as a gift. Right in the middle of a palmetto scrub stood a small cracker style house with a dog walk between two rooms surrounded by a few scraggly pine trees. The closer they got they could see bed sheets suspended slightly moving in the northern breeze. A sight that floods Rabbit with memories as he pictures his mother and the pain he experienced when he lost her. Several fat red hens scratched intently searching for their meal, darting from one spot to another in the large yard selfishly stealing a bug from one another. They laugh as the winner runs to one side and feast on her prize. A shaggy dog, if you could call it that sounded an alarm causing a heavy set round bottomed women onto the front porch carrying a gun in her hand and closely followed by three head of youngens. She stops at the top step, from under a sun bonnet she strains to make out the identity of the two strangers ridding into the clearing. The closer the riders got she was able to recognized who they were turning she handed the gun to the boy that was well concealed behind her large frame. She straightened her apron, smiling that familiar smile the boys recognized as their mother and found comfort in as they grew up. Gator spoke to Rabbit as they watched her waddle down the steps and across the yard in their direction, "Mollie looks so much like ma", he smiles and swings down from his horse and raced forward giving her a long hug. Rabbit followed suit and stood holding in his hand the chair bearing their father's brand when Mollie asked about he was hiding. She began to cry when she recognized the brand and held it as if were her father that had come back to life. The oldest of her children, which was named after his grandfather and they called him Little Crete. He took the horses and led them to the large set of pens shaded by two very large live oak trees. It didn't take long for the girls to take to their uncles and taking their uncles hands and walked up the steps to the awaiting rocking chairs. They talked of a time when they were all much younger and each spoke fondly of their parents. The youngest of the girls wanted to sit in the chair but Mollie would not allow it because this gift was too precious to her. Rabbit noticed how she stroked it as they talked. Their reunion was broken up when they heard the wagon coming down the lane. The boys stood and readied themselves for the unknown when Mollie told them to relax because it was her husband. Everyone walks to where he stops and climbs down wearing a wide smile as he recognized his two brothers-in-law. Mollie leaves the men to talk as she picks up the chair and takes the two girls in as they begin to prepare their supper. Even though it is still five days until Christmas tonight they will feast on venison, potatoes and fresh collard greens. The boys spoke affectionately of her biscuits so she will prepare a mountain of steaming biscuits that would be dipped in the honey they had robbed from a bee tree down on Shingle Creek during the fall when they visited the Yates.

Dark over took them without anyone really noticing when Mollie sent Dot the oldest of the girls to fetch the men. Willie led them to the open well to wash up and Rabbit whispered to Gator that he could really get use to living this way; which he readily agreed. Everyone ate their fill and the men retired to the front porch to enjoy a chew of tobacco. Gator related to Willie what had happened just a few weeks before and his reason for doing so was if something happened to them he would know and could assure Mollie that they were not bad and she didn't have to be ashamed of them.

The house only had one room for sleeping so Gator and Rabbit will spend the next few nights in the barn; which were a lot better accommodations then what they had been accustom to. It was late the first night they ultimately laid their head down. Sleep came easy for them and Rabbit's dreams were filled with adventures of his childhood.

The rooster announces the breaking of dawn as Rabbit jumps from his bed next to the fire just before his father steps from their room. He smiles at him as he passes while the boy rubs sleep from his eyes. The morning plan was to head to Bear Island because his father had promised to take him there and try to kill one of the tri-colored deer the area was known for. The fog hover's close to the ground as they emerge from the cypress strand situated behind their place onto the large scrub; which formed a jam in the junction of the three creeks; which flowed into Lake Hart. They had not walked far before happening upon their first young buck but it was not the one they were after. The sun was rising fast when the large pine island came into view. Rabbit's heart beat so hard he feared the noise would startle any deer within a mile of where they were. He followed close to his father into a thick myrtle bed. As they emerged there standing in a low area covered with belly deep broom sage was a large ten point buck having large patches of white all over his body. Rabbit had never seen such a beautiful animal and watched in amazement as he fed unaware of their presence right toward them when his father touched his shoulder and with a slight motion indicated he should shot him before he gets away. Rabbit slowly raised the gun and was about to shot when all of a sudden he was awaken by Gator shaking him trying to wake him up. Disappointed and aggravated at Gator in that he was only dreaming and did not really want the dream to end. He tried to ignore Gator's persistence but he would not go away. Gator softly laughed and asked, "Where ya been? Old brother, I been tryen to wake you fer awhile." Rabbit rolls onto his back tucking his hands behind his head and said, "Just dreamen." They joked with each other like they did when they were little boys. Gator liked to pick on Rabbit but the older he gets the easier to give as good as sent. After they got dressed and were rolling their bedrolls Willie opened the squeaky door allowing more the morning sunlight to overwhelm the shadows of the dusty interior. Off to one side they watched a mouse scurry up the wall and disappear behind a large horse collar. Willie said, "Coffee's ready, Mollie's been up fer hour's maken biscuits and fryen bacon. Better get to da house for da youngens eat it all. I's gotta go to Kissimmee and let em know I wouldn't be at work fer a few days." Rabbit straightened up and asked Willie if he could tail along because he needed to go to town and if it were all right he would saddle his horse and ride along. Willie was surprised at Rabbit's request and told him he could wait for him to eat a little breakfast. Willie told him he would saddle the horses while he ate breakfast. Gator looked curiously at Rabbit and asked what was so important that he just had to go to town. Rabbit reminded him that they had not brought gifts for Mollie's children and it would not be right for them to not have anything from their only uncles on Christmas morning.

The trip to town was made in silence, even though Willie tried hard to probe into what they had been doing the past few months. Rabbit did not want to seem as if he was not interested in casual conversation so he would just look away and mumble inaudible words that ultimately caused Willie to quite asking. The first house came into view when

Willie broke his silence and pointed ahead of them saying, "The third builden, this side of the road", Rabbit turned looking him in the eye's as Willie motioned to the left. "It is the store and if they ain't got it, it ain't been vented". Before they separated Rabbit finally broke his silence and told Willie that it is best he don't know what's been going on and asked him to promise him that he would not allow Mollie and the kids hurt. Confused, Willie agreed yet still interested in knowing something about his brothers-in-law but knew best then to keep pushing the issue and watched as Rabbit moved toward town.

Neither Rabbit nor Gator ever learned how to read and write. Schooling was foreign to those that lived so far out in the wilderness and even if there was one close the work to keep food available to the family took precedence. Even though life was hard it was a life that most wanted. The boys figured anyway they would not need these skills living and working in the wilderness. When people use numbers around Rabbit it makes him nervous and his pride does not allow him to admit his inability of reading and writing. When Willie said, "Did you hear what I say? The third house" Rabbit got a little irritated at Willie's doggedness but kept silent and hoped the house would be recognizable without him having to stop and ask.

Relieved, he was able to identify the store. He tied his horse in the front of the building. His eyes quickly surveyed his surrounding looking for anything that is out of place. For this reason Rabbit did not like going somewhere new. One thing he noticed was he drew curious looks from those standing on the porch. He could hear far better then most and was able to make out the conversation they were having, and he was the topic. Rabbit did not like men to judge him without knowing him. This gave him resolve to not back down form anyone who thought themselves better then he. The lead man looked back and forth between him and the men he was speaking to. Rabbit stopped and glared into the eyes and the next time their eyes met causing him to turn his back on Rabbit and change the subject. He seemed amused and you could see a slight smile appear on his face and with confidence he walked by the men tipping his head acknowledging him. Entering the establishment laughter roared from the left side of the large room causing Rabbit to turn in that direction staring into the dimly lit corner of the room. He could hear the clinking of glasses and smell the strong odor of homemade smokes. The smoke hung in the rafters and only moved when someone would open the front door. Behind the bar hung a broken mirror clouded by many years of thick smoke. After a swift scan allowing his eyes to probe deep into the shadows and comfortable he had nothing to be concerned with he turned his attention to the task at hand. He wanted to get the boy a pocketknife and the girl's a brush and a mirror apiece. For Willie he will buy a new bridle for his horse because he noticed he was riding with one that appeared to be falling a part and for Mollie he would get a bolt of cloth for new dresses and shirts for everyone. Placing the items on the counter the storekeeper added everything together and Rabbit pulled a twenty dollar gold piece and threw it on the counter making a distinct sound that drew the attention of the man standing closest to him. Rabbit noticed as he turned and inquisitively watched him almost as if he was sizing him up. The man finally spoke up and asked if he could buy him a drink and feeling confident about his ability to defend himself agreed and stepped toward him. The guy turned out to be a descent man and was just looking to be friendly during the Christmas season. While they were talking a young man entered into the business and everyone there could not help but notice. He was a loud mouth drunk that annoyed Rabbit but the subject of his conversation caught his attention. The man noticed Rabbit staring so he walked toward him and asked if he had a problem with him and why he kept looking at him as he lowered his eye's looking at the gun that hung on Rabbit's hip. Lifting his hand and resting it on the butt of the pistol caused the loud mouth to take a step back in a threatening manner. The loud mouth young man said. "Man, I don't want know trouble with you, I haven a hard time this mornen. I just found out my father was killed by bushwhackers north of here on the big creek. The blood flushed from Rabbit's face when he realized that he had discovered another part of the family of the man responsible for his own father's death. Rabbit had a choice, he could deal with it now and probably not be able to escape or he would bring trouble for Mollie and her family. Rabbit invited him to drink one with him and they began to talk about what had happened. Rabbit sealed their friendship when he told the young Roscoe boy when he revealed that deserter had killed his father during the war. The information was more valuable to Rabbit then killing the son of a man he had never met before but hated.

Willie walked into the store and saw the man Rabbit was talking with and abruptly walked to him staring at the man Rabbit drank with and harshly spoke to Rabbit saying. "It's time to go, now." Roscoe jumped as if he had seen a ghost causing the chair to scoot across the floor and finally falling over. "What? What do you want Willie?" "Nothen from you Roscoe, I just want Rabbit to leave now. It's none of you're business." Willie's actions made Rabbit wonder what was going on but agreed to leave with his brother-in-law with making a scene.

Again they rode without saying a word when Rabbit could take it no longer when he reached over and grabbed the reins of Willie's horse. What was that all about asked Rabbit? Willie told him he wanted to get far enough away from Kissimmee before he talked to him. He looked around and figured they were far enough away to tell his story.

"The man, if he could really be called that. He's a coward, a thief and no good. I think he was born bad and no good." Rabbit knew this to be true but if he told Willie this he would have to explain to him how he knew. "He killed a man several month's ago, but no one will do anything about it because of his father which is a lot meaner lives east of here. He has a few men that cannot be trusted with a rattlesnake and meaner. I have had a run in with him, he trouble and I don't want you to get mixed up with men like that. I know I ani't your pa but I feel responsible for you and Gator." Rabbit assured him that he liked him looking out for them but they could take care of themselves. Willie told him to not mention this to Mollie because she is extremely fearful of what this man could do in the dark. Rabbit let go of the reins and promised him that he would not have to worry.

Chapter 27

After arriving back at Mollie's place Rabbit called Gator to the barn and Willie never thought anything about it because he figured Rabbit was showing Gator the gifts he'd purchased while in Kissimmee. Rabbit shared with Gator every detail of what happened and how odd Willie acted when he first saw the stranger and recounted accounts of the young fellow's meanness. This angered Gator and he wanted to go right then and deal with him but vowed with firmness in his voice that before they left for home the problem would be taken care of. They both decided not to mention anything about this until after the Christmas celebration.

The next morning Rabbit and Gator woke Little Crete and headed to the woods as they had promised the night before. The morning was cooler than usual. The horses were feeling good and excited about being out on the open scrub once again. As always the horse's ears were perked and alert watching the distance for any movement. Rabbit like this quality in a horse because it was as if they had a warning of any impending trouble. It had been their wish to help their nephew kill his first deer. They believed this to be one of the most important rituals in a young boys life and they felt it was the least they could do for him since his father did not have time due to having to feed such a big family.

Daylight broke as they rode around the south end of the big lake. The sky was streaked with red, orange cutting through a line of gray clouds, a good sign of a cold front racing through. Rain would sweep across the lake and disappear before reaching shore and the only result was to disturb the great blue heron. It's majestic wings spread the full expanse lifting the bird as it's harsh cry echoed through the woods. It sailed through the air with effortlessness and landed some distance away resuming the statue like stance. Large bunches of ducks quickly took flight retreating from amidst the pickler weeds and lily pads making a wide circle than again landing close to the shore as the riders pasted and without missing a peat started diving and bathing them selves. The bonnets along the shore flipped and swayed as they yielded to the brisk breeze as it changed direction from the north then back from the southeast.

The excitement was evident as the boy constantly moved in the saddle behind his uncle Gator. They joked about his fidgeting but recognized traits of themselves in his actions that brought a profound since of pride. He kept asking in a low whisper of his Uncle Gator what gun he was going to use to kill the deer because he kept looking at Rabbit's gun and did not think he could shot the big rifle. Finally off in the distance they caught movement of several deer as they ran off with their tails flagging. The only thing they could think that caused them to do this was due to the whipping of the wind or possibly the deer saw them before they seen them. Little Crete apologized because he thought it was his fault because of their relentless joking, they assured him that the deer was not what they were looking for. From that time on they all begin looking for anything; which looked out of place and before long they saw a young spike buck chasing a doe. He was too enthralled in his pursuit to see the boy slid down from behind his uncle and grab the big shot gun that once belonged to his namesake. It was a little too heavy for him so Rabbit handed the reins to his horse to Gator and steadied the gun and whispered in Little Crete's ear when you are ready shot. Finally he pulled the trigger the blast of the gun knocked him to the ground. When his uncle Rabbit told the story he said you should have seen him go, "end winding".

When the smoke cleared and the boy was able to gather his self there lying on the ground was Little Crete's first deer, a small spike buck. Even though it was a small buck he smiled so wide you could barely see his eyes and couldn't stop saying, "thank you, Uncle Rabbit. Thank you, Uncle Gator".

As they returned home Gator shot six ducks and kept saying he hoped Mollie could cook ducks like their mother.

On Christmas Eve Willie took the children out onto the scrub and cut a small cedar tree. While there the children walked behind the wagon tossing litered knots for cooking and heating the drafty house. When they arrived home they decorated the tree with ribbon and flowers found on their trip that bloomed this time of year. The meal was as good as they could remember and the mood was festive. Rabbit enjoyed watching the kids open their gifts and run to him and hug him, saying, "thank you". Mollie and Willie expressed gratitude and plans were being made as to how the gifts would be used. Gator showed Little Crete how to sharpen his knife and he played pulled the peg with the boy for hours. The boys stayed for another week and started getting anxious wanting to get back to the backwoods. Early one morning they said their good-byes, saddled the horses, before they rode off Rabbit turned to Willie and assured him his problems would soon be over, then kicking his horse in the flank quickly disappeared around the large palmetto patch to the east of their cow pens. Confused and unsure of what he meant Willie just smiled and waved behind the boys.

Rabbit returns to Kissimmee for the first time since Willie came into the store and he learned that Willie had a problem Roscoe. There in the same seat and wearing the same filthy clothes he was wearing three weeks before he fund Roscoe. You could literally smell him as soon as you entered the room. Reduced to begging so he could get just a small drink and he had become an irritant to everyone. Rabbit could not believe how fast a man could go down hill when all he does is drink and from that point on he vowed to never touch the stuff again. He lived a long life and never drank another drop.

Roscoe recognized Rabbit and for the first time in several weeks the young man seemed to claim down and the brightness in his eyes returned. He walked over to greet Rabbit as he entered the room. But before he got close to Rabbit he stopped short and his expression of acceptance changed to a blank stare filled with pure hatred when he saw Gator. Everyone in the room saw this change. It was as if he saw a ghost, then he began to shake all over and acted as a caged animal. Before anyone knew what was happening he lunged at Gator, before anyone could say anything or called out a warning Gator drew the pistol that hung on his right side flew from its holster like a flash of lightening and he fired. The echo of the shot hurt Rabbit's ears as he ducked trying to avoid any retaliation or recourse. Before Roscoe's momentum stopped he had buried a large knife into Gator's shoulder, which surprised everyone. Rabbit rushed to his side as he sank to his knees with a loud thud and withdrew the knife that left a huge hole gushing forth-large amounts of blood. The keeper of the store stepped over Roscoe's body ignoring the last few breaths he struggled to take and bent down to see how Gator was doing. The store owner turned to one of the men that was drinking at the bar and sent him to get the justice-of-the-peace and sent another to get Aunt Penny the local mid-wife and only doctor in the area.

The pain that Gator felt was not like any he had ever experienced before. It hurt so bad that he almost passed out and sweat wildly poured from his forehead due to the pain. The justice-of-the-peace arrived before Aunt Penny was able to appear. He got statements from everyone there ignoring the lifeless body of the aggressor. It was determined that Gator's action was justified and no charges would be filed. In reality the justice-of-the-peace bent down and whispered a simple thank you for getting rid of a black eye on their community. Soon after Aunt Penny arrived and ordered gator to be brought out onto the porch because she would not feel comfortable with entering a man's drinking establishment. She finally got the blood stopped and Gator was comfortable enough for Rabbit to return to Mollie's home. Mollie and Rabbit returned with a wagon because she insisted to caring for her brother Gator until his strength returned. It took about three weeks for Gator to totally heal. During that time Rabbit got a job at the same saw mill Willie worked. Rabbit enjoyed the hard work but he looked forward to the freedom he knows by wondering and living off the land.

The morning the boys had planned to leave two men rode up into the front of the house. Gator recognized one of the men as the justice-of-the-peace from Kissimmee and the other was introduced as John Tanner who served as justice-of-the-peace south of Mellonvillie (modern day Sanford). The purpose for their visit was to ask the Roberts to consider becoming some sort of lawmen for the surrounding area in order to maintain order in this now growing part of Florida. Immediately Gator refused their offer and the reason was he did not want to be restricted in his pursuit of the men that had killed his father. But before John Tanner left he said he heard about what happened to their father and if they had any idea about revenging his death there would be no greater opportunity then behind a badge. Rabbit's heart skipped a beat and stared at the old man as he mounted his horse, facing the boys. "Think bout it, is all I have to say. Come to my home on the creek and we'll talk", was all he said. Everyone said their good-byes and the boys rode all the way back to the big creek without saying a word. Both secretly were considering the offer the two appointed lawmen at Kissimmee but either would say a word. On the second night out from Kissimmee they arrived home and after caring for the horses as darkness fell Rabbit finally broke his silence. He told Gator he thought the offer was worth considering and under the protection of the law they could do a lot of good for everyone. Gator's concern was he was not sure if they could complete what they had originally started. With that Rabbit turned over and faced the wall of the small house and fell into a deep sleep.

As the morning light brakes through the open windows and Rabbit could hear the steady drum beat of a rain on the tin roof. The rhythmic beat of the rain on the tin roof was hypnotic and very relaxing. Rabbit knew he could do little while it rained. He dearly despised working in side and did not mind things being in disarray. Convinced that this work belong solely to women but would not say such a thing in the presence of Mollie or any other women. Later in his life he would learn to not take advantage of women-folk thinking they are nothing more then hired labor.

In the distance he could hear the rumble of thunder. Through the open window he watched proof the cool breeze still blew as the moss moved slightly in the oak trees. He listened to the cabbage fans as the struck each other when finally one would give way and fall to the ground. It also blew in and across the front porch causing a few drops of rain to strike against the house forcing Rabbit the shut several of the shutters. He stretches conscience of the fact he would soon have to get up and relieve himself. Ignoring the call of nature he pulls the quilt up to his chin aware that a chill engulfing the room. He hopes this will be the last of the cold weather. He will welcome the warmth of spring knowing it to be his favorite time of the year.

The hunting was always better. The game sought the warming rays of the early and evening sun. In the summer time it was too hot and the winter time sometimes reached temperature too cold for Rabbit to be comfortable but the springtime was just right. He enjoyed watching the cattle eat with relish the flourishing grasses as the pounds just appeared. He enjoyed as well the weeks leading up to the yearly gathering of their cows. Another thing looked forward to was the possibility of revisiting the deep holes on the creek and fish for the large catfish. Again there were too many mosquitoes in the summer and too unpleasant in the winter. He remembers spending all night long fishing and relaxing under the cool nights. He recalls last spring while on one of his fishing trips they happened upon fresh hog rooting. He turned loose his old blaze faced cur dog and found delight in watching as the dog work the ground raising his nose to the air to wind. (Winding is when a dog uses the breeze to sniff for the odor a hog or deer leaves and locates the animal.) Yelping once he headed Yelping once then headed toward the patch of blue looking palmettos. Waiting as the dog worked the area then jumping the hogs that had rooted. (Jumping means finding the hog or deer and the chase is on.) It did not take long before the dog was able to stop and rally three large bars averaging about two hundred pounds apiece.(Rallying is when the hogs are able to bay out more than one hog at a time.) Rabbit was proud of what he considered to be one of the best catch dogs in the country. Turning the dog loose from the rope tied around his neck, he rushed in plowing down every small bush before him. Rabbit looked at Gator and the other men standing there and bragged about the fact there was not a hog this dog could not catch. Surprisingly he started to bay as well. (Baying is when the dog bark working the hog or cow because it had stopped to fight.) Rabbit looked at Gator astounded and said it must be a bad hog if he will not catch. Rabbit eased into the palmetto patch with a long cedar pole he had cut with a long piece of rope secured to the end. His intention was to rope one of the hogs in order to distract it long enough for the dogs a chance to catch it. Gator worked around to the other side of the palmettos to be on the backside of the hogs. Meticulously he worked the pole in and through the thick fans around over the nose and behind the ears.

Once that was accomplished he pulled it tight as the rope slipped and caught around the long cutters. Automatically the little cur dog ceased his chance and caught him by the right ear. The consistent baying was soon replaced by the shrill squeal of the massive hog that now tried it's best to escape its captors. The other two took their opportunity to break and run. Two of the bay dog quickly followed after the others and hastily persuaded the enormous hogs sporting two and a half inch tusks right out of the country. Gator rushed in and grabbed the hog by the back leg struggled to flip him onto his side. Rabbit drops the pole and pushes forward to help Gator. Once he was down he pulled a piece of nylon rope from his back pocket and tied his legs together. By the time they finished securing the first hog the dogs managed to stop the others and start baying again. If anyone had ever hunted wild hogs they know that a bar hogs will not run far from where they were raised. (A bar hog is boar hog that had been castrated.) They fought hard to get away from their pursuer by making large circles but you can usually catch them not far from where you jump them. Even though it had been almost ten minutes since the hogs broke and run the dogs stop the hogs only about two hundred yards from their first catch. Again they repeated the previous actions by entering into the palmetto patch with the long pole catching the second and then the third. By the time they had finished they had three bar hogs bearing the mark of their father. Rabbit rolled the first hog onto his tied feet and grabbed him in the flanks while Gator took hold of both ears and hoisted it and set it on the right shoulder of Rabbit. Situating it to a comfortable position on his shoulder he walked out of the palmetto patch to a clear spot and repeated it until all where were they could get the wagon to transport them back home. Both knew this was too much meat for them to eat before it ruined so they planned a trip east to the Yates homestead and the other families to share with them. Gator especially looked forward to visiting the Partin's because he really liked one of the girls but never acted on this for fear of being rejected.

Rabbit smiled as he remembered and while he was still lazily daydreaming he had not notice Gator was not in his bed. Suddenly he heard unfamiliar footsteps moving across the front porch. The silhouette crossing in front of the window Rabbit did not recognize the man. He felt this intruder might be a threat. He knew instantly that it was not his brother because the trespasser was several inches shorter than his own height. Rabbit never sleeps very far from his pistol. While keeping his eye on the door he reaches out taking it in his hand. Slipping from underneath the quilt he crouched as he moved into the shadows and waits until the unidentified person tries to enter the room. He extended his arm forward while pulling back the hammer. The old pistol makes a loud clanking that caused the intruder to turn toward the noise. He confidently called out and Rabbit recognized it to be John Tanner. Rabbit moves into the open area of the room as he passes where he had slept picking up his britches pulling them on. Relieved, he dropped the hand holding the pistol and greets the old man with the respect due him because of his age and position. They exchanged pleasantries and invited him to sit and enjoy a hot cup of coffee. While they talked and enjoying their second cup of coffee Gator swung open the door causing it to slam did not noticing they had company until he fully entered the room. Throwing a couple of wood ducks on the floor commenting how he wished there was a woman around to do the cooking. The old man stood extending his hand to greet Gator.

Being a man of few words John gets right to the reason for his visit. He began by telling them about what happened just north where the two creeks met. Several weeks ago someone killed two men and blew up a few of the stills in the area. John looked Gator right in his eyes telling him he was not interested in finding the men responsible for the killings. His only concern was he had heard that a man named Reynolds was spreading the word he was looking for anyone who had any part of this foolishness. He was promising to kill all involved and their families. Rabbit's heart skipped a beat. Gator wanted to know what this information had to do with them and why he thought it important enough to come all the way out here. Clearing his throat the old man continued by saying, the man who made the threat owns a small trading post north of Mellonville on the St. Johns River and a place outside of Kissimmee. He continued by telling them he had just been appointed as the new Justice of the Peace. The only other law is a Deputy Sheriff in Kissimmee and he has a lot to worry about there. I want you to know that I am too old to get too involved in this idiocy. But the way I figure, it would be better to strike first.

The two boys looked at each other trying hard to figure out what the old man meant when he dropped a bombshell. Staring them right in the eyes he said. "I know it was you boy's who done the killen up on the creek. Both of the boys looked away a sure sign of guilt. Then Gator turned defiantly toward John. His attitude changed as he started to say something. John broke the silence by saying. "You need not worry I will carry dat fermation to my grave, no one will ever know. But I'z need your hep, we need to get this man fore he comes here and hurts some innocent people."

Rabbit was certain from the beginning the old man knew something about what happened at the creek by the way he acted and by what he said back in Kissimmee. Gator was confused by what the old man wanted but did not have to wait long before he clearly out-lined his plan. "I want you to go and kill him before he comes here. No one will ever know that we ever had this conversation. I will deputize you. It'll be all legal."

Gator turns and walks to the door. Placing his hands on either side of the door jam, he leans forward looking out into the yard wishing this day had never come. Rabbit could tell Gator was thinking hard about what the old man had asked. Rabbit liked the idea of having the law on their side. It was his preference to be protected by the law.

Gator turns and looks straight into John Tanner's eyes and said, "I have great respect for you and believe what you say about not telling anyone but I'll do it my way, no questions asked. I wouldn't be curial or mean but it will be fast and clean." John Tanner stood up, reached out his hand and agreed to Gator's terms. They followed the old man out into the yard and watch in silence as he struggled to lift his weary frame onto the back of his horse. Tipping his hat he disappeared as quickly as he appeared and was gone.

The rest of the day was spent contemplating and planning for the probable things that could happen. Night came as an unwelcome foe and each slept restlessly. Rabbit could hear Gator toss and turn. He talked to himself all night. His words never made sense to Rabbit. He wishes he was back in Gridersville with his father and mother, when life was a lot easier and less complicated.

During breakfast the next morning Gator told his brother he had made up his mind to head for Mellonville. He figured it would be easier to go alone. Gator wanted to honest with his brother telling him the purpose for this trip. He was going to gather information about Reynolds and try to figure out if they could complete the task asked of them. He knew it would be easier if he traveled alone. He continued by suggesting it would be a good idea for one of them to head to the old place. Check things out and see if everything was still in tact. He struggled to smile as he said when this was all over his plans were to return home. He still dreams of raising cattle like his father. Rabbit spoke often of trying to bring back the old orange grove. He readily accepted his proposition, knowing Gator could take care of himself. Rabbit had gotten homesick and looked forward to seeing familiar things again.

After saddling his horse he slowly headed due south toward Wewahoottee. While riding across the large scrub called Pockataw Flats he noticed logging crews dotting the scrub cutting the massive virgin pines. The sound of falling pines was like the drops of rain falling off the oaks onto a tin roof. Rabbit shivered. He could not believe what these men were doing and it angered him. By their carelessness and greed something that he loved was being raped and defiled. He compared his part in killing evil men to the cutting of these pines and believed this act of destruction would have a far longer effect on men. He heard no bird sing. The meadow lark did not call out, the bobwhite could not be heard in its constant call for a friend not even a butterfly flitted from flower to flower or a yellow-fly. The sound of chopping, coughing and cursing could be heard in the once peaceful scrub. Rabbit felt the same in seeing this as he felt on the big creek just a few weeks before.

It had been several months since he last past this way and the landscape had changed so much it sickened him to see such destruction. He circled wide around where they were destroying the trees he feared what makes a man do such damage may rub off on him. He had seen men die and it was not as hurtful to him as seeing his beloved wilderness destroyed. Finally he entered the nature cut through the swamp leading southwest to Bear Island. He found solace as he past through the immense palmetto patches that shown evidence of wild hogs rooting acres of paint-root. The strong smell of boar hog hung heavy in the air as he past a large wallow pond next to a well used trail. Several pine saplings bore the scares of large hogs striking their tusk against them and covered with mud. The countryside was dotted with cypress heads encircled by myrtles so thick the canopy shaded out any growth, only the brown discarded leaves form a soft cover and perfect place for deer to retreat from the heat of the day. Several of the small cypress trees bore the scrap marks of a buck rubbing his horns. The smells, sights and sounds were intoxicating and wash over him refreshing him. It was here he could relax and find real purpose in life. Memories flooded his mind transporting him back to his childhood and the many hours spent hunting here as a boy. His eye became sharper wanting to see the buck before he himself was discovered. If he was presented the opportunity to kill one he would.

As Rabbit passed through the large ferns growing along the low area bordering the creek; which ran from Lake Hart to Lake Mary Jane, he knew he would soon be home. The bay tree bloomed with its dirt white flower that contrasted against the deep green of the leaves. The steady hum of the honeybee as it gathers its bounty drew Rabbit's attention wondering where the bee tree might be then quickly forgotten. Taking hold of the horn of his saddle and securely pushing his boots down into the stirrups balancing his self he drives his spurs gently into the horse's flank. Lunging forward into the shallow tannic water that appears to be running swifter then he remembered. The ripples produced movement in the lily pads, startling a large mouth bass causing it to swirl and swim to deeper waters. Looking down he watches the white sand boiled up from underneath the horse's hooves and quickly washes away removing any evidence of his presence.

As a small boy he watched fascinated by the minnows as they darted, jumped and chased each other along and around lily pads. The crawdad as it darted avoiding capture.

To avoid the thick palmettos and gull-berries laced with briers he eased through the lily pads growing densely along the shoreline. With each step he took, the large-mouth bass struck all around him. His eye was still sharp noticing every movement because he saw the banned water snake move toward the shore avoiding this strange trespasser into his world. Off to his left he watched a she coon fishing the bottom of the shallows teaching her little ones the art of survival. Finally he is able to leave the dark water and enter white sand his horse stumbles then corrects itself. Entering the high scrub covered with scrub oaks and low bushed palmettos with small islands of live oaks. Again he noticed a lot of fresh hog sign and wondered if there were any around that still bore his fathers mark. There were not as many hogs when he was a boy because his father allowed them to shot as many as they could. It provided fresh meat for the family and kept the smokehouse full. Squirrels barked and scurried along the ground in an escape and disappear into the thick undergrowth. He would see them here, than the next time he saw them they would be atop a high pine barking a persistent protest. A fox squirrel ran carrying a large brown mushroom in his mouth to a perch so he could enjoy his prize. Quail moved effortlessly through the thicket and at the last possible moment takes flight with wings of great fury. The sound of quail taking flight is enough to startle even the most seasoned woodsmen. In the distance Rabbit could see the familiar hammock of his childhood and pushed his horse to a faster trot. Before he get closer he saw a column of black smoke rising out of the thick canopy. So many emotions inundated his mind. His first reaction was to race in and run the interlopers away from his home, but he must be cautious. He dismounts from his horse and leads him down a small path to the back of the barn. Securing him to one of the small guava trees filled with bloom his father had planted when he was just a boy. He withdrew his rifle from its sheath slipping into the back of the barn through a still loosened board. He had used countless times as a child. The front doors of the barn stood open giving him a good view of the yard directly in front of the house. Staying in the shadows he adjusted his eyes to the darkness that engulfed its interior. Standing in the shadows he recognized the women standing on the edge of the porch and smiled. He was relieved when he recognized the woman sitting on the front porch as Mollie his sister. Stepping from the shadows of the barn he watched as Mollie acted strangely. She looked as if she was crying and this frightened Rabbit. He steps into the yard and called out to her caused her to jump. She rushed for the front door of the old house when she recognized Rabbit's voice turned and ran to his embrace. She almost knocks him down sobbing. She leans hard on Rabbit crying uncontrollably. He pushed her back shaking her asking with a shout, "what happened? Why are you here? Where's Willie?" She cried hysterically. Rabbit could not comfort her when he caught movement in the corner of his eye, forcibly moving Mollie behind him. With little effort quickly withdrew his pistol pointing it right at the boys head when he recognized Little Crete stepping from the house. The boy never saw the gun aimed at his head. If he did it did not affect him. He simple brushed it aside taking hold of his uncle, holding on as if he did not want to fall. Both were filthy and wore dirty clothes, Mollie had prided herself in the cleanliness. By now Rabbit was really confused and grabbed Mollie by the shoulders shaking her back to reality. He asked again, "What's go'en on? Where's Willie and the girls? Is there something wrong? For God's sake, why are you here?" It took several minutes for her to gather herself when through her sobbing she told him the girls were dead. Collapsing into the rocking chair she dropped her face into her hands. Through tears she told him about a man by the name of Reynolds and how he came to the house. For no reason she knew of burned them out. It was late one night and the only to escape was Little Crete and herself. There was nothing left of the others so she was unable to bury her little girls. She began to cry again as Little Crete patted her only the shoulder trying hard to comfort her. Rabbit felt the blood drain from his legs. He almost fell to the ground. Anger soon replaced that feeling of alarm. His first thought was he wanted his nemesis dead but quickly he realized he had a present responsibility of caring for his sister. Lifting Mollie from her chair he helped Mollie into the house setting her at the table. She sat just staring off into nothingness and never noticed as

Rabbit went to the front yard and shot several squirrels for their supper. After Mollie and the boy ate Rabbit convinced them to lie down. The moment their head hit the pillow they fell into a deep sleep. Rabbit sat up the entire night watching his sister fight her adversary, taking cool water and wiping her sweating brow. They slept until late the next afternoon when Mollie finally woke up and filled in the blanks left by their first telling of this meanness.

Mollie told of how several men swept into the clearing without warning. She does not recall hearing any gunfire but the fire consumed the house in a matter of moments. She begins to sob again as she continues, "later

I learned that Willie was shot in the back as he ran from the barn into the yard to confront the men perpetrated this crime". The first torch burst through the front window right into the girl's bed, they had gotten out of bed and before I could get to them they were burned to death. She stops and sobs and the tears flowed uncontrollably. Rabbit speaks softly to Mollie bringing her back to the story. The only reason Little Crete was not hurt, he was on the back porch taking a leak. A slight smile crossed her face as she looks fondly toward Crete and said proudly that he has been so brave through this whole thing. I managed to jump through the window and away from the flames as she lifted her worn dress turning her leg toward the only light produced by a single candle in the dark house revealing an open festering sore needing immediate care before it got worse. She continued by telling him the only thing she was able to save was the horse they rode here. Rabbit remembers seeing a thin sickly horse tied in the barn he since had taken to lush grass and allowed to eat. Rabbit asked if they told anyone about what had happened and she told him that they hadn't. She told Rabbit the only place she believed they could be safe was the old place so before daylight she and Little Crete slipped away and had been here ever since. Little Crete spoke up and said he was hungry again as he grabbed a hold of his uncle and wept bitterly.

The average person passing by the hammock would not notice it because it is so secluded and remote. If you did not know it was there you would not be looking for it. Mollie and Little Crete had been at the old place for about a week before Rabbit had come. She told him all of the food they had brought with them was almost gone and she had not been feeling well enough to gather enough food. After cleaning Mollie's leg Rabbit and Little Crete gathered some wild mustard and cut a swamp cabbage; which he prepared setting it on the back side of the wood burning stove. He killed a small doe, skinned it and hung it on the back porch. He left instructions with Little Crete about preparing food for his mother. Rabbit told Mollie he decided to head to Wolf Creek and to see if Aunt Penny would come back with him and tend to her wound and right after Rabbit told her what he planned she fell into a deep asleep. Rabbit encouraged Little Crete telling him he believed him capable of caring for his mother and assured him he would be right back. He secured fresh meat to hold them over while he was gone and the best way to fix the meat was to boil it. He made him promise that he would watch it close making sure there was enough water to keep it from burning to the bottom of the pot. He had Little Crete follow him to the garden area beside the barn. Remembering his mother had an aloe plant she used to treat burns when he was a child. Fixing a clear cooling paste for her burn and while applying the first layer she winched in pain but soon relaxed again and fell back asleep.

He saddled his horse and rode hard the rest of the afternoon determined not to stop until finally arriving at Wolf Creek. The moon was full and hung high in the sky as if it knew Rabbit was on a mission of mercy. Illuminated the open scrub, he found it easy going until he reached the first cypress strand concealing a flowing creek he had to cross. It was almost midnight as he plunged into the river and immediately his horse was swimming. He could fell every muscles of the small cracker horse underneath him tighten as he drove forward against the steady flow of the river. It was as if the horse understood the urgency of the trip and was willing to do his part no matter the cost. Finally finding his footing he methodically moves in and around the cypress knees submerged under the blackened water until the small horse makes its last lunge onto dry ground. Standing in waste high ferns Rabbit dismounted and checked for any injury that might have occurred while in the water. He removed from his saddle a few pieces of dried corn cob, sticking his hand out the horse hungrily ate this token of appreciation, followed by a hearty pat on the neck. Rabbit spoke as if the horse understood his words that he need to push him a little more but he would get all the rest he needed soon. Rabbit depended upon the little horse to pick out the easiest route out of the swamp and onto the scrub; which was more open. They rode steady for several hours when the rising sun broke through the darkness and revealed that he had traveled further then he had thought. By mid-morning the next day he rode into the clearing and ignored the pack of dogs as they barked and growled at this intruder into their world. He tied the horse at the front porch and kicked occasionally at the nipping dogs but their protest did not deter Rabbit. Calling out for help aroused the occupants of the house and the first person to emerge was Aunt Penny. Rabbit introduced himself again to her and she spoke harshly telling him she knew who he was but was curious as to why he was here. He explained to her his purpose and asked if she could come with him and help? When she heard his plight he could see her irritated expression was immediately changed to one of compassion and readily agreed. It took her two boys only a half hour to get her packed and loaded. She fixed a polis and gave Rabbit instructions on how to apply it and sent him on his way. One of the boys told Rabbit he was familiar with the area and they would find them in a day or so.

At day light the next morning Rabbit was back in the hammock and had used the first of the polis which seemed to bring some relief to Mollie, but Rabbit was still concerned and impatient pacing until he heard the sound of the old noisy ox drawn wagon. Him and Little Crete met them as they drew up in front of the barn. Without a word Aunt Penny made her way to Mollies side seeing the wound and touching her brow that was extremely hot she turned to Rabbit and told him she believes she has come in time. The next few hours will still be critical. She sent her son, Oscar to the creek to gather deer moss and other plants while Rabbit moved Mollie from the cool room next to the hearth in the cooking area and made her as comfortable as possible on the few quilts he found in a trunk belonging to their mother. Aunt Penny dismissed the three hovering males telling them all they could do now is to get in the way. As Rabbit reluctantly left the room Aunt Penny told him she was hungry for a good mess of blue-gills and wondered if they could go and catch a mess for their supper. They halfhearted grab a few cane poles and some worms Rabbit scratched from behind the barn and walked to the white sandy sloped bank of the creek not far from the house and watched the small corn cob bobbers bob on top of the steady flowing water. It did not take long before they had about fifteen bream as big as your hand and they were heading back toward the house when they saw Aunt Penny sitting on the front porch smoking her pipe. Oscar looked at Rabbit and said that was a good sign, if his mom smoked this early in the day. They cleaned the fish and Rabbit and the other enjoyed a good meal of fried fish and grits. For just a moment Rabbit enjoyed a normal life.

After three days Mollie's fever broke and the worry Rabbit had seen in Aunt Penny's eyes had disappeared. The wound on her leg still showed signs of infection, so she sent Oscar out to gather more wild herbs; which would be used to help draw out the infection. Again she had to speak harshly to Rabbit and Little Crete because of their hovering and would not allow them to see her for three more days. She would give them an hourly report but she worked hard to save the infected leg. About a week and a half later Mollie was able to sit up and Aunt Penny allowed her to walk to the porch and sit in the cool of the evening. Everyday saw Mollie gain back her strength and Aunt Penny's family had come to see how she was. Aunt Penny left instruction for Rabbit in caring for the still healing wound and loaded in the wagon to head home. Rabbit had killed a deer and two hogs the day before and used the meat to pay Aunt Penny for her services. Half was accepted and Aunt Penny made Rabbit promise that he would change her dressing daily for another week.

Chapter 28

Gator left at the same time as Rabbit, but he head north. His first stop was at the Tanner's place were he talked to Grandpa John about the actual location of the Reynolds place and his proposition of becoming a lawman. They agreed on the terms of their appointment and Gator was sworn in on the spot. It was also agreed that Rabbit would be sworn in as soon as Grandpa John could catch up with him. After receiving what information he had, Gator rode away from the clearing. As he rode, his mind was trying to put the pieces together and come up with a plan. He had ridden all afternoon and entered into a cabbage strand that bordered the St. Johns River. He was amazed by the size and height of the cabbage trees. Stopping for a cool drink of water, he lay down and rested in the cool breeze and watched as they sway back and forth. In the distance he could hear a red tailed hawk, better known to crackers as "chicken hawks" scream its presence. He remembered his father telling him the reason for the cry was to scare its small prey from under fallen cabbage fans and nest high in the trees. Squirrels, rats and mice would get nerves and bolt from their hiding only to be seen from a long distance away and quickly swooped up and eaten. He listened as the water gently slapped against the fallen trees that extended out into the current and wished that he had a fishing line to catch the blue gills that hid under and around their branches. He determined that next time he was to a place he could purchase some they would be put in his wallet for such a time as this in the future. He wondered if they had already gotten too far into this venture to withdraw but something deep inside of him demanded he stay the course and avenge their father's death.

When night fell he had built a small fire from the few littered knots he had gathered on his trip. When slept finally came he slept with one eye open aware he was close to Lemon Bluff and the Trading Post owned by Reynolds to relax. After a long night of restlessness he decided to take a walk to see what he could learn. One thing Gator prided himself in was to know the lay of the land and always have a way of escape. As it started to get dark he spotted a single light off in the distance. Sometimes he could see it clearly but next the light seemed to disappear. As he moved toward the light, he cautiously moved among the cabbage trees and around the thick cedars; which allowed him enough cover to get close. It had been several weeks since the last rain and the underbrush and fallen cabbage fans were dry and made a loud noise. Finally he came to a place he could clearly make out a small house not far from the high banks of the semi-swollen St. Johns River. Darkness seemed to fall early here on this part of the river. The hoot of a single owl could be heard in the distance and the mosquitoes deafening buzzing around his ears only hindered his ability to hear anyone or anything approaching. He had learned early in life to ignore the buzzing and in turn could sit for hours without swatting at a single skeeter. He removed from his front pocket the old pocket watch belonging to his father and held it up to the moonlight that shone bright casting streams of dull light throughout the cabbage hammock. It was 11:30 when he noticed the lamplight move toward the outhouse and heard the hinges screech as the figure paused hanging the lamp on a nail just outside the door as an indication the privy was occupied. Here's his chance, Gator eased forward toward the outhouse and snuffed out the lamp not making a noise. This left the man inside in complete darkness. This strategy worked perfect as Gator stood next to the door waiting for whom ever was inside to exit. He could hear the man inside cuss wildly when he realized the light had blown out. As he opened the door, Gator brought the butt of his pistol down hard on his head making a loud cracking sound. With a thud the large framed man hit the ground and Gator quickly gathered his prey. Taking a rope from his back pocket he secured his hands behind him, tying them tight as it was his hope to incur as much pain as possible. Dragging his captive to where his horse was tied but unable to lift him onto the saddle due to his size, Gator secured a rope around his captive's shoulders and using the horse hoisted him up and pulling his horse under him. Laying him across the saddle they started toward the scrub wanting to put as much distance between them and anyone that might discover he had disappeared. The moon was high in the eastern sky and filled even the darkest shadows of the scrub oaks with light. This was good for traveling but it worried Gator because if someone were following after him they would be able to locate him and get a jump on him. Sticking close to the thickest areas he was able to make good time and conceal his route.

The others in the cabin were unaware of the disappearance of their comrade and it was not until after daylight they discovered he had disappeared and started the search. The only sign they were able to find were the drag marks from the outhouse to a large oak tree giving them some indication of what had happened but confused when the drag marks simple disappeared. Gator was able to relax a little when he crossed the creek, entering the openness of the scrub and began the last leg of his journey.

Rabbit stopped by the cabin on his way to try to find Gator only to discover him sitting on the front porch. The first thing Rabbit noticed was a man tied to a post in the front yard.

Gator heard Rabbit coming and stepped to the bottom step to meet his brother in the yard. Before Rabbit could say a word Gator excoriated him, demanding why he had been gone so long and where the hell had been. He shot back, irritation in his tone as he told him about what had happened to Mollie's family. Gator's mood changed and without a word he withdrew his pistol from its holster. Stone cold, he walked to the man tied to the post and without hesitation put a bullet in the back of his head. The man tensed up, jerked, the slummed forward his dead body straining hard against the rope that bound him. Gator turned toward the creek, holding the smoking pistol down by his side walking straight to the edge of the clearing and violently vomiting. Shocked and oblivious to why Gator had suddenly killed his prisoner, Rabbit stood speechless until Gator was able to gather himself and explain who this man was. He went on to say, anger raged inside while you told of the burning of Mollie's house and the girls. He stopped and Rabbit understood the outrage that overtook his brother but still watched unbelievingly as Gator again walked to the lifeless body hanging from the post and kicked it until Rabbit ran and restrained him and shaking him until he stopped.

After several minutes Gator's expression changed as he turned and walked to his horse and returned with a rope he always had tied over the horn. Removing his pocket knife he reached down and cut him loose causing the limp lifeless body to topple forward. He secured the rope around the man's neck and pulled him down to the creek where he stuffed his body into a gator cave but before he left that spot fired his rifle into the murky hole as the body disappeared into the muddy water. Leaving the gator cave Gator rode aimlessly out into the flat woods well into the night. Returning before daylight the next morning Gator found his brother sitting by a fire in front of the barn lost in his thoughts and unconscious of anyone's presence.

Exhausted Rabbit fell into his bed and for the first time since his father's death he slept an entire night without being haunted by dreams.

The next morning the silence of their refuge was broken by the sound of horses rumbling forward and the firing of guns. Stunned Rabbit jumped up and instinctively grabbed his guns and without considering the consequences he rushed onto the porch.

Gator had been up for a while and was inside the barn when he was startled by this intrusion and grabbing his shotgun he steps out the door of the barn. Before he could get his first shot off Gator felt a burning pain in his shoulder. The man on the lead horse had fired his pistol point blank before identifying himself, striking Gator. As he fell forward he able to get one shot off that struck the lead rider in the leg and tearing a massive hole in the side of his horse. The horse toppled forward landing next to its rider. Surprised by what had just happened the three remaining men focused on Gator who lay still on the ground but did not fire a shot.

None of them noticed Rabbit as he came from the house. He emptied his repeating rifle into those sitting atop their horses striking one in the head; causing it to explode, disappearing from his shoulders. His headless body fell forward and to the ground as if slow motion making a dull sound as he hit the ground, his horse ran off in the direction he came. He hit another in the stomach causing a shrill scream followed by a deep gurgling sound escaping the gabbing hole. Dropping his rifle and with the speed of lightening his hand withdrew the large pistol and in one fluid action emptied the handgun killing the remaining men. The man that Gator shot in the leg managed to drag himself toward the cover of the palmettos bordering the clearing. As Rabbit walked forward he mechanically reloads his pistol stepping just in front of the retreating injured man and spoke harshly, asking "Who are you?" With defiance still in his voice he answered, "McDonald". Rabbit lent down and looked right into his eyes and asked why he would come here and do such a thing. With great effort and in much pain the man begged to be put out of his misery when Rabbit assured him he would feel no pain soon but he had to have some answers. Through labored breath the man explained, he had followed sign of a horse that had been involved in a kidnapping near Fort Reed. He went on to say someone had taken his brother and figured it was the men here. Life was swiftly passing causing Rabbit bent down closer to hear the man's softening voice than he looked into the eyes of the man that was in great pain and asked, "Do you know a man by the name Reynolds?" All Rabbit could make out was Reynolds was his brother-in-law as life slipped from him as he took his last breath. When it was all over Rabbit dropped to his knees and stared into nothingness.

He was brought back to reality when he heard his brother call out to him. As he stood up Rabbit dropped his gun to the ground and walked in a meaningless way toward the last place he remembers seeing his brother lying to the ground. Across the yard he saw that Gator had managed to drag himself and was leaning against the open barn door. All he could see was the red stain that covered the front of his shirt, his heart skipped a beat. He ran across the yard and knelt down ripping open and removing his blood soaked shirt, luckily the bullet passed clean through his upper torso and did not strike any vital organ. Remembering what Aunt Penny had taught him about stopping blood he rushed into the barn and returned with a handful of spider-webs. Wadding the web he placed it on the wound as Gator commented on how this wound did not hurt as much as when he was stuck with the knife. The pain he felt was from where the bullet grazed one of the shoulder bones and would be a pain he would have to live with the rest of his life. While Gator rested on the front porch Rabbit began to bury the four men who had entered their tarnished but peaceful domain. Their intent was to kill anyone they found without even first making sure the kidnappers of their friend was actually there. Gator was awakened by the sound of the ox cart as it somberly entered the clearing. Pushing himself up on his left hand he watched as Rabbit busied himself with loading what supplies and possessions they had accumulated by living here on the big creek. Tying the two horses behind the cart nervously bucking in protest but calmed down when Rabbit raised his voice commanding them to settle down. Constructing a crude bed for Gator to lie under where he would stand to drive the cart. Rabbit awkwardly loading him as gently as possible at first, but haphazard due to his constant complaining and persistent reminder of the fact he was injured. Rabbit knew that Gator would not forget the harshness in which he was treated but figured when the time for retaliation would come he would just have to deal with it. It was late that afternoon when they finally were able to leave. The wind was blowing from the southwest which was a sure indication of rain; which would help to cover their movement, not allowing anyone the ability to follow them to the old home place but bad for Gator because if he got the chills while weak it could prove fatal. It was a chance he had to take and continued to press forward.

Rabbit did not want what happened at Mollie's house happen to their childhood home so Rabbit took a more indirect route through the scrub to the opening that lead to the big lake. Coming to the northern edge of the lake he cautiously turned to the south east following an old Indian trail his father had discovered many years before. It began to rain even harder when he pulled under a sizeable grove rather large cedar trees. Within these trees Rabbit was able to drape a piece of heavy canvas over the bed of the wagon shielding Gator from the torrential down pour.

The rain caused the small creek the same one Rabbit just a few days before wadded across to swell beyond passage. The white foam atop the rapid flowing water passed him on the surface of the creek toward the west disappearing out of sight into the lily pads bordering the edge of the lake. Turning east they skirted the edge of the smaller of the two lakes. The going was hard and thick with dwarf cypress trees surrounded by switch grass and saw grass. Only a narrow passage his father had discovered many years snaked its way and the oxen never shown sign of struggle and bore their burden patiently. Having to detour due to the flooding took them a day more but Rabbit believed it safer keeping the location of the homestead secret. He knew he had to get Gator out of the cool rain, his weakened state scared Rabbit so he did not stop until he was able to get him home.

Mollie heard the rattling of the old cart over the sound the rain made hitting the wooden shingles and as it rounded the final bend in the trail. Afraid that someone had discovered their hiding place she ordered Little Crete to hide in the woods and not return until she called him. Reluctantly he followed her instruction and just before disappearing into the thicket he turned to see his mother grab the gun his Uncle Rabbit left and slip into the barn. This was the first time in his life he disobeyed his mother and remained just in the edge of the clearing well out of site and stared in the direction of the coming noise. Immediately he recognized his uncle and came running to greet him and yelled for his mother to leave her hiding place. Rabbit smiled as she exited the barn carrying the big gun and walked over the Crete grabbing him by the ear chastising him for his disobedience. The boy was more embarrassed then hurt but Rabbit could tell both were relieved. Rabbit did not stop the ox until he had maneuvered the animal to the front of the house. The whole time Mollie was franticly asking the whereabouts of Gator and why he was not with him. Dropping the gun in the mud she pulled back the canvas she saw Gator lying in the bottom of the cart and the blood stained dressing across his shoulder. Both lifted him from the cart and managed to get him inside next to the fireplace.

Chapter 29

Gator slept for the next few days as Mollie tended to his wound using what she had learned during her own injuries keeping it free of infection. Rabbit headed to the woods knowing that he could find some meaning to what had happened back on the creek. He hunted providing fresh meat for them to eat. Rabbit spoke to Mollie about the need to go to town and get the needed supplies. He would not go to Kissimmee or Campbell Station because he was still fearful that the men responsible for killing Willie and the girls and may discover their location and try to finish what they had started. In a way he wished they would come while he and Gator was there so this whole business would be over. In his wildest dreams he never thought things would happen as fast as they were happening. But he knew he was quickly becoming weary of killing.

The plan was to head for the Wewahoottee trail leading east and when he came to Jim's Creek he would turn due south. He rode lazily throughout the day enjoying watching the game but still aware of the reason for the trip. Just as the sun was setting the second day Rabbit emerged from Jim's Creek swamp entering a large pine flat covered with the yellowish green palmettos and gull berries when he saw a massive herd of cattle. On three sides he could clearly see the glow of small fires. He thought to himself that it would be nice to have a hot cup of coffee and someone to talk with. The camp belonged to the Yates. They live near the St. Johns River marsh on Tosohatchee Creek most of the year, the rest of the year they lived on the east coast. Rabbit was glad this was friendly camp and they welcomed him.

As they sat around the fire he learned they were trailing this bunch of cows to the west coast. Curiously he enquired whether they needed of another hunter. Mr. Yates told him they would be hunting for another week before they would actually be heading out and if he wanted to tag along they could use the extra help. Rabbit spoke privately with Mr. Yates sharing with him the reason he was traveling to Deer Park and needed about a week but if the offer still stands he would catch up with them in the Kissimmee Valley.

He saddled his horse and left camp about daylight. Many of the hunters were already hunting for the small bunches of cows that were spotted the afternoon before. Rabbit was determined he would not stop until he had delivered the needed supplies. Crossing Cox Creek he entered the wide expanse of open pasture dotted by cypress heads, off in the distance he could see a long cypress strand that seemed to encircle the prairie. As far as the eye could see there were small herds of wild horses and deer filled the horizon. He had never seen so many deer in one place in his entire life. It was evident by the spinning and prancing of his horse that even he felt a freedom in this place not experienced before.

Late that evening as the sun was setting casting its long shadows across the open expanse of the prairie he watched as a she bear along with her two cubs amble from one cabbage hammock to another. She saw the rider and stood on her back legs, in a threatening stance then dropping down on all fours she disappeared into the light haze as it rolled in covering their retreat. He tugged at the canteen that around the horn, gave it a hearty shake seeing how much he had left then turned it up taking a long satisfying drink. In the open he continued to ride north hoping to make up lost time spent watching the she bear. Satisfied he had traveled far enough away from where he had seen the bear he stopped and made camp for the night. One thing he had not realized until he stopped was how tired he was. Sleep came easy and Rabbit liked the feeling he had by knowing he was free for a while from chore he and Gator had taken on that now defined their life.

The next morning making sure the fire was all the way out and walking into the middle of the small cypress head he filled his water bottle from the small spring bobbling out of the middle. He reached the store at Deer Park around nine o'clock that morning, using the last of his gold coins he purchased the supplies needed and secured a little extra for the two month trip west driving cattle. He did not take the time to stop and enjoy the scenery but hurried home. One thing worried him, if he left how, could he be sure his family would be safe.

Rabbit shared his plans with Gator and Mollie and assured them he would be back within six weeks. Saying his good-byes, making sure he had all he needed he turned south toward Narcoossee. He figured they had long enough to south of Kissimmee and this would be the first place he would look. Finding the herd on the south end of the big lake he rode into camp and was recognized by Mr. Yates and greeted with a handshake. As he dismounted he noticed several hunters he had not seen the first time he spent the night at their camp east of here. One particular man took interest in the gun hanging at Rabbit's side and did not fear his special attention irritated Rabbit. His continual watching made Rabbit very uncomfortable but knew Mr. Yates would not tolerate any mischief in his camp. Taking a seat to where he could keep the stranger in full view, he watched him over the top of his drink. The uneasiness stayed with him until he had finally gotten his belly full of the aggravation, stood slowly as to not seem threatening and walked over to confront the man. The stranger abruptly stood and then smiled at Rabbit. He extended his hand in a friendly gesture and asked Rabbit if he recognized him and because Rabbit was annoyed he responded with a sharp "no". Rabbit's demeanor abruptly changed and became non-combative when he reminded him they had met several days before Christmas at the store in Kissimmee. He said, "Don't you remember I bought you a drink?" Rabbit softened because he did recall how friendly the stranger had been but could not recall ever hearing his name. They spoke for several moments when the man introduced himself as Mat Reynolds. Instantaneously Rabbit took on a step back, taking on a defensive stance because the man who had killed his father was a man named Reynolds. Rabbit enquired as to where he had come from and the man assured him he was not from these parts. He continued by telling him he had heard of several men was looking for a man by the name of Reynolds and by what he had heard he was definitely glad there were no connection. He went on to say the men sounded like they piss and vinegar flowing through their veins. Assuring him he was not a part of the punch from north of Mellonsville. Shifting in his seat he reached into his wallet and produced a newspaper clipping from "The Kissimmee Valley". The article tells about how an unknown group of men were hunting the Reynolds Raider for an unprovoked murder of one of the area cattlemen at the end of the War Between the States. Rabbit dropped his head because this meant more people may be suspicious of him and his brother. This caused a wave of fear and apprehension to strike Rabbit. He knew this news had to share Gator to protect his family. It was real strange to Rabbit if this stranger was not connected to this whole thing, then how, does he know so much about those outlaws living north of here. The relaxed feeling Rabbit had when he first entered camp was now replaced by apprehension and distrust. Mr. Yates could see this agitation and pulled the two men aside and explained to them he had no need for trouble and if they could not get along they would have to find work somewhere else. Rabbit gave Mr. Yates his word and his intention was to fulfill his agreement and work hard to prove his self. Rabbit then took his place in the drive.

A hard day's work was familiar to Rabbit and with his likable personality it did not take long for him to be promoted to a lead on the south side of the herd.

Two weeks into his new adventure on one of the many scrubs they would have to traverse they began to hear and see sign of wolves. The cattle sensed the presence of the wolves and everyone was concerned whether or not they would stampede. Sure enough late one night, one of the watchmen raced into camp spraying dust over and atop the sleeping men, arousing them and within minutes every man was in the saddle including the cook, circling the herd. Just the presence of the hunter calmed the herd but due to the density of the thicket it was decided not to move the herd until good daylight. Rabbit felt waves of relief when the first sign of light began to break in the east. Streaks of orange shot high into the sky and outlined the deep gray storm clouds rising from the horizon. Flights of thousands of cattle egrets dotted the sky, their destination unknown to Rabbit. Hundreds of whooping cranes catching an up draft cries aloud as they rise higher and higher into the air soon disappears from sight. A lone bald eagle whistles atop a high pine tree. Martin's dive and dart up and down hungrily grabbing up the mosquito that swarms as the cows aimlessly pass by. He looks around and the hunters are still in the saddle from the night before as they ate a cold meal of biscuits and guava jelly. Lazily the cattle rambled eating lavishly on the lush grasses that grew so abundantly. Daily he could see most of the cows getting fatter and healthier. There were about six head that looked sick so the were cut out of the herd and several of the hunters drove them to Sick Cow Island near Fort Drum. This island was well known by cattlemen all over the area to have certain elements in the water and plants that helped to heal sick cows. Several years before an old Indian told a man about this island and led him there, from that time forward it was open to all how cared to drive a herd there.

After separating from the sick cows Mr. Yates ordered the men to pick up the pace. He sent Rabbit and Mat Reynolds ahead to pick up several smaller herds he had contracted to purchase the year before. An appointed place was determined to meet up and off they rode ahead. During this time Rabbit learned a lot about Mat Reynolds and figured he was telling the truth about himself but he still could not completely trust him. While at Fort Meade Rabbit was introduced to an eighteen-year-old girl by the name of Sarah Drawdy, instantly he experienced something he had never known. Mat joked about how silly he acted around her and encouraged him to pursue her because they would have to be leaving at daylight. Rabbit did not understand what he meant and grew angry when his suggestion was explained to him. Just before Rabbit mounted and rode off he assured her that he would be back and take her back to Gridersville. She smiles at him and gently kisses his cheek. All Rabbit could think about was the pretty young lady he had left behind with a promise.

It took another two weeks to complete the drive to the west coast and as soon as he received his pay he headed back to Fort Meade. As he rode up the trail and into the settlement two shaggy looking men caught his eye. Their pistols hung loosely on their hip and he recognized the guns as being Confederate issue. He kept his eye on them as he rode past where the two men stood. The hair stood up on the back of his neck and he had a real uneasy feeling. Stopping in front of a small white washed house Rabbit swings open the gate from still sitting in the saddle and enters into the front yard when he heard one of the men called out to him. Doing this he lost sight of the men for just a second when he heard a voice that is horse and scruff demanding him to turn around and look at him. He could feel his blood begin to cool as he causally turned not wanting to make a move that could be taken the wrong way and faced the stranger. Rabbit could not speak; even if he could he would not provoke this adversary at Sarah's home. The other man now stands in the gate blocking his escape. Rabbit finally broke his silence as he steps down from the porch and tells the men he does not want any trouble. The man standing in the gate asked stupidly, "what do you mean trouble?" Rabbit responded sharply telling the man standing in the gate it was himself that had followed him and was provoking this situation. We just want to talk was his answer as his eyes dropped to the Dragoon hanging at Rabbit's side. The empty look of the aggressor now shows sign of concern and his attitude changed becoming almost apologetic and began to back out the gate. His actions confused Rabbit who was unaware of the three men now standing behind him having repeater rifles leveled at their head. Just then a man stepped up jamming a pistol into the ribs of the man in the gate. His first words were a rebuke for their behavior followed by a command to drop their guns. It was at this point Rabbit learned that Sarah's father was the captain at the fort and that these men had tormented others long enough. Now they had brought this danger to his very doorstep he would act swiftly and divisively by arresting them and sending them away. As they were being lead away one lunged for an armed guard, managed to wrestle a pistol from him. Turning toward the scuffle Rabbit was surprised by the brazen attempt of the man as he raced toward them holding high the pistol. Feeling threatened Rabbit pulled his pistol like greased lightening and discharges three shots, each finding its mark in the middle of the aggressor's chest. He was dead before he hit the ground with Rabbit standing over the dead in the street, a man Rabbit had never met, one that did not have to die. At that moment Rabbit realized that trouble seemed to trail hard behind him and he knew Sarah would never be safe around him. He just turned, unties his horse, climbs atop ignoring the cries of Sarah for him to come back and rides off. Not far from Fort Meade he gets down from his horse and angrily kicks at the dirt then falls to his knees and cries bitterly. Something happened that day to Rabbit, something he could not explain but his heart seemed to have died that day outside of Fort Meade.

Rabbit carelessly ambled into the clearing, Gator stood up and watched confused as he unconsciously dismounted, removed his saddle, tossing it next to the barn. Gator knew something had happened to his brother but Rabbit refused to talk to him. The next few weeks the only time anyone would see Rabbit was as he came from the woods to sleep at night.

It was the first of the week and the signs of spring had begun to reveal themselves when a stranger rode up in the front yard and spoke to Gator. After a few moments of small talk he asked if Rabbit Roberts lived around here. Surprised Gator did not give much information as he questioned the stranger. It was at that point he introduced himself as Mat Reynolds. At once Gator's reaction was that of Rabbit's that night in camp and Mat assured him that he was no kin to the Reynolds from Mellonville. Uninvited Mat walks up the steps and sat next to Gator. He notices the pistol under his coat, which made Gator uncomfortable. Mat asked again if Rabbit lived here and asked if he had been acting strange lately. Gators expression changed and he looked inquisitively at the man sitting next to him uninvited and awful nosey.

Mat told Gator what had happened at Fort Meade and how he had left a young lady he had promised to marry when he returned from the west coast. Gator began to understand how he had seen Rabbit act as they spoke the rest of the day, watching for Rabbit to return from his daily search for sanctuary in the creek swamp.

Like clock-work Rabbit emerged from the thicket to see Mat and Gator now standing on the edge of the porch staring in his direction. For the first time in weeks Gator saw his brother relax and his hopelessness disappeared when he recognized Mat. Finally he took the time to just sit and they spoke of some of the happenings during his absence from the home place. For the first time in his life Gator did not want to continue hunting the murders of their father. He recalls how he felt when caught doing something wrong as a child and the torment he experienced when he knew he had disappointed his father. This is how he feels now and wishes this whole mess that he so stubbornly drug Rabbit protesting into was over. He told Rabbit he wanted him to return to Fort Meade and see if he could fix his relationship with Sarah Drawdy. Rabbit stood abruptly and with sternness in his voice and said, "No, what we have started must be finished, it seems like death follows us where ever we go. I can't afford to love anyone any more or lose another." With that he rushed into the darkness and disappeared out on to the scrub.

Chapter 30

Springtime passed into the dog days of summer. The heat waves rose in shimmers across the scrub east of the old place. The heat was almost unbearable and very little could be done without getting "bear caught". (Bear caught is a way old-timers use to describe heat stroke.) Not even a songbird would try to sing in this heat for fear it would become over heated and die. It was so dry you could hear what little grass was left crunch and crackle under foot because it was so bridle. The palmetto and cabbage fans shriveled taking on a lighter green color looking kind of dirty due to the drought. Rabbit comments how he noticed the palmetto berries dropping off and how difficult will be later to fatten hog without a good crop of berries. It will be the same with acorns. The hearty oak yields to the dryness its leaves curled and fell to the ground at the slightest of heated breeze. It had become difficult to relax and maintain any activity other then the daily chores.

All the work put into preparing the ground for the garden. The hours Rabbit spent behind that stubborn mule turning over and in the ground the cows had fertilized. The many trips he walked back and forth from the open well and back to the garden was now all for nothing. The young plants in the garden could not be kept alive even with the daily watering.

Day after day the storm clouds would gather to the east and the sound of the rumble of the thunder could be heard off in the distance, but no rain. A steady hot wind blew from the due west colliding with the eastern wind causing it to rain in other areas but it had been weeks since the last drop fell. The deer, hogs, turkey and other small animals once found in abundance scattered across the open scrub and filling the lower swamps are now concentrated around the three lakes not far from their home. With a great deal concern Gator and Rabbit watched as they slowly began to dry up. This created an uncommon problem for Rabbit and Gator because where the game gathered so would the hungry bears, panther and wolves. They now are more aggressive. Nothing was safe from a thirsty and hungry predator. Early one morning Little Crete came, running back to the house britches down around his ankles naked as a jay bird. The door slammed shut announcing his entrance echoing through the house waking up everyone. He looked terrified. Because while he was at the outhouse a panther screamed in a clump of palmettos right next to where he was and it sounded like a women screaming in distress.

Rabbit rushes from his room where he had just managed to fall asleep and all he could do was laugh at Little Crete when he finally realized his was naked. Gator did not find any of this foolishness funny and scolded the boy for his outburst. Mollie simply said the Gator, "a panters a mit bigger and badder then a spider". Gator turns gives Mollie a dirty look then returns to his room. Little Crete still red faced due to the fact everyone had seen him naked but puzzled at his mother's statement and Uncle Gator's response. Rabbi rubbed his head as he passed by him returning to his bed telling him next time he has to crap, take a torch and gun.

The creek they once had to swim now is bone dry. The few fish caught in the deep holes along the creek bed draws buzzards by the hundreds. They feed continually on the rotting fish adding to the stale stench of drought. One day while walking the edge of the lake and picking up the dieing fish as fertilizer for their garden a red fox became very aggressive and ran at Little Crete almost biting him. Luckily Gator was able to shoot him. Gator used this incident to teach Little Crete the signs of rabies and how he should hand a like situation in the future. As they returned to the house he thought to himself his fears became reality if they did not get rain. From that day forward until they got sufficient rain he and Rabbit had another responsibility watching for rabies.

The well that had faithfully supplied cool refreshing water for the household was getting muddy. There was talk of digging it deeper if the rain did not come soon but no one wanted to expend that much energy but knew the day was coming.

The cattle that roamed far from any human presence lost their fear of everything in order to find what little water there was. Little Crete was out riding the edge of Lake Hart when he came racing back to the house begging his Uncle Rabbit to follow him. He wanted to show him something. As they left the scrub following the sandy trail leading out onto the edge of lake, Rabbit was surprised to see several head of cattle way out belly deep in the lake eating the lily pads.

They spoke as if admiring the animals for their drive to survive when all of a sudden the water around the cow furthest away erupted. Both jumped, startled by the sight of several large gator tails splashing about in a furry. The dying bellows of the cow was soon silenced as the cow just disappeared. It took only seconds for the cow to drowned and be ripped to pieces. There were six more cows in the water as they just stared in disbelief at what happened. The only thing Rabbit could figure was they were in shock. Finally one by one they began to make their way back toward the shore when the second was attacked. It was hard for the smaller gator to overpower the six hundred pound cow as she struggled to live longer than the moment. Finally she broke free only stagger a few feet before collapsing from loss of blood. Rabbit was determined not to allow the gators to eat her so he carefully eased close enough to the cow to put a rope around her head and drug her onto the shore. Before leaving her to the buzzards he made a long spilt down her back bone and removed the loin for their supper. Rabbit shivered when he realized they another threat he had not previously thought of and now would be watchful for. Still shaken they hurriedly turned their horses and headed for the safety of the sandy shore. After carrying the fresh meat back to the house to Mollie they continued east toward the creek. They traveled its distance through thick myrtle beds, dried ferns. The briars still green with no leaves. Large thorns would reach out tugging and tearing their pants and some would even manage to stick in and tear skin. The sweat the poured would seep and run over the cuts causing them to burn. What they discovered was Lake Mary Jane's fate was worse than the big lake they had just left. Allowing the horses to drink and cool themselves in the shallows they skirted the edge until the mud forced them to enter the scrub. Something caught Rabbit's eye and he strained to make it out. He turned back to the west and followed a small trail around the edge of the lake until he could hear splashing sounds. Dismounting and tying his horse to a small pine sapling and taking his gun in hand. He pushed through the thick palmettos and just the slightest of effort caused a man to sweat so bad he felt as if he was going to be sick. Just then he stepped out on to the bright white sand shore of the lake he realized what he had saw. Another cow driven by her thirst sank in the muddy bottom of the drying lake and is not sunk down to where her head is just above the surface. Rabbit raises his gun aims and pulls the trigger. Another cow lost but at least this one will not suffer any longer.

Just before they turned to head back to the horses Rabbit heard another shot in the direction of the switch grass marsh. Confused as to why anyone would be out in the marsh. There were no trees for shade and he was sure all the water was dry. Wanting to dismiss the shot due to the heat he heard another and believed it to be a distress call. After getting to the horses he instructed Little Crete to head back to the house and tell his Uncle Gator to come as fast as he can and follow the savannah southeast. Before he disappeared around a palmettos patch Rabbit warned his to stay as far away from the big lake as possible.

Rabbit tried the most direct route but the thick mucky mud made it almost impassable. He back tracked finally making it to the high narrow savannah and noticed the deep cut ruts of a wagon. A few wilted cabbage and palmetto fans lay along the trail as if someone was cutting a trail. Ahead of him he could see a small column of smoke rising from a make shift camp. He could hear a child crying and wondered if the heat was playing tricks on him. Knowing something must be wrong he abandoned common since and rode right up in the camp. Jumping from his horse he wanted to find the source of the crying when all of a sudden a small little girl ran from the bushes almost knocking him to the ground. She held to him so tight as he reached down to pry her loose. He tried to claim her but she was just son frantic. He gave her some water from his canteen when Gator and Little Crete rode up. The little girl would not allow Rabbit to get more than a foot from her before she would cry out. Rabbit carried her as they looked for her parents. Gator called for Rabbit but the closer he walked to the area he called from the more the little girl would fight. It was decided to carry the little girl back to Mollie and they would return and see if they could locate her parents. They just could not believe someone would abandon that little girl way out in the middle of nowhere to just die.

Gator rode ahead and called for Mollie. She ran from the front porch because she heard panic in his voice, only to see Rabbit riding into the front yard carrying a frightened and dirty little girl. The only place that had no dirt was the path of tears where they had rolled down her cheeks. Mollie looked bewildered, yelling, insisting that he explain why he had the little girl and where her parents were. Gator came from the barn leading his best dog that would be used to trail the missing folks. Rabbit told Mollie he had no time to talk but they would be back as soon as they could. Then he would tell her everything. The little girl clung to Mollie as she took her from Rabbit. Mollie walked to the well and drew a bucket of water. Mollie lead the little girl to the front porch where she washed her and while she was drying her off she remembered the small dress she was making for the girls when they were killed. The small dress is the only possession she had to remind her of her daughters. It was a perfect fit. Mollie held her close and questioned the little girl but all she would do was to stare with lifeless eyes which broke Mollie's heart. How did Rabbit and Gator happen to find her? Who was she? Where is her mother? With that thought Mollie pulled the child close to her bosom as a tear rolled down her cheek. The little girl could tell her nothing. She hovered over the girl as she ate the last of the biscuit drenched in wild honey, then she climbed into Mollie's lap and feel asleep. She smiled and stroked the blonde curly head as she sighed and went limp in her arms.

The men rode cautiously approached the wagon unsure of what they would find. Maybe the father and mother had just slipped away for a few minutes and where now back at the wagon missing their child. Like before there was no one to be found. They did find the horse used to pull the cart half eaten and an old double-barreled shotgun. Rabbit looked for extra ammunition but was unable to find any. Grabbing the heavy shotgun he wondered how the small girl was able to pull back the hammer much less shot twice without getting hurt. Breaking the gun open he found there were no spent shells in the gun and the end caked with mud rendering the gun un-shot-able.

Where did the shots come from and how was such a small child able to shot the gun without getting hurt are questions he will ponder for the rest of his life.

He called for Gator who had walked a little further down the savannah in search of some clue as to the whereabouts of the child's parent's. Mystified he pushes his way back through the thick growth of grape vines, briars, palmettos and cabbage trees when he happened to see a set of legs sticking up out of a loop-lolly. (This is Florida quicksand. Murky thick mud produced from what use to be a spring covered with lush green grass .) A wave of horror struck him as he was barely able to call out to Rabbit. Finally he was able to managed to make a scratching call that brought Rabbit at a full run. They both could not believe what they were seeing. Undoubtedly the father had fallen into the sink hole and the mother tried to help free him from the suction created by the deep black muck and in a panic he sucked her down with him. Shaken Rabbit grabbed the women's legs and pulled with all his might and was unable to break her free. Perplexed as to what to do they determined to just free her as best they could and bury them together in the murky grave so any wolf or other scavenger would not eat her. Gator cut a long pole and together they push until the last of her feet disappeared under the surface. Both men had seen men die and had even killed a few of them but neither had witnessed such a thing before. They swore Little Crete to silence and gathered what little earthly possessions remained in the wagon. At this point they decided to head for home.

Soberly they rode back down through the thick vines and vowed to never come here again and promised each other when they saw such a place as this any other time they would avoid it. Rabbit stopped abruptly and stared toward the southwest and watched as a thunderhead built. You could actually see the clouds churning and the flashes of lightening as it shot across the sky. He secretly hoped the rain would soon come a wash away any evidence of this tragedy. He also kept the thoughts to himself regarding the lightening and the threat of wild fires which they did not need at this time or any other. He knew there was no way a fire could be stopped if it ever ignited the dry scrub. Lost in his thoughts as they rode silently back to the house. He recalls to memory the fire; which had swept through when he was a small boy and the destruction it caused. It moved so fast it swept over quail still sitting on the nest and the cows and hogs caught unable to escape the fury.

Eventually they arrived back at the house and were met by Mollie and her inquiries as to what they had found. Little Crete jumped from his horse and wrenched causing Mollie to waddle as fast as she could to his side. When he had finished he began to sob as Mollie grabbed him into her arms looking back at Rabbit and asked. "What in God's name happened?" As she turned her attention back to the boy who was crying uncontrollable. Rabbit only asked one question. "Where's the girl?" Mollie then spoke up and told them they had washed her, feed her and she is now asleep. He acknowledged her as he turned toward the barn to put the horses in the pen and feed them. Gator gets down and hands his and Little Crete's reins to Rabbit and tell Mollie and Sarah to sit down and he will tell them of all they found. With dismay they listened as Mollie held Little Crete tight. She kissed him and repeatedly told him she was sorry he had to witness such a thing as that. Rabbit joined them on the porch. Sarah noticed that he had been crying himself and in the midst of such calamity she realized she loved him even more. It was decided that Mollie would raise the little girl as her own and when she is old enough and could understand she would tell her of the day's events. Rabbit asked if they could call her Sadie if she was unable to tell them her real name. It was several months before Sadie said a word. Mollie seemed to have taken the responsibility good and there seemed to be renewed life and hope back in her actions.

Before dark that very afternoon it started to rain and it rained steadily all night. Rabbit watched the rain fall and with it some of the feeling of hopelessness and helplessness washed away with every drop.

For the first time in weeks they were able to sleep the entire night without having to cool themselves sparingly not wanting to waste this precious commodity. The next morning the wind picked up and the bridle limbs and scorched cabbage fans began to fall still driven by the strong wind blew as projectiles across the clearing. Moss now soaked through and swayed violently by the fierce wind extended parallel to the ground. Places water had never stood now flooded and for the first time in his life he saw water flowing across the trail into the scrub. Small springs of water boiled out of the ground and fish swam across the front yard of the house. Little Crete had somewhat forgotten the events of a few days past and found pleasure in chasing the large catfish passed the front steps. It rained for three days and three nights and only out of necessity would anyone venture beyond the front porch. Life for the next few weeks returned to normal.

There was plenty of time for Gator, Rabbit and Little Crete to make plans for a trip south. They will go to where Rabbit had seen the largest of the three herds of wild horses. With each passing day Little Crete grew more anxious and spent his time questioning his uncles about everything from being sure he was going to be able to get his own horse. His expression changed when he thought of the possibility of the horses being gone, than what would they do. Gator grew impatient with the boy's persistence and would constantly refer him to his Uncle Rabbit.

At long last the appointed morning had arrived. As each gathered their own gear Gator had finally had enough of Little Crete's aggravation and snapped at him for his childishness and excitement. This immediately gendered a harsh retort from Mollie; which at once caused Gator to feel ashamed for not simply overlooking the boy's enthusiasm. Before he mounted his horse he walked to where Little Crete was standing and apologized for his behavior, turning he picked up his rifle and rode away.

Amazingly the area southeast of the old homestead was still scorched from the drought. It appears as if it had not rained like at the old place. They found a small herd of horses without much difficulty. Even a blind man could see them by the dust cloud produced as they moved. The once fat sleek horses clip off what little grass remained but still look as if they are just bags of bones. Once it was determined they bore no man's mark it took little effort to get the horses moving because the farther north they traveled the more grass they found. It took all of four days to make it back within sight of the marsh with the savannah. Instead of skirting the edge as usual they turned due north keeping to the open scrub. Neither Gator nor Rabbit actually wanted to be away from home any longer than necessary but both knew they would lose several horses if they were pushed too hard. The moment the first willow pond came into view the horses would not leave until they ate their fill of the verdant grass and almost overnight the horse begin to show visible improvement. Not having to be anywhere anytime soon Gator decided to slow their pace and enjoy the freedom of being under the stars once again.

The next evening as the sun streaked purplish-reddish amber orange across the western sky and for the first time in a long time Rabbit believed life was worth living again. Gator while on one of his walks killed a fat doe and the smell of cooking venison filled the air. The tranquility of the camp was broken all of a sudden when Little Crete stood to his feet and with a very serious face announced he had picked out his horse and his uncles could have pick of any of the others they wanted.

Gator smiled at Rabbit; as they listened to the little man give further details about how he came to his decision. He looked serious and right in the eye of his Uncle Gator and said, "Member da uter day? Dat little blaze faced black hos? Member how she aw-ways tried ta lead, I think she'll make a good hos." With that he sat down and took a big bite of steaming piece of hot venison fresh from the fire. Even though Rabbit could tell it burned him, he never complained. Both men agreed with his choice and they bragged about how he had an eye for horses. He smiled and told of all he had planned for Jim the little horse.

It took them two weeks to complete the pen they would use to break the horses. By this time the horses had gained weight and started to look normal. Their strength came back and each would prove to be a challenge to break. Each person had their own way of breaking horses. Some would break the will of the horse and then being the

process of retraining. Rabbit was not in favor of this technique because he had seen many a good horse ruined. He liked using a round pen to teach the horse who the master was. At first they would get the horse use to being touched; which could take several days. After they could get a halter on they would begin to run them in the pen. For some horses they learned right away, bit for other it would take up to a week.

The little horse Crete had chosen was easy to teach. About two o'clock in the afternoon after Rabbit had worked the little horse for about an hour after lunch he decided to try a saddle. The horse fought a little but quick submitted to the weight of the saddle and never fought again. Rabbit called for Little Crete to join him in the middle of the pen. He showed him what he needed to do next and as if he had done it all his life he worked the horse one way then another. First he called for his submission which the little horse willingly gave. The sun was beginning to set when Rabbit told him it was time to ride him. With apprehension the young boy climbed up on the back of the horse. He only offered to fight once but immediately became docile. Rabbit still in the middle of the pen worked the little horse first one way then the other instructing Crete to make him give his head toward the fence. Both Rabbit and Gator watched amazed as the boy and the horse worked as one unit. Gator climbed on his horse and they rode out into the scrub and the longer the boy rode the horse the more convinced he became Little Crete is more of a horsemen then he would ever be.

The next day it was the same. Gator wanted a new horse one fit for the remaining task before them. Rabbit was satisfied with his horse but feel in love with a small paint mare. The cut all of the studs but one, a slick bay muscular horse that had already shown signs of dominance, a trait Gator liked. After marking and branding the small herd they turned all but the horses they had picked out. They were almost through with the last of the horses when Little Crete call from atop the round pen, there were several riders passing on the trail headed for the house. Rabbit instantly recognized the two lead riders. The first was Mat Reynolds. Turning he asked Gator if he recalled the fellow who come looking for him several months before. To which Gator mumbled under his voice that he never trusted him. The other was Captain Drawdy from Fort Meade. The other men he did not recognize but if they were with Mat they had to be good fellows. Gator was not convinced Mat was as good as Rabbit thought and was leery of any stranger remaining very cautious.

Rabbit had finally returned to his old self and life around the old place seemed to be getting back to normal. Gator still does not know what all happened to him while on the cattle drive but the one thing he did know was that Rabbit had never kept a secret from him before and he did not like the fact he never elaborated on it.

Recognizing Sarah's father Rabbit greeted him with the respect due his position. When he first saw Captain Drawdy he straight away thought of Sarah and looked beyond the men standing before him to the slow ambling wagon hoping for any sign that she had come. Waves of disappointment flooded him because he could not see her. Deep down inside he wished he could go back to that day and comfort Sarah rather than break her heart. Not listening to any of the conversation taking place he wishes she would come to him and they could be together. After everyone was introduced and Gator felt at ease with the strangers they were invited to the front porch. Captain Drawdy told of his leaving his post at Fort Meade and entering private life. He shared his desire to become a cattle owner and was presently interested in finding a place to settle down. He inquired about the land surrounding their home which to Gator was odd. He was very pleased to hear they knew of no one who had claim to it.

No one had noticed the young woman but Mollie as she steps gracefully down from the covered wagon. Mollie instantaneously knew who she was and as she would tell Sarah later, "I have never seen anyone a pretty". It was not until she called Rabbit by name that he was even aware of her presence. He turned and stared in disbelief not knowing what he should do. Throwing caution to the wind he then ran to her, taking her into his massive arms almost crushing her. She did not mind, because his clumsiness and lack of refine is what she fell in love with. His clumsiness did hurt but dismissed it bragged he was good looking and that is all that matters. Rabbit could not take his eyes off of her and felt as if a ton of bricks had been lifted from his chest. He could finally take a deep breath and it not hurt. Mollie was overjoyed for Rabbit. Standing in one place stomping her feet and clapping her hands. She was so excited she pulled Sarah from Rabbit's arms giving her a long hug using her short soft plump arms. Mollie was the only one who knew how Rabbit felt and confided in her about his intention if ever he saw her again. He longed for her to be by his side. It had been since before she had to leave Kissimmee that she was able to talk to another woman. Without considering anyone else Mollie quickly ushered Sarah inside the house leaving the men folk to their talk. Rabbit did not want Sarah out of his sight for fear he would lose her forever but Mollie's persistence finally managed to run him out of the kitchen.

Gator showed Captain Drawdy the clearing next to the barn inviteng them to stay. Everyone in the party but Sarah busied themselves about setting up camp. Captain Drawdy had not done anything but rode through the area and had fallen in love with the land. Asking many questions about the surrounding area and the closest land office to which Gator replied in Kissimmee. Due to Captain Drawdy's service he was entitled to one hundred and sixty acres.

After several days working and riding the area it was decided he would take a trip to Kissimmee and file his claim on the land between the old place and the big lake and if the price was right he may purchase more. He learned the land where they were once belonged to a logging company and was now for sale for taxes. The price was a dollar an acre so Captain Drawdy, purchased six hundred additional acres on the other side of the Roberts land. Upon his return they would begin the task of building a permanent house so as Sarah would not have to sleep in the back of the uncomfortable wagon. Something Mollie would not allow giving her one of the rooms next to her. Assuring Sarah's father that she would take full responsibility for Rabbit's action and if the were at all off color he would sleep in the barn after he had gotten a whipping from her. To which they all laughed but Rabbit because he knew his sister enough to not push it.

He would build a set of cow pens just in case he was able to purchase a few head. They spent weeks cutting down cabbage trees using these to construct a house until the lumber he ordered was delivered. After digging a large hole in the ground the reason being was to help regulate the temperature. As they set the logs on their side, with each log they set the house begun to take shape. Within a week they were able to move from the tents into the house.

Chapter 31

It was clear to all, even though Gator did not approve Mollie and Mat Reynolds had become interested in each other. Everyone knew eventually the two would end up getting married. Gator detested the way in which Mollie acted in front of Mat often chiding her for the way she acted in front of her son. He thought it pushy and told her over and over again she could be no plainer in her intentions. To which she would reply, "I may not have another chance at a father for Crete." To that statement, Gator turning slapping at the air with his hat in hand telling her Little Crete had him, than slam the door and stomp off the porch. Mollie knew Gator meant well but until he himself experienced loneliness he would never understand.

One morning after breakfast Mat invited Mollie to accompany him to Kissimmee. His reason for going was to pick up some supplies and see if he had any mail because he was expecting a letter. Gator protested strongly and forbade her from going. His rationale was quickly explained by reminding everyone of the men who had killed Willie and the girls might recognize her. Follow them back to the hammock. Mat had remained silent for several reasons but felt it is place now and interrupted Gator's angry outburst. He guaranteed everyone especially Gator he would not allow any harm to come to Mollie. To which Gator knowing he would not be listened to turns and walks away mumbling. Mollie smiles as she remembers how their father would act when their mother would disagree with him. He knew it would not pay to argue Mollie.

Mollie acted like a child as she prepared for the trip. After speaking privately to Sarah of her feelings for Mat she hoped it would not be considered too forward of her going on this trip without one of her brothers. Also feeling guilty regarding what she considered betrayal to her dead husband. Sarah persuaded her she did not want to live out in this rough country without having someone to care for her and Little Crete. Gator continued to object and did not care who knew his concerns and tried hard to convince Mollie that he and Rabbit would be enough for her and Little Crete. Sarah listened as long as she could then spoke sharply to Gator informing him that he or Rabbit could not provide everything Mollie needed and he needed to just get out of the way.

Gator had never had anyone speak to him in that way and it irritated him but knew better than to say anything else. He simply left the room, saddled his horse and rode out into the scrub. Mollie smiled and clapped her hands like a little girl even though she could hear him mumble under his breath his opposition. Mollie had Mat wait as long as they could hoping Gator would return before she left because she wanted to assure him everything was going to be alright, but he never came. She did not know he sat just out of sight and followed them as far as the small creek south of the old place and in a way felt satisfied with his sisters choice.

Three days had passed since Mat and Mollie left for Kissimmee when Gator heard the wagon rattling down the old dirt trail and finally entering into the clearing in front of the house. Mollie had a wide smile on her face which was strange to Gator when Sarah rushed past him stopping next to her as she grasps the hand of Mat. Everyone came from all directions when they heard Sarah scream and all they saw as Gator throwing his hat to the ground and stomp away. Rabbit was confused and asked what happened. Sarah ran to him with such excitement almost knocking him over, grabbing him around the neck announcing Mollie had gotten married and tonight there was going to be a celebration.

Sarah began to shout orders and within a few hours a feast was spread on the plank table Sarah had removed from inside and life was peaceful.

Two of the men that worked for her father played the fiddle and after they had eaten their full they danced late into the night.

Gator still did not trust Mat; which Mollie was aware. She tried hard to dispel his deep embedded concerns.

Chapter 32

The hot days of summer slowly receded into the cooler days of fall. This time of year there were a lot new challenges but the time honored practices brought the family together. First they needed to gather the cows and use them to prepare the garden spot for planting the collard and mustard greens that grew well in the cooler weather. While the women set out the tender plants and Little Crete toted water from the open well the conversation center around how good fresh greens will be.

Mollie and Sarah followed the men driving the wagon as they entered the scrub in search of their cattle. It took all of that day and well into the next before they were able to gather twenty-five scrawny cows and their half-grown calves and start back toward the old place. Off in the distance they could hear the sound of cattle lowing and the creaking of whips. Rabbit and Mat separated from the herd and headed in the direction of the lowing. Aware of the threat of rustlers they would not take a straight route but would make a wide circle hoping to come up behind the drivers. Rabbit relaxed when he recognized Mr. Yates as he rode ahead of the vast herd of cattle beginning trailed by up to fifteen men. When Mr. Yates was parallel with them Rabbit rode out in a non-threatening manner when Mr. Yates and three other riders galloped in their direction, gun in hand. They exchanged greetings and Mat commented about the size of the herd they were driving. Mr. Yates told them he was headed to the west coast to sell them for shipping to Havana. Rabbit commented to Mr. Yates this was an odd time of year to trailing cattle and inquired as to why he was doing it now. All he said was, "Times is hard."

Mat asked if he knew of any cows for sell when one of the riders spoke up saying he had about one hundred head for sell back of the St. Johns River marsh and if was interested he would sell them for ten dollars a head. Mat rode up next to the man who had given this information and an agreement was reached for delivery of these cows and the selling of his mark; which was crop spilt in the right ear and crop sharp in the other and the star brand as well. He arranged to stop back by on the way back and if they wanted they would ride together and Mat and the others could trail them back. Mat assured him he would have the thousand dollars ready for him when he returned and they shook hands. Before the Yates party left he reminded Rabbit he would be gathering his cows south of the Kissimmee Valley in the spring and he looked forward to him joining them; which Rabbit guaranteed him he would be there and he would be bring his nephew and they said their goodbyes.

Mat was so proud of his deal he had made with Ben Cox and could not wait until he told Mollie he was now a cattleman. Rabbit spoke of their expanding their land holdings because he planned one day to marry Sarah and raise his family on the old place.

Chapter 33

It had rained almost twelve inches since the rain began to fall and the creeks, bay heads, cypress strands and swamp's are over flowing and the flat woods are began to flood. The cattle have now moved from the marshes of the St. Johns River and the Kissimmee River Valley out into the sandy savannahs bordering the low areas. The Roberts, Drawdys, Bass', Yates, Browns, Hensons and Tanners join together in gathering their cattle from all directions. None of these families but the Yates' had large herds of cattle but the cattle they had were honestly gained. Together they drove them to the big pens built by John Henson on the north east corner of Lake Hart. The high sandy ridge covered with scrub oaks, pines so tall one got dizzy standing at the base looking to its heights. The pine needles covered the ground and as the wind blew through their heights it created a whistling sound that seemed to relax even the hardest of cowman. Everyone looked forward to working cows in this area and the time spent fishing and camping when the work was complete.

It took several days to hunt the allusive scrub cow; which could run as fast as a deer and as long as a long-winded coon hound. Every palmettos patch, cabbage head, cypress head and deep swamp was combed and every cow driven out onto the big prairie until all the hunters could make the final drive to the pens.

To the cattleman the chorus of lowing cattle and the cracking of the long whip were beautiful and meant they could pay their bills and purchase more cattle if desired.

The mood in camp the first night was cheerful as the last of the cattle were counted and the gate was closed and secured. Some men climbed the cypress pole pens and talked with pride as they numbered the cows and calves each easily. Identifying their own cows by the pattern of specks on their backs or whether one has a white face or not or by the shape of the horns. Mr. Yates finally spoke up and all agreed they would start first thing the next morning, than each headed to their respective campsite for a good hot meal, story-telling and finish the night with rest. One of the best mammiers in the territory was a man by the name of Mose Gunn. He was born and raised around a small settlement called Bartow. Everyone liked this half Indian when he got a little shine in his belly. He regaled them with stories of adventure and suspense, no one really knew if any of his tales were true but they sure keep the listeners spell bound. While they sat listening to Ol Mose tell his story; a lone rider raced into camp startling everyone causing dust to roll up and over those sitting around the fire. He was hysterical finding it hard to breath as he told of how several rustlers had shot and killed three of the hunters in his group and had stolen thirty head of cows belonging to the Partin's east of where they now camped. It took only a few minutes to gather seven riders including the Robert's brother and Mat Reynolds. Following the man who had brought the news to the last place he had seen the rustlers they were able to find the three dead men shot in the back. This angered Gator because he could not understand this unprovoked act of murder and he set out that night looking for any sign of these murdering cattle rustlers. The moon hung high in the eastern sky and its light was enough to make it easy to locate sign the cattle were being moved at a rapid pace. John Tanner instructed the riders to stop and silence their horses perhaps they may be able to hear the lowing of nervous cattle. Sure enough off in the distance almost a half mile they could hear the popping of whips. They set an easy pace for the riders to stay in the saddle as they moved forward in the shadows of this moon lit night. They could remain concealed until the last possible moment. It took the rest of the night to finally catch up with the rustlers when they finally stopped to rest unaware they were being followed. All seven riders surprised the rustlers without having to fire a single shot. Everyone including Gator noticed how one of the men seemed to recognize Mat Reynolds when the silence was broken by three rapidly fired shots from Mat's rifle. His actions caused a moment of confusion as each side thought first about running then survival. Mat's deed produced the reaction of wrath from more than a few of the riders. Mat pushed through the dazed crowd and stood over the convulsing body of the dying man and for no apparent reason just stood over him as he took his last gasping breath. To everyone's surprise the usually calm and reserved Mat, his expression change almost crazed animal like, then instantly changed back to his mild manner personality. Apologetically he tried to assure the astonished assembly he saw the dead man going for his gun. With a shrug of his shoulder he callously said, he needed killing anyhow.

Gator still holding tight to the old shot-gun wades through the crowd stops, taking a few seconds to gather his thoughts he faces Mat and demanded he explain the real reason he shot the man. Was it because he recognized you, damn man, are you are hiding something from everyone. In Gator's anger he grabbed him by the collar literally lifting him off the ground all the while drawing his fist back to hit him when Rabbit grabbed his arm, whispered something that caused Gator to calm down. Gator turned to Rabbit with a stern look on his face and without concern of hurting anyone's feelings he voiced his option and how he felt about Mat and now more than ever he was sure Mat was hiding something. He would never trust him until he came clean about everything. Rabbit thought it was strange as well but quickly dismissed any question because he senses something but he did not believe him to be a bad man.

Rabbit swung up on his horse and he and Mat followed the other riders away from the camp where the rustlers had been tried, convicted, executed then given a proper burial. Rabbit found it hard to separate the impassive killings he and Gator had been a part of and the hanging of those men found with stolen cows. The only thing that helped him justify it all, was simply each were all mean men and if not stopped they would continue killing innocent people like Mollie, Sarah and his father.

John Tanner in his wisdom could see the turmoil in Rabbit's eyes so he drew up on his reins and told him sometimes hard decisions had to be made by a few in order that those you love stay safe. Sometimes innocent men get caught up in the wake of the moment but what helps is for him to remember what his mother taught him as a little boy before he left Georgia, "it is God who will be our final judge and he knows it all".

Mat knew best to stay away from Gator the rest of the time spent working cattle; which was extremely difficult because everyone was dependent on each other. Instead of spending the last night at camp Mat returned to Mollie so he could tell her about what had happened and come clean with her.

The Robert's and Reynolds's calves were now pushing 100 pounds and need to be worked. The yearling bulls were castrated and marked with a crop under bit in the right ear and a crop split in the left and branded with a "CR". Then they were turned loose as money in the bank for future use. Rabbit followed the bunch of cows as they meandered from the pens off onto the scrub, his mind was flooded by the thoughts of all that had happened over the past few years and comes to this conclusion, marrying Sarah, having lots of children and raising cows is all he wants to do the rest of his life.

The first frost blanketed the ground at the full moon in December 1895 turning what little grass left in the cow pens to an orange brown almost as if it had frozen in just a moment. Rabbit and Little Crete hooked the single tree to the trace chains on the old wagon, their fingers burned because of the cold but they knew had to go onto the scrub to gather littered knots. Any other time both Little Crete and Rabbit would be excited about getting away from the boredom that sometime filled their time around the clearing but today there seemed a kind of dread. The brisk northern wind blew across the open scrub cutting like a sharp knife through the tattered denim jackets straight to the bone. The longer the day went the colder it got forcing both to seek the shelter of the lower swamp in hopes to find a way to be shielded from the wind. Entering into the shadows of the large towering trees and the moisture from ground seemed to make it even colder so they made up their minds to endure the cold. The quicker they gathered what they needed the quicker they could get out of the cold, this thought pushed them on. Little Crete pointed out the different birds that huddled in large bunches trying to stay warm. There were cardinals, blue-jays, mockingbirds, and morning-doves, birds that usually stay away from each other perched close to stay warm. They watched for as long as they could stand the bitterness of the wind when Little Crete said in a saddening way he could barely hear the peps of the now freezing dying birds.

At last they pulled the wagon to the front of the house. Even though Rabbits hands burned due to the frigid cold he insisted Little Crete go ahead inside to warm up and he would be in as soon as he had unhooked the ox and secure him in the barn. Mat heard them coming, so he was standing just outside the front door and he called for Rabbit to come inside for a few minutes. A little irritated because he did not want to get warm then cold again but at Mat's insistence Rabbit followed him inside. As he walked in Mat handed him a new denim jacket purchased for him while in Kissimmee the last time him and Mollie visited. After piling the littered on the porch at the back door they all huddled around the fireplace and Mollie cooked a big pot of venison stew. The smell of stew filled every inch of the house. The four walls became torturous to the four men as they tried hard to fill their time without irritating the other. Gator and Little Crete worked on the worn harness. Rabbit sharpened knives for Mollie warning her she needed to be very careful. Mat was handy with tools so he mended the two broken chairs and the table Mollie had tripped over causing it to shatter. She cried for two days concerned her weight, Mat assured her that it was not her weight but the age of the table. Telling her he still loved her and not to worry it could be easily fixed.

Even though it had been darker than usual all day when dark finally come Mollie commented that it seemed darker for some reason. Soon she would discover why because it started to rain and it rained steady all night long. By morning there was ice all over the ground. The stout branches of the mighty oak bent under the weight and across the hammock you could hear them yielding to the burden and crashing to the ground. Even when the rain stopped and the sun began to break through the rapidly passing clouds the sound of melting ice gave the allusion of rain. Fortunately none of the gigantic limbs atop the house fell but there was a concern relieved when it started to warm. The temperature changed little over the next few days. The only difference was the sun was not hidden behind the low fast moving clouds driven by a stiff northern wind. Everything that was green before the rain is now a yellowish brown.

The cold weather did not last long but the effects of the ice could be seen as far south as the cane field on southeast side of the big lake in Kissimmee. The cattle fared well by going deeper into the swamps and surviving on the grasses there untouched by the cold. While riding a circle about five miles from the old place the riders found evidence of the effects of the cold on the small animals and game they depended on for fresh meat. Rabbit commented to Gator that it would be hard for a couple of weeks but he believed things would recover well.

Everything began to bloom and things seemed to return to normal. The scrub blanked by yellow and purple flowers. Mollie and Sarah would spend hours walking among the beautiful flowers just talking and Sarah would tell her most secret dreams about her and Rabbit. Mollie enjoyed this time, a time that should have been shared with her two daughters but thankful for Sarah's friendship.

The wild jasmine with its white flowers and the brilliant yellow flowers of the honey-suckle covered the scrub oaks growing along the side of the sandy trail leading to the hammock and the fragrance swirled in the sight breeze filling the clearing and bringing a feeling of ease. All the damage from the freeze began recovering by March of 1896. The killings which; had taken place the year before were all but forgotten and Rabbit had relaxed, finally feeling comfortable enough not to wear his pistol.

No one heard the riders as the raced into the clearing when the first of the gunshot fired. The sound of bullets whizzed past everyone because they were caught by surprise. Following the impact of the rapid firing of the guns the wood splinter from the pecky cypress showering Rabbit as he scurried for cover, grabbing for his hip only the remember he had hung his guns just inside the door moments before. Hundreds of shots stroke the house crashing through the newly installed screen over the open windows used to keep out the mosquitoes. As Rabbit entered the house he saw Mollie grabbed Little Crete forcing him down hitting the floor hard almost knocking the wind out of him, as she covered their heads, shielding herself from the spray. Between the pops of the guns centered on the house they could hear the shouts of men cussing causing more confusion but their shouts helped Rabbit locate them in the mayhem. Rabbit crawled to where his pistol hung on the wall and as he drew it from the holster he stood in the open window and mechanically he fired in the direction the men still sitting carelessly in their saddle. The two closest to the front porch lurch as the 44 caliber shot ripped into their chest causing them to fall backward then forward and eventually falling to the ground. One was dead before he hit the ground but the second still holding his pistol yelled defiantly and with hatred cursed until his voice trailed off and he laid dead. Dropping down behind the base of the window and quickly reloading the hot pistol. Before he could stand again he heard the blast of the big shotgun; which gave him the poise confidence to stand again and quickly unload the pistol in the direction of the remaining rider as he dropped from his horse then scrambles to the covering of the large palmetto patch next to the back side of the barn. The shots Rabbit fired dusted his heels forcing him to quicken his escape, making for cover. Rabbit almost laughed out loud because he could not believe that the aggressor's arrogance now turned to cries of mercy, which in Rabbits eyes shown their true cowardice. His hatred for these men boiled within him and all he truly wanted was to end the coward's life. Yet deep inside he felt his stomach began to heave. The next two blasts were evidence that Gator had found the retreating ambusher. He emerged from the barn behind the following the injured man to the front of the house. Righting himself Rabbit pushed open the door and rushing out into the sandy yard carefully scanning the area for any possible threat. It was all over when Captain Drawdy and his men rode into the clearing with guns drawn. Rabbit looked into the face of Captain Drawdy as a tear rolled down his cheek and the look of disbelief imprinted upon his face. Sarah followed behind her father and raced to where Rabbit stood as blood stained the white shirt still unbuttoned. He was unaware he had been hit, never feeling the pain until Sarah called his attention to the blood. She grabs the shirt and in one fluid motion removed it. Her forcefulness caused Rabbit to blush. Grabbing his forearm she turned him toward a single beam of sunlight that had found its way through the thick canopy. Examining the wound turned his blushing to waves of nausea due to the pain. No one noticed Little Crete as he stumbled from the front porch to his knees all covered with blood. Gator was still standing where he had deposited the man he drug from the thicket when he finally noticed his nephew and called out to him. Rabbit was closer as he turned was able to reach the sobbing boy first. Forcibly he lifted him from the ground looking him over for the source of the blood and found no wound. Everyone stood dumbfounded as he stood without saying a word when he slowly lifted his arm pointing toward the front door. While Rabbit was still holding Little Crete, Sarah rushed to the porch looked inside the house when she let out a shrill scream and the reason was lying on the floor in front of the fireplace, she saw Mollie in a pool of her own blood.

Everyone stood stunned trying to understand why this had to happen and who would do such a cruel thing. Mat had gone to Kissimmee several days before and was not due back for another day. Rabbit was unable to go find Mat due to his injury so the task was left to Gator. Gator did not care for Mat because he did not trust him but out of respect for his sister and respect for her love she had for Mat he rode to Kissimmee accompanied by two of Captain Drawdy's

Sarah accepted the responsibility of preparing Mollie for burial. After retrieving water from the rain barrel she washed her body and put the dress she was married in on Mollie. Sarah's father helped to place her on the table in the cooking area. She fell into the chair that Mollie had treasured, the one that her brothers had given to her for Christmas, the only thing that was able to be retrieved from their burned out home in Kissimmee and sobbed. She had never been involved in such as this and had never had anyone so close to her, died. Even though her mother had died when she was a little she was too young to remember. The Captain busied himself in building a coffin out of the wood he had delivered for building his house.

Later that night Gator returned to the faint glowing of a single candle in the cooking area with word from Kissimmee that Mat left the day before heading home, earlier than planned. He followed his sign until it disappeared as he crossed the creek. What troubled him was what he found on the other side. The wagon Mat was driving was turned over and his horse dead in the creek. There was no sign of him it was as if he just disappeared from off the face of the earth. He thought to himself, how much more tragedy can this family take and how this added news would affect Little Crete but he had to face this responsibility and lead this family through. They gathered what supplies Mat had purchased at Kissimmee and righted the wagon and would send some of the others back to get it later. While he was securing one of the packages a new dress Mat had gotten for Mollie fell to the ground at his feet. It was as if someone had taken a large hammer and struck him right up side the head. For the first time in his adult life he began to cry uncontrollably, those standing near him was confused but out of respect quickly rode away leaving him to deal with this situation by himself. Reaching down he gathered the dress gently in his stained hands, folded it and placed it in his wallet {a wallet is a pouch used by cow hunters to carry their supplies.} The silence of the moment Gator could hear strange splashing down the creek. His heart fell as if it would explode in his chest. He remembers of Rabbit telling how the large gators in the lake instantly killed the cow last summer consuming it in mere moments and his thoughts were that Mat had floated down stream and he was being eaten. He pulled his pistol from it holster and fired a single shot into the air; which caused the men that had just left to return at a full run. He explained what he had heard and before anyone could say another word he plunged his horse into the water and headed in the direction of the splashing. He was not prepared for what he saw, even though he was extremely relieved that what the gators were eating was not Mat, but who was it? All but the head and trunk of the body remained as the three gators rolled and ripped the body apart. The longer this mystery lingered without answers the madder Gator became and the greater his hatred grew. Turning to the men that stood close all shocked by what they were witnessing, he said with a resolute tone, "I'm gonna hunt'em down and kill ever last one of'em if its da las thing I do". With that he spurred his horse making him jump straight out of the water and onto the bank. The tone of his voice frightened one of the men so bad when he returned back to the house he told Captain Drawdy that he believed Mr. Gator to be possessed with the devil and pure evil.

Gator entered the house, walking over to Little Crete, leaned over and spoke something into his ear. The boy had still not spoken since the shooting nor had he cried and this worried Gator. His biggest fear was Little Crete's life becoming as messed up as his if he didn't learn how to deal with what was going on inside of his head.

Gator stares off into nothing, recalling all the feelings he experienced after the death of his father and shivers. He feels unqualified to speak to his nephew due to his involvement in so many killings. Dropping his head into his hands he whispers a simple prayer for help when Little Crete reached out touching him on the shoulder and said, "things'll be all right Uncle Gator" and then he began to cry; which did Gator welcome. He pulled the boy onto his lap and held him, assuring him that everything will get better and he could count on him to care for him. Rabbit eased up onto his elbows and smiled knowing now they could help their nephew to grow into a strong man.

Next Gator he walked over and sat down next to Rabbit who was still groggy from having the bullet removed from his arm and gently patted his head as a declaration everything was well. The bullet had missed the bone but had damaged the muscle, Captain Drawdy was confidant he would heal as good as new and by the end of summer he would be back to normal. Gator walked over to where they had laid Mollie and hoisted her into his arms and as a flood of emotions washed over him and he began to cry again, but as quick as he started it stopped

They buried Mollie next to her mother and the empty graves bearing only wooden markers of her two little girls and Willie. It was a sad day for everyone as they stood next to the graves wondering within themselves when this madness would end. What happened today only enhanced the hatred Gator felt and enraged the burning need for revenge.

Everyone became aware of the fact that Mollie had been the glue holding this band of misfits together. This unfortunate event gave Sarah the chance to step up and prove her-self worthy to Rabbit in hopes he would finally ask her to marry him. She had pressed the issue more lately with the help of Mollie but Rabbit was reluctant due to the fact of his constant fear of her getting hurt as the result of what they had committed to do to the men that had murdered their father. Mollie tried hard to convince Rabbit there was more to life then getting revenge and she was sure that if their father were alive he would tell him the same thing. It did not help either, that he was afraid of Sarah's father and did not like the idea of having to ask for her hand. Taking charge she moved her stuff into Mollies room, picked up her chores and no one not even her father voiced any opposition. She struggled at first but quickly adjusted to all that Mollie had done without anyone recognizing it and for this her respect for Mollie grew daily.

The sun was beginning to set. The gray dismal clouds covered the retreat of the sun; which cast long shadows into the hammock when Gator announced his intentions of going after those responsible for this evilness and vowed that with every inch of his being not one of them would see this date next year. Little Crete had grown close to his uncle and run to his side begging him not to go. Rabbit tried to convince him if he would just wait until he was well enough to ride, he would join him. He would not listen, but did agree to allow one of the Captain's men to go, his name was Daub. He was a tall slender man with gray hair. He often said of himself he did not have much book since but he sure could handle a gun. Gator was certain he could handle a gun and knife better then him self and would give him the chance soon to prove this true.

Chapter 34

Gator and Daub saddled their horses, secures the supplies they figured necessary for several weeks on the trail, a roll for sleeping and extra clothing. Rabbit asked Gator what he intended to do first when he explained to him he would travel north to the big creek and visit with John Tanner seeking his advice. They said their good byes and climbed into the saddle, before turning toward Bear Island he leaned down and spoke specifically to Little Crete and told him that what he had to do would not take long and when he returned they would head south and hunt for several days. Reaching down with his right hand he patted his head and smiled, Little Crete reciprocated assuring his uncle that he would wait. Turning north he passed through the sandy scrub leading to the ford near Bear Island. He had a choice; he could veer to the east and follow a high narrow savannah bordering Lake Mary Jane, which would open out into the southern end of the Pocka-taw Flats. It had rained almost six inches since they buried Mollie and he knew that the flat woods would be flooded and he would have to spend longer in the saddle. Or, he could skirt the eastern edge of Lake Hart moving from one tussock to another spending only about an hour in deeper water. This way leads him further north causing him to have back track a little before entering the western border of Pocka-taw Flats but this helps him to avoid the deep water. The only thing it would cost him following the later path would be an extra day on his trip. Daub pointed north and sought Gators attention to buzzards circling on the east shore of Lake Hart. His curiosity was peeked choosing for him the direction he would take. He put his spurs to the sides of horse causing him to lunge forward into the deep water. Finding its footing they pushed forward and it did not take as long as Gator thought to make it to high ground. The closer they moved toward the circling buzzards the more they were able to smell the strong odor of rotting flesh. The sound of approaching horses caused the buzzards to take flight and land in the gigantic pines. In a small clearing they noticed a small mound of pine straw and dried palmetto fans covering a deer killed by a panther. The horses where unsettled due to the strong aroma left by the big cat and their reaction caused Gator to resume his push forward. Daub finally spoke up and asked Gator about his plans, he reminded him the sun was beginning to set and they would need to make camp soon. Gator pointed across the flat woods toward a lone cypress head due east and told him that he wanted to make it that far before he stopped. There was fresh water there and plenty of game so they would have venison for supper. Daub suggested he make a big circle south then again east and when he got equal with the cypress head he would turn north and meet him there before dark; which Gator agreed. Gator watched him disappear out of sight and finding an old cow trail he rode with his legs scrapping the gall berry and palmetto fans. The yellow flies swarmed darting in and out of the range of Gator's hand. Their bite was harder them the mosquito.

As soon as Gator found a place he felt safe camping the night, he gathered an armful of littered knots. There were several big live oak trees bordered by thick palmettos inter-woven with grapevines and briars. The opening into the clearing was only about fifteen foot wide. This would make it easy to observe anyone trying to enter his camp. Gator was not afraid in starting a fire for cooking and keeping the biting pesky bugs away. Taking two small scrub oaks he stripped them of their leaves and tied them to two pegs he hammered into the ground. Between the two sticks he laid out his bed and covered it with the mosquito net

About dark they could hear the howls of several wolves off in the distance. Just beyond the canopy Gator watched with amusement at bullbats swooping and diving making a sound that is indescribable but unforgettable. Somewhere out on the open scrub a whippoorwill's lonesome cry could be heard when the wolves would be quite. That night they eat the breast of a turkey Daub shot as it flew up to roost for the night and enjoyed meaningless conversation.

A slight breeze began to blow out of the south just before the sun began to rise. The sky streaked a bright reddish-orange fading into an ashy gray horizon with not a cloud in the sky. Daub stood and poured a steaming hot cup of coffee, holding it to his nose he took a deep breath and finally spoke to Gator as an old friend. Up until this moment he had been evasive and unwilling to speak casually about any subject. Gator had tried to have a conversation with him because he was use to hearty arguments and exchanges with his brother as they traveled across the scrub. Daub told him that he agreed with what he wanted to do but it was because of these actions so much death followed him and if he did not find an end to this madness it would consume everyone he loved. With that Daub sat down, taking another long gulp of the scalding coffee and begin to tell his story. "I'm sixty-two years old and I have not been back to where I was born since I was fifteen. I got mad at my father about feeding da hogs, so I run away. I wondered around until I was taken in by a family da owned a cotton plantation in Alabama. I fell in love with the foreman's daughter and we had planned to be married when I turned nineteen, with just a week before." He stopped what he was saying and with a lonesome look, he stared at the fire and Gator could see a single tear roll down his right check. With a sigh he took another sip from the cup, wiped the tear away and continued. "The owner hired another man to get more production from the workers, but he was a mean man. He took a shine to the foreman's youngest daughter and was constantly warned to stay away. Everyone was uneasy having him live in the main house and no one trusted him but it was part of his pay. Late one night I heard a scream from the barn. I ran to the barn pushed open the door in time to see him lying on top of her. Without thought I picked up a singletree and bashed his head in. Then I pulled him off of her the same time her father rushed in seeing her lying there on the floor barely breathing. He grabbed her and shouted at her asking why she would do this to him. I stood there and could not believe what I was hearing, his daughter had just been raped but he was only concerned as to what people would now think of him. This enraged me, realizing I still had the bloody singletree in my hand I hit him until he collapsed and fell next to the now unconscious girl. Dropping the bloody singletree I knelt next to her lifting her in my arms as she took her last breath." He dropped the cup and looked wildly into his hands now open before his eyes and said. "She died in my hands." He then looked Gator right in the eyes and the empty gaze surprised him and with a kind of softness he had never witnessed while talking to Daub he spoke. "You're an honorable man, I can see good in you and there is a family that loves you. If you continue your present path you will loose all that you have. Killing, whether it is justified or not, will kill a little bit of you every time. I know; cause that's all I have done since my first killing in the barn. Gator, if you got to kill this man you're after, then let this be the last. Get out of da killen business as soon you can." His voice trailed off as he stood and walked away, the shadows cast by the large oaks concealed him from Gators view. He then turned and watched the fire flicker and danced in the slight breeze, the smoke whipped from side to side swooping down to the ground the shooting straight in the air as the aroma of the littered fire filled the air. He dropped into deep thought as he contemplated the advice he received and was unaware of Daub standing next to him with the horse saddled. After another cup of coffee they mounted and headed out into the open low-bush flat woods. The wiregrass, huckleberry bushes, dog fennels, some briers and broom sage conceals the trail that leads further onto the open scrub toward the hardwood swamp concealing the headwaters of the Econlochatchee River. Gator rides forward unaware of his surroundings as he considers what Daub had said, when he was brought back to reality as Daub rode up and said, "Gator". Gator pulls back on his reins and looks in the direction Daub was looking. Off to the south making their way along the thick growth of palmettos used to conceal their presence they could see a column of travelers. Gator was sure they had already been seen and there was no reaction but a deliberate retreat. His curiosity caused him to move a little closer and he recognized them as Seminole Indians because of the multicolored wardrobe. They counted twenty-three women and ten full-grown men, two Negro's and several children. Gator did not know if they were friendly or not and did not have the time to find out when all of a sudden the band stopped, startling Gator. Quickly they dismounted hiding their horses behind a large myrtle bed as they slipped through the myrtles they could see movement that was strange in nature. Just beyond the extent of the myrtle bed was a switch-grass pond that ran all the way to where the band of Indians had stopped. Several of the men looked as if they were digging a hole while others busied themselves around an op-long shaped bundle decorated in bright brilliant colors; the red and yellow stood out against the green background. Minutes passed into hours as they watched the strange happenings that at times were hidden from their view because the band was constantly moving around the wrapped bundle just fifty yards away when all of a sudden they chanting stopped. An older man stood spoke a few words in their language, turned and continued their pilgrimage south. They watched as the slow moving band disappeared into the thick hard wood swamp. Gator's curiosity made him abandon common since, leaving his hiding place he walked to the area where the Indians had concentrated. In the middle of the trail they had just walked on he found a small area if disturbed soil. Gator looked in the direction the Indians had disappeared, than leant down scratching in the disturbed ground. Just about a foot below the surface they found the reason for their strange ceremony, they had buried one of their own. Gator staggered back then jumped to his feet shocked by this discovery, Daub could see the surprise in his expression and walked to where he was and replaced the dirt over the dead Indian. Tradition has it that if an Indian died on the trail that they would be buried on the trail so the spirit would always know the last direction their family had traveled.

Gator and Daub turned north giving the place a wide birth and headed for the shallow ford at Cow Pen Branch. It was after noon when they came to the shallow crossing south of the Magrit place and crossed the creek. {Most people do not realize that before Disston Hamilton started digging drainage canals in 1881; which changed the landscape of Central Florida. The Pocka-taw Flats now known as Wedgefield flooded due to the fact it was the headwaters of Econlochatchee, Jim, Cross, Cox, Turkey and Toshochatee Creeks.} They pushed on because Gator needed to speak to John Tanner about all that had happened lately.

The sun was beginning to set when they finally rode up in front of the Tanner homestead. Several family members with gun in hand stepped from the shadows to meet the strangers invading their solace. The closest to Gator was John Tanner's eldest son, Oscar. Before Gator dismounted he declared who he was and why he was there so late in the day. Henry extended his hand making Gator and Daub feel welcome and for the first time in several days able to relax. Henry barked orders and two teenage boys stepped up and took the reins of the tired horses, turning toward the barn. Daub grabbed his rifle from the sheath laced to the side of his saddle and followed close behind their host. As they walked up the steps they were invited to spend the night if they were a mind to, Gator readily accepted because he was tired of eating cold food. Staring out into the yard watching as everyone hurried about his or her nightly chores when the silence was broken by Gator's enquiry about John Tanner. Henry looked at Gator kind of astounded at his inquiry and told him they had just returned from Lake Tracy {close to Brooksville, Florida} and burying him there. Henry could see that Gator was disappointed at the news and asked if he could help in any way. Settling back in his chair Gator first told him of what they had seen south of Cow Pen Branch. Henry told them this was a custom of the nomadic Indians. When one of the party dies away from their base camp are buried in the trail and out of respect for the dead as they leave the burial that all walk over the grave. Some say it is to conceal it, while others say it is their belief as they pass over the dead then the spirit of the dead would know what direction to follow. They made small talk until a call came from inside to cook kitchen announcing the nightly meal was ready. It was completely dark when the men returned to the front porch, lit their pipes and talked some more. Each took a swig from the freshly obtained shine from a family friend further north. When Henry stood up, pointing toward the side room informing his visitors they could spend the night in the side room, because children would sleep in the barn. Just before they all disappeared into their respective quarters Henry spoke up and said they would speak of the other matter first thing in the morning, and with that the lamp was blown out and darkness quickly rushed in and filled the void left by snuffing out the light.

Rabbit lifts himself to a sitting position and calls for Gator; Sarah rushes to his side and places her hand on his forehead. Sweat pours from his brow and the bedclothes he was wearing was soaked as well. Sarah calls for Little Crete to tell him she needs him to run down to her father's place because she needs him. He looks past her as she is talking and looks with great concern at his uncle. She could see in his face distress and apprehension, she stands and grabs him taking him in her arms and holding him as he begins to cry. He sobs uncontrollably and wildly swung his arms, it was all Sarah could do to consol and assured him that if he would do what she asked of him, his uncle would get better.

Little Crete pushes back from her with resolve flushing over his face he wipes his tears away with his shirtsleeve, apologies and turns and bolts out the door. Captain Drawdy sees the boy running up the trail and hurries to him while the others who are hard at work and asked what is wrong. Little Crete stops, takes a deep breath and tells him what he had rehearsed all the way there but before Captain Drawdy could ask another question the boy turns and was gone. A thousand things run through the boys mind as he dips and weaves in and around the over hanging limbs of the scrub oaks and black jack oaks that line the trail. It becomes a game to him and for a short time forgets the hurt of loosing his mother and possibly now losing his Uncle Rabbit. He stops along his way and examines the tracks of a lone boar hogs that had crossed sometime during the night. He imagined himself hunting the hog and baying the hog in the saw grass pond just off the trail and how proud his mother would be if he could return with a report of capturing the hog, then all of a sudden he remembers, fear engulfs his mind. Relief comes when he hears the wagon coming up the trail and then he again begins to run toward the house. Captain Drawdy sees the boy start to run again and slaps the horse with the reins used for driving the wagon in order to offer what assistance he could to Sarah in the care of Rabbit.

Before Little Crete entered the house to find out how his uncle was he runs to the open well, pulls down on the long sweep used to draw water from the bottom of the deep well. With a resolute grunt he drew out a fresh bucket of cool water and strained his young muscles carrying the full bucket to the front porch. Sarah standing on the front porch awaiting her father drawn from the house she too heard the wagon making its way down the trail. She finds some pleasure in the situation when she sees life had returned to the attitude and manner of the boy. Before her eyes she watches as he transforms into a little man and offers to help him up the steps but he refused because it was now his responsibility to do the chores he once shared with his uncles.

As Captain Drawdy passes Little Crete he pats his shoulder and the boy smiles because it was his Uncle Gator's way of letting him know he was doing a good job. He bounces from the porch and hurries to the barn to tend to the horses. Taking a big scoop of corn from the crib and pours it in the wooden troughs he takes the wooden bucket over to the well, draws another scoop of water only to spill it as he transfers it to the watering bucket. He learned a valuable lesson and only draws a manageable amount and he's off to make sure the horses have water. Stepping from the barn he watches several squirrels running and jumping from limb to limb. Ever since his Uncle Gator left they had not enjoyed the fresh meat they had grown accustom to so he marched onto the front porch, swung open the door reached for the single shot shotgun leaning next to the front entrance and announced his intentions. Rabbit was now sitting up and he smiled at Sarah as her expression of pride turned to worry. Before she could voice her opposition Rabbit with nothing more than a whisper assured her he will be ok.

He was proud of himself as he set the four squirrels on the front porch and began to skin them. He called to Sarah as he had heard Rabbit many times call to his mother declaring they are ready for her to begin to prepare the nights meal. Captain Drawdy made the comment that what happened today was good for everyone, especially Little Crete.

Days turned into weeks as Rabbit continued healed from his wound. He was able now to walk by himself and his first trip was out into the yard. The short strolls he took down to the creek with Little Crete, was a little too much too soon. Sarah still worried about Rabbit for the reason he would stare for hours at a time down the old sandy trail. She would often hear him convey his concern and need to go and find his brother. About three months had past when he stepped onto the front porch and announced he would be gone for a couple of hours, saddled his and Little Crete's horse and rode off into the scrub. Just before they disappeared Sarah walked up and looked him in the eye and asked him to promise he would only be gone for a couple of hours, when he smiled and said I'll be back soon. He told her he was going to look at the cows Little Crete told them about last night.

They talked as they wadded through the small creek turning east. They stayed to the well-defined savannah around Lake Mary Jane. Sometimes passing through the dried up fern beds as finally entering the scrub, Rabbit could see the bunch of cows lazily feeding on the lush grass and eased as close as he could to see what mark they bore. He commented to the boy as to how proud he was they fared well during the summer and it looked like they were going to have a good bunch of calves this year.

The boy just shook his head in agreement and pointed beyond the first bunch to a much small bunch feeding past a rather large cypress head. He asked if they could ride a little farther and to see what mark they had. Without warning Rabbit put the spurs to the flank of his horse and bolted away. Surprised Little Crete kicked his horse causing it to lurch forward and in just a few steps had caught up with his uncle as they rode at a slow lope for quite a distance. Satisfied with the cows they had seen Rabbit returned to the house just before noon and in the front yard was a strange horse. Flash back, to the time of the last attack put Rabbit on the defensive as he ducks behind the barn. He commands Little Crete to stay hid until he was called for, Rabbit dismounts and circles to the left of the barn, passing behind the back of the small house he peers in through the open door and there sitting at the table talking to Sarah was Mat. Rabbit was taken aback by the sight of Mat, first Rabbit thought he was dead, second he looks like he had lost about thirty pounds and looked like a skeleton. Another thing strange was he was fresh shaven and wore clean clothes. The next thing Rabbit noticed was the new shiny pistol he had strapped to his side and it looked military issue. Rabbit stepped onto the porch; which caused an immediate response from Mat. He stands dropping his hand to his gun than relaxing when he recognized his old friend. The first question out of Mat's mouth for Rabbit was, "where's Gator?" Rabbit ignored the question, walked to the front porch and hollered for Little Crete telling him he could take care of the horses and come in. Turning Rabbit walked to Mat stuck out his hand and greeted him as if he had not been missing for as long as he had. Sarah continues telling Mat what had happened and how they thought he was dead because all they found was his wagon and a dead horse. At that point Mat shifted in his chair and looked Rabbit in the eye and asked again if he knew where Gator was and if so, might Rabbit tell him. He had some information he must share with him and it was urgent. Rabbit assured him he had no knowledge of his whereabouts other than a good idea. Mat stands and nervously fidgets with his gun and reiterates his need to see Gator. This was peculiar to Rabbit and he insists Mat sit down and tells him what was bothering him. Hesitantly he sits down, clears his throat and began by telling him old man Reynolds is dead. This information interested Rabbit as he asked Mat to continue. Turning the collar out of his thin jacket he revealed a silver badge and the inscription "U.S. Marshal". He continues by telling how he was sent down here by the Governor in Tallahassee to put a stop to all the killings and his main responsibility was to capture or kill Reynolds. After he met Mollie things changed for him and he knew if he did not get to Reynolds before Gator did all he loved could be destroyed. The information he was receiving, Reynolds was not going to stop until all the Roberts were dead. Reynolds is responsible for the fire in Kissimmee and Mollie's death. With this statement Rabbit could hear the hesitation in Mat's voice. Rabbit drops his head and a wave of freedom filled his entire body as the end to a part of his life he never cared for was finally over. Mat spoke up again and said he had something else he had to tell him and he was afraid the information would not be as easily received as the news of Reynolds death.

Rabbit looked at Mat and said, "what, that your Ben Reynolds son?" The surprise on Mat's face told the entire story and when he was finally able to speak he asked, "How long have you known? Does Gator know?" Rabbit assured him he was not one hundred percent sure until this morning when he looked into his eyes but Gator had questioned the possibility ever since the first time he met you. That was the main reason he never really befriended nor accepted you, but he promised Mollie he would not do anything to harm you. Mat drops his head into his hands and begins to weep just as Little Crete enters the house. His eyes light up when he saw Mat and ran to his side his arms wide open embraces him to the point of almost choking him. Mat takes the boy in his arms and at that moment everything seems to be unimportant. Little Crete tells him of his morning adventure. He told of how Uncle Rabbit had promised to take him on a trip to see John Tanner. The news took Sarah aback as she turns and stares at Rabbit, he smiles at her and mouths to her "we'll talk later" and smiles. She did not think the news was anything to smile about and stands walking out the door. Her last words before leaving were with annoyance, "I'll be outside if you want to talk". Rabbit knew if he was going to have any peace about the matter he needed to go now and tell her the true reason for his going to see John Tanner.

He softly grabs for her arm as she steps from the porch. Gently placing his large hands around the waist, pulling her close and says, "I wanted to ask your father first but the cat is out of the bag. I want to marry you and I was going to ask if he knew of a preacher who could make it proper." Stunned she reciprocates with a passionate hug followed by the most loving kiss. Rabbit had never experienced such a feeling. A sensation rushed through his entire body, one he had never known but from that moment on he never doubted his love for her.

Chapter 35

The next morning Gator was awakens by the crow of a rooster. He lay in bed waiting for the sound of someone stirring. Daub sat up and stretched breaking wind loud enough to shake the floor. Gator made some sarcastic comment telling him if they spend another night he was sleeping out in the barn. "We's been out in the open and I's never knod you to snore as loud as you do, I like ta never got ta sleep" joked Gator as he stood. Daub mumbled and rushed out into the yard and the silence was broken by the sound of him relieving himself followed by another loud fart. He enters the room and says. "My father told me there are five kinds of farts, and do you know what they are?" Gator's curiosity was peaked and told him he knew of only one. Daub smiled and while putting on his boots said, "a poot, a toot, a fart, a rattler and a tear-ass" followed by a thunderous laughter because none saw the three boys standing at the door being entertained by their visitors. Gator stood to chew the boys when he heard the booming voice of Henry Tanner as he commanded them to busy themselves with the chores of the morning. They scattered like quail rousted from their hiding place beneath a clump of wiregrass. Henry's voice shocked Daub causing him to drop his left boot, it was echoed by a booming fart like a horse under strain rumbling like distant thunder. Henry looked into the room and asked what kind was that? Daub smiled, you could see a slight blush on his face as he finished tying his boots. Reaching for his hat and quickly walked into the yard.

In just a few minutes they sat down to a table full of food. The men always ate first and they talked of their many memories of John Tanner.

Gator ended this part of their conversation by say he will truly be missed.

Gator's expression changed as he inquired about any information he had about old man Reynolds. He again stressed the need to find him and finish what had been started many years before. Henry told him he had heard a U.S. Marshal had been sent to find Reynolds and arrest him or kill him. Word of all the killings was beginning to worry those who would eventually come to settle this area. This news caused Gator to question Henry more, pressing him for what information he had. Henry told him what he knew and assured him if he heard anything else he would send him word. He suggested Gator return home and allows the law to do its job. This was totally opposite of what his father wanted and Gator wondered if he should talk to Henry about it but figured it would be best to do as he suggested and allow the law to handle the situation.

It pleased him because he could finally see the end to the killings and would allow him and Rabbit the freedom to accumulate the herd of cattle; which was their fathers dream. He said, "if this is true I will be back in the fall to purchase a few cows from you". Henry acknowledged him with a nod and stood from his place at the head of the table and walked out into the yard calling to the boys. "You can eat now and as soon as you are through we'll head to the creek and cut firewood."

Gator and Daub spent the morning resting under the shade of the large oak trees, enjoying the steady breeze which blew from the south. Daub commented about the muffled sound of thunder off in the distance and leaned forward from his resting place looking to the sky and finished by saying, "we need some rain".

Their hosts returned from the creek bottom followed by a wagon full of wood. This wood will be dried and used for cooking. Henry talked with Gator and Daub a little longer as they watched the boys stack the wood next to a lone pine tree east of the house. Daub saddled the horses and waved back at Henry just as they entered the thicket bordering the scrub.

The next morning Mat, Rabbit and Little Crete saddled their horses and headed toward the ford of the creek leading onto Pocka-taw Flats. Their purpose was two fold, first to find Gator and give him the news about Ben Reynolds, then to see John Tanner about a preacher who could perform a wedding. Just before dark Gator saw three riders enter the scrub to the south west and immediately recognized one of them as his brother Rabbit. Unsure if they had seen him yet he turned straight at them wanting to close the distance between them so not to have to ride into their camp after dark. Rabbit was as observant as his brother and saw the riders moving toward them at a rapid pace. A sick feeling settles deep in his stomach and he takes an evasive move allowing him plenty enough room to escape if need be. As soon as he was on high enough ground he recognized Gator allowing him to relax a bit. Gator was relieved to see Rabbit up and getting around until he recognizes Mat of whom he was still very leery and feels hatred surging through his body. He pulls hard on the reins forcing the horse to slide to a stop. Daub watched what was happening and positioned himself between Gator and Mat. Pretty confident if Rabbit was riding with him there was a good reason and there was a need to talk. Finally they reached each other Gator rode right up to Little Crete ever watchful of Mat and inquired how the boy was. He could see and was thankful he was back to his old self and very proud of his skill on a horse. Little Crete smiled a mile wide smile as his uncle praises him. He starts to give a minute-to-minute account of their trip when Rabbit had to silence him so the men could share the news they had learned. Daub greeted them then excused him self from their presence riding out into the flat woods hoping to kill a young deer for their supper. Finding a good safe place for their camp they unsaddling the horses and build a fire. After getting settled down Mat shared the news about Ben Reynolds while flipping his collar revealing his badge. Gator said, "So, you're the marshal? Why didn't you tell us?" Mat assured him that he wanted to many times but felt he needed to keep silent because he did not want anyone to think he married Mollie just to keep them in sight. He went on to say, "I truly loved your sister and looked forward to living the rest of my life with her and be a father to Little Crete". He reached out taking the boy by the back of the neck pulling him to his side.

As soon as Daub returned with a young fat doe the each whittled a stick then pushed it down in the ground piercing meat allowing it to sizzle next to the flames. Three-day-old biscuits lie on palmetto fans catching the dripping grease to heat and soften them making them fit to eat. Coffee grounds roll and do the hominy flips in water drawn from the creek named Cox Creek, when Rabbit asked Mat why he had lost so much weight. He begins by saying; "I'm sure you found my wagon" hesitating to see if he got a response; which he did. "I was about to cross the creek when five men rode up beside me when I recognized the leader as my father. He hadn't seen me since I was knee high to a grasshopper but he was so consumed with his hatred for anyone that had anything to do with you", looking right into Gators eyes. Gator shifted in his seat on the log; which was drug up next to the fire and Mat continues. "He knew he was close and any shot fired would take away the surprise so he took the butt of his shot rifle and knocked me out. I guess he thought he killed me and left me for dead. I don't remember anything else until I woke up several hours later at the Simmons place over on Wolf Creek. Ms. Penny believes that when he hit me on the head it shook something loose and because of that I can eat like a horse and stay as skinny as a snake. I get bad headaches and can't see as I once could but everything still works as good as ever." He stops to turn his meat and readjust his biscuit, than he poured him a heaping cup of hot coffee. The others just looked at him in disbelief when Little Crete joined the conversation by asking him how he came to be a Marshal. Taking a deep sip of hot coffee almost taking his breath he answered, "My mama left when I was just two years old back to Atlanta and when I got old enough she allowed me to go to school. I got a college degree in common law and when they learned who I was they asked if I would be willing to come back here and see if I could help put an end to all this foolishness. I guess you're curious about how Ben Reynolds died? After leaving the Simmons I headed back to Kissimmee because I had to refit myself, I had not had a gun in my hand since I last left Kissimmee. I was able to buy a horse from the Yates and when I arrived in front of the store in Campbell Station I recognized my father as he stepped into the road right in front of me. He recognized me, turned and ran for his horse where he had foolishly left his gun. I than heard a shot to my left, I jumped from my horse as I withdrew my revolver, than watched surprised as he stumbled forward falling face first in the dirt. Off the front porch of the store stepped a man by the name of Crow Shivers holding a shotgun still pointed in the direction of the body now staining the dusty road. Turning my attention to the man I would later learn he was my mama's brother who was sent down here to tell me she had died." After talking to the only law in the area we rode out into the scrub and spent the night talking.

Taking his cup of coffee in both hands he takes a long gulp of the black comfort. "In that moment I lost my mama and father and now you tell me I have lost the love of my life, Mollie", he stands and disappears into the darkness. Everyone eat their supper in silence and welcomed sleep with a new since of freedom.

The next morning the sun shines bright through the bay trees, cypress and water oaks that shielded the campsite from the rising sun. The small fire was rekindled and Daub was awakened by the strong smell of the coffee boiling. He jumps up and hurries toward the palmetto patch some distance from the camp. Little Crete laughs out loud that draws his Uncle Gator's attention, "what ya laughen bout?" He points toward Daub as he rushes by, bent over and the expression on his face revealed the pain he was experiencing. Almost every step he took he expelled gas and mumbled something about a loose puckering string. Everyone laughs out loud and the mood of the camp was jovial when Gator called a gathering of everyone and shared his plans about gathering a herd of cattle. Rabbit told him of the two small bunches close to the house and his conversation with Mr. Yates south of the big lake in Kissimmee. They spoke of the vision and the prospect of fulfilling their father's dream of making a living from owning cattle in Florida.

Chapter 36

Sarah had finally finished her morning chores and slips from the house leaving behind responsibilities that engulfed her entire existence since Mollie's death. With joy she served the man she loves and wants nothing more then to make him happy, especially now that she knows he wants to marry her. She stopped to remove her lace up boots so she could feel again the warm sand between her toes, a pleasure of her childhood. As she walked steadily toward the creek ambling lazily just yards from her home. She reaches back and loosened her brownish-red hair allowing it to fall down the middle of her back. Settling down in the lush green grass growing abundantly along the bank of the creek, thankful the old scrawny cows had not found the grass. She's captivated by the beauty and watches as the current moves the hanging willow limbs back and forth, making small wakes that continually lap the shore, the movement hypnotizes her for the moment. Staring deep into the tannic water trying hard to see under the surface, the only thing revealed was her own reflection revealing the mess her hair had become. Lowering her feet into the cool dark running water she takes a deep breath as she relaxes, feeling every muscles begin to relax. She closed her eyes and listens to the deafening shrill cry of the Katie-did and shivers at the image she has of them in her mind. The songbirds continued to sing undisturbed by her presence. Bouncing around on the ground scratching in the dry leaves searching for an unsuspecting worm or bug for their dinner. She loosened the top buttons of her blouse, feeling the refreshing breeze to blow across her body, touching her skin that had not been touched by the unforgiving Florida sun. She drifts off and falls asleep. Immediately she began to dream of what it was going to be like when she finally became Mrs. Rabbit Roberts. She is suddenly awakened by a different sound of rustling in the leaves behind her. She jumps up and surveys her surrounding and does not see anything but the small birds still frolicking; which was a good indication there was no danger. Reluctantly she relaxes again taking solace of this place. Picking up her boots she indolently walks back toward the house when she caught the whiff of a sweet scent of wild buttercup. Attentively she looks for the yellow flowers growing on a vine when finally she spotted a blanket of yellow reaching to the top of several trees along the trail. She runs to the flowers, grabbing a handful of flowers taking a deep breath allowing the aroma to fill her senses with the beautiful fragrance emanating from the small yellow flowers. She watches and is entertained by the busy bee as they bound from flower to flower. Life to her could not get any better when out of the corner of her eye she sees a huge black bear standing in the middle of the sandy lane strangely it was looking in the opposite direction. Panic and fear gripped her heart she had never experienced these feeling before causing her fear to intensify. Should she scream? Should she turn and run? She had no idea of what to do when things got a lot worse. The bear stands on his back feet still looking in the other direction when he all of a sudden dropped down on all fours turning in her direction and started running right at her. Now she cannot run nor can she scream, all she can do is drop under the weight of her now heavy legs; which now feel like a thousand pounds and she collapses. Aware of the possibilities and what could happen but unsure of the outcome she lays still. The large bear ran right past her as if she was not even there, overcome by the musky smell she almost throws-up. Not wanting to move and draw attention to her if he had stopped close to her, she lies still. The next noise she hears is the sound of horse hooves and the concerned voice of Rabbit. She jumps up looking in the direction the bear had run, hiding behind Rabbit when he began to laugh uncontrollably. This infuriated Sarah because to her this was serious and her first reaction was to slap his face; which she did and Rabbit's response was astonishment. Realizing what she had done she covers her mouth and her eyes were wide open. Her expression started Rabbit laughing again that was joined by the other riders who had caused the bear to run over her in the first place. They refocused when Little Crete come bouncing up to them causing his horse to slide to a stop in front of Rabbit and yells, "come on Uncle Gator's put the dogs on the bear and he's leave'en the country."

While on the scrub two riders joined up with Rabbit, Gator and Little Crete by the name of Crow Shivers {son-in-law of Henry Tanner}; which was the man who is said to have killed Ben Reynolds and Newton Tanner {actual brother of Henry Tanner}. They were out hunting. Rabbit swung up into the saddle, reached out his hand to Sarah allowing her to swing up behind him when Crow said, "looks like ya caught yer she bear". Everyone but Sarah laughed at the comment and her only reaction was to flush with anger. Rabbit turned and headed for the house so he could drop Sarah off and join the hunt. The Captain had come for a visit with Sarah for the afternoon and became worried when he could not find her. He was relieved when he saw her sitting behind Rabbit. Out of respect for her father he dismounted and helped Sarah to the ground. Before he could turn to greet her father Sarah pulled him to her and gives him a long kiss. Unaware of what had just happened her father cleared his throat believing their actions inappropriate in front of these strangers. Rabbit pushes back as Sarah smiles at her father and he introduces himself to the two older men. They excused themselves and turned and gallop toward the sound of the running dogs. Rabbit removed his hat, apologies to Captain Drawdy and in the same breath awkwardly asked him if he could marry his daughter. He turns to his daughter who was wearing the broadest smile he had ever seen, reminding him of his wife. He knew she loved him and now the trouble seemed to be over he agreed and invited everyone to his place that night to celebrate.

Rabbit jumped into the saddle and wheeled his horse in the direction of the sound of the dogs in hot pursuit of the bear that had threatened his soon to be wife. The direction the bear was taking confused Rabbit because the bear was running toward Lake Hart. It was thick with grapevines and myrtles. At times he had to circle wide to the west onto the high sandy hill covered with acres of broom sage and tail Johnson grass. Any chance he could he would turn toward the lake hoping to cut off the bears escape, but the myrtles and willows were so dense his horse who had never backed down from a challenge fought against his control wanting to find an easier way. Turning again toward the sandy ridge the bear had done the very thing he thought it would do, he circled back and was heading for Bear Island and the towering oaks and pines. The bear was almost a half mile ahead of the lead dog. Rabbit put the spurs to his horse and as he was running as hard as he could, loosened his whip. His plan was two-fold. First he hoped his brother had stopped to listen for the dogs and the direction they were heading. He hoped then he would hear his whip. Second, he wanted to try to heat up the bears butt by popping him with the whip. Well, things didn't go like he had planned and as soon as the whip hit its mark the bear stopped, wheeled and stood on all fours challenging his pursuer. When he stood up he could stare Rabbit right in the eyes almost catching him with its first swat. In the mayhem Rabbit dropped the reins as he grabbed for his gun. The horse wheeled suddenly freeing Rabbit from his seat and he hit the ground. Luckily the bear was still too concerned with the pursuing dogs to pay Rabbit any attention. Right then Gator's best bear dog leaped over Rabbit and took a secure hold on the nap of the bear's neck. The bear screamed trying hard to rid himself of his adversary when the next one hit him hard from the other side. Unfortunately that dog was not as fast and able to escape. The bear reached out with its front two paws taking hold of the smaller dog and with his massive jaws clamped down on the throat killing him instantly. In the midst of the ruckus Rabbit had time to right himself and catch his horse that wanted real bad to get away from this threat. Covered by a layer of sand that had stuck to him due to the sweat pouring from his body soaking his shirt he was able to reach for his gun but before he could get a good bead the monster freed himself from the first dog and disappeared into the thicket.

Rabbit climbed onto the saddle. His arm that had been wounded in the shooting several months before hurt him and he realized he had no more strength on that side. By the time he was settled in the saddle the other had joined him and in thunderous chase they were off again. The bear was being pushed hard by the dogs and were heading straight back to Bear Island. Because Rabbit had come from that direction he led the other back across the open broom sage flats and quickly closed the gab the bear had established. The bear crossed the creek tearing down the small brush before him leaving a well-defined path for them to follow, over and around the tussock's floating I the shallow water. It looked as if he was going to run straight across the island. He made a wide circle then heading right back in their direction. The dogs changed their barking from a running bark to a steady baying, meaning they had finally treed the bear. The dogs were in a mad frenzy trying hard to climb the live oak the bear had picked for the battle that soon would ensue. The bear nestled comfortably in the fork and watched the dogs tear at the base of the tree and every once in a while he would almost seem to yawn adding a loud hiss to aggravate the dogs. Daub cut a long sapling and talked Gator in climbing to the lowest limb and he begins to punch at the bear's bottom. He ignored the dogs not feeling a bit threatened and focused all his fury on Gator. Rabbit swears he smiled as he lunged from his roost to the limb just above Gator's head. It growled and he could feel it's hot breath giving Gator little chose but to drop the prodding stick; which caused the dogs to run for cover but as soon as they saw things were clear they were right back focused on the bear that had now moved within just feet from Gator. Everyone on the ground was starting to get worried as no amount of aggravation could deter the bear from its present mission and that was to execute as much harm to Gator as he could. Gator had other plans as he let go of the only thing that kept him from falling and allowed gravity to take control. He landed right in the midst of a pack of dogs that had worked themselves into tumult. All but one dog scattered at Gator's harsh words knowing that he would never tolerate any dog that did not mind. The only one left baying the old bear was a half blind jip. The only reason she was allowed to live was she always produced pretty and healthy puppies. To everyone's amusement they learned that day undoubtedly she going deaf too because she never heard the loud thud of Gator hit the ground from falling out of the tree yet stood there loudly barking right in his ear. When Gator reached out to slap her on the nose it scared her so bad she run right over him hollering as she passed, all along thinking the bear had a hold of her. Everyone laughed but Gator when he took the old shotgun from Little Crete's, cooked both barrels, aimed and fired. The explosion of the old shotgun rung throughout the trees on the island as it echoed to silence. The bear just fell forward wedging its self between two large limbs. This further infuriated Gator and he stomped off cussing the bear with every breath. Daubs laughed out loud, he suggested Gator climb back into the tree and roll him out. His proposition was met with a look of confusion; which promptly changes to irritation. He turns toward his spooked horse taking hold of the lose reins. Replaced the gun in its sheath climbs into the saddle and barks an order to Little Crete causing the boy to jump straight into the saddle. Daub knew better but could not help when he let an echoing laughter. Gators reaction was to bust through the thick patch of palmettos closely followed by the boy.

Daub was glad Gator did not want the old stinking bear because Daub planned to skin it and cure it for Sarah's wedding present. He struggled to climb the large tree using the pole Gator had dropped and pried him loose. He skinned the bear right where he fell leaving the bloody meat for the buzzards and privately hid the skin in the barn. He would spend most of his time working and tanning the hid because he did not know when the marriage would occur.

Chapter 37

The morning dawned as any other for Rabbit even though he experienced a flood of nervousness he had felt only a few times before. He dealt with anxiety by staying busy. He walked to the barn and fed the horses. Noticing that one of the young mares was favoring her back foot. Opening the gate and making sure it was latched back he entered the pen. Softly he spoke to her as she timidly stepped forward. Reaching out he hooked the lead to the halter and led her to the gate post. After tying the horse Rabbit placed his hand on her neck walking down her side sliding his hand. Standing right next to the flank of the horse he reaches down taking hold of the foot just above the hoof. She yielded and relaxed leaning her weight toward Rabbit waiting patiently as her searched for the source of her pain. Setting the foot down he hurried to the tack room retrieved a curved knife and cleaned out the packed manure from each hoof. He must have hit a tender spot because she turned her head nudging Rabbit in the back as protest. He returned the knife to its place pulled the watch from his pocket and was astonished that cleaning the hoofs only took a few minutes.

For Sarah it was the most beautiful morning she has ever seen. Today her dreams will come true. She will marry the love of her life. She sits on one of the chairs Uncle Mose had built her for a wedding present. She stares into the mirror her father had hauled by wagon from Orlando giving her some of the comforts she was use while living at Fort Meade. To her everything was perfect and she begins to cry she wishes Mollie could have lived long enough to see this day. She never wept for her mother because she never knew her. Sure she thinks it would be nice to have her mother there on the day she is to wed. But her mother was foreign to her as if an Indian mother would walk in and try to assume that role. Now Mollie was different. She remembers the first time they met and instantly created a friendship and bond that not even death could break. Her only wish was that Mollie could have seen her dress and could have been her maid of honor. There was a gentle knock at the door. As she leaned placing her ear to the door she asked who it was. The voice on the other side was Rabbit's. He told her he understood he could not see her but he just needed to hear her voice. Throwing caution to the wind she swings open the door grabs Rabbit by the shoulders literally dragging him inside his room. They stand holding each other in each other's arms. A passionate kiss that affected Rabbit in a way he had never known. With that she pushes him away from her satisfying embrace then whispers in his ear, "tonight". She smiles bounces to the door and told him he must leave and not get caught. As the door opened there standing was Sarah's aunt that had just arrived. Sarah liked this aunt because she was not prim and proper as the other two. Giving Rabbit a soothing smile followed by a shake of her finger. Jokingly she follow Rabbit to the front door and her purpose was to answer any question that would rise about the reason for him being back next to Sarah's room.

He steps onto the front porch and watches the low clouds moving fast from west to east. Only allowing the sun to occasionally shine through revealing the perfect day Sarah had always dreamed of. In the front yard of Rabbit's house, he and the other men had dug a pit. Filled the pit with seasoned oak wood that now burned gray-amber coals sizzling as the meat cooked slowly. Smoke hovered just below the canopy for just a few minutes before the wind drove it into the scrub. The smell of cooking beef and pork filled the clearing causing the men to continually draw their pocket knife from the pocket and sample the near finished meat. The Tanner's commented on how they could smell the cooking beef way before they arrived. The preacher paced nervously from pot to pit commenting he hoped the preacher was not long winded today because the food sure smelt good. The first two or three times his comment was funny but when you had heard it all day be began to aggravate even easy going Mose. Who finally had to tell the preacher to find somewhere else to go.

Daub and several other men stood over the pit, turning the meat so it would cook equal on all sides. Gator and Little Crete busied themselves with the preparation of the swamp cabbage cut the day before. The small ax slide across the stock of the cut cabbage and the boots removed to reveal the heart that was cut into a large cast-iron wash pot. A white steam rose from the pot as you heard beacon and wild onion sizzling, seasoned by salt and a small amount of sugar. Taking a large wooden spoon Gator stirred the contents of the pot. When the beacon had cooked through Gator would add the cut cabbage and bring the concoction to a hard boil and then the fire would be removed allowing the tender cabbage to cook gradually. All the ladies gathered at the Drawdy home to help Sarah dress for the ceremony. Ole Mose said it sounded too much like a hen house for him to stay around so he picked up his fiddle and hurried to the barn to tune it up for the dancing later.

The longer the day went the more anxious Rabbit grew. His edginess began to irritate Gator and he threatened to take Rabbit down to the creek and cool him off. Rabbit was about to respond to Gator's threat when their attention was directed to the rattling of a motor vehicle as it entered the clearing. Henry Tanner said, "boys, stop your playen companies here we don't want them to think they come to a funny farm." Reverend R.W. Lawton from Oviedo and the other men were introduced to the rest of Sarah's family. The men joined into the talk around the fire while the ladies followed Captain Drawdy back down the dirt trail to his home. Rabbit felt intimidated by the fancy dress and he was not sure how to act around them. Uncle Joe and Uncle Hubert helped him to relax when they withdrew a pouch of chewing tobacco, took off their jackets and spit brown streams of spit every few minutes.

The preacher chose to stand close to where the cooking was happening. Several of the men stopped taking shots of shine just because he was present Daub didn't care. While all the other men shied away from the shine hid away under some piled wood trying hard to hide it from the preacher, Daub drank defiantly. The preacher lightened the party by commenting how he liked a man that was not afraid to be himself around a preacher. This statement had the reverse effect on Daub and he said if he could not make the preacher mad by drinking wasn't as fun, he just wouldn't drink. The preacher nudged Henry and smiled all the men standing around where the meat was cooking erupted into thundering laughter.

After a few drinks Crow Shiver, Mat Reynolds uncle had married one of Henry Tanner's oldest daughters and Mose Gunn a half breed Indian from west Florida began to tell stories. Mose told one that enthralled everyone and caused the men and young boys present to lose track of time. He served as a scout during the First Seminole Indian War and was ordered to track down this one Indian who kept stealing the fort's chickens. He would wait until just after dark grab a chicken and run like the wind. All you could hear was the chicken cackling then they just disappear. The phantom banshee developed quite a reputation and many fools believed he was a ghost or some kind of witch. He continued by saying he personally got tired of hearing all that foolishness and vowed to catch the thief. The next night just like the nights before they heard the muffled cackle of a hen as the thief ran through the thick underbrush. Ole Mose leaped from the shadows and move toward the last place the chicken was heard. Within just seconds the thief and chicken disappeared, this baffled Ole Mose. Turning back to where he last heard the chicken, than stealth-fully retracted his steps and found a half fallen Bay tree with a small cave like hole under the roots where he thought he heard a chicken. The mosquitoes were so thick you could brush them off your face but he eased a few feet away and squatted in some palmettos and waited. The sun started to rise, there hovers a dense fog making it difficult to see more than a few feet in front of your face. You could hear the dew as it drops from the high limps almost like rain. The first few streaks of sunlight cuts through and fills the hardwood hammock when all of a sudden he could see the image of a small boy slip from the hole, head first. Mose almost gave himself away when he had to keep himself from laughing out loud. The boy had dark round eyes and looked like a screech owl looking out a hole. He got so tickled the boy noticed him and as he ran past the old man took a hold of his long brown hair. As he fell back e chicken was tossed into the air

He looks around, his eyes as big as dinner plates and was convinced he had gotten away scot-free when he disappeared again into the hole when Ole Mose stood up and quietly strolled over and stood over the hole and when the boy stuck his head out I wacked him. We'll, he let out a scream like you aint never heard, I thought he'd never shut up and thought I was going to have to crawl in there with him to shut him up when all of a sudden I got whacked on the head, harder then I had ever felt and was out cold. I finally woke up about noon and learned one thing from that encounter and that was don't think yourself to always be the hunter, cause there's always someone hunting you. The mood was somber until Crow made a comment about he wishes he could a seen Ole Mose trying to wiggle his big butt into that small hole and everyone just thundered with laughter. A few more stories were told when they started focusing on Rabbit and his wedding night when the hour finally come when the preacher with his booming voice called for all to gather. The preacher turned to Rabbit and whispered something in his ear that made him blush and he turned to the crowd of men as they begin to leave in a single file line and smiled a wide grin he raised his arms over his head motioning for all to draw close. Rabbit is the first to see Sarah as she entered the clearing. To Rabbit it seemed as if the clouds were rolled back and the sun shone brighter than he had ever seen. Her hair was down and flowed down and across her shoulders. The dress she wore was an off white and button up covering her neck. It cascaded in layers from her shoulder down almost hitting the ground revealing for bare-feet; which garnered a devilish smile from Rabbit. The small beads glistened and sent shimmers of reflected light off of them taking the breath from all who looked at her. In her hair she had a single yellow honey suckle and in her hand she holds a large magnolia flower big as a dinner plate. The Lanier family had come for the day and brought their music instruments. One of the boys began to play a soft tune on the fiddle and the rest for Rabbit was a blur. He could not take his eyes off of Sarah when he was brought back to reality when the preacher had to repeat for the second time, "You may kiss your bride". The fiddle played and the gathering of about twenty people erupted in applause and over the roar of the crowd you could hear Daub said, "Now the party begins".

Chapter 38

Two weeks after the wedding Gator rode up in front of the house and called for Rabbit. A familiar anxiety came over Rabbit because he recognized a certain tone in Gator's voice. Everyone but Rabbit accompanied Mat to Fort Christmas. Their purpose was to drive back the one hundred cows he had just bought back to the scrub close to the old place. While crossing the big scrub three strangers took pop shots at them. This cowardice act irritated Gator but he would not go after them as long as Little Crete was with him. Gator was not going to allow any harm to come to the boy. He tried hard to persuade his uncle he would be able to take care of himself, to which his uncle replied. "When you can pee without squatting, then you can decide for yourself". The boy knew better than to argue.

Rabbit gave Sarah a three year old mare. She cherished the animal and refused to allow anyone to tend to her horse but herself. The afternoon she received the gift her and Rabbit rode to the creek crossing and after a bit of persuasion the horse finally lunged forward jumping half the creek at one time. Her and Rabbit made a wide circle on the scrub. Sarah loved the woods as much as anyone. The flowers blooming and the birds singing and the gentle breeze made for the perfect day. Lost in the beauty when the first flash of lightening shot across the sky and Sarah insisted they head home at the first flash of lightening.

Sarah mounted her horse and followed Rabbit to Captain Drawdy's place where he kissed her and assured her he would be back in a few days. He then turned to Little Crete and made him promise he would go back to the house every morning and just before dark, milk the cow and water the garden.

Gator, Rabbit, Ole Mose and Crow headed across the small creek and into the deep fern beds bordering Lake Hart. This had always been the quickest way the Tanner's on the big creek. Their plan was to gather a few more men and together they would take care of this problem. This trip will not be filled with sight-seeing of casual conversation. This was a serious situation and this type of spineless action must be met with swift justice. It was just about dark when the four riders made it to the Tanner's. Gator told his story. Henry suggested they wait until first light and than they would have the advantage of knowing the land. There seemed to be a since of gravity to the nights meal and their sleep was un-restful. All Rabbit could think about was what if these men get away from them and find Sarah and do horrible things to her and just the thought stirred old emotions that frightened Rabbit.

After breakfast the next morning while a few of the men saddled their horses a rider came into the clearing at a rapid pace and very excited. Henry recognized the rider and assured Gator and the other men he was friendly. Henry introduced him as Will Evert McGrit and shared with Gator that the young man was a close neighbor. Before Will could dismount he begun telling of how three strangers bushwhacked and fire several shots at him. He went on to request their help in tracking them down and dealing with them when Gator spoke up and extended his hand out introducing himself. Informing him that is the reason they are saddling their horses and invited him to ride with them. He said it would b helpful if he could show them where they shooting took place.

Will lead them right to the spot where the shooting took place. Sure enough right there on the ground were eight spent cartridges and confusingly sign of two men. Will tried hard to convince them that the other set of foot prints were those of a friend that lived out in the scrub somewhere but some would not listen. Rabbit followed the bare foot prints of who Will called the ghost. Gator followed by Crow Shivers headed in the direction Will pointed saying the shots came from. It did not take Rabbit long to return and confirm Will's story because just inside the creek swamp all sign of the so-called ghost just vanished. About the same time Rabbit arrived Gator rode up and told those waiting they had located the corpse of a man who had been shot in the gut. Turning in his saddle he motioned not too far from where they were Crow saw the smoke of a camp fire. With this information everyone turned and rode hard in the direction of the camp but before they were able to identify themselves Crow and Gator rode in and shot them in cold blood. This action surprised even Rabbit. He questioned why he did what he did without first finding out what was happening. The actions of Gator Roberts sickened and angered Henry Tanner. In stunned disbelief he spoke in a unchangeable tone stating he did not want to have anything to do with such cold men that could kill without reason but this killing he believed was not justified until they had proof.

The words Henry Tanner spoke cut like a knife into the stomach of Gator. He felt remorse and tried to explain to Henry but his words feel on deaf ears. He then turned to Rabbit looking for some understanding but his stare was met with bewilderment. Rabbit found he had no words but a lot of questions.

With that Gator, Crow, Ole Mose rode off in a westward direction. Rabbit could hear Mose in a barely audible voice ask, "What's wrong with Rabbit? We just fixed a problem, now no one has to worry anymore." Gator left never saying another word.

Rabbit stayed behind and helped to bury the three men they had witnessed killed in a way not all agreed with. Assuring Henry Tanner he would find out why Gator did what he did and let him know his answer, to that Henry just replied, "Gator's, just a killer. He'll be nothing else but a killer. It would be best if he not come to my place again. Do you understand what I am saying, Rabbit?"

With this Rabbit dropped his head in shame then removed his hat wiping his brow with his sleeve. As they returned to where the horses were tied and they spoke about the upcoming spring cow hunt. Henry guaranteed him the events of the day has not changed his intent of participating in the hunt but he had better speak to Gator before and assure him that type of action will not be tolerated in his camp. With that he wheeled his horse. Leaving the area as fast as he could; followed close behind by Will Magrit and the others men who had come. The place where the men were killed was named from that time forward, "Dead Men's Branch"

Rabbit spurred his horse and maintained a steady gallop until he finally caught up with Gator and the others. Rabbit tried to lighten the mood by telling Gator of plans for the spring cattle hunt. He told him they would camp the first few days at Cow Pen Branch driving whatever cows gathered to the pens. He continued by saying, Sarah and the other women will set up camp when Rabbit realized that Gator was not listening pre-occupied deep in thought. So Rabbit questioned him hard to as why he did what he did. Finally Gator pulled hard back on the reins turning to him and all he could do was to stare. Frustrated Rabbit turned his attention from Gator and rode in silence the rest of the way home. Sarah noticed the subdued demeanor of the men when they entered the clearing. She tried to change the mood of the men by challenging Rabbit or Gator to a race down the trail and back but neither even responded, simply walking in opposite directions. Rabbit sat on the edge of the porch just staring out into nothing when Sarah sat next to him placing her hand on his leg. Rabbit jumped finally his eyes cleared and Sarah could tell he was his old self. Gently she asked what happened out while you were out there. Rabbit's answer was simply, "I think I have lost Gator."

The night before Rabbit and Gator were to ride out and met the other hunters at Cow Pen Branch they busied themselves with preparation. Gator had not said two words in the past few weeks and Rabbit figure like always he will get over his anger and soon they would talk again. In the same barn within just feet of each other the wagon was filled with two dutch ovens, a barrel for water that would be drawn from the creek, and enough supplies for the two week trip. Sarah packed a moss filled mattress and quilts so she and Rabbit would stay warm in the early morning dampness. Little Crete was excited and keep asking when they would finally leave. Sarah asked if he got what she told him to pack and her question was met by a confused look. She listed the items again and smiled as he jumped from his horse almost spooking the ox team and disappear into the house. He returned just as fast as he tossed a small package in the back of the wagon scurrying back atop the horse.

Gator was responsible for his own sleeping gear. Rabbit noticed Gator packing everything he owned and wondered what was going on when he walked up to Gator and asked if everything was ok. Gator smiled for the first time in a long time and assured him he was just preparing for any rain they might get while being out on the scrub. While they rode toward Cow Pen Branch Gator talked as if his tongue had just been freed from prison. To Rabbit this was a welcomed relief and they spoke of their childhood. Little Crete listened and hung on every word his Uncle Gator said. Finally Rabbit felt if life was returning to their hectic world.

The last of the calves were being released. The lowing of the gathered cattle fades in the distance. Everyone seemed satisfied with another successful year and the fine calves they would have to sell in the fall. They all agreed on a date for the fall hunt and promised to keep a sharpe eye out for each other's cows. They spoke of the chuffers needing planting and the hogs that need working. No one noticed when Gator dismissed himself from the conversation. He rides up to where Sarah was packing up for the trip home dismounted. He walked up to her and said good-bye. She straightens up and looks at him perplexed, wondering why he would say such a thing knowing he still lives in the extra room with Little Crete. He turned and rode away. He then found Little Crete, dismounted taking the boy in his arms he hugged him. Little Crete stood baffled and it shown all over his face. Gator at last spoke telling him he had to leave for a while but he would be back soon. He made him promise to listen to his Uncle Rabbit and keep learning all he can. Because one day he will have to make it on his own and he needed what knowledge Rabbit could impart. The boy started crying and this embarrassed him. He turned and walked to Sarah who had left her work because she had watched Gator's conversation with Little Crete and realized what was going on. Rabbit was still taking with Henry Tanner when Gator approached them leading his horse and hat in hand. He extended his hand first to Henry and apologies to him for his action back on the scrub several weeks before. Rabbit and Henry could tell that he was sincere about his remorse and knew that nothing else needed to be said. Gator then turned to Rabbit grabbed him and hugged him hard squeezing him tight. As abruptly as he grabbed him he pushed him away from him. Rabbit was a little shocked by his actions until Gator spoke again. He choked up while he told Rabbit he was leaving taking Ole Mose back to Bartow because he was tried and wanted to go home. He made jokes about it, saying, he was getting a little forgetful, than he was heading south to see about purchasing more cows. He did not know when he would be back. Rabbit tried hard to talk him out of having to leave but Gator would not listen. He helped Ole Mose climb up into the wagon driven by Crow. Crows wife, Henry's oldest daughter had died in child birth and feeling out of place Crow decided it would be best if he left as well. Gator mounted his horse and rode away.

Chapter 39

The ride back to the hammock was a solemn one. Rabbit rode aimlessly trying to understand why Gator thought it needful to leave so abruptly. He really did not care about what others thought because they were not an everyday part of their lives. On several occasions Sarah had to holler just to keep him from riding right into a tree.

Without speaking to Sarah Rabbit decided to sell the old place. He would sell all but the house and the plot of land the graves were situated on. Their total property equaled five acres. Captain Drawdy was glad to pay what Rabbit asked; which increased his land holds to four hundred areas. Rabbit had talked to Emmett Tanner and was told of two hundred acres not far from him new place for sale. If he had cash he could purchase the entire piece for twenty five cent an acres.

Rabbit could not stay there any longer because of all the memories. Sarah finally agreed on one condition, once we get to where they will move they will not move again. She was ready to start a family and she knew it would be difficult if Rabbit could not find some peace. Searching the entire piece of property Rabbit fell in love with a large live oak hammock. He liked the location because it backed up to Joshua's Branch. With the money left from the sale of the property in Gridersville he had lumber brought to Lake Cane landing. He along with the help of several families around the Fort Christmas settlement hauled the lumber from the St. John's River. The hammock buzzed with the sound of saws and hammers. With each day the cracker style house began to take shape. It took all of three weeks when Sarah was finally able to move out of the lean-to into the new house. The house looked just like the house her and Rabbit lived in when they first got married. With pride she stood at the wood burning stove and cooked their first meal in the new house. Setting the table with her finest china it glimmered as the lamp light faintly shone in the eating area of the kitchen. She was very excited because she had an announcement to make.

They sat together as Rabbit swelled with pride because this was the first time in his life he had built something and provided for his family by his own hands. Finally he was the provider just as his father once provided for his family. He now knows how his father felt.

Rabbit pushes his plate forward to the middle of the table indicating he was finished. He started to get up when Sarah spoke. "Rabbit, I am going to have a baby." The news not only shocked him but it took Little Crete and Sadie by surprise. Rabbit looked confused as he stared at Sarah not saying a word. Sarah broke the silence and said, "Well, did you hear what I said?" Rabbit was shaken back to reality, stood up and embraced Sarah gently not wanting to hurt her. He told her to sit down and take it easy when she informed him that she was don't dying she was just having a baby." She continued, "I am not going to break and I know when I cannot do something, so don't treat me like I am fragile."

Six months past and the time for the baby to come finally arrived. Rabbit sent Little Crete to the Tanner's to fetch Aunt Dovie to come and help with the birth. An hour later the sound of a rattling wagon invaded the clearing. Uncle Isaac stood in the front of the wagon urging the oxen to hurry along. Right behind him sitting in the back of the wagon Aunt Dovie fumbled with the contents of a black satchel. As the wagon rolled to a stop Aunt Dovie eased to the back of the wagon waiting for help down. Rabbit was the first to get to her in a panic. Aunt Dovie dismissed his alarm simply asking where his wife was. Never stopping for his direction she marched right uo the steps opening the door. Once inside she needed no one to tell her where Sarah was. She could hear her heavy breathing. Aunt Dovie sent Rabbit away knowing she did not need his help. Uncle Isaac busied himself with hauling water and brought in the supplies they had carried for the birth. Two hours later Rabbit heard the first cries of the new born baby boy. Aunt Dovie finally allowed Rabbit in to see both mother and child; which they had named Samuel Oscar Roberts. Horror flooded him when he first saw how pale Sarah was but drew strength from her comforting smile. She pealed back the small quilt revealing a pointed head red baby. He questioned if he was ok because he looked strange. Aunt Dovie told him if your head was pushed through a knot in a board he would look funny too. Rabbit reached over and kissed Sarah knowing now he loved her even more.

Just before supper that night when she believed Sarah was strong enough Aunt Dovie allowed Little Crete and Sadie in to see the baby. Instantly Sadie fell in love with the baby and from that moment on she became his surrogate mother and a big help to Sarah as she adjusted to being a new mother. She called for Rabbit and asked if he could go and give the news to her father to which he agreed and he and Little Crete would leave at first light.

Sarah wakes at the movement of her husband as he sits up in bed pulling on his cotton socks. He turns and smiles at her hearing the familiar sound of the open springs as they squeak underneath her in the frame of the rod iron bed. She rolls to her side as she watched him make his way toward the door. She smiles as she remembers the first time she shared this bed with him and whispers a simple prayer of thanksgiving. Rolling again then gently touches his pillow. Continuing to smile she watches him remove his sleeping shirt, hanging it on the twin hooks on the back of the door. Closing her eyes she counts every step he takes as he makes his way across the wooden floor; anticipating the next creak she welcomes as an old friend. Opening her eyes she strains to catch a final glimpse of him pulling on his breeches in the darkness. Following him with her eyes now adjusted to the dimly lit room as he yanks on the top left draw were she had so lovingly placed his shirts the day before. She had washed them by hand then hung them in the spring warmth remembering how they sway in the breeze. He swings open the door and disappears into the darkness. The next sound she hears is him opening the door just down the hall, with his stern but doting voice says, "Wake up Crete. It's time to get up".

She rolls over, taking hold to the corner of the sturdy bed hoisting her hefty frame to the sitting position. What she used to do with no effort now takes her breath. She slips from the high bed putting her feet down on the gritty floor only reminding her she needs to sweep. Finding her house shoes she works her toes in, stands and shuffles in the darkness into the kitchen carrying her pee pot. The first sight she sees is her husband bent over stoking the fire in the wood burning stove. In the flicker of the fire she admires his large frame. They pass without saying a word as she makes her way to the white outhouse specially constructed for her alone. She closes the door knowing this was her exclusive place, no one can bother her here and she can begin her day as she had for years and that was quiet and praying. Sarah shivers when she sees a spider scurry from one corner to the other disappearing into her web. Quickly she pulls her pants up and adjust her nightgown taking one last look in the direction the spider had vanished vowing to have one of her kids come a kill the spider.

When she returns to her world her day started by filling the kettle with water. Scooping in two large scoops of coffee into the kettle than straining to hoist it and place it on the open flame beginning the long wait for it to boil. She tugs on the cast iron frying pan freeing it from the pie safe. Dipping a glob of lard from the bucket next to the back door she clanked the wooden spoon making an echoing sound to ring through the house. Using her hands she mixes her famous biscuits, rolling, pressing and turning over the flour mixture. Satisfied it had been mixed enough she slide them into the oven. Without having to ask Crete, he had not forgotten his chore first thing of a morning and returned from the smokehouse carrying a side on fresh smoked bacon. She slices the bacon thick because that is the way her family likes. Shuffling across the floor to the pie safe she retrieves a small bucket of eggs and fries several hard piling everything on one plate than setting it in the center of the large table. As always they ate in silence.

The silence was broken when Rabbit final spoke to Crete reminding him of what he expected done before he returned. Acknowledging his uncle with an understanding smile Crete picks up his plate placing it in the boiling water atop the stove and heads for the barn to hook up one of the new large mule his uncle recently purchased when he begun this new venture of farming. Sixty acres were cleared west of the house and he wanted it readied for planting. They would plant watermelons the first year hoping to make enough to recover some of the cost of the mules and seed. The next two years they will plant sweet potatoes. Between planting those cash crops they would plant chuffers and indigo for the cows and hogs. Rabbit followed Crete to the barn giving him final instructions then saddles his horse.

Today he will head to Magnolia Ranch and look over a new bunch of cows he an Emmett Tanner had just purchased. This bunch of cows will increase his herd to four hundred brood cows, fifteen bulls and one hundred steers. Crete watched his uncle climb into the saddle, secretly longing to ride go with him but resigned to the task at hand.

He leads the huge mule from its pen after putting the bridle into his mouth. Tying him to a leaning post in the front he carries an old wooden bucket so he can reach the neck of this large animal. Hoisting up the leather collar than placing it around the mule's neck and buckling it securely at the top making sure it did not slide. Next he lifted the hames make sure that it sets evenly in the groove than buckling it as well. Taking the trace-chains down from the nail he and his Rabbit had placed for their storage. The small double hooks fit into the slots on the hames and the steal circles hung on the tips. With each step Jake got lost in the rhythmic clanking of the trace-chains. His aunt was standing on the front porch as he past, called for him and handed him a jar of cool water instruction him to find a shaded place so the hot sun will not warm it as fast.

Opening the gate he laid down the wire gap leading the mule through. Walking down the side of the fence he looked for fresh sign of deer or hog entering the field. Finding two good trails and making a mental note of their location. He hopes he will get a chance to tell his father and get permission to come and sit here just before dark and kill fresh meat for the table.

The plow still stood right where he had left it the afternoon before. Maneuvering the mule into position and giving a gentle tug on the long reins the mule backed into place. Taking the trace chain from its resting place and connecting it to the single tree then doing the same on the other side he was ready to begin. Pushing down on the handles of the plow he spoke to the mule prompting him to step forward. Without any strain or effort the big mule pulled the bottom plow down the long row to the other end. He laid the plow over on the right side hollered "gee" and the mule turned quickly facing the opposite direction. It was the same all morning. The sun now high in the sky he takes the last of his water and savors every last drop.

As he makes another turn he sees his Sarah as she enters the fence. She waits patiently peering from underneath her large bonnet. Standing next to her he sees his younger cousin, Sam just as he darts out into the freshly plowed field when all of a sudden he hears him scream. His mother takes a few steps out into the field when she reaches out and takes a hold of the boy stanching him backwards, back toward the gate. She turns to Crete, motioning for him to come and by the way she was acting it was an emergency. He pulls back on the reins secures them to the handles of the plow and runs toward the commotion. Seeing the threat long before he gets to where his mother is and turns toward the fence and breaks off a branch. Telling them to back away, Crete, races pass them and with a solid swing over his head brought it crashing down upon the head of a large rattlesnake. Stunned and leaving instruction for his aunt to watch close to where it goes if it moves before he gets back then runs toward the side of the house where he had left his hoe the afternoon before. Returning he was able to cut the snakes head off. Still shaken she tells him to tie the mule in the shade and wash up for dinner. Before she turns to leave in a threatening way she warned him to not bring that snake to the house. He respectfully replies and turns heading back to where he left the mule, Sam right behind him. He kept asking if he could ride the mule. Crete unsure if the mule would tolerate the extra weight and not wanting to get into trouble if he fell off and got hurt, Crete told him no.

As they walked toward the gate they found another rattlesnake not as big as the other but still over five feet long. Crete pulled his pocketknife from his pocket and cut the two rattles each having nineteen and a button. Crete handed one of the rattles to Sam reminding him not to shake it next to his eyes. He began to brag about finding and killing two big rattle snakes and how he could not wait until his father returned so he could tell him of it. Crete knew better that to disagree and simply turned and headed to the open well next to the house. The well was able three feet wide, standing about two foot above the ground and about twenty feet deep. They used a long sweep to dip down into the water drawing up only about two and a half gallons at a time.

Just as they sat to eat they heard the rattling of Rabbit's spurs as he steps down from his horse. Sam jumps from the table ignoring the call from his mother to return pushes open the door allowing it to slam. Rabbit had not fully stepped down from the horse when Sam jumped at him throwing the rattles Crete had given him into his father's lap.

Crete looks at his aunt in disbelief because if he had done as Sam he would have gotten a whipping. She just shook her head as she sets another plate. As the door opened Sam was still telling how he alone had killed the rattlesnakes without the help of anyone. Crete stared in wonder as to why his aunt would not correct him as he tells these lies. Realizing that to correct his story would be met with harsh words from either his aunt or uncle so he just finished eating his meal. When he finished his meal he placed his plate in the sink returned to the well refilled his water bottle and headed back to the field. He was so aggravated by the action of Sam he did not stay to hear what his uncle had to say about the new cows.

He had made two rounds up and down the field when Rabbit rode up to him telling him that he needed to put the mule up and saddle his horse. They were going to spend the rest of the day looking at the cows behind the house. Crete smiled a wide smile and hurries toward the barn. In the trough Rabbit had put corn and filled the bucket with fresh water. Crete was thankful for the help he received because he wanted nothing to delay his time in the saddle riding next to his uncle.

Rabbit told him they would be ridding the fence right in front of the house because it runs all the way to the St. Johns River Marsh. The first place they came to was a place called Scrub Ford. It had not rain in several weeks but the ground here was still boggy. Crete noticed sign of two riders who had just passed by and made a comment of his discover when Rabbit turned to him. Complimented him on his observation and telling him he was proud of him. He told him they were going to meet some friends at Horse Hammock then they would continue on to cross the river opposite of Persimmon Hammock. They were going to gather what cows belonged to them and drive them back across the river to the old goat house. Crete was apprehensive about swimming the river but would not share his feelings with his uncle. He did not want to be seen as a weakling. As they circled a large myrtle passing through belly deep broom-sage he could see the opening into the hammock. Just as they entered they could hear the faint dull sound of an ax as it chopped into the cedar tree. Haflie and Olly were repairing a hog trap that had been destroyed by a rather large hog. Rabbit had been seeing the sign of this hog for weeks and there were plans being made to bring the dog and see if they could jump him and catch him. After they were satisfied the hog trap would hold the trap was baited and set and they rode away.

Once on the other side of the river Crete and Olly turned south and begun looking for any sign of cows. The others would head north and after making a wide circle they would all meet at the flag pond on the big prairie. The sun was beginning to set as the last of the cows reached the other side of the river when Crete was instructed to continue with the others and in the morning he could leave for home. As Rabbit turned to leave he looked right at Crete and told him he was proud of him for all he did today especially for killing the two rattlesnakes. This warmed him and he was glad someone recognized what he did.

Chapter 40

Crete was only seventeen years old but could do the work of a full grown man. His greatest pleasure was spending time atop a horse working cows. His short arms made it difficult for him to swing the long braided cow whip so one day his uncle cut one of his old whips down for him. He practiced whenever he got the chance and got so good he could hit a grasshopper before it could jump. He used it sparingly on the cows because he did not want to be accused of causing the cattle to break and run.

The next morning he was awake before daylight. They ate what little they had from the day before when Haflie told him he needed to head home. He entered the swamp riding an old trail to Bee Tree Log when he happened to see a tanned form pass before him near a bonnet pond. He thought at first it was a deer and pulling his twenty-two. He saw it again out of the corner of his eye just before it disappeared into a palmetto patch. His horse sensed the animal long before he did and began to side step. Crete figured it would be best not to stay here much longer. He gently nudged his horse not too fast because he did not want to give the panther anything to chase skirting the pond to the north. He still looked behind him only to assure his self he was not being followed. The trail led out into a big scrub when he finally relaxed. As he rode along thinking of how proud his uncle would have been of him if only he could have killed the panther. His attention was drawn by the circling buzzards ahead of him. Cautiously he rides in that direction and finds a dead cow. He thought to himself she must have die giving birth or something but he could not find a calf. Getting off his horse he was able to get close enough to see she belonged to his uncle. Just as he started to leave to report this to his father he heard the faint bellow of a small calf. Lying not far from her dead mother was a small white faced brindled heifer calf looking up from behind a small clump of wire grass. Quickly he dismounted again gathered the small frail calf in his arms lifting it on to the front of the saddle doing as his uncle had done many times. The crossing of Buncombe Branch was difficult but he managed to cross without losing his grip on either horse or calf.

The dogs announced his coming long before he actually entered the clearing. Stopping in front of the house he noticed Rabbit's horse saddled along with the mule. Disappointed he could not go again with his uncle but resigned to his responsibilities, he called out. Just then the screen door swung open and shut with a boom. Out shot Sam; which caused the three animals to become spooked and side step, throwing their heads in reaction to the slamming of the door. "You're in trouble, Crete. You're in trouble, Crete." He chanted in almost a rhythmic tone not noticing that his uncle had followed him out. With his long boney fingers he thumped the boy on top of the head producing and even louder yelp. Retreating from his uncles' reach he found little solace behind his mother's rather large frame when she took a hold of his ear and gave it a twist and a confused look on Sam's face. Crete dare not laugh out loud but he was extremely pleased that finally his little cousin was punished for his meanness.

"What you got there, Crete?" asked Rabbit as he walked down the wooden steps. He told him the story as he lifted the small calf to the ground. Once there he examined the calf and determined she was in good shape for being a dobby. Just as Crete was about to speak Sam asked if he could have it as his own, when his request was met with a scruff, "no". Rabbit continued by saying, "This is Crete's and it looks like he has a good start to his own herd. Take her back to the pens and we'll see if ole Bet will take another." Crete hoped with all he was the old milk cow would take her so she could grow big and strong. Without much effort Bet took the small calf after smelling her for a bit. When they were sure the cow would take the calf Crete was told to go in and eat some breakfast and afterwards they would ride together. He looked confused as to why the mule was tied out front of the house. As he ate he asked his aunt why the mule was ready to plow when she told him she was going to plow some this morning. He insisted he be allowed to stay and plow so she would not have to be in the hot sun when she told him she would not be out there that long because Uncle Bunyan was coming and he was going to finish the field.

Rabbit and Crete rode together taking a different route. Rabbit never spoke much while riding but today he was very talkative. He began by telling Crete of the time when he was a little boy and of the first time he every sat atop a horse. "I was real nerves. My butt stuck to the saddle. It is not like riding on the saddles they have today. The McClellan saddle did not have a horn causing calluses to form on your butt. I nearly fell of two or three times but my father told me once I got the hang of it I looked like a tick on a dobs back. I knew better than to show any fear or hesitation, sort of like I can see in your eyes when I asked you to do something. I know it is hard for you to live the part of a man being still a boy, but you'll be thankful one day." Crete was somewhat embarrassed that his uncle had noticed his reluctances and vowed that very moment he would not let him down. Then again he was pleased his uncle recognized his contribution to the family. His only wish was if Rabbit would take a firmer grip on his younger cousin Sam. Rabbit continued, "I got you a job that will put a little money in your pocket and help the family out as well. Next Monday I will ride with you to Magnolia Ranch and Friday at noon you can leave. This will allow you to be home about dark." Crete stopped his horse causing his uncle to pull up as well. The stopped facing each other and Crete asked, "What do I do?" "Well your main responsibility will be to provide fresh meat for the cow crew. You'll have to cut a few swamp cabbage so we need to sharpen the ax when we get to the house. Gather wood for the fire and a couple of days a week you will work with the cow crew gathering and working cows. It is hard work but I believe you can handle it" he answered Crete. Rabbit turned toward Horse Hammock and continued without another word.

Their first stop was the hog trap Little John had built in Horse Hammock. There they met him there because he spent the night in which he was famous for. Every time a hog would throw the trap he would cut and mark the boars and reset the trap. John told Rabbit he had cut five nice boar hogs and marked a total of twelve. One of John's calling cards and something Rabbit did not like the fact he always bobbed the tail making it harder to recapture them later. It was a scary thing to have a big hog caught by the dogs and reach behind expecting a tail and there is none. This could cause a man to get real hurt if he does not react fast enough.

They relished the last of the coffee as they waited for the sun to rise above the horizon and for Clearance to arrive. The day was wearing on and they could see the boiling of the storm clouds to the southwest. Clearance rode up wearing his slicker and complaining about the rain he had to ride through just to get there. He told them he thought it was a bad idea to continue doing what they had planned today because he was afraid it was going to rain early. They were sure to get drenched.

Rabbit was serious about getting his cow back across the river before the rainy season hit and flooded the river marsh. If it rained enough down south Big Prairie would flood and stay that way for several months. There was not one cowman in this part of the state that could afford to lose too many cows. Last year he waited and it cost him several good cows. If he could not it would mean he would not see some of his cows for up to a half a year and he did not like that idea.

John dosed the fire and packing his gear. They made a straight line to the large willow ponds that searched for about two mile south along the west side of the St. John's River. They would have to cross through them in order to get to the open marsh and Osteen Island. Carefully in a single file line they made their way through large ferns. Sign of fire still marked the dead cabbage tree stumps, some twenty feet high. In areas the horses would almost disappear into large holes formed by the muck fire several years ago taking a storm like the one they are fixing to experience to finally put it out. Osteen Island had a small cabin and it had just come into view when the first lightening strikes hit, followed by a loud clap of thunder. It echoed of the hammock and willow pond behind them. Crete's horse hopped to one side almost dislodging him from the saddle. The situation was getting direr so the usual jesting was not offered. Each man knew the gravity of the condition of the weather and wanted to get out of the flashes that are now coming one right after the other. Crete could feel the electricity in the air as every hair on the back of his neck stood up. Within just a few minutes the cabin and island before them disappeared. The rain fell in such volume immediately they were all drenched to the bone. Crete could not remember a time when he was as cold as he was right then.

Clearance jumped from his horse untied the rope holding the gate closed and everyone entered the pen. It did not take long for them to unsaddle the horses throwing them in a leathery heap at the entrance of the cabin. Little John spread out his gear and busied his self with getting a fire started. Luckily someone had stocked it with plenty of lightered. In one corner Crete found a stack of corker sacks he used to cover him when he removed his wet clothes. It offered little warmth until the fire filled the cabin with its warmth. It rain steady for the rest of the morning and into the late evening. Just before dark Rabbit saddled his horse and spoke to Little John and Clearance about his growing concern for the cows on the other side of the river. If this keeps up there is only a few places for them cows to get out of the water. If enough of them crowd those small hammocks they will starve. He would ride back to his place and send word to Emmett Tanner and Evert Yates to join with us in driving all of our cows off those islands and back into the scrub where they will have half a chance. Crete had started to get dressed when his uncle told him to stay with the others and he would be back as soon as possible. He reached into his wallet and handed Crete what food he had brought and looked at Little John asking him to keep an eye on the boy. To which they both agreed.

Rabbit had not taken but a few steps from the cabin door when he vanished into the dense growth of the willow pond. It continued to rain all night and at first daylight Crete became concerned because all around them was water. From tree line to tree line was nothing but a solid span of water. Only the tops of the cabbage and cypress trees could be seen. This concerned John because he now knows the seriousness of moving the cows back across the river to higher ground.

Crete had to go relieve himself real bad so he rushed out of the cabin door just as he heard John call out telling him to be careful about snakes. He had not taken but a few steps when there coiled was a large moccasin. All over the ground there were pigmy rattlesnakes, rattlesnakes. Banded water snakes every kind of snake you could imagine. They have come to the high island for refugee from the flood waters. Crete shivered just thinking about the snakes. He tip toed back to the door watching every step he took. He asked John if he could kill some of the snakes when he looked at Clearance and said that is a good idea. He asked. "How do ya figure on killen'em?" Crete did his whip stepped outside and with pin-point accuracy and on the first pop cut the pigmy rattler right in half. John took his whip which was about sixteen foot long and with every pop cut the heads right off the snakes. All together they killed twenty-two snakes of every shape, color and kind.

The sun now shone bright. The water glistened as if it were glass. The silence was broken by the sound of splashing coming from behind the cabin. All there knew it was too early for Rabbit and the others to be back. John pulled his rifle from its sheath. Standing off tone side the sound of splashing grew until finally it reached dry land. Transfixed in the direction of the sound they stood still when all of a sudden six deer bounded into the clearing. Realizing they were not alone but too exhausted to care they moved to one side and disappeared into a small clump of palmettos. Crete could not believe what he had just seen. Deer that usually run at just the sight or scent of a human now ignore their greatest enemy for jut a few moments of rest. By the time night had come coons, possums, rabbits and three buzzards had joined them on the small island. John slipped from the cabin and Crete jumped when the shot rang out. He had decided to have a little fresh meat so he killed a little maiden doe. He said it would probably starve.

The fire ragged when they heard the first of the calls from toward the river. Crete could hear the sound of ores hitting the side of a wooden boat. They stepped from the lit cabin into the darkness. Straining to see they could hear the muffled conversation of two men. Slowly the boat fought the current as the lantern cast it glow about the boat. John looked at Clearance and said."Hamp and Lamb." To which Clearance replied, "Wonder if they seen any of our cows?" The two old men nosed the boat on the shore. Stepped from the boat and greeted each other. They were invited to stay the night and share a hot meal. They told of the dead cows, hogs and deer they had seen while traveling from Lonesome Slough. The water is deep and swift. The only place they did not have to fight the current was south of Blues Head. The water is clear up into the cypress at Little Prairie. But if you take your time you could make it there in a half days ride. They told of a small bunch of cows stranded on a myrtle island. They assured them as well the mosquitoes are going to be bad. That night their prediction came true and Crete had a hard time sleeping until John shared his mosquito net.

By the third morning Rabbit and the others had not made it back to Osteen Island so John decided to head toward the small myrtle island and drive that bunch to Near Slough. It was not as easy as Crete thought it would be. The stubborn cows did not seem to understand they were there to help them. The myrtles were so thick they could not use their cow whips. Finally getting off their horses they wadded through waist deep water finally able to drive them out into the open water. John and Clearance put the whips to them and it did not take long for them to get tired of the continual striking of the whip on wet hid before they figure it was best to go in the direction they were being pushed.

It was dark when they made it to Paw Paw Mound. Just a small part of the entire mound was visible. Again they found it covered with snakes. Everyone was too tired to enjoy the killing as several days before and after just a few minutes it became a chore. When they finished killing the snakes they had killed fifteen rattlesnakes. One was the biggest any of them had ever seen. It measured ten feet six inches long and had twenty two rattles and a button. Clearance said if he was heading home he would have skinned it out. Hamp pulled out a sack and picked the giant snake up by the head and allowed it to fill the sack. He looked at Clearance and told him he would skin it and dry the skin for him.

The next morning Crete saw several riders emerge from the tree line, enter the water and head straight toward them. Half way there he watched as the horses struggled against the current. Swimming, they at last found their footing on higher ground. A wake rushed before them Crete recognized his Uncle Rabbit and Emmett Tanner. As they got to dry land dismounted and greeted each other. Crete was relieved by the help his uncle was able to gather because he felt he was not as good a help as he should have been yesterday. They greeted each other when John complimented Crete for his grit and ability with a whip. As his uncle passed he put his hand on his head messing up his hair giving him a big smile.

Emmett walks to the fire takes the boiling pot of coffee from next to the fire. Pours his self a cup of the hot drink and drinks it with great relish. They turned and stared over the water and watched as a dead cow floats by. Emmett clears his throat and tells Little John and the others that the Yates will soon join them. He believed that most of the cows will be along the cabbage hammock running to Persimmon Hammock. He also mentioned the pine islands at the furthest eastern edge of Big Prairie. He thought it best to gather as many as they could drive them back to here because it is narrower here than any other place on the river. If any of their cows were found further north the best place to cross would be Cow Creek. Everyone agreed and plans were to begin at day light the next morning. It was close quarters having ten men and their horses on less than a half acre but it would have to do. That night the dogs were restless because the noises coming from the water as the once fearless animals sought their own place out of the water. Their desperation did not alleviate their instinctual fear.

The fire shone bright as its light flickered making the trees looked as if swaying to some unheard melody in the small cabbage hammock. In the silence of the morning the only thing that could be heard is the whining of a horse and it swishes its tail at the biting bugs. Crete was luck because he slept next to a smoldering dried cow patty. Its smell repelled the biting mosquitoes. Someone coughs on the other side of the camp awakening Crete. Sitting next to the fire he could see Emmett, Evert and his uncle Rabbit. A sense of pride filled him as he believed he was in the presence of the best cowmen in the territory.

Daylight finally broke the horizon. The colors were a brilliant orange-yellow. Buzzards circled in every direction. Hundreds, more than Crete had ever seen in his entire life. A breakfast of cold biscuits and bacon was all they had time for. They broke up into four groups. Emmett, his two sons and his brother-in-law Crow headed due north for about a mile. There they would enter the long cabbage strand heading to the pine islands. Evert and his crew rode due east and would ride through the middle of the cabbage strand until they came across Emmett's sign driving everything the find a head of them. At that point they would join up and begin the long drive back to Paw Paw Mound. Little John and the three other men who had come with Evert would head south to

Possum Bluff make a long swing and drive whatever cows he found back to where they camp the night before. Together they would be more able to drive what cows they find a cross the swollen river marsh. The plans were to move them all the way to the south end of Pock-a-taw Flats.

Emmett and his crew had not traveled long before they came across their first bunch of cows. There were only about twenty head. Each looked as if the flood had already started affecting them. Without any resistance the cows calmly relented to what little pressure was placed on them. It was as if they understood what these men were trying to do for them. Crete listened as the men spook of the severity of this flood and the possible long lasting effects this could have on everybody. Before noon they had gathered about a hundred head. Rabbit was concerned because not one of his cows was found. Off in the distance the lowing of cows and popping of whips could be heard long before anyone could actually see them coming. Crete watched as the riders circled the herd as Emmett's crew pushed their cows to form a herd of about three hundred. Rabbit rode along side of Evert and asked if he had found any of his cows. Not one of the Robert's cows was anywhere to be found. This began to worry Rabbit because these cows were meant to pay this year's taxes.

They had hoped to be able to cross the river before dark but as they emerged from the hammock the sun was beginning to set in the west. The actual sunset was hidden by a thunderhead reaching high in the sky. Each of the men would had really preferred to cross but knew it would be fooling to try this late in the day. They circled the herd trying to settle them down but something stronger then the will of the men drove them on. One cow started across the marsh and one by one mechanically trudged through the belly deep water. As darkness fell they were no longer able to see the cows as they pushed forward. It was determined they could do nothing in the dark and it would be easier to gather the strays in daylight. They camped another night at Paw Paw Mound.

The next morning only a few cows milled about their camp. It seems that all of the others just disappeared into thin air. Camp broke. The few cows gathered and started back across the river. Nature made it easy for the men to re-gather the cows and drive them to the flats where there is plenty of grass. Rabbit was concerned because not one of his cows was anywhere to be found. The men were tired so all agreed to meet in a week.

Two weeks later a rider rode up in front of the house and informed Rabbit that all of his cows were spotted close to Magnolia Ranch.

Rabbit contacted Emmett Tanner and it was agreed they cows would remain in the big scrub north of the Kissimmee River until spring and them they would be worked with the Magrit cows and then driven back north. Rabbit made several trips to see Will Magrit and he along with Crete helped to repair the set of cow pens. While chopping cypress post Crete's ax slipped then sheered off striking his leg slicing him open. Rabbit with the assistance of Will Magrit used a hair from the tail of his horse to sew up the cut. It took several weeks for Crete to be able to return to helping repair the long lane to the pens.

Years passed and Rabbit along with some of the other men in the area were hired as Ranger Riders during the Texas Tick fever days. They traveled all over the state enforcing the states requirement in dipping the cows, horses and mules. Men who were once friends now face off as enemies. Each trying hard to preserve a life style they loved. Rabbit was involved with a few shootings but everyone he was involved with tried hard to follow the law.

While on one of his trips away Sarah got sick and passed away. This affected Rabbit and he abandoned the place in Christmas and moved back to Gridersville so he could be close to Sarah's grave. He continued growing his herd. Selling all his heifers to Will Magrit and his steers were driven to Kissimmee and shipped north. Rabbit was now a lot older and knew his days were soon to be over. He wanted to make sure Crete and Willie would be able to continue in the cattle business so he contracted with a few cowmen to help manage his operation if something happened to him.

Rabbit was now about seventy one years old. He awakened early that spring morning and saddled his old horse. Crete tried hard to convince him to take the truck but he refused to listen simply saying if you're goen with me you better hurry and saddle up. Rabbit called for Willie and told him to saddle the little bay. The boy ran toward the barn reminding Rabbit of himself the first time he was allowed to go with the men. The rode silently not following the new road the county had constructed but cutting through the scrub toward the lake. Since Captain Drawdy had passed away Rabbit inherited the property and had moved his entire operation here. There were still some open range cows bearing his mark on the Pock-a-taw Flats. They crossed the small creek now widened to a cross canal making their way through the large ferns. Crete could see his uncles strength return and wished he would tell him what he is thinking but Crete had riden along side Rabbit enough to know he does not speak while riding.

About the Author

R. Wayne Tanner was born into a pioneer family having a long history reaching back as far as 1834 when his great-great-grandfather came to Florida as a Scout during the Second Seminole Indiand War. He enjoys a deep heritage in the ranching and farming of Central Florida. Being a 5th generation Florida Cracker raised enjoying and experiencing country life in Christmas FL. He is also Baptist Preacher.